CYNTHIA HARROD-EAGLES

Dynasty 5:
The Black Pearl

sphere

SPHERE

First published in Great Britain in 1982 by Macdonald & Co (Publishers) Ltd
First paperback edition published by Futura Books 1982
This edition published by Warner Books 1993
Reprinted by Sphere in 2007

3 5 7 9 10 8 6 4

A CIP catalogue record for this book
is available from the British Library.

ISBN 978-0-7515-0642-6

Printed and bound in Great Britain by
Clays Ltd, St Ives plc

Papers used by Sphere are from well-managed forests
and other responsible sources.

MIX
Paper from
responsible sources
FSC
www.fsc.org FSC® C104740

Sphere
An imprint of
Little, Brown Book Group
Carmelite House
50 Victoria Embankment
London EC4Y 0DZ

An Hachette UK Company
www.hachette.co.uk

www.littlebrown.co.uk

SELECT BIBLIOGRAPHY

Historians' Works

Ashley M.	*England in the Seventeenth Century*
Bryant A.	*Restoration England*
Chapman Hester	*The Tragedy of Charles II*
Fussell G. E. & K. R.	*The English Countrywoman 1500–1900*
Hill Christopher	*The Century of Revolution Reformation to Industrial Revolution*
Holdsworth W. S.	*History of English Law*
Jordan W. K.	*Charities of Rural England*
Kenyon J. P.	*Stuart England*
Laver J.	*History of Costume*
Morrah Patrick	*Prince Rupert of the Rhine*
Notestein Wallace	*English Folk*
Owen David	*English Philanthropy 1660–1960*
Shaw W. A.	*Calendar of State Papers*
Trevelyan G. M.	*England under the Stuarts English Social History*
Turner E. S.	*The Court of St. James*
Watson F.	*The Old Grammar Schools*
Wedgwood C. V.	*The King's Peace The King's War*

Contemporary Material

Reports on Endowed Charities Vol. iv. West Riding of York
History of my Own Time – Bishop Burnet
Memoirs – John Evelyn
Through England on a Sidesaddle – Celia Fiennes

Memoirs – Count de Grammont
My Life – Edward Hyde, Earl of Clarendon
A French Ambassador in the Court of Charles II – J. J. Jusserand
Natural and Political Observations – Gregory King
Diary – Samual Pepys
Memoirs of the Verney Family – Lady Verney

To my friends of the RPO
with thanks for much kindness.

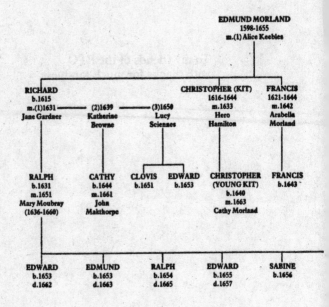

EDMUND MORLAND
1598-1655
m.(1) Alice Keebles

RICHARD
b.1615
m.(1)1631 ———— (2)1639 ———— (3)1650
Jane Gardner   Katherine   Lucy
                Browne   Scienes

CHRISTOPHER (KIT)
1616-1644
m.1633
Hero
Hamilton

FRANCIS
1621-1644
m.1642
Arabella
Morland

RALPH
b.1631
m.1651
Mary Moubray
(1636-1660)

CATHY
b.1644
m.1661
John
Makthorpe

CLOVIS
b.1651

EDWARD
b.1653

CHRISTOPHER
(YOUNG KIT)
b.1640
m.1663
Cathy Morland

FRANCIS
b.1643

EDWARD
b.1653
d.1662

EDMUND
b.1653
d.1663

RALPH
b.1654
d.1665

EDWARD
b.1655
d.1657

SABINE
b.1656

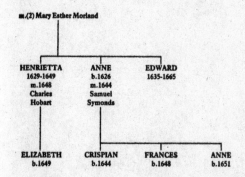

m.(2) Mary Esther Morland

HENRIETTA
1629-1649
m.1648
Charles
Hobart

ANNE
b.1626
m.1644
Samuel
Symonds

EDWARD
1635-1665

ELIZABETH
b.1649

CRISPIAN
b.1644

FRANCES
b.1648

ANNE
b.1651

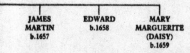

JAMES
MARTIN
b.1657

EDWARD
b.1658

MARY
MARGUERITE
(DAISY)
b.1659

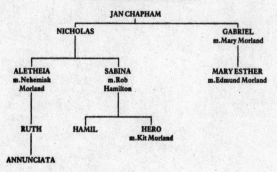

How Annunciata was related to the Morlands

JAN CHAPHAM

NICHOLAS

GABRIEL
m.Mary Morland

ALETHEIA
m.Nehemiah
Morland

SABINA
m.Rob
Hamilton

MARY ESTHER
m.Edmund Morland

RUTH

HAMIL

HERO
m.Kit Morland

ANNUNCIATA

BOOK ONE

Lion Statant

Ah how sweet it is to love,
Ah how gay is young desire!
And what pleasing pains we prove
When we first approach Love's fire!
  Pains of love be sweeter far
  Than all other pleasures are.

John Dryden: *Tyrannick Love*

CHAPTER ONE

The yard was full of horses and servants and the ladies of the house were coming forward one by one to the mounting block as their mounts were led up. Two elderly servants were watching the scene from an upper window. The yard was full of deep cool shadow and the soft, vivid smell of a June dawn, but the sun had reached over the roofs of the outbuildings and was warming the top bricks of the house, and the two women had pushed open the casement and were leaning their elbows on the sill to enjoy it.

Below them Annunciata Morland jostled her cousin Cathy out of the way and took her place at the block, lifting her slender hand to the servant who was holding her pony, Nod. It was cleverly done, and no one below would have noticed it, except Cathy herself, and Cathy was used to being slighted. But the two women saw it perfectly, and one tutted and shook her head. 'What that young lady needs is a whipping. She's too uppish by half, and poor Miss Cathy—'

Ellen regarded the other woman sourly. 'Poor Miss Cathy' had always been a plain and sickly child, and had therefore never attracted the love and attention of the Morland Place servants, who had a natural prejudice towards healthy, bonny children. Leah herself had never had any time for her and had slapped and bullied and berated her through her childhood to her present adolescence without ever calling her 'poor' Cathy until now. Ellen knew the reason for the sudden sympathy: it was pure jealousy. Normally, Ellen would not allow anyone but herself to criticize Annunciata, but only that morning at Shawes Ellen had been worsted in one of her increasingly

3

frequent arguments with her young miss, so she confined herself to saying 'Aye, well,' in a noncommittal way.

They watched Annunciata mount gracefully and take the reins as the servant spread her skirts around her. She was plainly dressed, as was everyone nowadays, with no feathers or lace about her, yet she managed to make the black broadcloth seem like a Court dress and her stout dun pony like a milk-white fairy horse. Her luxuriant dark curls tumbled out of her plain black cloth hood as if nothing could contain their bounty, and Ellen's heart swelled with pride as she was led to one side and Cathy took her place. The contrast between the girls was marked, and Ellen forgot her grudge against her young miss and thought instead, why shouldn't she take the place of that unlikely scarecrow?

'There's some,' she murmured, 'as whipping hasn't helped along much.'

Leah bristled. She was older than Ellen, and her position as governess and mother-of-the-maids at Morland Place made her an infinitely superior person to Ellen, who held a similar position but only at Shawes, a damp old ruin of a house on a small and unimportant estate.

'What your Miss Annunciata needs,' she said firmly, drawing herself up with dignity, 'is wed. Fourteen's old enough. My mistress was wed at fourteen and none the worse for it.'

'Aye, but thy mistress has no book-learning,' Ellen pointed out. 'My Miss is right clever, and her thinkin' is wick as an eel.'

'I don't hold with over-much education for ladies. It does 'em no good,' Leah said.

'The old mistress was book-learned,' Ellen pointed out with pleasure. Leah's face darkened. It was ten years since Mary Esther Morland died – the same year they killed the King – but she missed her still. She had nursed Mary Esther as a baby and been with her all her life, first as nurse, then as personal maid, then as housekeeper and

4

companion, and finally as governess to Mary Esther's children. Losing her was like losing sight.

'Aye, well, there never was one like the old mistress,' she said as if dismissing that argument. 'But your miss – why, everyone knows she was to wed Young Kit, ever since she was born. Why does your mistress delay? Fourteen's old enough, and the lad's nineteen – why don't they marry and be done with it? He's a good match, and he'll look elsewhere if she's not sharp about it.'

'Maybe my mistress has other plans,' Ellen said secretively. Leah looked at her sharply.

'She'll not find a better match,' she said stoutly. 'Young Kit's got the city property from his father, and the Butts estate from his mother, besides the Scottish lands. And now his mother's dead he'll be looking to wed—'

'Nay, but he had to sell Watermill to pay the Roundhead fines,' Ellen interrupted, 'and Aberlady was burned down after the battle at Dunbar, and Birnie is overrun with presbyters, and Lord knows if he'll ever get it back, so maybe my mistress is thinking twice about the match. After all, when you think who Annunciata is—'

She stopped abruptly, aware she had been on the brink of an unforgivable indiscretion. Leah narrowed her eyes.

'Who is she, then?' Ellen did not answer, and Leah went on, 'Well all respect to your mistress, and pretty as Annunciata may be, she's a bastard when all's said and done, and no one knows who her father was.'

'Maybe so, maybe not,' Ellen said smugly.

'Are you saying you know?' Leah demanded.

'Maybe I know, maybe I don't,' Ellen said infuriatingly, 'but the fact is Shawes is not entailed, and Miss Ruth can leave it to anyone she likes. So my miss is an heiress as well as the prettiest, sharpest thing in the county, and Miss Ruth will not rush into weddin' her, and that's it and all about it.'

Leah breathed hard, aware she had been bested, and that what Ellen said was true. Shawes, though a small estate compared with Morland Place, was a very good inheritance, and there were the warehouses on King's Staith besides. Annunciata was an important heiress, and she knew it, just as she knew she was and always had been the prettiest thing on two legs. Leah looked down into the yard again and saw how Young Kit and Edward – Mary Esther's last child – both hung around talking to Annunciata while they waited for the rest of the party to mount up. Annunciata flirted with them both, playing one off against the other. Meanwhile, on the other side of the yard, Cathy and her ten-year-old cousin Elizabeth Hobart sat their horses, ignored. It was the same thing all the time. When there was dancing, everyone fought to claim Annunciata's hand, and only the losers approached the other young ladies.

Now the last of the ladies was mounting – Leah's own mistress, the mistress of Morland Place, wife of Ralph Morland, the Master. Leah felt a twinge of anxiety along with her pride, for the mistress was pregnant, and Leah never liked to see her ride when she was pregnant. The anxiety sharpened her tongue, and she turned away from the window with one last barbed comment and a jerk of the head towards Annunciata and her knot of faithful attendants.

'Miss Ruth wants to watch she's not more rushed into wedding the lass than she plans on.'

'What dosta mean by that?' Ellen demanded furiously, but Leah walked away, massively dignified, without replying, and Ellen could only mutter after her. 'Tha s'd watch thy spittle doesn't poison thee, tha sidey owd bitch.'

As the party clattered out through the barbican and over the drawbridge, Mary Moubray was conscious, a little guiltily, of a sense of relief. She knew she ought to feel that Morland Place was her home, and not a prison, and she knew that it would break her husband's heart if he thought

6

she was unhappy, but she could not prevent the lifting of her heart and struggled not to let it shew too obviously.

They were riding up to Harewood Whin to collect elder. It was one of the periodic tasks and was often left to servants, but Ralph, always eager to please Mary and always looking out for some way to make amusement for the household, had thought of making it into a party. The laws had been growing more and more strict over the last ten years, until it seemed that almost anything that was pleasurable was banned by the Puritan government. At first they had been able to ignore some of the laws, but then General Cromwell – Lord Protector he styled himself – had set his major-generals over them, with armed soldiers to enforce the laws, and heavy fines and even imprisonment for infractions.

Morland Place had suffered. A large portion of the estate had been confiscated, as a punishment for the family's royalist activities, and later fines had been raised against them for the same thing, and for the continuance of the forbidden Anglo-Catholic celebration in the chapel at Morland Place. Much of the family's plate and jewels had had to be sold to pay the fines, and it had been hard at times to scrape through. The worst thing had been the attack on the chapel a few years back, when armed soldiers had broken in during the early Mass. They had damaged the altar, stolen the altar-furniture, and torn out the rails, making a bonfire of them in the yard on which they had burnt the copes and altar-cloths and prayer-books.

It had been a terrifying thing, but even worse were the human consequences. The Master of Morland Place, Edmund, had suffered a stroke while trying to save the ancient wooden statue of the Blessed Virgin. He had had one stroke the previous year which had left him partly crippled; the second attack killed him, and he was found in the Lady Chapel lying face-down, the statue hidden and safe under his body. The old priest, Father Michael Moyes, had been arrested and imprisoned, and not all that money and pleading could do could get him released. He was an old man, and prison life was too harsh for him. He had died in his cell the following winter.

Other deaths had followed indirectly. Hero Hamilton, Young Kit's mother, had felt the shock deeply, and had gone in terror of a second raid on the chapel at Shawes. She had died in her sleep two weeks after the raid, and everyone believed it was fear that had killed her. And Mary herself, who was heavily pregnant at the time, had slipped her child early. The baby had never been strong in consequence, and had lived only twenty months. Through all this, and through the hardship and fear that had followed, it was Ralph who had held things together. From cheerful, indolent boyhood he had been thrust by events into responsible manhood. His father had left Morland Place after the death of Mary Esther, passing over his inheritance to Ralph and going to London to live, and with the death of Edmund, Ralph became Master of Morland Place in truth. It was a heavy responsibility, but Ralph had always retained his natural cheerfulness, and everyone increasingly grew to rely on him to give them hope through the difficult years. Ralph had shewed no signs of feeling the strain except once, last year, when the news came of the death of Lord Cromwell: then he had cried 'Thank God!' and had fallen to his knees, covered his face with his hands, and wept.

Mary glanced at him as he rode beside her on Red Fox, his big chestnut gelding. He was a tàll man, over six feet, and big-built, with broad shoulders and long, strong bones, but there was nothing heavy about him – he was as lithe and graceful as a cat. He was much like his grandfather in looks, having the same silver-fair hair, wide grey eyes, fine-boned, Grecian face and golden skin, but where Edmund had been a cold, proud statue of a man, Ralph's face shewed his lazy good-humour. His grey eyes were flecked with gold, and had the long impassive stare of a leopard, and the lines around them were laughter lines, his long, sensuous mouth curling upwards at the corners.

Mary Moubray had been fourteen when she first met Ralph, a month before their wedding. She had been born and bred in the wild Borderlands, and her home was at Emblehope, in the bleak and barren uplands between North Tynedale and Redesdale. Her father had owned a large estate there: he had been killed in the last battle of the war, near Carlisle. Her mother had been half-sister to Samuel Symonds, who married Mary Esther Morland's eldest daughter Anne, and when Mary's mother died, Sam Symonds had become her guardian and had taken her to live on his estate at Bell Hill in Coquetdale, a greener place then Emblehope, but as wild and bare.

Then, when she was fourteen, everything had changed, and changed so drastically that she had spent almost a year in a state of bewilderment that amounted to shock. Sam had told her, kindly enough, that he had arranged a match for her. As her father's only surviving child she was his heiress, and a good match was not hard to come by – she was to wed Ralph Morland, eventual heir of all the great Morland estate. Thus far the news had not displeased her, for she had always known that some day she must marry; the shock came in the fact that they were to leave for Yorkshire on the morning, and she was to be wed within the month.

Sam and an armed guard had escorted her on the long ride down to York. It was necessary in those troubled times to have armed men with you when you rode through the wild lands, but to Mary, in her bewilderment, it had seemed as though they were soldiers come to take her to prison. The idea had coloured her first year in Yorkshire. It was a strange land to her, a soft, wet, green land, and she had felt stifled, and hated it. All her life she had known the wild airy uplands, their emptiness and silence; now she had to grow used to the crowded, noisy, stinking lowlands. Hitherto she had had nothing to do but enjoy herself, and had spent most of every day out of doors, riding, hunting, hawking, or simply walking over the moors and hills. Now she was confined indoors with a bewildering number of tasks to perform. She was translated, at a stroke, from a careless girl to mistress of a great household with all that that entailed.

And she had been married to the huge, golden, powerful man who terrified her. Deeply unhappy as she was, she was unable to escape, and so she retreated inside herself, hid herself behind a mask of immobility, concealed her fear and confusion with a slow-moving dignity which suited her new position and kept most of the multitude of people at a distance. Oddly enough, the only person in the household who entered into her feelings was Edmund. He had been born and brought up at Morland Place, but his father came from Northumberland, from Tods Knowe, only an hour's ride from Emblehope, while his mother came from the wild moors of Birnie, in Stirlingshire. He had inherited much of his parents' love of solitude, and was himself an intensely reserved man. A strange kind of silent sympathy had grown up between them, and Mary had found that when she was especially driven and unhappy, she could take refuge with Edmund, for with him she could sit and be quiet, and no one would dare disturb her.

Ralph caught her eye now and smiled. 'Are you all right?' he said. 'You must tell me if you feel uncomfortable.'

She nodded. She did not smile, but then she rarely did, for the mask she had assumed had become habit. 'I am well,' she said.

'Good. I know Leah did not want you to come, but we shall not ride fast – in fact we shall not go out of a walk all the way. I do not think it can hurt you.'

'I am glad to be out,' she said. It was an understatement. Her eyes glowed with the pleasure of being in the fresh air again, and Ralph knew it. He had grown skilled in interpreting the minuter expressions of her face.

'Tomorrow, if you like, we might go hawking out on the moor. Leah would never let you hunt, I know, but we could get up very early and steal away – just you and I and a few servants. Would you like that, my hinny?'

She only nodded, but her eyes were happy. He was always kind to her, quick to sense what she wanted and try to provide it. In the early years of their marriage she had been too confused and unhappy to notice, and had blamed him for her unhappiness, for it was he who had married her, and it was he therefore who confined her to the house and made her pregnant. But as time went on she realized that he had not chosen the marriage any more than she – it had been arranged between Edmund and Sam Symonds – and that he did his best to mitigate the circumstances for her.

She had not found pregnancy hard, except in the curtailment of her freedom. She was a tall, healthy girl, and carried easily: Leah said hill-folk always did, because of their strong sinews and upright carriage. But for the same reason childbirth went hard with her, and her labours were always long and painful. Her first child, named Edward, was born in January of 1653, and she was barely recovered from the birth when she conceived again. Edmund was born in December of the same year, and Young Ralph in October of '54. The fourth baby was due in November '55 but was born a month early. Ralph had named him Edward too, for Edward was the family name, and he wanted to be sure that it survived amongst his children.

After the miscarriage she had had a couple of months' grace while she recovered; but she conceived early in the new year and her first daughter was born in September of '56, and was named Sabine. Ralph had had to go to London that winter, to sort out some business matters with his father, who acted as the family's factor in London, and

Mary had had a delightful winter of hunting and riding and freedom. Oddly, though, she had discovered herself missing Ralph, and the big warm bulk of him in bed beside her, and when he returned in the middle of February she greeted him so lovingly that she was soon pregnant again. That summer her second son Edward died, and on the 11 November, St Martin's day, she had borne another son, whom they had Christened James Martin. Her sixth son had been born in November '58, had also been named Edward, but had lived only a month, dying just before Christmas; and now it was June, and she was four months pregnant again.

Ralph loved his children, and adored her for bearing them to him, but Mary wished there could be time in between one labour and the next conception for her to savour a little freedom. As for her children, she was proud of them, and glad that she had had them, of course, for an infertile woman was a useless thing, universally to be despised, but she had little real affection for them, except for Martin. He was the only dark one of the brood. Ned, Edmund, Young Ralph and Sabine were all the image of their father, big-boned, golden-skinned, blond and pale-eyed – beautiful children and much admired, especially by the servants, who clucked over them happily and spoiled them as much as they could when Leah was not watching.

But Martin, who was coming up for two, had been a small, dark, wrinkled baby at his birth, and as he grew he took on his mother's looks. He was a slenderly made child with unexpectedly dark skin, silky black hair, and dark-blue eyes the colour of a young kitten's. He was not as boisterous as the other children had been at his age, and there was a sensitivity and thoughtfulness in his fine-featured face which, with his dark colouring, made him seem alien to the brood. The servants sometimes talked about him being a changeling, but they could not dislike him, for he was the sweetest-natured of all the children, and Lambert, the tutor, praised his quickness and intelligence. Ned had not been able to read until he was three, and Edmund still wrote an abominable hand, but Martin, who was not two until November, both read and wrote well, and knew three French songs already.

They passed through Ten Thorn Gap, and now they were no longer on Morland land, for the North Fields had been the part of the estate that Parliament confiscated. It was owned now by one Master Makthorpe, a Puritan and Parliamentarian of rigid convictions. He was the local Justice of the Peace, and made an uncomfortable neighbour for the Morlands, not least because it was well known that he coveted more of the Morland lands than he already had. Ruth and Ralph were both of the opinion that it was Makthorpe who had initiated the raid on the chapel, but they kept their thoughts to themselves, for fear of frightening the household.

The sun was beginning to dry the dew off the grass by the time they reached Harewood Whin – a wild, tangled wood through which ran a little beck called the Smawith. It was the home of badgers and foxes and deer and, from time immemorial, the hares that gave it its name, and there were many ancient and holy trees in it. It was from Harewood Whin that the Morlands fetched home the may on May Day, and from there that they cut their holly and mistletoe for Christmas-tide. Morlands had hawked and hunted there, children played there, and lovers met there, time out of mind.

They threaded their way through the overgrown paths, and soon had to dismount and lead their horses, for the boughs hung too low to allow them to pass. The great elder tree was near the centre of the wood, where it was darkest and most mysterious and, as they neared it, Mary felt the power of the place. They walked in silence, and the wood was quiet, no birdsong to shake the peace, so that the sound of their passage – the rustle of leaves, the crack of twigs underfoot, the clinking of bits, the occasional, startling ring of shod hoof on stone – seemed unnaturally loud. Then they came out into a little clearing, and there was the great elder in front of them.

Ralph signalled to some of the servants to take the horses to one side, and then gestured forward Clem, the steward's son, who was carrying the garlands. He did not need to tell anyone to be quiet – no one wanted to speak or laugh in that strange silence, and even Annunciata was standing wide-eyed, forgetting to pull at her curls or look sideways at Edward. The elder was the most venerable of all the trees in the wood, and it had great power, both to good and to ill. Its leaves, berries and flowers, and even its bark, were used in a great number of medicines and salves, and sprigs of it warded off evil spirits; but the elder-mother, if offended, ate little children, and it was also reputed to be the tree from whose wood the Cross was made, and from whose branches Judas the traitor hanged himself.

Clem came forward and snatched off his hat, and bowed three times, very reverently, before the tree, and in a loud voice began the prayer to the elder-mother, praising her power to good, and begging her to allow them to pluck her leaves and flowers. To placate her, they had brought her garlands of honeysuckle and wild garlic flowers, and Clem wound these around the boughs from which they intended to take what they needed. This done he stepped back, picked up his basket, and looked towards Edward. Mary shivered suddenly. It was very cold in this shadowy place, and she was glad she would have nothing to do with the plucking of the leaves, for she had too many children to risk. Clem, too, was married, and had two sons, and his mother had been a woods-woman from up Wilstrop way, and he would have been very loath to perform the necessary task, as Ralph well knew. So Ralph had asked Edward, who was a bachelor, to do it. Edward stepped up cheerfully but quietly with the knife and scissors. He was not much of a believer in the old rites, or magic, or the pagan country powers, but even he took off his hat and bowed to the tree before beginning.

When the basket was full the two men bowed again, Ralph spoke the prayer of thanks, and they all departed gladly. They passed through quickly to the north side of the Whin, and when they broke out into the sunshine, everyone's spirits lifted as if they had successfully avoided some danger.

'Shall we breakfast here?' Ralph asked, pausing by some grassy hummocks on a slight rise above the beck. 'What need to go further? Clem, you could spread the cloth there, on the level ground. Barnabus, take the horses and tie them in the shade.'

Talk and movement broke out as if released by his words. The servants bustled about preparing things, spreading the cloth and bringing out the food, taking the horses and pointing out the best spots for the ladies to seat themselves. Ralph spread his doublet for Mary to sit on. 'The grass is still damp here – you might catch a chill.' She allowed him to fuss around her, too glad of the fresh air to mind anything. Beyond the beck Low Moor stretched flat and bare towards Hessay, and beyond Hessay was Marston Moor, where so many Morlands had died. Mary heard Young Kit saying, to Annunciata:

'Over there is where my father fell. You've never been that far, have you? I'll take you there one day.' Mary glanced round in time to see a quick tussle between him and Edward as to whose coat Annunciata would sit on, a tussle which Edward won as he won almost every contest between them. Edward was as beautiful and wicked in his way as Annunciata was in hers, and Mary knew from first hand how dangerous he could be. Although he was Ralph's uncle, he was actually four years the younger, and was so astonishingly like him in looks that strangers always took them for brothers. He had the same colouring, moon-pale hair and grey eyes, and the same firm, classical features, but he was smaller and stockier in build. During the winter that Ralph had spent in London, Mary had found herself more and more often in Edward's company. He had taken her riding, hunting and hawking; he had danced with her in the long saloon, he had played cards with her, had played the lute to accompany her while she sang through the long dark evenings. Mary, missing Ralph as she did, had been in danger of falling in love with him.

He was easy to love – handsome, amusing, witty, attentive, and with an unexpectedly feminine approach to many things which made him easy for a woman to talk to. Afterwards, on more mature consideration, Mary had decided that he had intended her to fall in love with him, even that, had things gone that way, he would have made love to her. It puzzled her even while it shocked her, for it was a kind of wanton wickedness that did not accord with the rest of Edward's nature. He was not a cruel person, and he had no spite against Ralph – he and Ralph were the best of friends. In the same way, he tormented Young Kit by continually tempting Annunciata's wavering affections away from him and towards himself, even though he and Kit had grown up together and done their lessons side by side in the same schoolroom. When they were both children, Edward had protected the more timid Kit from the rages of their hot-tempered tutor, often provoking a beating for himself to distract attention from Kit; while Kit, the more intelligent of the two, had frequently done for Edward the work which he was too stupid or lazy to do himself.

Mary saw now how it puzzled Kit to be thwarted continually by his best friend, and how he tried to make excuses for Edward that would prove him innocent of any design against him. It puzzled Mary, too. She did not think Edward was in love with Annunciata, any more than he had been in love with her that winter. She wondered if it was in him to be in love at all. There was something odd about Edward, something restless and misdirected in him that she could not quite put her finger on. She had had a little dog, when she was a child, that had been caught in a trap when it was a pup, and damaged its leg. Because it was so young, the leg had healed, and the pup appeared quite sound, except that when it ran there was something odd about its gait, a limp so well adjusted to that it was impossible for a stranger to determine which leg had been damaged. Edward gave her the same feeling. There was something broken or damaged inside him that he had compensated for, so that all that appeared was this undefined strangeness.

The servants were bringing round the food, and while Mary watched Edward said to Kit, 'Don't you think one of us ought to help Cathy and Elizabeth? They have no one to attend them.'

'Oh, yes, of course,' Kit said, and after a brief pause, realizing that Edward was not going to move, he went to station himself beside his two cousins and help them to the food. Edward, with a strange little smile, sat himself down beside Annunciata, and began to talk to her in a voice too low for Mary to overhear. Annunciata seemed to have no objections to the arrangement, judging by the sidelong glances under her lashes and the dimpling smiles she gave her companion.

'Here you are, dearest,' Ralph said, bringing her a cup and napkin, and beckoning Clem over to them. 'What will you have? Some cold beef? A little of the brawn pie? Those pasties look very good. Have you the wine there for the mistress, Clem?'

Mary waited until Ralph was settled beside her and they were both eating before she said quietly, 'Husband, don't you think you ought to have a word with Edward? He is paying far too much attention to Annunciata these days.'

Ralph glanced across in surprise, and then shrugged and smiled at Mary. 'Oh, I don't think she minds. I think she enjoys it.'

'Kit minds,' she said succinctly.

'Kit knows, as does Edward, as does everyone, that Annunciata has been promised to him since she was born.

17

They will marry one day, when it is good time. He has nothing to worry about.'

'She encourages Edward,' Mary said. Ralph looked again. Annunciata was laughing at something Edward had said, and her cheeks were very pink and her eyes were bright. Her prettiness made Ralph smile.

'She's a high-spirited little baggage, and as pretty as spring flowers. Of course she enjoys Edward's attentions. It's flattering for her. But she knows she is to marry Kit. Edward has no estate – she couldn't marry him even if she wanted to, and for all her frolics, she knows her own value as an heiress: she wouldn't marry a penniless man. No, dear heart, it's just fun. Don't worry about it.'

There was nothing more that Mary could say. Not for anything would she tell Ralph about that winter she had had with Edward, and unless she told him, she would never be able to convince him of the danger lying in wait for Annunciata. So she let Ralph change the subject, and ate her breakfast in silence.

'It all looks so peaceful,' he said, gesturing with a piece of barley bread towards the open country lying still and empty in the sunshine, 'that it's hard to believe that chaos is so close. You remember when the Protector died, I thanked God for it?' Mary nodded. 'Yet now I almost wish him back.'

Mary gave him a questioning look.

'Ah yes,' he went on, 'whatever Old Noll was, he was one man, and a strong man, able to hold his men in check. Since he went we have had his weak son, and now a gaggle of even weaker generals divide the power between them, and determine our fate by the force of arms. The Rump recalled!' he exclaimed in disgust. 'That party of paltroons, vicious, self-seeking, incompetent, and corrupt! Where will it end? Any man with a troop of soldiers under him can seize what he likes, and the law and justice will be swept aside.'

Edward, overhearing him, left his private conversation

with Annunciata and said, 'It has always been that way. It is no worse now than before.'

'Not always,' Ralph said. 'We had a King once, and a Church.'

'I am too young to remember it. You are too, I suspect,' Edward said. 'Since the war began, there has been no law but the law of force. Why should you expect things to be different now? With Devil Cromwell gone, the factions will break out more unrestrained than ever, and we shall be called to arms to decide who will rule us next. Perhaps it is best that way. Perhaps we shall have a proper war, with battles and cannons and charges and counter-charges. What good are we now, for peace? A war will use us up in the best way possible.'

Ralph stared, astonished by the bitterness in Edward's voice, and glad that no one but Mary and Annunciata had overheard it. It would not do to alarm and depress people needlessly. 'Don't speak like that, Edward. Another war is unthinkable.'

'Not unthinkable. Not even very unlikely,' Edward said.

Annunciata's face had sharpened as she listened, and she said now, 'Do you really think there will be another war? Would you fight?'

'Why not?' Edward said lightly. 'A mercenary's life is not a bad one, I hear tell. You would like it too, Nance. There are always lots of balls and parties when there is a war.'

'Really?' Annunciata brightened. 'That would be good. Life is so very dull nowadays, with no dancing or singing or anything nice.'

'A war would be the very thing for you,' Edward went on solemnly, and Ralph relaxed, seeing that he was joking now, and the danger had passed. 'You would be the queen of every ball, and the toast of every mess, and you would dance with the brave and gallant soldiers, knowing that you sent them to their death with sweet memories.' Annunciata's face was rapt as she imagined the scene, and

Edward, ever more solemn, went on, 'And I – I should be the bravest and most gallant of them all, and die a hero's death, and be discovered with my hands clasped around a miniature of you, in my last endeavour to raise it to my dying lips.'

'Oh!' Annunciata breathed, her eyes filling with tears as she was carried away by her own imagination.

'And you would weep for me, sweet Nance, and realize once it was too late that you had truly loved me. And you would renounce the world for ever, and enter a convent in France.'

Now he had gone too far. The rapt expression left Annunciata's face, and her lips tightened as she saw that he was teasing her. 'No I would not, then,' she said firmly. 'I should be glad that such a reprobate had gone to his just reward, and I should marry the first man who asked me, just to spite you.'

Edward burst out laughing, and said, 'I'll wager you would, too. Beware your temper, my sweet cos, or it will lead you to ruin.'

'Now, Edward, don't tease her any more. To be sure, young ladies' dignity is not to be bruised.'

'Oh, I knew he was teasing all along,' Annunciata said airily. Mary was not so sure. She had been watching Edward's face, and more than ever he puzzled her, for the bitterness that had burst out from him had never left his eyes, even while he was laughing his most merrily.

CHAPTER TWO

They were to ride back a long way round, for Mary's sake, and the sun was so pleasant that they skirted the wood rather than ride through it. When they came round onto the east side Ralph's two great brindled hounds, Bran and Fern, suddenly pricked up their ears and began growling, and a moment or two later the humans picked up the sound of altercation some way ahead. As they rode on it became clearer. Bran and Fern barked and ran forward, and Ralph and Edward spurred their horses into a canter as they heard someone screaming.

As they came round a corner of the wood they had to rein back sharply, for they found themselves in the middle of a herd of pigs, milling about across the path and running first this way then that as two heavyset men tried to contain them. It was the pigs, they were glad to discover, which had been screaming. But there were four of the men, and they were armed, and the two not engaged with the pigs were standing over a very old man and a very young girl-child. The old man looked terrified, but he was arguing fiercely; the child was crying, and even from a distance Ralph could see that the tears were washing clean tracks down an extremely dirty face.

'Hoa there! What's going on?' Ralph called. The soldiers looked up at his cry, but held their ground unperturbed, while the pigs, freshly agitated, milled first towards and then away from the horses' hooves. Red Fox flared his nostrils at the sudden whiff of pig and skidded to a halt, going up into a half rear as he tried to turn away but was prevented by Ralph's hands and heels. Horses hate pigs: soon both horses were whirling madly, snorting and rearing, while the tough little black hogs shot like skimmed stones from under their feet, screaming like burning martyrs. The din and confusion were indescribable as the armed men cursed, the child wept, the old man lifted his reedy voice in plea, the dogs barked, and Ralph shouted to the rest of the Morland party to keep back, lest their horses be affected by the pigs too. He sweated and cursed as he tried to hold his maddened gelding, having horrible visions of Mary thrown from her horse and losing the child.

At last Ralph managed to move Fox away and jump down, and Barnabus dismounted and came forward to take the reins. Fox, his eyes goggling, dug at the ground with his fore-hooves, shaking his head and snorting as if he had inadvertently sniffed at an ants' nest. Edward threw his reins to Barnabus too, and the two men went forward on foot, Ralph calling Bran and Fern to him. They ran to heel and stood beside him, bristling and growling indiscriminately.

'What's going on here?' Ralph asked, pushing his way through the pigs, who were calmer now and had fallen back on rooting for food. The old man turned to him as to authority. Ralph knew him – one of the cottagers from Rufforth, the nearest village.

'Oh Master, thank the Lord you've come! You'll see justice – you'll tell 'em. Sixty years and more I've been grazing my pigs here. Sixty years – and my grandfather before me. I never heard the like of it. You tell 'em, Master. You know.'

'Know what?' Ralph asked patiently, and then to the men, 'Whose men are you?'

'Master Makthorpe's,' one of them answered, as if there was no more to be said.

'Aye, Master Makthorpe sent 'em,' the old man said disgustedly. 'Foreigner, incomer that he is, and thinks to tell us all what to do, and this wood common grazing, always, always, since time began, Master, you know that.'

'Of course it is,' Ralph said. 'The Whin is common

grazing. The villagers have always grazed pigs here. Why, what is the trouble?'

'They're telling me I can't take my pigs in,' the old man said.

'That's right,' said one of the armed men. 'This is Master Makthorpe's land, bought and paid for, and you're trespassing, old man, you and your damned pigs. And so are you, Master, so why don't you take your pretty folk off and leave matters be that don't concern you.'

Ralph stared. 'Just a moment, what are you talking about? Master Makthorpe didn't buy the Whin.'

'Oh yes he did,' the armed man replied smugly. 'All the land up to Low Moor, that's what it says in the bill of sale. And the Whin is this side of the moor.'

Ralph considered. 'But even if he bought it, there are still rights of common. He can't take those away.'

'Can't he?' the other man said succinctly. He jabbed at a rooting pig with the toe of his boot. 'Best take your hogs away, old man. I like a bit of roasted pork to my supper.'

'You can't stop the villagers grazing their beasts in the Whin,' Ralph said firmly. 'The rights of common stand, even if the land if bought.'

'We can stop them, and we will,' the second man said. 'And who is to prevent us? You, Master, and your brother? And the two dogs of course.'

The other two men came up to join the speaker, and the four of them stared impassively. Edward, behind Ralph, touched his elbow gently. There was nothing they could do, unarmed, against four armed men.

'I'll go to law about this,' Ralph said bitterly.

The second speaker smiled, almost gently. 'Master Makthorpe *is* the law,' he said. Then he turned again to the old man. 'Go away, gaffer. Take thy pigs and thy bairn, and go home. And tell your friends that they had better stay away from the Whin from now on. We don't want any accidents, do we? Go on, go home.'

Ralph and Edward walked back to the waiting group. Ralph clenched his fists in fury.

'God damn him! I'd like to shew him! He can't do this to my people!'

'You know he can,' Edward said, and then the bitterness filled his voice again. 'It is what I was telling you. Any man with soldiers can take what he wants. It is beginning, Ralph, just as I said. Makthorpe is the law, just as that man said. Who can you complain to? Who will take your side? And who will take the poor people's side? Not Makthorpe, that's for certain. He has no value for the people, nor loyalty, and they none for him. He knows nothing of master-and-man. It's a new world from now on.'

Ralph stopped still, staring at the ground as he tried to think his way out of the situation. He was not a great thinker, and the troubled times he had grown up in had prevented his taking in too much education, but he had absorbed sound principles from Mary Esther, who had been as a mother to him.

'What can we do, Edward? We can't abandon the people to that wolf.'

'There is nothing we can do now. Perhaps the times will change. But for the moment there is nothing. If it comes to war again, then we can march out and fight.'

'But I hate doing nothing!' Ralph ground out between his teeth.

Edward laughed. 'I see that, old war horse. You have my mother's spirit. Remember when she held the chapel against Fairfax and all the might of his army?'

'Mam wouldn't have let this happen,' Ralph said, remembering right enough.

'Times were different then. We still had a King to fight for, and Fairfax was a gentleman. Ah, God, I am glad she is not here to see how things have gone to the bad. It would break her heart. For this, think you, they all died, Kit and Malachi and Frank and Hamil and all our men!' There was a silence as they stared at each other, remembering the dead. Then Edward said softly, 'We were born too late, you and I. We should have fought and died too. Better than this!'

Ralph roused himself. Less given to thinking than Edward, he lived more for the present, and his sanguine temperament would not allow him ever to despair. Besides, he loved life. 'No, no, don't say that,' he said. 'Things will get better. And meantime, we have the womenfolk waiting for us and worrying. We'll think of something. We'll find a way. Come on, Edward, look cheerful. I don't want Mary to fret.'

They got home at noon, in time for dinner. Mary took Elizabeth and went off with the basket of elder to the store rooms and the others went into the house, arriving just as the children were let out from their morning's labours and came running down the stairs. They burst out from the staircase hall into the great hall like a pent-up river, their voices shrill from the strain of having been silent all morning, and Bran and Fern jumped forward to bounce around them and thrust their blunt muzzles lovingly into the fresh young faces.

The four eldest were as like as four peas out of one pod, especially as they were all dressed alike, in dresses of stout brown woollen, with holland pin-afores and white linen caps. From under their caps the pale hair fell, straight and shining as water; four identical faces, honey-skinned, were wreathed with smiles; from above broad cheekbones, four pairs of long grey eyes viewed the world with candid good humour. Only their sizes were graded, though there was so little difference between Ned and Edmund that folk often said they had been meant to be sent into the world as twins; Edmund, having been delayed eleven months, did his best to catch up by growing faster than the rest.

The children caught sight of their father and their noise

stopped as if by magic. It was the first time they had seen him that day, and so they came forward respectfully and knelt in front of him. Ralph put out his hands and rested them on each head in turn and blessed them. The silence lasted one moment longer, and then they were up again and clamouring for his attention, eager to tell him what they had been doing. Ralph grinned down at them, not trying to sort out one voice from another. They all did lessons with Lambert, all equally unwillingly.

'My poor bairns,' he said happily. 'You've inherited your father's brains I'm afraid. You will all be famous dunces!'

Sabine's shrill voice rose over her brother's to attract his attention. 'But Papa, why do I have to do lessons with the boys? Women don't have to be able to read and write. When I grow up I shall be married and never read anything ever again. Can't I stop having lessons, Papa?'

Ralph stroked her head. 'Don't let Leah hear you saying that, sweeting. No, you cannot stop your lessons. Don't you want to grow up an accomplished lady?'

'No. I want to be rich, and have lots of horses, like you.'

Edward laughed and said, 'She has you there, Ralph.'

Ralph grinned. 'Well, little one, to be rich you must marry a rich man, and he will want you to be clever and accomplished so that you will grace his big house. Morland ladies have always been well-educated. How shall you be a great lady if you cannot read and write?'

'Mama cannot read and write,' Sabine said judiciously. 'Isn't she a great lady?'

It was time to cut free from the dilemma. Fortunately, at that moment Ralph caught sight of the last of his brood, standing back a little from the fray, holding the hand of his tutor and watching the scene quietly.

'Ah, there is my littlest one!' Ralph said with relief. 'Come forward, Martin, for my blessing.'

Martin let go of Lambert's hand and walked quietly through the crowd of children and dogs to kneel before his father. Even in his bunchy petticoats, there was something of dignity about the tiny child, and he walked with an uprightness that reminded Ralph of his mother. Mary had the proud easy carriage of the hill-people, and always held her head up like a queen, moving so lightly and quietly that she hardly seemed to touch the ground. It was clear that Martin, when he grew up, would be like that too. Ralph laid his hands tenderly on the small head. Under his white linen cap, Martin's hair was a dark, rich brown, so dark it appeared black, and it had a soft curl to it that made his fingers stray almost of their own accord to touch it. Ralph spoke the blessing, and Martin turned his face up to regard his father with those disconcertingly blue eyes.

'Thou art thy mother's child,' Ralph murmured, and stooping down he picked the boy up and held him in his arms so that their faces were on a level. Martin looked at him solemnly, unsmilingly. 'Have you worked hard this morning? Have you done your lessons well?'

'Yes, sir,' Martin said.

Ralph grinned. 'Then I don't know whose child you may be, for both your parents are terrible dunces. You must be a changeling, as they say.' And Martin, not understanding the words, but knowing that his father was joking, smiled suddenly, a smile so sweet that it would have charmed a bird from its branch. Ralph kissed his brown cheek and put him down, then addressed the tutor. 'Have you a good report of them all, Master Lambert?'

'Yes, sir, upon the whole. I have not beat them at all today.' Lambert was a dark-haired, pale-skinned Welshman, so gaunt and emaciated that he looked as though he might die at any minute. He was a Catholic who had lost his position with the growing severity of the law, and had tramped the country since, passed from household to household, keeping only one pace – and sometimes a small pace – ahead of imprisonment. Fear and deprivation had undermined his health; he had spent much time in hiding, even more on the run. It was through Mary's pleas that he

27

had got his present position, for he had come to Morland Place one night with a letter of recommendation from a neighbouring family in Redesdale. Mary, like most Borderland folk, was a Catholic, and she had begged Ralph to take Lambert on. Ralph had been doubtful about endangering the family, but at length it was agreed that Lambert would have the position as tutor, and keep the fact of his priesthood a secret even from the servants. As no one knew him in the neighbourhood, the thing was feasible, and so far he had not been discovered, though there must have been many who had their suspicions.

'Not beat them?' Ralph said, half jokingly. 'How will they learn if you do not beat them?' But as he spoke he hugged Martin to him, and then set him down, as gently as if he were made of eggshells. Mary came back into the hall at that moment, and Ralph was filled with such an upsurging of love for her, the mother of his children, that he wanted to do something special for her.

'My dear,' he said, the idea coming to him as he spoke, 'look what great lads your two eldest are grown! Do you not think it is time they were breeched?'

Ned and Edmund stared at him, their eyes growing rounder with excitement.

'Really, Papa?'

'Do you mean it, Papa?'

'Why, yes, of course. Ned, you are past six, and Edmund is well grown for his age. I think it is time you put off your petticoats and put on manly dress. What do you think, Mary, my love?'

'If it pleases you,' Mary said, but Ralph could see that she was pleased.

'Then we shall send for the tailor this afternoon,' Ralph said, and smiled down at his two eldest sons as they jumped up and down and cried out their thanks. 'And now, shall we go in to dinner? I think it is past time.'

Clem went into the city after dinner and brought back the tailor to measure the two boys for their first ever suit of breeches and doublet. He also brought back some news, which he beckoned Ralph aside to hear.

'The word all along the road is,' he said, 'that Master Makthorpe is not best pleased with you, Master. The word is that he is offended at your interference and has sworn to bring down your pride. I beg your pardon, sir, but I thought you would want to know.'

'Yes, of course,' Ralph said, puzzled. 'But I have done nothing against him.'

'You took the poor folk's side against him, Master. That would be enough,' Clem said. 'Master Makthorpe knows that we all view him as an incomer. And there have been raids on his barns, and one of his ricks set afire. If he can suppose it done at your bidding, sir, he will.'

And only an hour later there was the sound of horses in the yard, heralding a visit from Makthorpe himself.

'He comes like Lord Percy, with a retinue of armed men,' Edward said disgustedly. 'Will you see him?'

'Of course,' Ralph said. 'I must.'

Ralph received him in the hall with all formality, with Edward and Kit at his shoulder and all his male servants around him. The latter stepped forward firmly to bar the entry of Makthorpe's followers.

'If you please,' Ralph said quietly, 'your men must leave their arms outside.'

'What? What?' Makthorpe said blusteringly. 'Disarm my men? What would ye be about, Master?'

'No man enters Morland Place armed, nor ever has, unless he enters by force,' Ralph said in the same quiet tone. Makthorpe stared for a moment, and then made an abrupt signal to his men to fall back.

'Then they shall wait at the door,' he said sharply. He and Ralph stared at each other, equally matched in this situation. Makthorpe was a big, red man, who might have been called a fat man except that his fat was hard. He was like a rose-hip, and as bald as a rose-hip, and the skin of his bald pate was darkened by the weather to an unpleasant, freckled brown-red. He wore the Puritans' garb of dull black and brown, and the white linen of his collar and cuffs was soiled and stained. His finger nails were black-rimmed, and he carried about him the sweet, greasy smell of the unwashed.

'Now then, Master, I have come to talk to you,' Makthorpe said, his scrutiny apparently over.

'Say on, then,' Ralph said.

'I speak to you alone. My words are for your ears,' Makthorpe said, casting a comprehensive glance around the hall. 'We'll go somewhere, just you and I alone.'

Ralph glanced quickly at Edward. 'I have no secrets from Edward,' he said, taking a significant half step towards him. Makthorpe sneered.

'Happen tha hasn't, but that's nowt to do wi' me. My words are for thy ears alone, Master, so doos tha come wi' me privately, or am I to go?'

It was the contemptuous use of 'thee', having nothing to do with friendliness, and Makthorpe's lapse into the vernacular was his way of shewing that he was too powerful to care what Ralph thought of him. In such circumstances, 'master' was almost an insult, but Ralph, knowing the basic weakness of his position, kept calm and, with a silent nod to Edward, led Makthorpe towards the stewards' room. As soon as they were alone, Makthorpe began.

'Now then, Master, you have had a brush with my men this morning, so I hear.' He stood with his legs straddled and his hands on his hips, looking massive and immovable, and the arrogance of such a stance in another man's house riled Ralph.

'Your men were preventing a commoner from exercising his rights of commons. Harewood Whin is, and always has been—'

'Harewood Whin is mine,' Makthorpe said, cutting hard through Ralph's exposition.

'You cannot erase rights of common. They are one of the basic rights of the people, based on—'

'I can do anything I like,' Makthorpe interrupted again. 'You had best get used to that idea, Morland, for it will cause you less pain if you get it straight. I am Justice of the Peace and I can do what I like. I have powerful friends in high places, and you have none. You are a proscribed person, a royalist delinquent, a payer of fines, Ralph Morland of Morland Place, and the sooner you humble your pride and acknowledge who is the top man around here, the better it will be for you. I don't like being opposed, not by anyone, and especially not by a Morland. Don't interfere with my men, or my land, or my orders. Do you understand?'

'I must stand by my people,' Ralph said quietly.

Makthorpe's face reddened with sudden rage, and he roared, 'Your people? *Your people*? You talk like a bloody king – your people!' His rage abated as suddenly as it had come and he went on in his normal voice, 'Well, what do I expect from a Morland? Nay, Master, must I spell it out to thee? I 'ave much of Morland Place already, and I will 'ave more, sithee. Interfere wi' my men, and tha plays into my hands.' He strolled over to the window, and appeared to change the subject. 'You have a tutor for your bairns, a man called Lambert?'

'That's right. It is no secret.'

Makthorpe turned, surprisingly swiftly for such a large man, and his eyes narrowed. 'Nay and it's no secret that the man is a Catholic priest. No use to deny it, Ralph Morland – his story has caught him up at last. Aye, and what's more, it's no secret that your wife is a Papist.'

Ralph paled, but controlled himself to say firmly, 'It is not a crime to be a Papist.'

'Aye, I know what you mean. It is not a crime to be a Papist, but it is a crime to hear the Papist mass. A crime for any priest to speak it, and a crime for any man – *or woman* – to hear it.'

31

Now Ralph was genuinely surprised. 'I don't know what you mean,' he said. There had been no Mass said at Morland Place since Edmund died.

'No use to look innocent,' Makthorpe said. 'It is common knowledge. Not all your servants are tolerant of Papism. Many of 'em hate it as much as I do. Now I've left you alone so far, but if you bother me, I s'l have to bother you. And you know what the penalties are for recusancy, don't you? Think on.'

And with that he turned on his heel and strode out, leaving Ralph bemused and shocked. Was it possible that Makthorpe was right? Was Mary secretly hearing Mass with Lambert? Was that why she pleaded to have him taken on? And then he shook the idea away. Impossible! Mary would not deceive him so, put the household in such danger. He followed into the hall, and watched in silence as Makthorpe and his men departed.

'What did he want?' Edward asked at length, provoked by Ralph's silence. Ralph looked quickly at him, opened his mouth to speak, and then shut it.

'He wanted to frighten me,' Ralph said.

Edward smiled, not a pleasant smile. 'And were you frightened?'

Ralph said nothing.

That night when he and Mary retired, he watched her with more than his usual attention. It was his custom to get into bed first, and to sit up propped against the pillows, drinking his final draught of wine-and-water while he watched her moving about the room, brushing her hair, singing to herself, picking things up and putting them down. Her hair was long and dark, reaching, when loose, almost to her knees. She had once, when she was pregnant and it was very hot, put it up out of the way for coolness, plaiting its great length and then winding the plait about her head like a crown. It was a strange style, unfashionable and odd, but it suited her, and Ralph liked it, and so she had continued to wear it thus, and it fascinated him to see the close, shining coil unfastened and come tumbling down, to be shaken free and brushed into a glossy mane.

But tonight, though his eyes followed her as usual, his expression was withdrawn, and his mind was in a turmoil. It shocked him to discover how little he knew her, and it shocked him even more to discover the jealous workings of his own mind. He loved her, and ought therefore to trust her, and yet he did not immediately dismiss the idea that she might actually be hearing Mass with Lambert and thus endangering him and all the family. And, his mind went on relentlessly, if she deceived him in one thing, might she not deceive him in another? He wanted to halt the terrible thoughts, but did not know how.

At length Mary looked across at him, and seeing the strangeness of his expression, she halted in what she was doing and said, 'What is it? Did you want to say something?'

'Yes, Mary.'

'What then?'

'Mary, I—' He stopped again, and she waited, patiently, watching him. She looked so young and childlike in her white, lace-trimmed bedgown, with her hair falling like a dark cape about her. She put a hand under the mass of it and flung it back over one shoulder, an unconscious gesture that turned his heart in him with love for her. She was his wife; her belly was beginning to swell with another of his children; he loved her. It came to him suddenly that the trouble was his trouble, and that he must not burden her with it. She was dark and silent and strange, alien to him and to Morland Place. She was the captive of his spear, and she bore the captive's fate in silence, but he could not make her bear the victor's burden too.

'It is nothing. Come to bed, my heart.'

She stared for a moment longer, and then obeyed him, dismissing the interlude from her mind. In the darkness

Ralph held her and thought, if it is true, I do not want to know. And if it is not true, I do not want to be ashamed. Either way, I cannot tell her. She is entitled to my loyalty, at least.

And the next morning he was closeted with Edward for a very long time.

The breeching of the boys took place four days later, when the tailor had had time to make up the new suits. It was made into something of a celebration with family and friends gathering for a festive supper and singing and dancing. The two boys were formally divested of their petticoats, and with so many hands upon them that the process was hindered rather than helped, they were dressed in their manly clothes. The tailor had done a fine job, and nothing was forgotten, from broad-brimmed hat right down to the matching fur muff. Then Ralph brought out the special surprise, the two swords he had bespoken, half-size and perfectly balanced for the lads, and he buckled them on and then sent Ned and Edmund to walk about the room so that they could all admire them.

'They look so tall,' Mary said, and there was the hint of a tremble in her voice, for now they were her bairns no longer.

'And much prettier than in their petticoats,' Ralph cried. 'I think these skirts should be burned, the ugly old things – don't you, my boys?'

'Yes, yes, burn them!' the children cried. It was the signal for an outbreak of the kind of horseplay they all loved, and soon they were marching round the room, Ralph in the lead, bearing the despised petticoats on the point of his drawn sword, waving them like a banner. The children marched behind him, Ned and Edmund proudly, with their hands on their own swords, like great generals, and the rest behind, snatching up musical instruments as they passed and playing impromptu marching music. Even solemn little Martin trotted at the back, beating out the steps on the tambour.

The guests and servants fell in too, and the whole procession made its way out into the yard where a brazier was dragged out and the petticoats were burned with some mock-formal speeches from Ralph. Supper came next, a special supper as it was the first Ned and Edmund had ever sat up to. They sat very erect and quiet, red-faced with pride, on either side of their father, and were too moved by the importance of the occasion to eat much. Sabine sulked furiously at not being allowed to sit up too, and took her dismissal with Ralph and Martin to the nursery so badly that Leah was forced to give her a whipping rather than the sugar-plums she had secreted in her pocket for a compensation.

After supper everyone retired to the long saloon to spend the evening with singing and dancing and making merry. When the dancing was beginning, Ralph watched with amusement and some exasperation how all the young men and boys gathered eagerly round Annunciata, asking for her hand, leaving others girls partnerless. It would not do, he thought, making his way towards the group. For one thing, there were her cousins Cathy and Elizabeth, young ladies of the house, who were being slighted. And for another, there was Young Kit, drooping disconsolately a little way off, watching with hurt eyes like a dog banished from the fire. Annunciata was enjoying her power, sparkling at one young man and then another, and Ralph had to conceal a smile as he strode through them, pushing his way gently up to Annunciata and taking her hand.

'Now then, gentlemen, I'm afraid I have to announce that Mistress Annunciata Morland is going to disappoint you all. Her hand for the first dance is promised to me, and who can argue with the Master of Morland Place?'

He led her away, and the others scrambled off good-humouredly after other partners; even Kit, glad that Annunciata was to dance with someone he could not regard as a rival, went to seek out Cathy with good will. Annunciata walked beside Ralph to the head of the set, her eyes sparkling with happiness at the distinction of dancing with Ralph himself. As they took their place she turned her face up to him and smiled, and his heart melted. By God, he thought, but she is lovely! Her eyes were dark brown, almost black, warm, hypnotic and shining, fringed about with long dark lashes; her face was long, finely shaped, with high cheekbones and a straight, proud nose and chin, but her mouth was full and long and curling, delicately etched and yet sensual. With that mouth and those eyes, he thought, she could make any man in the world fall in love with her. And she was not yet fifteen!

'Well?' he murmured to her upturned gaze.

'Thank you for dancing with me,' she said.

'I had to prevent a fight breaking out,' he said with mock sternness. 'Are you not ashamed to draw all the young men away from your cousins? Poor Cathy and Elizabeth had no one to dance with.'

'Oh, them,' Annunciata said carelessly. 'They would have had, once I'd chosen.'

Ralph laughed aloud. 'You mischievous little baggage,' he said. 'How calmly you take it! Well then, if you will not pity them, pity poor Kit. He suffers agonies while you flirt with every man in the room. Why cannot you be kind to him?'

'Oh, but he is so dull,' Annunciata said, frowning.

'Nonsense,' Ralph said. 'He is a very intelligent young man.'

'He cares for nothing but books,' she said.

'Not true. He likes to hunt and to dance and – well, to do everything you do. He is a good looking boy, too. What more do you want? The truth is that he is too good for you.'

'He is not!' Annunciata flashed out, and he smiled, and she saw he had been provoking her.

36

'Anyway, you should not flirt when you are to marry him.'

'We are not betrothed,' she said quickly.

'No, but everyone has known from the time you were born that you were to marry him. He expects it. Everyone expects it.'

Annunciata moved her head restlessly. 'Perhaps. But he is not – oh I don't know, Ralph. He isn't fun. He is not like Edward.'

'Ah, Edward,' Ralph said softly, looking down the set to where his uncle was dancing with a pretty young woman, the daughter of a neighbour, and making her blush. 'Edward is a different proposition.' He looked down into Annunciata's face quickly enough to catch the wistful expression with which she was watching Edward. 'You could not marry Edward,' he said, 'even if Edward wanted to marry you.'

'I know,' Annunciata said, and made again that restless, escaping movement of her head. 'If only—' she said, and stopped. Ralph looked at her with unexpected sympathy.

'If only Edward's person could be united with Kit's fortune?' She looked up, surprised and wary. 'But life isn't like that, little cos. So if you will make life easy for yourself, dance with Kit and be kind to him, and do not chase after Edward's heart. Be contented with Kit's.'

'Kit doesn't love me,' Annunciata said, and said it so naturally and easily that Ralph stared, his gaze sharpening. Kit not love her? It was axiomatic that Kit loved Annunciata. But she was clever about people – did she know better than the rest of the world? Was there nothing more in Kit's disconsolate drooping than hurt pride?

'Well, then,' Ralph said, trying for lightness, 'be contented with my heart and Kit's hand in marriage. Will you dance with him next?'

'I want to dance with you again,' she said.

'I am flattered, you minx, as well you know I would be, but I shall not dance the next. So will you dance with Kit?'

'All right, if you want me to,' Annunciata said. At the end of the dance Ralph led her up to Kit, and seeing the pleasure on the young man's face decided Annuciata had been wrong about Kit's not loving her. Annunciata was not ungenerous, and having been persuaded into dancing with Kit she did it with good grace, and was pleasant to him and smiled at him and laughed at his jokes, and so Kit glided down the set with the rapt expression of a man in paradise. But she could do those things without occupying much of her mind, and her eyes under their carefully-drooped eyelids were sharply observing the rest of the room. She was looking particularly for Edward, to see who he was dancing with this time, but she could not see him anywhere. Then, just at the end of the dance, she saw him and Ralph slip out through the far door, the south door.

When she had curtseyed to Kit and escaped from him, she drifted up to a servant who was standing near the buffet, helping to serve the cooling drinks.

'Where did the Master go, and Master Edward?' she asked casually.

'Master said he was going to look at one of the horses, that he said was restless earlier on.'

Annunciata nodded and drifted away again. She waited until everyone was milling around choosing partners for the next dance, and took her own opportunity to slip out of the south door. The great staircase was well-lit, with candles in brackets against silver sconces, and there was always a chance of a servant coming by and asking her what she wanted. Quietly, her feet soundless on the drugget, she slipped into the great bed chamber, through the dressing room, and out into the little stone passage that led to the old spiral staircase, the chapel stairs. It was quite dark on the staircase, but she had gone up and down it a thousand times, and her feet were sure. In a moment she had passed swiftly through the great hall and was going out by the buttery door into the moonlit yard.

She was running towards the stables when she heard the

sound of hooves, and some instinct made her pull back into the shadow of the house as the great bulk of a horse came out of the stables, its hooves clattering and skidding on the cobbles. It was followed by another, and they paused in the yard as the two men leading them pulled down the stirrups and mounted. Annunciata watched in silence as they rode out under the barbican and were silhouetted briefly against the lighter sky beyond. There was no mistaking the air of tension about the two men that spoke of some secret purpose in this unexpected outing; just as there was no mistaking the great height and breadth of shoulder in Ralph's silhouette.

Without further thought, Annunciata lifted her skirts and ran towards the stable block where her own pony was stalled.

CHAPTER THREE

Her pony, Nod, knuckered softly in greeting as she pushed into his stall and reached for his halter rope. There was just enough moonlight to see by, and it glinted from the bit of his bridle, hanging up on the wall above his head. Annunciata could not have reached it without finding something to stand on, but in any case, she reasoned, there was no time to bridle him, or she would lose sight of Ralph and Edward. Nod was quiet, and she had ridden him since she was five: she was not afraid.

She led him out of the stables, and the sound of his hooves on the cobbles was so loud that she was sure they must hear it within and come running out to stop her. Forcing herself to move calmly – for if she startled the pony her adventure would be over – she led him across to the mounting block. He stood quietly while she got up on the block and scrambled awkwardly across his bare back. She had never ridden cross-saddle, and it felt most peculiar, but she thought it must be easier than side-saddle, and she was the best horsewoman in the county. Taking a twist of his coarse mane as well as the reins, she kicked him into a walk, and as soon as they were clear of the barbican she pushed him into a canter, keeping him on the grass so that the riders ahead wouldn't hear her.

It was harder to see them than she had expected, and she almost ran into them, for they had been passing through the shadow of a treed dip in the track when she caught them up. Luckily Ralph hadn't brought the dogs with him, and she was able to haul Nod round off the track and amongst the trees. She saw him turn his head sharply and look back as if he had heard something, but they did not stop. The next moment they were out into the moonlight and she had them in plain view. It was easy now – she had only to hold well back and keep to what shadow she could find, and she could follow them wherever they were going.

She thought at first they were going to Shawes, but then they turned off the path towards Ten Thorn Gap. Here they crossed a long stretch of open ground, and Annunciata had to hold Nod right back, for if either of them turned there they would certainly see her. So she had to stay back in a hollow until they had passed through the gate in the brake of high black thorns, and by the time she herself had gone through, they were out of sight.

She pulled Nod up and stopped to consider. The most obvious ways they could have gone were either straight on towards the Whin and Rufforth, or north towards Knapton and North Fields. The Whin seemed most likely, for if this clandestine outing was not connected with Makthorpe's illegal operations there, she did not know what it was about. She was about to turn Nod towards the Whin when something gave her pause. She never knew what it was, then or afterwards – perhaps something heard or seen at the very limit of her senses – but after a moment's hesitation she turned Nod's head northwards, and began walking along the track towards the North Fields.

The country here was open champion, and on either side of her rolled the fast-ripening corn crops, oats and barley, their strips turning and curving with the contours of the land so that they looked like giants' rake-marks. In the moonlight the crop shone silvery-gold, and as she rode along she made a fantasy for herself, that the land was the back of a dun horse and the crops were his coat, which his giant master had just finished currying. Now there was an almost square area on her left where the crop was not oats or barley or even beans, but wheat. Dikes had been cut to either side of it, and it was obviously lovingly cared for. Very little wheat was grown in those parts, and what there was was generally used to make the master's soft white bread, and was guarded like gold, even the gleanings being gathered by servants for the master and not left to the poor folk as was customary with other crops. Annunciata had only had wheat bread on a few occasions, at celebrations and feasts at the big house, for Shawes had no wheat crop, and in any case half-and-half or clap bread was considered good enough for children. When I am rich, she thought to herself, I shall have white bread every day.

Then she was roused from her reverie by the sound of sheep. Beyond the wheat was an enclosed field, called the Bur by the local people, and on a rise in the middle of the field was a stone shippon. When this land had been Morland land, the Bur had been used to contain sheep that had to be held separate for some reason – ewes to be bred, for instance, or young sheep to be marked. In bad winters the breeding ewes had sometimes been driven in there for shelter from the weather and the wolves, and the field had been enclosed for so long that it was actually hedged with a stone wall, into which were let several wooden gates.

There were two horsemen by one of those gates now, and from the murmur of sheep voices there were ewes inside. At once, like a flash of light, Annunciata knew what Ralph and Edward had come for. They were going to let Makthorpe's ewes onto his wheat. She had heard, as had everyone, of the other attacks that had been made on his property – the ricks fired, the becks fouled – and she wondered if they were Ralph's doing as well. But then she shook the idea away. It was not the sort of thing Ralph would do. Even this, the letting of the sheep, could not be the whole plan. Perhaps, she thought, this was the diversion, to attract attention and take Makthorpe's men away from somewhere else. At any rate, they would need her help. She rode forward confidently. Two men without dogs could not hope to direct forty ewes.

Edward saw her first. The two men were moving gently along the sides of the flock, not speaking much, and the sheep were running quietly so far, moving straight forward, though at any time they might all suddenly swerve one way or the other in that maddening, inexplicable way sheep had. Ralph was further from her, beyond the sheep. Edward turned his head, perhaps attracted by her movement, and quite clearly in the still air she heard him exclaim. 'Holy St Mary!'

Then Ralph looked, and they both paused for a second as Annunciata rode forward.

'I came to help you,' she called softly.

'Go back! Go home,' Ralph called back. 'You must be mad, child. Go home at once.'

'Don't be silly. Now I'm here I might as well help you. Nod's a good sheep pony.' He was, as Ralph ought to know, for he had seen her often enough helping the shepherd for fun. He was standing now like a rock as the sheep flowed past him like a river, and the ewes, after the manner of their kind, were steadying to his calm and using him as a marker.

Edward saw all that in an instant, and called to Ralph, 'Let her stay.'

Ralph lifted a hand in a gesture of resignation as he and Edward exchanged a glance. There was nothing they could do about her presence until the sheep had been moved, or they would lose the whole flock, but after that – she would have to go. Annunciata turned Nod gently and chivvied the edge of the flock as it came too far over her way, while on the other side Ralph trotted Fox forward to station him at the dike at the edge of the wheat crop. Annunciata did not see exactly what happened, but suddenly Fox went into a half-rear, and then staggered, slipping on the lip of the dike. He scrambled for his balance, but with the surge of sheep passing him and jumping the dike he could not get firm foothold. He fell, and Ralph disappeared under him.

There was a moment's pause while both watchers expected to see the horse scramble up and Ralph reappear, but then the horse whinnied, and Ralph cried out, a groan of pain hastily bitten off in the remembered need for secrecy. Fox did not get up, though his head came up, nose pointing skywards, and there was the sound of his struggle in the darkness. In a flash of intuition Annunciata knew what had happened. Fox had cast himself in the dike, and could not get up, and Ralph was trapped underneath. She kicked Nod into a canter and rode straight through the sheep, scattering them like pebbles under hooves, caring nothing if she lost the whole flock, for she knew that a cast horse will thrash about in panic, and a man trapped underneath could be crushed to death.

Breaking through the sheep, she could see Fox's hind-quarters sideways in the dike as they had slid from under him, while his forehand was turned the other way, one foreleg folded under him awkwardly. Even as she halted Nod and slithered to the ground, she saw the horse lift his head again and thresh madly, and heard again the groan of pain from Ralph, invisible in the darkness of the dike under his big gelding. She must stop Fox from moving at all costs. She dropped Nod's halter rope and flung herself at Fox's head, and putting all her weight against his neck and head, pushed it to the ground and pinned it there. His head immobilized, he kept still, though she could hear him snorting in terror.

'I've got him, Ralph,' she cried. 'Are you all right?'

'My arm,' Ralph groaned. 'Broken. My ribs – I think—'

Edward reached them at that moment and flung himself from the saddle. His horse pulled back, snorting, from the strange dark shape in the dike, and Annunciata called to him, 'Fox is cast. Can you get in and free him? Ralph is trapped underneath.' Edward tried to approach, but his horse pulled back. 'Let him go,' Annunciata pleaded.

'I can't,' Edward said. 'He'd be off across country. I'd never catch him.' Ralph groaned again.

'Oh God,' Annunciata cried. 'We must do something, quickly. Wait—' Fox was quieter now, trembling under

44

her, but not trying to free himself. 'Edward, can you get near enough to hold Fox down while I get into the dike? Stand on his neck or something, just keep him still.'

'You can't—' Edward began, and then shut his mouth. The situation was critical. 'All right.' Coaxing his horse, he moved nearer, and as Annunciata slid off Fox's head, he got one foot up on the neck just behind the head and put all his weight on it. He had not expected it to be enough, but Fox seemed to accept his immobility, and though he trembled and snorted, he did not move. Annunciata crawled round him and into the dike. Running her hands over Fox's shoulder she located his trapped foreleg and eased her hands along it.

'Hold on, Ralph, not long now,' she murmured in encouragement, but Ralph did not reply. She wondered if he had fainted. The pain must be bad. Her hands passed round the knee and down the slender cannon bone. Ralph was under his shoulder and flank. It was the tip of the hoof that was caught, dug in behind a stone in the wall of the dike. The stone was immovable, so all she could do was to brace herself and try and lift the hoof far enough for the trip of the shoe to clear it. She strained, feeling her own muscles begin to tremble with the effort, but her arms were strong from riding.

At last there was a grating sound, and she felt the hoof come free. Fox felt it too, and tried to pull his foot away from her, but she kept hold and turned it back under his body to get it straight. Left to himself he might easily wedge it back into the same position.

'Is it done? Are you ready?' Edward's voice came urgently from above.

'Wait,' Annunciata said tersely.

'For God's sake, hurry. We mustn't be discovered.'

'Wait,' she said again, more firmly. She must find out the position of Ralph's body. If any part of him were under the hind hooves, he might be badly hurt when the horse used them to lever himself up. She crawled round and

45

reached under the horse. No, the hind hooves were clear. She pushed her hands in to locate Ralph's position. If she could hold him still while the horse got up, it would be better for him. She stretched herself as much as possible over his body. He did not speak or move – she guessed that he was unconscious.

'All right,' she said, trembling a little. 'Get him up.'

Edward took his foot off Fox's neck and as the horse lifted his head he caught hold of the bridle and pulled.

'Come on, Fox, good lad. Up you get, old fellow.' Fox moved cautiously, and then, feeling the improvement of his position, dug his forehooves in and scrabbled his hind hooves round under him. There was an instant's pause, and then he heaved himself up and scrambled out of the dike. It was a terrible moment for Annunciata, like being trapped in a bottle with a thunderstorm, and the world seemed filled with the huge, hot, horse-smelling weight of him, while her puny, fragile body alone stood between the man-crushing power of the gelding and Ralph. Something hard hit her shoulder a numbing blow, and she closed her eyes and crouched lower, and then suddenly the horse was out and clear and the fresh night air blew round her again.

Ralph groaned again, awakened from his faint by the pain. Carefully Annunciata felt around his body. The outflung arm was the one that had been caught under Fox's shoulder, and it had an odd angle to it where it had been broken. His other arm had been crushed against his ribs, but the rest of him was straight, and she hoped he might have escaped further injury.

'Can you get up?' she asked him. 'If I hold your arm? Is anything else broken, do you think?'

'My chest hurts abominably, but otherwise I think—' He tried to sit up, and cried out with pain as his arm moved.

'For God's sake, hurry,' Edward cried, holding the two horses. 'We will be found any moment.'

'I'll have to tie your arm with something,' Annunciata

46

said. She thought frantically for a moment, and then lifted her skirts and felt for her petticoat laces. There was nothing else that would come off easily, and she cursed women's clothes, that took so long to put on and take off. At last she freed one petticoat and drew the unwieldy mass of linen out.

'Jesus!' she heard Edward exclaim in mixed anxiety and exasperation.

'Wait!' she snapped again, and drew the petticoat round Ralph's shoulders. 'Is the horse sound?' she called up, and then to Ralph, 'I'll have to hurt you, moving the arm.'

'He seems all right. He's trembling, but he's standing square. Oh hurry, hurry!'

Annunciata took firm hold of the broken arm, biting her lip in squeamishness at the horrible unnatural feel of it. She began carefully to fold it across Ralph's chest. He groaned in pain, and she knew how much it must hurt him, for he would have tried not to make any sound as she did it, and the groan had been forced past his lips. She heard the rough end of the broken bone grate, and it made her shudder, but she had the thing in place now and was pulling the petticoat round it and securing it as best she could with the waist-laces.

'There now,' she said, and Ralph turned his head away from her and vomited, simply as a dog, from the pain.

'Sorry,' he panted at last.

'Can you get up?' she asked. She got her feet under her and passed an arm round him, wincing as he put his weight on her shoulder.

'What's the matter with your arm?' Edward asked her.

'Nothing,' she said impatiently. Ralph was on his feet now. She helped him out of the dike, and Fox snorted and goggled away from him, swathed strangely in white. He'd never manage Fox with one arm broken and God knew how many ribs. A little way off Nod was waiting, his loose halter rope hanging, his head drooping as he dozed, resting one hind hoof and then the other. Either of the other horses, let go like that, would have been half across the county by now. Oh thank God and St Francis for good, gentle ponies! 'You'll have to ride Nod,' she said to Ralph. 'I'll take Fox.'

'But you can't—' Edward began. It was all he could do to hold the two of them, upset as they were. Annunciata silenced him with a glance.

'What else can we do?' she said. She helped Ralph over to Nod, who was small enough for Ralph to be able to get astride him without too much pain. Kicked into motion, Nod would find his own way home – all Ralph would have to do would be to stay on. Annunciata gave him one doubtful look as he crouched in pain on the pony's back, and then she turned back to Edward and the two horses. Fox looked enormous and her shoulder was throbbing with pain now as the numbness of the blow wore off. She put out her sound hand to the reins, and Fox laid back his ears and snapped and jerked his head away. She met Edward's eyes and they exchanged thoughts. The other horse, Bayard, was no better.

'Help me up, will you?' she said. 'He's much too tall for me.'

There was nothing else to be done. Edward took hold of her bent knee and lifted her to the saddle, and she settled herself and took the reins.

'Come on then,' she said. Edward mounted and they walked forward. Annunciata called to Nod, who watched them for a moment and then started after them. She tried to still her hurt shoulder by pressing the arm across her waist, but the jiggling was still extremely painful, and she had no stirrups to steady herself. Fox was quieter than he might have been, suffering from shock, but he was still no easy ride, especially when she had only one hand to control him with. It was a nightmare journey that seemed to go on for ever. She clamped her teeth shut against the pain, and prayed that she might not fall off.

Annunciata winced as Ellen eased her torn sleeve away from her shoulder, and at Ellen's sharp glance, took her lip between her teeth to avoid shewing further weakness.

'I've no sympathy for you,' Ellen said.

'I asked for none,' Annunciata retorted, and then cried out involuntarily as Ellen tugged again. The cloth of her sleeve was sticking to the wound with dried blood, and as it came free she felt the warm flow begin again.

'Whatever you meant by it I s'l never know,' Ellen grumbled on. 'Rushing about alone at night – riding astraddle like a – like a – Dear God 'a' mercy, what have you done to this arm?'

Annunciata screwed her head round and squinted down, and felt a little sick at the sight. A deep flap of skin had been gouged up and it gaped like a mouth, pouring fresh warm blood, while all around a spectacular bruise was already blackening.

'Fox must have caught me with a hoof as he got up,' she said, trying to sound nonchalant. 'Ouch!'

'Bide still, tha troublesome maid!' Ellen said crossly.

'You're hurting me!'

'I've to see if there's owt broken. Bide still.' Ellen flexed the joint and turned it and Annunciata yelped again with the pain.

'You will break it if you do that. Leave me be. I'll be all right.'

'No justice if you are! The Devil looks after his own, they say, and it 'pears you're sound enough, but for the bruising. Well, you'll have enough pain to remind you of this night's work, if there's not worse to pay. However you could think of such a thing – but then you didn't think. You never do. Who will marry you, when you've made a scandal of yourself, do you think?'

'I can marry anyone I like,' Annunciata said crossly. Ellen dipped a cloth in the hot water held by a pop-eyed maid and began gently to swab the wound. Annunciata braced herself and did not cry out, and Ellen could not help admiring her courage, even while she deplored her behaviour.

'Aye, you like to think so, my maid,' she muttered, peering at the bloody flap and dabbing carefully. 'You think yourself the best match in Yorkshire, I doubt not, but you'll find otherwise when the young men shake their heads. Because believe me, no man wants a wildcat for a wife. Men want a gentle, proper maiden to wed, and if you don't mend your ways, you'll find no one wants you, not even Master Kit.'

'I don't care if I never wed,' Annunciata said.

'Don't care was made to care. You'll care right enough.'

'I tell you I won't. I don't want to marry. I want to stay single and enjoy myself. Married women don't have any fun.'

'Fun!' Ellen exclaimed, scandalized. 'What a way you talk, Miss! Fun indeed! You'll wed all right – but you'll wed the worse if you don't mend your ways.'

'I don't want to marry,' Annunciata persisted. 'My mother didn't – ouch!' Her hand flew up to her cheek as Ellen slapped her with all the force of her sinewy old arm. As her cheek reddened slowly with the mark of four fingers, she stared at the old woman through tear-filled eyes.

'There's for saying, tha scandalous child. Never speak so again, doos tha hear me? Never.'

Annunciata opened her mouth and closed it again. She had rarely seen Ellen so angry and determined, and thought better of arguing with her. After a long pause, Annunciata said very softly, 'You know who my father was, don't you?'

Ellen's eyes were suddenly sympathetic, but she flicked a glance towards the little maid, who was having the most exciting evening of her life so far, and said, ' 'Appen I do, 'appen I don't. Now hush till I finish binding thee.'

Ellen bound the bruised shoulder tightly, and pulled the torn sleeve up. She had just sent away the maid with the bowl of bloody water when the door opened and Ruth,

Annunciata's mother, came in. Her face was stern, and very pale under her tan. She seemed to have aged that night. Her eye brushed coldly over her daughter and rested on Ellen.

'Have you done?'

'Aye, Mistress. There's nowt broken, nowt but a big bruise amiss—'

'You'll need to find a shawl to cover that torn sleeve for the moment. Ralph wants to see her. Go with her and stay with her, and when he has done, put her to bed. Tomorrow morning we will ride home. And then,' she turned her eyes at last to Annunciata, who flinched at the anger in them, 'and then, I'll give you the beating you deserve for this night's work.'

'Nay, Madam,' Ellen protested, 'don't trouble yourself. I'll beat her myself tonight.'

'No,' Ruth said. 'You would be too soft with her. I'll do it, and see it done properly. Go now and fetch the shawl.'

Ellen scurried off, her eyes anxious. Annunciata waited awkwardly, wanting to speak to her mother but afraid to meet those hard eyes. Ellen, be too soft? she thought. Ellen had always viewed it as her duty to counteract the rest of the world's admiration for Annunciata. At length she looked up at her mother, and saw Ruth's gaze averted. She was staring at the ground, both thoughtfully and unhappily, and Annunciata's heart turned in her, for the one person in the world she really loved was her mother, and she could not bear to think it was her own delinquency that was making her unhappy now.

'I'm sorry, mother,' she said quietly.

Ruth looked up and stared at her consideringly, and then she sighed. 'Perhaps you are. But if you knew beforehand what the consequences would be, you would still do the same.' It was not a question, and Annunciata could not think of anything to say. 'Something will have to be done about you, that's for sure.'

Annunciata's mouth went dry. She did not know what

her mother meant, but the only thing that came to mind was that her mother might send her away, to a convent abroad or something like that. But there was no time to speak, for Ellen came back with the shawl and draped it carefully over her shoulders.

Ruth said, 'Go now and speak to Ralph, and then get on to bed. I'll make you up a draught. Ellen shall give it to you.' And she turned away and went without another word.

Ralph was propped up in bed, his eyes heavy from the strain and from the draught Ruth had already prepared for him. Mary and Leah between them had set his broken left arm and splinted it, and it lay beside him on the bed like something that did not belong to him. His other arm and his ribs and back were severely bruised, but they did not think there was anything else broken.

When Annunciata came in he roused himself enough to smile and say, 'Come closer, cos. I want to thank you.' Annunciata walked up to the bedside between the hostile ranks of women and servants, all of whom deplored what she had done. She held her head up and looked neither to right nor left. Ralph's eyes went to the bulky bandage on her shoulder, and he frowned anxiously. 'Are you hurt, child? What has happened to you?'

'It is nothing,' she said. 'A small cut and a bruise. Fox must have struck me as he got up.'

Ralph's eyes glowed. 'Take my hand,' he said. 'I can't move to take yours.' Following the gesture of his eyes, she reached out her left hand and took his right one, which lay across his body for support. His warm fingers closed round hers and he squeezed them tenderly. 'You saved my life, little cousin,' he said. 'For that there is nothing I can ever do to thank you.' Meeting his eyes, Annunciata felt his warmth spreading through her, and she smiled.

'There is no debt,' she said.

'I shall never forget it,' he said. He looked round at the lowering faces and raised his voice to say, 'Will you all move a little off. I would speak with my cousin privately.' With ill grace they complied, and Ralph, still holding her hand, said, 'Sit on the bed, so that I can speak lower – but be careful not to move my arm.'

She obeyed him, feeling unexpectedly comfortable. So close to him, the warmth of his big body seemed to envelop her. Suddenly she wondered what it would be like to be in bed with him, and the thought, taking her unawares, made her blush before she was able to thrust it away. Ralph's eyes never left her, and almost as if he could read her thoughts, he pressed her hand again and his smile turned into a grin, lighting the gold flecks in his grey eyes and driving away the lines of shock and tiredness.

'Will you get into trouble, chuck?' he asked her softly.

She shrugged, and then wished she hadn't. 'Mama says she will beat me, but I don't care.'

'Ah, poor you! It's all my fault.'

'No, it isn't. It's my fault for doing what I knew was wrong.'

'You're a brave little thing,' Ralph said admiringly. 'You don't make a fuss. You should have been a boy.'

'That is why my mother is to beat me,' she said, laughing at him.

'Listen, sweetheart, I meant what I said. You saved my life, and I shall not forget it. I shall find some way of making it up to you, for the beating at least, if not for the hurt shoulder.'

'Will you get into trouble?' she asked, suddenly grave.

'I hope not. Things are bad enough.'

'What had you meant to do?' she asked very softly. He shook his head slightly.

'Better you do not know. I would not have you involved more than you are. Now, chuck, kiss me once, and then off to bed with you. I am falling asleep.'

She leaned forward to put her lips to his cheek, and at

the last moment he turned his face and took her kiss on his lips. A warm tingling passed through her at the touch of his mouth, and she thought that she had never smelled anything so sweet as his skin. Then she drew back, released her hand, and stepped away from the bed. On her way out she passed Mary, and their eyes met. Mary's face was always impassive, but just for a moment she looked at Annunciata with a strange expression, partly speculative but part – could it be – envy?

In the little room where she slept when she stayed at Morland Place, Annunciata stood swaying with weariness while Ellen undressed her. Cathy and Elizabeth were asleep in the bed on the far side of the room, and Annunciata and Ellen stood in a small pool of light from a shaded candle, as if they inhabited a tiny island in the sea of darkness.

'Well now, what did the Master want with you?' Ellen asked as she pulled the sleeves down. Her voice was the merest murmur, barely moving her lips. 'He were looking at you such a way—'

'He was thanking me for saving his life,' Annunciata said.

'Saving his life, tush! Such a way to talk. You're vain enough as it is, you don't need any encouragement to think well of yourself.'

'I don't,' Annunciata said wearily.

'Aye, and you do, or you'd not think you were a law unto yourself, and go rampaging off like a mad hare—'

The conversation was settling itself along familiar lines, and Annunciata felt close to tears.

'He said he would find some way to make it up to me,' she said in desperation.

'Happen he can come between you and your beating tomorrow,' Ellen said caustically, and then was sorry, for it is not a pleasant thing to have to look forward to. 'Eh,

54

lamb, I'm right sorry I could not save thee that – not that tha doosn't deserve it an' worse—' she sharpened her voice out of sheer habit, but went on, patting her young charge's sound shoulder – 'but after all, wi' thy poorly arm and all – I s'd think tha's had enough punishment. Happen the Master would speak to thy mother for thee?'

'No,' Annunciata said quickly. 'I wouldn't let him anyway. It would be too shaming.'

'Well, well, as you say,' Ellen said soothingly, and helped her off with her gown. It was difficult to get the nightgown on, for Annunciata could not lift her right arm at all now, but they managed at last, and Ellen helped her into bed and pulled the covers up, smoothing and petting them as if they were Annunciata herself. 'There then, child, sleep thee well, and God bless thee. Th'art a sight too good for any man, though I say it, and even if Master Kit could marry thee, I'd say you were twice too good for him, and so I s'd tell anyone, so there.'

She stopped abruptly, and in the electric pause that followed, Annunciata's eyes opened wide and she stared at her nurse in wonder.

'What do you mean, Ellen?'

'Nay, nay I mean nothing, nothing at all.'

'What do you mean, if Master Kit could marry me?' Ellen primmed her lips and Annunciata went on firmly, 'I shall not let it be until you explain, and so you might as well tell me now and save yourself pain. Come, dear Ellen, what did you mean? Tell your little girl.'

Ellen sat down suddenly on the bed. 'Eh, but tha's a silvery tongue for such a steely mind. Well, I'll tell thee, for I think tha s'd know any road. But never tell anyone I told thee, not thy mother nor anyone.'

'I promise.'

'Master Kit cannot marry thee, nor tha marry him, for you are brother and sister together, so now then.'

She folded her lips and her arms, and Annunciata stared uncomprehendingly.

55

'But – Kit and me? – What—?'

'Coom, Miss, think it for thyself.'

'You mean, we had the same father? Kit's father was my father?'

'That very thing. But think on, it's a secret. I just thought tha s'd know, lest tha fall in love wi' him.'

'But how do you know?' Annunciata asked at length.

'Because thy mother loved him when she were a lass, and she never loved anyone else, not all her life long.'

Annunciata considered. 'Is that all?'

'It's enough. Doost think thy mother would lie wi' a man she didn't love? But there's more.'

'Well?'

'On the night tha was conceived, Kit's father were in the house. He and thy mother talked alone together. On the very night tha was conceived. And all this long while thy mother has let folk think you were to marry Kit, for the very reason of turning their minds from the truth of who your father was. But she's never said it in so many words. Just let folk think it, and not gainsaid it.'

Annunciata thought back, and saw that this was true. She stared at Ellen with eyes as black as dark water. 'Kit my brother?' she whispered at last. 'I can hardly believe it.' And her tired mind ranged over the years she had grown up with him, and she wondered if that was why she had never felt able to love him as a future husband.

Ellen took the candle and tiptoed out, leaving Annunciata in darkness, for the moon was down now and it was quite black outside. The draught her mother had made up for her was beginning to take effect, and the jangling pain in her shoulder was dimming to a throb. Her mind was drifting in a pleasantly cobwebby way which prevented her from worrying too much about the events of the evening or the problems the morning would bring.

Kit my brother? she thought again. Kit's father, who died at Marston Moor, my father? If it were so, her father died before ever she was born, and she did not want that to be true. She thought of her mother, who had shared her house with Kit's mother, Hero, all Annunciata's life. No, she couldn't believe it. Her mind was hovering on the brink of sleep, but the thought came as clearly as the sound of a bell across the darkness, clear with certainty: Kit my brother? *I don't believe it.*

CHAPTER FOUR

Makthorpe paid his visit four days after the accident. Ralph, still in bed, had expected some kind of reprisals and had warned the servants, and particularly the watchman on the gate, to be alert. Clement, the old butler, came to him to report that Makthorpe had been seen riding towards Morland Place.

'But this time he's come like a Christian, Master,' Clement said. 'Only four men with him, and they not armed, though they're wearing some kind o' livery, for all the world as if he was a baron.'

'Prince Palatine more like,' Clem put in quietly. 'That's how he fancies himself.'

'And he not even a gentleman,' Clement went on indignantly. 'Why, he has no coat-armour, and his father, they do say, was nothing but a—'

'All right, Clement,' Ralph interrupted, trying to get back to the point. 'If he comes like a Christian we shall have to receive him like one. You had better get down to the hall, and tell the mistress to receive him with as much honour as he shews.'

'I don't like it, not one bit, Master, straight I don't.'

'Line up as many of the servants as you can, and make sure they're tidy.'

'I'd sooner he came threatening, then we'd know where we were.'

'And don't forget to apologize for my not receiving him myself.'

'The wise shepherd fears the smiling wolf.'

'Get on, Clement, and stop muttering,' Ralph said affectionately. 'I shall beware this smiling wolf, don't you worry. Be off, now, or he'll be in the hall before you.'

Clement went out, still muttering. Clem, hesitating on his way out, met Ralph's eyes. 'Father's right, you know, sir. He must be very confident if he can afford to come without arms.'

'All we can do is brazen it out,' Ralph said. 'You know nothing, anyway, so you can tell nothing.'

'I can guess, though.'

'So can Makthorpe. Every man's guess is his own personal treasure, so let him keep it to his breast. Go on now, and help your father.'

Left alone for a little while, Ralph brooded on the implications of Makthorpe's visit. He had expected him to come earlier, and armed, angry and threatening. Could it be that he did not know who had let out the sheep? Perhaps it would be possible to brazen it out. But then, as Clement said, Makthorpe was the wolf: you could never trust him.

He came in, genially smiling, bringing with him his own distinctive miasma of dirt and old sweat. Ralph, who was a fastidious and cleanly person, shivered at the smell as a horse shivers at the smell of pig.

'Well, well, Master Morland, here you are sick abed! As soon as I heard I had to come and visit you, like a good neighbour, and see how you fared. Your arm, is it? Broken! Dear me, how troublesome for you.'

'A horse fell with me, and rolled on it,' Ralph said. 'It was kind of you to come.'

'Not at all,' Makthorpe said, and then, in case it sounded like a mere form of politeness, he expanded. 'Not kind at all. Merely curious.' The smile slid off his face like a lizard slithering down a crack, and he waved the attendant servants off with an imperious hand which no one felt like disobeying. Then he surveyed Ralph with the cold and calculating eye of a fell-monger. 'I wanted to see how you carried off your act. Creditably, I must admit. The first act, servants in hallway, a household carrying on as normal despite the Master's unfortunate accident. The second act, Master in bed, pale faced but brave. Yes, yes, a very good act. Have you ever been to a playhouse? No, of course, you are too young, they have been closed these many years. And rightly too, or do you disagree?'

'I have nothing to say on the subject of playhouses,' Ralph said.

Makthorpe smiled wolfishly. 'Very wise. Opinions on that troublesome topic should be kept *in petto*, especially when your visitor is Justice of the Peace, charged with the moral welfare of his people.'

Ralph writhed to hear Makthorpe talk about 'his people', but he held his tongue. So far nothing had been said to suggest Makthorpe knew what was going on, only that he was suspicious. The very next words dashed his hopes, however.

Makthorpe narrowed his eyes and said with an air of coming down to business, 'So, then, Morland, you ignored my warnings not to interfere with my business again. You interfered, and in a very troublesome and, I may say, expensive way. Forty breeding yows running loose about the countryside, and the Devil's own job to round up again. And an acre of wheat trampled and eaten, fit for nothing now. Do you know, I have had to turn my stirks on it – there was nothing else it was fit for. All my good wheat – and wheat as dear as gold dust in the markets. Shall I have to eat dark bread this winter, Master Morland? And shall it be your fault?'

'I don't know what you're talking about,' Ralph said.

Makthorpe sneered. 'Don't trouble yourself with denying it, Master. I know it was you and your young friend. As I told you before, not all your servants love Papists.'

'You said that before,' Ralph agreed. 'What did you mean by it?'

'Just that a powerful man has to have friends in many places.'

'Spies, you mean.'

'Call 'em what tha likes, Master,' Makthorpe said

contemptuously. 'One of thy servants eats my bread; one of thy hounds feeds at my hand. I know.'

'You could never prove it,' Ralph said, his mind working furiously.

'Couldn't I? Don't be a fool. With a man to testify, and my own picked jury, what chance do you think you'd stand?' He looked at Ralph easily, the man with the power. Ralph felt his anger rising, but he was at a disadvantage, lying on his back, immobilized by his arm. 'When I first heard,' Makthorpe went on, 'I was that angry, I wanted to come right over here and haul you off to prison there and then. But I cooled a bit, and thought a bit, and that's why you did not see me until now. And now I see you, I think happen tha's been punished enough. A broken arm is a nasty thing, and never heals sound, does it? And besides, I've bigger stakes in you than an acre of wheat and forty sheep. I want Morland Place, all of it, and I mean to have it.'

'Not while I live,' Ralph cried furiously.

Makthorpe smiled unpleasantly. 'Why, what a funny thing you should say that,' he said. 'Nay, but I won't threaten. That's for little men. You know what I can do. I have my faithful servant in your household, who will report to me whatever you do, and sooner or later I'll get the evidence I want. And then I shall have you, and I shall have Morland Place. And that woman of yours, your wife, so-called—'

'Don't you dare to speak about her like that, you – Ralph boiled over in fury.

Suddenly the mask was off Makthorpe's face and he snarled like a wild animal. 'I do her too much honour to call her a woman. She's a Papist, and they are fit for nothing but to be fed to the dogs. Nay, it would dishonour a dog to feed on filthy Papist flesh!'

It was all there, the common people's unreasoning hatred of the Catholics. Makthorpe's father had been a flesh-merchant, and Makthorpe had been brought up with all the prejudices of his class. While his adoption of Puritan ideals went only skin deep, his hatred of Papism was bred into his bones. Ralph fell back on his pillows, pale and exhausted. 'Get out,' he said. 'Get out of here. And don't ever come here again.'

Makthorpe moved away, the mask back on, the geniality of his power like a thick slime over his words. 'I'll come back, and when I do it will be as master of this place.'

'I'll kill you first,' Ralph said wearily, without passion.

Makthorpe grinned. 'Aye, you'll need to, for nowt else will keep me out.'

And he turned away, beckoned to his servants, and walked out. For a moment there was silence in the room, and then with a helpless gesture towards his manservant, Barnabus, Ralph leaned over the side of the bed and vomited.

'We've got to find out who it is,' Edward said, not for the first time. He was sitting beside Ralph's bed, and they were alone in the room. That was the terrible thing, having suspicion cast on the servants, when they had all been completely trusted before. 'We've got to find him out and get rid of him.'

'I know that, but how?' Ralph said wearily.

'Is there anyone you don't trust? Anyone you've ever had doubts of?'

'No, of course not. If there had been, I'd have got rid of him. You know that.'

'It was a useless question anyway,' Edward said. 'You're far too trusting. You'd trust anyone.'

'How should I not?' Ralph said, running a frustrated hand through his hair. 'All the servants are old friends. I've known them all my life. The old ones have been in the family for years, and the young ones are their children, or the children of local people. No one likes Makthorpe. I can't believe anyone would betray us to him.' A thought crossed his mind. 'Perhaps it isn't true! Perhaps he said it only to confuse and upset us, to make us distrust our own people and perhaps give ourselves away in the process.'

Edward looked at him levelly. 'Do you believe that?'

Ralph's face fell. 'No,' he admitted. 'He knew, all right. About our midnight ride. Someone told him. No, he was telling the truth when he said one of my hounds fed from his hand.'

'All right, then we've got to work it out. Who went out of the house? Who would have been able to get word to Makthorpe?'

'Lord, any of them! All the outside servants, and most of the men in the house are out some time or other. And we don't know when Makthorpe got the word. He didn't come here for four days. It could have been any time between then and now.'

'That's true,' Edward said, and lapsed into silence. At last he said, 'It's hopeless. We'll just have to watch them all, and see if we can detect any suspicious behaviour.'

'We can't watch them all,' Ralph said. 'There are too many. Besides, there are some we can rule out. I refuse to believe it could be Clement, or Clem, or Jakes, or Jack – or Arthur, or Barnabus—'

'Aye, aye,' Edward stopped him, grinning, 'or any of them. We are back where we started, Ralphie. You refuse to believe it could be anyone. As I said, we shall have to watch them all. And we shall have to watch our step.'

'I wonder,' Ralph said suddenly, 'if he knows about the part Annunciata played.'

'He didn't mention her,' Edward said thoughtfully. 'And yet, if it was one of our servants told him, he must know.'

'Unless the servant did not think it worth mentioning. Let's hope so. Not for worlds would I have her in trouble. I would sooner she never even knew of Makthorpe's existence.' He brooded for a moment, and then his face lightened. 'By Our Lady, but she's a brave lass!'

Edward's glance slid sideways. 'She shamed me,' he said. 'I should have done what she did, Ralph. But I hesitated.'

'No, no,' Ralph protested. 'You did right not to let go of the horses, Ned. We should have been in a terrible mire without them. It was no shame on you.'

'I didn't think of the horses, not right away. I was afraid, Ralphie. I saw those threshing hooves and I was afraid. But Annunciata just jumped in.'

'She thinks more quickly than us, that's all,' Ralph said soothingly. 'You would have come to help me in another moment, wouldn't you? You'd have given the reins to her to hold and jumped in yourself.'

'Yes – but—'

'There you are then. It was no shame, Edward. We are what God makes us. Come, come, Nuncle, cheer up! No one thinks the worse of you.'

The old, joking nickname made Edward smile, and they dropped the subject, though Ralph could see that Edward had not forgotten it. He resolved not to mention again in Edward's presence how brave Annunciata had been, or that she had saved his life, for he loved Edward and not for worlds would cause him pain. But he had not forgotten what he owed Annunciata, and he resolved to give her some token of his appreciation at once, until he thought of some more permanent way to thank her.

Annunciata had almost completely rejected Ellen's theory about her fatherhood. From time to time she did look at Kit speculatively, and wonder, for there was a very faint resemblance between them. They were both fine-boned and dark-haired, and she did feel very sisterly towards him. But she would always reject the thesis. The resemblance between them was not marked, and she was bound to feel sisterly towards the boy she had grown up with from the moment of her birth.

Annunciata knew very little about her mother. Ruth was a very private person, and spoke rarely about herself, never about her feelings.

Why had she done it? Annunciata wondered. How had it ever come about? Had she loved the man, secretly, though there was some terrible bar to their love? It occurred to Annunciata that perhaps Ruth had merely, simply, wanted a child. If she had wanted a child of her own, to whom to leave her estate, but had not wanted the trouble of getting married and sharing her power with a man, was it not possible that she had chosen a man and got herself pregnant by him, just as she might put a favourite mare to a good stallion, for the colt she would get out of it?

The thought persisted in Annunciata's brain, and made her feel uncomfortable for some time. It was the kind of coldly logical thing her mother might do; and what did that make Annunciata? And then her sense of humour asserted itself, and she told herself that if her mother had done that, she would at least have chosen the best stallion in the land to cover her. Maybe Annunciata had royal blood! That would please Ellen no end!

Ellen came bustling in and discovered Annunciata, chin in hand, daydreaming and smiling.

'Eh, what art thou about? Sittin' smilin' like a heathen. Stir thissen up, child, and get on. We s'l be all behind, and we've to be at Morland Place this morning. Has said thy prayers?'

'Yes, Ellen, of course,' Annunciata said calmly, getting to her feet.

'I wonder,' Ellen said, narrowing her eyes. 'And has read thy devotions?'

'Yes, Ellen.'

'What was the subject?' Ellen said quickly. Annunciata smiled disarmingly.

'Patience,' she replied. Ellen's suspicion waned no more than a fraction.

'Aye, well tha's read wi' scant attention, I'll be bound,

and it'll have done thee no good, to judge by the smile on thy face. What was tha thinking about?'

'Oh, nothing. Isn't it a beautiful day?'

'Never mind beautiful day, how come tha sits thinking nothing, when there's more to do than tha can finish in a day? The Dark Gentleman will find thee something to do if I don't. And get up, miss, at once, and look to thy skirt! It's all up at the back! Eh, but th'art more trouble than four lambs at one yow.'

'Why are we going to Morland Place?'

'Because the Master has bid us. There's that sewing to do before you go, so get busy and stop asking questions. Where's needle at?'

'I wonder if we'll ride to the Ash Woods? Edward said he saw the marks of a boar there. I wonder if Ralph's arm is well enough to ride yet? I wonder what we'll have for dinner.' Annunciata stared dreamily out of the window.

'I'll give thee something to wonder at if tha doesn't pick up that needle at once,' Ellen grumbled, lifting a threatening hand.

Annunciata shook herself out of her reverie and picked up the needle and the top piece of plainwork in the basket. She had a certain amount to do every day, and though she hated sewing, Ellen and Ruth between them always saw to it that she completed it, and so it was best just to get on and not annoy Ellen, who could be troublesome when roused. She sat down on the stone window-seat where the meagre light from the slit window was best, and jabbed the needle into the linen shirt. Ellen watched, her expression softening. There was, despite all her wickedness, a kind of goodness in Annunciata, she thought, a kind of uncomplaining, getting-on-with-things attitude that Ellen valued, for it was very much a Yorkshire trait, and people tend to value in others what they value in themselves. 'That's my good girl,' she said, watching Annunciata stitch away at the seam. 'It's all good practice for you, for when you're mistress of Shawes, you'll have to do your daily task, just like now.'

Annunciata looked up and smiled her best smile, an unaffected, sweet smile that never failed to win Ellen.

'When I am mistress of Shawes, I shall be just like my mother. And, Ellen, I don't believe Kit's father was my father.'

'Well, and tha's a great deal too good to be any man's child,' Ellen murmured, and her wrinkled face softened even further. 'Get thy task finished, my wee lamb, and I s'l put out thy blue dress to wear to Morland Place.'

It was her best dress, and Annunciata loved it. 'Will Mother mind?' she asked cautiously.

'Thy mother won't notice,' she said briskly. 'Not if tha went dressed in sacking an' binder twine.'

Ralph was up and about again, with his broken and splinted arm supported in a sling of cloth around his neck.

'Just like Mary when she has a new bairn,' he joked. Mary, like many of the people of the far north, generally carried a new baby around with her at first in a fold of plaid or linen. Leah tutted a little at the habit, thinking it was not becoming to the dignity of the mistress of Morland Place, but Ralph liked it and would not forbid her. It suited her slow-moving, easy grace.

He was in the hall to greet the party from Shawes, and he at least noticed Annunciata's dress.

'Why, how smart and pretty you look,' he said, making Annunciata flush with pleasure. 'That colour suits you.' There was much more he could have said, but he was aware of disapproving glances from several quarters, and so he hastened to make much of the rest of the party before saying, 'Annunciata, I should like to speak to you alone for a moment before we dine. Will you come to the steward's room?'

Annunciata, who had stationed herself beside Cathy so

that the contrast should shew up her beauty, was startled from a reverie, and stepped forward, holding her head high as she became aware of all eyes on her. Fern pushed up against her as she followed Ralph across the hall, and she placed one hand on the bitch's head, aware of what a pretty picture it made. Fern, for once, co-operated in the plan, and walked sedately, keeping her great rough head under Annunciata's small white palm until they were out of sight.

Cathy watched the studied exit, exasperated. She was perfectly well aware of why Annunciata always chose to sit or stand near her, and even from time to time feigned friendship with her. Elizabeth suffered in the same way, though less frequently, for while Elizabeth's painful shyness and lack of wit and conversation were a perfect foil for Annunciata's personality, her face was, if not beautiful, at least sweetly pretty. Cathy had suffered so many illnesses as a child that she had never grown well. She knew that she was sickly-looking, pale and thin and undersized, and beside Annunciata's blooming healthiness she looked like a weed that has grown in the dark. Besides that, she had taken after her mother in looks, and her mother had been as plain as clap-bread. Cathy had her mother's rather chinless, rabbity look, pale-lashed eyes, freckled skin. Her hair, which she had lost in a childhood illness, had grown back coarse and fuzzy and sandy-coloured. Added to that, she had no best dress, and the russet wool she had on only made her look more ginger than ever.

Cathy tried hard not to feel resentful, and not to dislike Annunciata, for she had been brought up with sound religious principles by Mary Esther. She knew that it was wicked to question the ways of God, and yet she couldn't help feeling that He had been unneccessarily unkind in making her up so ill. Need the contrast have been so great? she found herself asking, in spite of all her efforts. Cathy, though not outstandingly clever, was clever enough, and having been diligent in her lessons was accounted accomplished amongst women, even amongst Morland women.

But Annunciata, as if her health and beauty had not been enough, was also endowed with that casual quickness of intelligence which allowed her to grasp things easily and remember them effortlessly. Without having tried half as much as Cathy, she was twice as learned; without practising the hours that Cathy did, she both played and sang better than her cousin. Cathy could have endured to be uglier than Annunciata, if only she could have been cleverer.

She sighed and looked across at Elizabeth. She was small and plump with brown curly hair and a round face and a sweet, shy expression. Her mother, Henrietta Morland, had died in childbirth, and her father, Charles Hobart, had very soon afterwards married a rich young widow with two sons of her own, and had proceeded to have two more sons by her. Having, therefore, no use for Elizabeth, her father had sent her to Morland Place to be brought up and educated. It had been well known from the beginning that her father did not intend to provide her with a dowry, and therefore it was very unlikely that she would be able to marry, so she would spend her life at Morland Place unwed, as a lady companion to one or other of the Morland women.

Because of this Elizabeth, like Cathy, had always been slighted by the servants; but unlike Cathy she felt no resentment. She knew her humble position, and having no great brilliance of mind she accepted it, and was only grateful for what little attention she got. When Annunciata stood or sat near her, she reddened with shyness, but was pleased at being sought out. It exasperated Cathy, but it would have been as wrong as impossible to teach Elizabeth to hate Annunciata too.

'How is your shoulder?' Ralph asked Annunciata when they were alone. He stood by the fireplace and leaned against it with his sound arm, so Annunciata had to come further into the room to face him. She positioned herself so that the sunlight coming in through the window would light her hair. The side pieces were fastened back with four pink rosebuds that Kit had sent to her while she was dressing, and she was aware of how well they looked.

'It is mending,' she said. 'It is still very sore, and there is the most frightful bruise. Such a good job one mayn't wear décolleté dresses nowadays,' she added, 'for the bruising would show even through lace.'

Ralph laughed. 'Oh little cousin, you are so vain! I swear you would be willing to suffer twice the pain if only it didn't mark your pretty skin. Confess now, would not the greatest internal pain be preferable to you to the smallest blemish on your face?'

Annunciata frowned. 'I don't know what you mean,' she said crossly. 'I am not at all vain. I am perfectly well aware that it is a sin against the Holy Ghost—'

'You are perfectly well aware of how pretty you are at every moment of the day. Why else do you stand next to my sister in the hall? And why else do you stand where a ray of sunlight will touch the roses in your hair? No, don't move – I like to look at you. Who picked the roses for you?'

'Kit,' Annunciata said, trying not to smile and failing.

'So you are being kind to him at last?'

'Is it kind to accept his flowers?'

'It is always kind to accept a gift. I know we are told that it is more blessed to give than to receive, but it is a great art to receive elegantly and graciously. And I have asked you here today to give you a little practice in that art.'

'You have a gift for me?'

'Ah, how that lights your face! You like to be given things – and why not? Sweets to the sweet. It gives people joy to give, and your avarice is in excellent order, as Edward would say. Yes, I have a gift for you, a small token of my gratitude for your help.'

He reached up onto the high shelf above the fireplace and brought down a cedar box, opened it, and held it out

70

to Annunciata. She came forward and looked into the box, and then looked hesitantly up at Ralph.

'Yes, go on, take one out. They are for you.' She reached in and drew out one of a pair of bridle ornaments, and held it up so that the sunlight glinted from it as it turned and swung from her fingers. It was a disc of gold which fitted over the loop at the corner of the crownpiece, and from it hung three golden chains onto which were threaded, at intervals, polished beads of dark pink coral.

'It's beautiful,' Annunciata said. 'It is the prettiest I have ever seen.'

'They belonged to Mam,' Ralph said. It was his name for Mary Esther, a pleasant compromise between Madam and Mother. 'She had a pretty chestnut mare called Psyche that she always rode, and I remember these ornaments dancing and jingling as Psyche pranced along. Mam said they looked like bunches of half-ripe raspberries. My grandfather gave them to her, and so I give them to you. They should belong to a pretty woman.'

'They are so pretty,' Annunciata said, taking the other out of the box and holding them both up. 'I don't know anyone who has anything so fine.' She smiled at the thought of how grand it would be to have such fine bridle ornaments – real gold, and real coral. Then a slight frown of anxiety crossed her face and she looked up at Ralph again. 'But—' she began.

He grinned. 'Don't worry, they are mine to give. So much of our family treasure has been sold, but one or two things I held back. The black pearls, for instance, I would never sell, and the amethyst collar, and the Queen's emeralds, and the Percy jewels. And some of Mam's things. I could not part with them to strangers, but they should be used. She would be glad to think of you having these.'

'Thank you,' Annunciata said. It was little, but it was enough. She put them back in the box, and Ralph closed it and gave it to her.

'And the next thing,' he said, 'is to get you a good horse.

71

It is long past time that you had a lady's horse, not that old pony. Think how you would look on one of my fine chestnuts, with the ornaments catching the light.'

Annunciata saw in her mind's eye. It made a fine picture. How Edward would admire her; how she would lead them all a merry dance at the hunts! Ralph watched in amusement as her vanity took charge.

'I don't know that my mother would allow—' she said, hesitantly.

'I'll handle your mother,' he said. 'It can be an exchange, to salve her pride. I'll find something for old Nod to do – turn a mill or something.'

Old Nod! Annunciata had forgotten him, but now in her mind he turned his old head and looked at her with that sweet, trusting expression she knew so well. He had taught her to ride, had taken care of her through countless rides and hunts, keeping up as best he could on his strong, short legs. She had shared many hours of solitude with him, riding over the familiar fields, standing together at the top of a rise and looking over the great sweep of the land below. She thought of him carrying sacks and bales, or endlessly turning a mill, and she swallowed hard. Her vanity fought briefly with her affection, and lost by a narrow margin.

'No, thank you,' she said. 'I'll ride Nod. I am contented with him.'

'But you will not be able to use the ornaments on him. They would look out of place,' Ralph coaxed gently. It was true – it would be ridiculous to dress up the old dun pony, and she would not, for anything, make him ridiculous. Her head went up a little.

'I know it,' she said proudly. 'I shall keep them until – for another time. But I do thank you.'

'Just as you please,' Ralph said. 'Shall we go and join the others now?'

Annunciata followed him out, a little puzzled. She had half expected him to be offended at her refusal of his gift, but as he passed her she saw that he was smiling quietly to himself. Now what on earth, she wondered, was there in their conversation to make him look so pleased?

CHAPTER FIVE

Through the long, hot summer weeks, the harvests came in – the hay, the different grains, and the fruits. It was a time of hard work and much pleasure. Everyone was busy. The Morland men took off their jackets and worked alongside their employees; the schools closed so that the children could be released to help, for there was no idle hand at harvest-time. Everyone must join in so that the earth's bounty could be gathered and safely stored before the weather changed. Even young ladies might, at harvest-time, abandon some of their carefully-taught dignity to share the gentler part of the labour, and the more seemly part of the pleasure.

Ralph loved harvest-time. He could spend every daylight hour out of doors in hard, healthy exercise. He frequently abandoned his shirt and stooked alongside his men, naked to the waist, and his skin darkened to the shade of clear honey and his hair was bleached silver-white by the sun. Edward preferred to supervise the building of the haystack, for he loved to see things grow, and stacking was a creative art, building the circular base of woven branches, turning the hay-swathes inwards so that the whole structure would slope outwards and shed the rain, building upwards slowly and carefully so that hay could be drawn out for use without collapsing the rick. There was, moreover, plenty of opportunity for sampling the buxom delights of the village girls who worked alongside the men, or brought them up their dinner of meat and bread and ale or buttermilk. As he said to Ralph, 'Hay seems to have an extraordinary effect on young women's modesty. It never fails.'

All the harvesting was communal labour, and at harvest-time even long-standing enmities were put aside. Morland men helped to bring home the Makthorpe harvest, and vice-versa, and side by side they laboured on fields of yet other landowners. Hunger was the common enemy of all, and a spoiled harvest meant hunger through the long, dark winter that faced each of them.

Cathy and Elizabeth were happy to tuck up their skirts and work alongside the young village women in the flailing yard, scooping the golden grains into the shallow bowls and then emptying them into the grain bins. It ruined their hands, of course, but it was worth it for the sense of freedom and companionship. At dinner time they would sit down with the others and devour bread and cheese and great wedges of apple pie, and drink buttermilk that had been kept cool by suspending the pitchers down the dark, cold well. It was pleasant to be looked up to by the village girls, instead of being slighted by the servants, for even the prettiest of the cheerful, freckle-faced lasses thought Cathy and Elizabeth the epitome of gentle-born elegance. The village lads, too, were fun, shy and monosyllabic at first, hurrying from embarrassing encounter to the safety of work, swinging their heavy flails with much display of rippling muscle. On the first day they had been too shy to take off their shirts before the ladies, but by the end of the week they were working stripped to the waist, and chaffing the great ladies almost as freely as the Dolls and Bets and Mollys.

The little children worked out in the fields, gleaning, and made themselves useful by fetching and carrying. Mary, great with child, appeared only at midday when she helped bring the dinner out to the men. Ralph encouraged her in this, having a private theory about the beneficial effects of sunshine and fresh air. When she appeared he would put down his fork or rake and find her a pleasant spot in which to sit, spread his coat for her, and sit at her feet, plying her gently with food and drink and talking to her about the day's activities. At dinner time Morland

75

Place sat silent and empty in the strong sunlight like a great deserted ship, every living soul being out of doors. Even the dogs and cats would be stretched out somewhere outside; the pigeons and peacocks would have sought the shade of trees; only the swans, gliding effortlessly along the mirrored surface of the moat, would be moving, their white reflection breaking dazzlingly in the glassy ripples.

Annunciata had not found it necessary to help with the harvest at Shawes, in which she had found an ally in Ellen, whose pride in Annunciata was no degree less than Annunciata's in herself. But when the harvesters moved to Morland Place and everyone made themselves useful, it was no longer possible to sit in the shade with a book. She declined to join Cathy and Elizabeth in the flailing yard, having no desire to spend the next two months repairing the damage to her hands. Besides, she knew quite well that Cathy and Elizabeth did not like her company, and their company had no charms for her when there was no man to impress.

She would have liked best to be on the stacks with Edward, but that was not possible, and so she offered her skills as a horse handler. Officially her task was to hold the head of the horse that drew the hay-cart while it was loaded in the field, and then lead or drive it to the place where the rick was building and hold it while the cart was emptied. In fact, it meant that she had nothing to do for most of the time, for though Edward and Ralph went along with the fiction that the horse needed to be held, it knew its job too well and would not have moved away even if a cannon had been set off behind it. It suited Annunciata perfectly, for she went from the field where Ralph was working to the place where Edward was working, and in each place she could sit in some pleasant, shady spot and bask in the admiration and attention of the men working there. She had borrowed a plain, wide-brimmed straw hat from one of the village girls to protect her white skin from the sun, but it did not stay plain for long. Kit gave her some ribbons for it, and then men in the fields brought her flowers. It became something of a competition amongst them as to who could find her the prettiest offerings, and she spent much of each day decorating her hat with plaits of wild flowers, dog-daisies and moonwort and poppies and corn-flowers.

Then came the morning when the last of the hay went to the rick, and the rick-thatcher arrived, and by dinner time everyone was gathered around the rick watching him begin his skilful work.

'So that's done,' Ralph said, pushing his hair back from his face with a grimy hand. 'And a right good harvest, too. Tomorrow we'll get Lambert out here to bless the rick, eh, Ned? Yes, what is it, Barnabus?' His man jogged his elbow and he turned to see Mary approaching over the fields.

'Our dinner is arriving,' Edward said, throwing Ralph a warning look, for it was not wise with so many people around to speak of Lambert's priestly calling. Ralph did not understand the look, but his attention was distracted anyway by the sight of his wife.

'By all the saints, she's getting to be a grand size!' Ralph exclaimed as his wife picked her way towards him, followed by servant women carrying the baskets. 'Did you ever see such a wonderful sight, Ned?'

'Never,' Edward said dutifully, but with such a marked lack of enthusiasm that Ralph laughed.

'Ah, wait until you're married yourself, then you'll know how to appreciate a fair round belly, full of brats.'

'That is a pleasure confined to married men,' Edward said. 'Now this is more like what I care to contemplate.' Ralph followed the direction of his eyes, and saw Annunciata, drawn from her seat in the hedgerow by the sight of Edward and Ralph together at ground level. 'She's as vain as a cat, but by God she is pretty!'

Ralph glanced at him curiously, wondering at his vehemence. He had always assumed that Edward was as amused by the little girl's devotion as he was – but she was no longer a little girl, of course. Was Edward perhaps beginning to take her seriously? But here was Mary, looking hot and uncomfortable. The babe was not due for another month, so the doctor said, though Mary was so big that Ralph wondered if she might be going to have twins. Twins did run in the family, and it would be wonderful—

'How is it with you, sweetheart?' he asked, taking Mary's arm and escorting her into the shade of the cart. 'You don't look quite well.'

'I am well enough,' Mary said. She meant to be as impassive as always, but she sounded cross and tired. 'It is so hot today.'

'But the walk will have refreshed you?' Ralph said anxiously. Mary looked at him and away again. She was too big to find walking refreshing, and in any case it had become uncomfortable over the past few days, for the baby was very low inside her. But she could not speak of these things in front of the harvesters, and it annoyed her that Ralph asked questions on the subject.

'I had sooner stay at home,' was all she said. With Ralph's help she sat down on the grass and leaned her back gratefully against the wheel of the cart.

Ralph knelt beside her, screening her from the rest of the men and thus making a small privacy in which to ask her, 'Does something ail thee, hinny?'

'A pain in my back,' Mary admitted. 'Low down, like a gnawing in my spine.'

'How long?'

'All day, since this morning.'

'Is it—'

'The babe? No, it is not that pain.'

'What does Leah say?'

'Leah is gone over to Shawes, to help Ellen and Ruth with the store-cupboards.' She was suddenly irritated by his concerned face hanging over her. 'Oh I am well enough. Leave me be. You have been content to leave me be all day.'

78

'But sweetheart, the harvest—'

'Aye, aye, I know, the harvest must come first. Leave me be, I say.'

Ralph backed off, knowing that pregnant women are sometimes strange in their tempers, and saw to getting out the dinner for the men. Edward seated Annunciata nearby, close enough to look as though she was part of the group, but far enough away so that he could talk to her privately if he wanted, and the rest of the men gathered round and sat or squatted nearby. The serving-women unpacked part of their load, and then went off to take the rest to other fields.

'What have we to drink?' Edward asked, peering into a pitcher. 'Ah, buttermilk again. I shall be glad when we get to the cider-making. I never could like buttermilk. Let me serve you, cos.'

There was pigeon-pie, cold, to eat, and cold beef, and bread; there was the delicious, crumbly white cheese that Mary herself made after the recipe from Wensleydale; and the pink, sweet cheese that came up from the west country that you could cut into firm wedges; there were golden oat-cakes, Leah's special baking that no one, not even Jakes their cook, could quite imitate; an apricot tart, made from their own small, dark Morland apricots; and fat purple plums and bright yellow pears from the Morland Place orchards. Cider-making soon, Ralph thought, as he spread the food and picked out the best for Mary; no perry-making at Morland Place, though. They grew only eating pears. They had got their perry from Watermill House, before the Scots army had destroyed it and burnt down the orchards during the civil war; now they had to buy it from Somerset. Shawes made a little, but only enough for themselves.

Mary refused everything, but finally was persuaded to take a little of the Wensleydale cheese and some plums and an oat-cake, and she picked at them idly, too hot and uncomfortable to be hungry. She looked across the group to where Annunciata sat with Edward, both of them eating with good appetite and great pleasure, as if they had been labouring hard all day. They are alike, those two, she thought: they will always come out well from any situation, without any effort. Ralph was sitting beside her with his arm round his updrawn knees. The skin of his forearms was burned butter-brown, and she could see the hairs on them were bleached white, silvery-white so that they were almost transparent, making it seem that his skin had a silvery sheen to it. His profile was etched firm and beautiful against the dark-blue sky, his eyelids lowered over his sleepy, golden-grey eyes. Her own eyes traced the lines of his face, his long, straight nose, his full lips, gently parted, and she shivered suddenly with a feeling of foreboding. He turned to her, feeling the movement.

'What is it? You are not eating,' he said gently, and then started up with alarm, for Mary gave a strange little cry, more of dismay than pain, quickly cut off. Her body was rigid, her eyes fixed, as if she were listening for something.

'Mary, what is it? Is it a pain? Is it the babe? Mary!'

She turned anguished eyes to him, and then looked down at her lap, began to stand up, and changed her mind. Her lips moved once or twice as though she was not sure whether to speak or not, and then the words burst out of her despairingly.

'The waters have broken. Oh Ralph!'

Those men near enough to have heard looked away in painful embarrassment, and Ralph put his arms round her as if to defend her from the situation, for just a moment before he realized something must be done. If the waters had broken the babe would not be long behind: Mary must be got to the house. But there were not women here – they had all gone on to the farther fields. Someone must fetch them – and the doctor and midwife – if the babe was coming early Mary might need help. Thank God that at least Annunciata was here – she was level-headed in an emergency as Ralph well knew.

Ralph jumped to his feet and snapped out his orders. 'Sam, run you after those women and bid them go back to the house as fast as possible. The mistress's child is coming. Ben, go over to Shawes and fetch back Leah – run as fast as you can. And you, Barnabus, get back and saddle my horse and go for the midwife. Don't waste a moment. Mary, can you stand? We must get you into the cart.'

'What is it? Is the baby coming?' Edward came over to them, drawn from his private conversation with Annunciata by the sudden departure of the three men.

'We must get her back to the house,' Ralph said, his arms round Mary, drawing her to her feet. 'Help me get her into the cart. Annunciata, throw my jacket in there – and Edward's. Make it soft for her. Take her other arm, Ned.'

Between them the men helped Mary up into the back of the hay-cart, and Ralph said, 'You drive, Ned. Fast as you can.'

Annunciata had climbed up beside Mary, but was looking distinctly reluctant about it. The business of childbirth attracted her not at all. But as Edward went to climb over onto the driver's seat, Mary gave a terrible cry, and wrested her arm free of Ralph's hand.

'No! No men. I'll have no men. Get down, Ralph. Tell Edward to get down.'

'What—? Who will drive you? Mary—!'

'Tell him to get down,' she cried hysterically. She had felt the baby move into her passage, and she was terrified that it would come at any second. She could not endure for any man to see her give birth. '*She* will drive me.' She jerked a hand towards Annunciata, and then cried out again. 'Hurry, it's coming!'

Ralph still stared, amazed and troubled, but Edward realized what was happening. He vaulted down from the cart unhitched the reins and threw them to Annunciata.

'Get down, Ralph. Drive on, Nancy, as fast as you can. We'll follow.'

Annunciata gave Edward one desperate look of appeal as she caught the reins, but he did not return it. He whacked the horse on the rump, startling it into motion, and as Ralph too realized what was happening he jumped off the back of the cart. Annunciata yipped to the horse and slapped the reins, urging it into a clumsy canter, heading down the slight slope of the field towards the gap in the hurdles that fenced it; Mary clung to the sides of the cart, trying to brace herself against the motion, and trying even more desperately to hold back the inexorable movement of the baby inside her. Edward and Ralph were already running, but falling behind as the cart gathered speed.

Annunciata had little time to think of what might be going to happen, for all her effort was needed to guide the horse. She had driven before, but never a great solid haywain, drawn by a cart-horse that had rarely in its life moved out of a walk. The cart leapt like a live thing over the uneven ground, making her grab at the side rails to keep herself in the driving seat. She had no whip, and had to keep yelling at the horse, who was unused to laying out his legs in this manner and was automatically slowing. Then the field-gate loomed up before them. Should she stop the horse, walk him through the gap? But she might never get him going again. The gap must be wide enough for the cart, for it had come in that way. A cold hand seemed to clutch at her vitals as the hurdles leapt towards the rattling cart. She tugged frantically at the horse's mouth to correct his line, and at the last moment he swerved slightly and the cart dashed through the gateway clear. Annunciata heard Mary cry something, she could not tell what. Sweat had broken out on her forehead, unpleasantly cold in this warm sunshine. Thank God, there was Morland Place up ahead, gold-grey and peaceful like a great brooding bird, framed with blue sky and curds of white cloud.

The horse was slowing again, and Annunciata let him,

dragging him to a halt at the end of the drawbridge and remembering only just in time to put on the brake, otherwise the cart would have gone on moving and run the horse over.

'Can you walk?' she asked Mary, realizing that she was yelling and modifying her voice to continue, 'we can't get the cart through the barbican. I'll help you.'

She jumped down in a flurry of skirts, dropping the reins, for the horse was standing with hanging head and heaving sides and would not move again for some time. She ran round to the back of the cart and helped Mary to the edge, but at the thought of dropping down onto the ground Mary's courage left her.

'I can't!' she wailed.

'I'll go for help then,' Annunciata said with considerable relief. The one thing she wanted to do was to get away.

'No! Don't leave me!' Mary cried. Annunciata made a helpless gesture with her hands.

'If you don't get down, you'll have to have it there. Come, I'll help you.'

She reached up her arms and tried to take Mary's weight. Mary shuffled herself forward awkwardly, and then flopped forward. She was too heavy for Annunciata to support, and Annunciata went over backwards with Mary on top of her. Mary cried out, more with alarm than pain; Annunciata bit back her own cry, for Mary had landed on her shoulder, which was still not sound. It took her some effort to get herself up, and even more effort to get Mary up, but in the end they hobbled together over the drawbridge and through the barbican into the yard. Annunciata called out for help, wondering desperately where everyone was. Surely someone must be around.

'Hello, there! Is there anyone home?'

'Help me up to the bed chamber,' Mary groaned. 'Hurry!'

'Where is everyone?' Annunciata cried angrily. She did

not want to be left alone with this responsibility. 'Hello! There must be someone!'

Mary was almost doubled up now, and was clutching at herself with no more pretence at modesty. They reached the stairs and began climbing, and at last someone came, an old woman and an old man, standing side by side in silent wonder at the foot of the stairs. Annunciata almost cried with relief.

'The mistress – the baby is coming – you must help,' she babbled. The old couple stared up at her uncomprehendingly. 'Don't just stand there – do something!' Annunciata almost stamped with exasperation. 'Fetch help or something.'

They continued to stare at her, milky, bewildered eyes in ancient, wrinkled faces, docile and uncomprehending as oxen. Mary groaned, and Annunciata realized that no help was here. She took a firmer hold, both of herself and Mary, and barked an order that old people would understand.

'Fetch hot water, and clean cloths,' she said. 'Bring them to the great bed chamber.' She could think of nothing else. Surely someone else would come soon. She helped Mary on up the stairs. Never had they seemed so endless. The top of the stairs at last, and along the passage, and into the great bed chamber. She let go of Mary for long enough to wrench the heavy covers back from the bed, exposing the plain sheet. The covers were so heavy she hurt her wrists pulling at them. Then she helped the swaying Mary to lie down, and not knowing what else to do, began to pull of her shoes and stockings.

'It's too early,' Mary said, making Annunciata pause, puzzled, before she realized what she meant. 'It's not due for another month. If it should die! I don't want it to die!'

Annunciata said nothing. She dropped the stockings onto the floor and then began at Mary's buttons. She felt utterly helpless, and whenever Mary groaned she felt sick and frightened too. And then at last she heard what she had longed for – footsteps on the stairs, brisk, young footsteps, and she turned to the door and almost cried out with relief as her mother came in.

Ruth gave her daughter a glance of mixed surprise and reassurance as she strode briskly to the bed.

'Leah's on her way, and Ellen. I thought I'd better come on ahead,' Ruth said putting a hand on Mary's abdomen. 'I grabbed the nearest horse and galloped. A good job I did, it seems.'

'The waters broke out in the field,' Mary whispered. 'I've been trying to hold back.'

'All right,' Ruth said, and then to her daughter, 'Is anyone else here?'

'Only two old people. They were no use. I told them to bring hot water and cloths.'

'Go and hurry them up, and bring a sharp knife too, the sharpest there is. And some goose grease. As quickly as you can.'

Annunciata darted away, glad to have something to do. When she came back, her arms full of cloths and a pot of goose grease, her mother had got all the covers off the bed, and had taken off Mary's gown. Her sleeves were pushed up above the elbow and she was looking worried.

'They're coming,' Annunciata panted. 'They're bringing the water and the knife. Is she all right?'

'Good girl,' Ruth said absently. 'Is that the grease? Good, give it to me.'

'What's the matter?' Annunciata asked, looking from Mary to her mother's worried face.

'The bairn's stuck. With the water away, it's too dry to get out. You'll have to help me.' Annunciata backed involuntarily, and Ruth glared at her. 'Don't be a fool,' she snapped. 'Hold that grease pot.' The old couple came shuffling through the door, and Ruth whirled, keeping herself between them and the sight of the mistress. 'Put the water cans down there, and put the knife on the dresser. Now get out, and don't let anyone else in here, unless it's Leah or Ellen,' she snapped. As soon as the door was closed, she dipped her hands in the goose grease and pushed them up under Mary's petticoat. Annunciata, standing close enough now not to be able to avoid seeing, had to swallow hard as she saw the baby's great head stuck in the opening to Mary's body. She had not been present at a birth before, and she didn't like it at all; but she watched all the same as Ruth eased her fingers around the baby's head, working the goose grease between its skull and Mary's dried-out skin.

'All right, Mary?' Ruth said, and her voice was suddenly gentle, as Annunciata had sometimes heard it addressing a sick horse or labouring mare. 'Push when you're ready. It's almost through.'

Mary made some indistinguishable noise, and then a long, groaning cry as she braced herself to push again. Ruth's fingers worked down round the baby's head, and then Mary gave a sharp cry as the head suddenly came free in a gush of blood. The baby's head was face downwards, and Ruth quickly worked its mouth open, releasing another gush of blood.

'Dampen a cloth and wipe its face,' Ruth said sharply to Annunciata, who was staring in a mixture of horror and wonder. She scurried to do as she was bid, and as she tentatively wiped the baby's face, it opened its eyes for a second and seemed to try to move away from the touch of the cloth. Annunciata was enraptured. It was alive! The wonder of it pierced her – a new, separate life was here, where there had been none before.

'Is it a boy or a girl?' she asked her mother. Ruth gave her a glance of amused exasperation. 'How should I know, simpleton? How is it with you, Mary?'

'Well enough,' Mary croaked. 'I am so thirsty.'

'You shall have water in good time. There is work to be done yet. Are you ready to push?' Mary grunted. Ruth said to Annunciata, 'Here, take the head and support it as the baby comes free.'

Reluctantly Annunciata took the head in her hands – it

was bloody and slimy, and she loathed getting her hands dirty. Ruth was working her fingers behind the baby's neck, and then as Mary pushed again she helped ease the shoulders through. One more push, and it came slithering free in another gush of blood.

'It's a girl,' Ruth said. 'A fine big girl, Mary.'

'The blood's all over the sheets,' Annunciata said, unable to think of anything to say.

'Here, hold the baby,' Ruth said, guiding her hands underneath it. Reluctantly, Annunciata took hold of it while Ruth tied the cord and cut it, all her movements spare and efficient. She caught Annunciata's eyes on her and gave a small smile. 'It's much the same as foaling. Perhaps a little harder,' she said. 'Those sheets will never be any use for anything. You can never get the smell of birth blood off them.'

'Why is there so much blood?' Annunciata asked.

'It's God's way,' Ruth said indifferently. 'Mind what you are about! Don't drop the child! There now. Here, wrap it in this, and then you can shew it to Mary.'

Wrapped in a piece of torn cloth, the baby looked more human, and Annunciata felt much less reluctance to handle it. It was a big baby, and very sleepy. She took it to Mary, and shewed it to her, and Mary glanced wearily and turned her head away.

'I'm thirsty,' was all she said. Ruth nodded to Annunciata.

'Sometimes it takes a while,' she said quietly. 'That's God's way, too, in case the babe dies, then the mother doesn't suffer so much.'

'I'm thirsty,' Mary said again.

'You shall have some water, by and by. When the afterbirth is gone. Come now . . .'

Annunciata moved away, seeing that she was not needed just then, leaving the murmuring women and the blood-stained bed, and carried the new baby to the window to study it. It seemed a very peaceful baby. 'Shouldn't you be crying?' she asked it quietly. 'I thought babies did nothing but cry for the first few weeks.' The babe opened its eyes and stared up unseeingly into Annunciata's face. She was enchanted by it. She had never seen a birth before, except of animals. All newborn animals were lovely, but until now she had thought bairns singularly lacking in charm. But this one! She felt attached to it, she felt it was in some way hers, the more so since its mother had rejected it. She had already forgotten the pain and the blood, the terrible raw splits in Mary's skin and the smell of the birthing. The baby opened its tiny mouth in a huge yawn, and Annunciata smiled with a surge of love for it.

'I wonder what they'll call you,' she murmured.

A few days later the baby was Christened Mary Marguerite. 'Though the name is so much too big for her,' Ralph said, 'that I cannot believe she will ever be called much more than Daisy.' After her hurried and informal entry into the world, Daisy went on in a much more seemly way. The robes that should have been made for her had to be purchased ready-made, but there were plenty of fine things for the birth-chamber left over from previous occasions. Friends and neighbours came in a steady procession to visit the new child, bless her, admire her, and sit and talk to the mother, sipping caudles and nibbling honey cakes and comparing confinements. Gifts were brought in plenty, for everyone loved a birth, and no one from highest to lowest came empty-handed. There was always a great deal of public rejoicing when a woman was delivered of a healthy bairn; but the Christening was done secretly, after dark, with servants guarding all the doors, and no one but household and family attending, for it was conducted in the chapel by the old rites. Edward thought it folly, and said so, but Ralph only spread his hands apologetically and said, 'How can I deny Mary? And how can I give my daughter less than her siblings?'

The chapel was decorated with flowers, sweet chamomile and dog-daisies, and there were no torches, only candles, burning with little pin-pricks of lights in the velvety, incense-fragrant darkness. Annunciata sat amongst the memorials of those who were her ancestors as much as they were the new baby's, her eyes on the high altar and the little group gathered there. She felt very peaceful, full of a quiet joy, and for once entirely a part of what was going on. She had not lost the feeling of attachment to the baby, who was lying so quietly in her new robes in Ruth's arms, while the priest spoke the ancient words over her that made her a member of God's community.

Ruth and Edward, the sponsors, renounced the Devil and all his works on the babe's behalf. Ralph, the father, gave the child her name. Mary, still on a litter, watched from the shadows, her face marked with weariness as much as with pleasure. Her gown was of a dark red cloth which merged into the gloom of the unlit corner, so that her face and neck rose white and mysterious as if from nothing. She wore the Black Pearls around her throat, and they made her neck look as if it had been severed from her shoulders. Annunciata put the unchancey thought away from her hastily and crossed herself. There should be none but good thoughts here at Daisy's Christening – little Daisy, at whose birth she had assisted. Annunciata felt as if it was she who had given birth, rather than Mary. Mary had turned away from the child without interest. Annunciata looked at Ralph's big form cut out against the candlelight near the altar, taking the child back from the priest with his strong, sure hands, as easily as if the baby was a new lamb. Ralph the father, Annunciata the mother. She shivered at her thoughts, and began to murmur a prayer to distract herself.

When the ceremony was over, Ralph came to her and said, 'It seems I have to thank you again, cousin. If you keep on coming to my aid like this, I shall run up a fine debt to you.'

'There is no debt,' Annunciata said. It would have been unnatural to avoid his eyes, and yet she wanted to, though she did not know why. She had known Ralph all her life – he had been like a big brother to her, always there, teasing her and petting her and getting her out of trouble – so why should she suddenly feel shy?

He said, 'No, I know there isn't. But if there was, I should be happy to be in debt to you.' And he leaned down and kissed her cheek. It was a kindly, casual, friendly, brotherly kiss, but it completed Annunciata's confusion, and she felt the imprint of his lips on her cheek long afterwards, as if they had been hot enough to brand her.

CHAPTER SIX

By the time cider-making time came, Mary was up and about again, but this time she did not carry her new bairn slung against her hip. For some reason she had taken against the baby, had no interest in it at all. Leah told Ralph not to worry, that it was sometimes that way.

'You've seen it in animals from time to time, I dare say, Master. There's nothing to be done.'

'Lucky for poor little Daisy that she has you,' Ralph said. 'You'll look after her.'

'Aye, you can leave the bairn to me, and take the Mistress out a-hunting. That's the way it should be. It makes my life easier, I can tell you, Master, not to have her lugging the poor little mite everywhere with her.'

Ralph grinned. 'You never did like her barbarian ways, did you, Leah? Well, it suits us well enough, for I'm glad to have her with me again. I miss her.'

So he arranged picnics and they hunted the young autumn bucks over the open country. The weather was fine and warm and clement, and he was glad to get Mary out of doors, for she was looking peaked since the last birth. He thought she would like a trip home to Northumberland, for she had always suffered from homesickness, but the times were too troubled for such a journey. The huge standing army that General Cromwell had built up during his reign was in a ferment, for it had not been paid for more than a year, and the news from all over the country was that the soldiers were getting out of control and taking to looting and plundering. Rogues and vagabonds, too, were taking advantage of the unsettled times and the lack of firm government, so the roads had never been less safe for travellers.

But it was not Ralph's way to worry about things he could not change, and he dismissed the state of the country from his mind just as he did the menace of Makthorpe. There had been no reprisals over the Christening, and Ralph was happy enough to allow himself to think Makthorpe had been lying about the spy in his household.

Edward knew this, and it made him almost frantic. His reaction to trouble was always different from Ralph's. He feared and despaired more, and was more at pains to hide it and to compensate for it. His reaction to the trouble that, starting in the south of England, was creeping northwards, to the chaos which threatened to engulf them all, was to throw himself into a frenzy of enjoyment, and into a wild flirtation with Annunciata which left her breathless and dazzled and stopped only just short of scandal. Annunciata, congenitally restless and bored, was as eager for the intrigue as Edward, and it was easy for him to persuade her to more and more daring.

One unseasonably hot day found them far from home, farther than Annunciata had ever ridden before, and alone except for their horses. They were sitting atop a rise, comfortable on the short, sheep-bitten grass which Nod and Bayard, safely hobbled, were cropping at a little distance. The autumn sun beat down, burning the bracken gold, warming the grey stones of the wall behind them, slanting dazzlingly to the tumbling water of the river below. On the higher ground the harvests were always later, and beyond the retaining wall oats were growing still ungathered. The little breeze stirred the ripe heads into a long, slow whisper; amongst the hard green-gold stems a thousand wild flowers grew, adding their fragrance to the scent of crushed grass and upland thyme.

Annunciata sighed contentedly and pulled off her hood, shaking her hair loose from its confinement.

'It's so lovely here,' she said, 'and it's so good to be away from everyone. No Ellen! No nagging voice telling me what isn't seemly.' Edward, reclining on an elbow and watching her lazily, smiled his mysterious smile.

'She must have a lot of telling to do, with you,' he said.

'Sometimes it seems to me that there isn't anything I can safely do, except sit still with my hands in my lap,' Annunciata said. She screwed up her face and gave one of her wickedly accurate imitations of her old nurse. ' "Nay, ma lass, tha s'lt have the seemin' of a lady, if tha's not one at heart." Poor Ellen. After my mother, you'd think she would have given up.'

'She cares for you,' Edward suggested. 'And you do, for her.'

'I suppose so,' Annunciata sighed. 'It's just that—' She leaned back on her elbow and searched amongst the grass stems for one worth chewing. 'Sometimes,' she continued, 'I just wish I hadn't been born a girl.'

'The ways of the Lord are inscrutable, my Nance,' Edward murmured languidly. 'I'm glad you were. Here.' He pulled up a green stem and held it out to her, and, blushing a little under his gaze, she took it and crunched the sappy part between her teeth.

'How dry everything is up here,' she said, for something to say.

'Sheep country,' Edward said. 'They spoil grazing. That's why we fence off our good grazings for the horses and cattle. Sheep spoil everything.'

'Still – "It is the sheep has payed for all",' Annunciata quoted.

Edward smiled. 'I had that written across the top of my horn-book when I was a child.'

'So did I. It's practically the family's motto. Not appropriate in my case – Mother's fortune is founded on horses, if anything.'

'Ah, but Shawes was part of Morland Place once, and you are still a Morland.'

'Until I marry.'

Edward shook his head. 'Not you! You'll be a Morland

all your life, whoever you marry. Our family has a tradition of women such as you. Besides, Morlands marry their own. There are still enough men with the Morland name to provide you with a choice of husbands, little cos. Don't give up heart.'

Annunciata looked at him quickly and then away again, wondering what he meant. Did he refer to Kit? Or perhaps – to himself? At any rate, it was time again to change the subject. She looked down towards the river. She could see a great sweep of it from here, from the place where it ran dark and silent under the willows, to where it broadened out into pebbly shallows, flinging the sunlight in gold coins against the mellow stone of an old pack bridge, and then narrowing again to tumble whitely over boulders and natural weirs. She had lived with the sound of water all her life, and up here, out of the sound of it, she could hear it still.

Edward watched her contentedly. He had an artist's eye for beauty, and it pleased him just to look at her: for the moment, he needed nothing more. Her profile was to him as she avoided his eye. He loved the way her dark hair sprang away from her tall, full forehead, lifting back with the breeze and its own vigour, curling away down her back like a riot of dark water. He loved her straight, sharp, proud nose that, with her fine arching brows, gave her face such a look of aristocratic haughtiness; he loved her long, full, mobile mouth with its flamboyant sensuality; he loved her wide dark eyes, that belonged to neither mouth nor nose, but to some ancient and alien blood that ran in her veins. Still and dark with ancient wisdom were those eyes, bright with an atavistic wildness that belonged to some land of heat and blood and strange ritual. Those eyes had looked across desert sands, had watched the pyramids building. How alien she looked, here in the cool grey and green of the northern lands! Her strangeness excited him, stirred in him a primitive desire of possession: he wanted, simply, to own her, she who was stranger in her own country.

'I have never come this far before,' she said now, and Edward, brought back to reality with a bump, wanted to laugh aloud.

'You have gone farther with me than with anyone else,' he said, and at the faint edge of laughter in his voice she knew he was meaning something more than she did. He saw her confusion, and took pity on her.

'You shall go farther yet, one day. I predict it for you,' he said solemnly. She glanced at him cautiously.

'Can you see the future?' she asked. 'Have you the second sight?'

'And the third, and the fourth,' he said.

She looked cross. 'Don't tease me.'

'I wasn't. I can see a great deal of what's in store for you. A great future. Yorkshire will be too small to hold you. You will go far away from here. Perhaps even – to London!'

'And to Court?' She tried to pretend to be joking too, but she half believed him.

'Undoubtedly. And you shall be a great lady.'

'A duchess?'

'Well, perhaps a countess,' he conceded.

She snorted. 'And what for yourself, oh great seer? King of China perhaps?'

'No. Nothing for me. I have no future.' He tired of the game suddenly. 'Come here.' He reached his hand out, and as she leaned towards him he caught her round the neck and pulled her down to lie on the grass in his shadow. He leaned above her on one elbow, and she looked up into his face languidly. She was so trusting, he thought, half touched, half exasperated. She did not see the danger she was courting, did not consider the consequences of her 'wrong-doing'. She was all for the moment, doing whatever gratification bid her, trusting her own luck, or in this case, him, to keep her safe.

'What a child you are!' he said softly.

She frowned, a delightfully inappropriate reaction. 'Not such a child,' she said. 'You are not much older than I.'

'I was never as young as you,' he said softly, brushing a lock of hair back from her face with the back of his hand. Her skin was like cream and velvet, her eyes shockingly dark in so much whiteness. 'I was about your age when my mother died.'

'I don't remember her. Did you love her very much?'

A light had gone out when Mary Esther died. He didn't answer her question. He said, 'Even before that, I had seen so much. You don't remember the war. It was almost over before you were born. So many dead, so many betrayed, and my mother—' He stopped and was silent for a long time, his eyes on her face, but not seeing her. At last he spoke. 'You know the old wooden statue of the Holy Virgin that stands in the Lady Chapel?' Annunciata nodded. 'It is so old that there are stories about it. The servants say that on the day my father let the Parliamentarians in, the statue wept. Real tears. You will find some who say they saw it. There are marks on the face still.' Annunciata shuddered, and her hand moved, wanting to cross her, but it was held down by Edward's arms and body. Edward was not superstitious, and had scant belief in folklore. He said, 'They tell stories about what they wish was true. The statue did not weep, but my mother did, and the tears were her heart's blood. She was well and strong until the day they killed the King. Then she wasted away with grief and shame.'

Annunciata was as still as a mouse when the owl-shadow passes over it, and after a long moment his eyes seemed to come back to her, and he smiled at her apprehensive quiet.

'Sometimes,' he said gently, smiling, 'there is just a shadow of her in you, Nance, my little bird. There is something about you that just—' His words trailed away, and he leaned down, slowly and delicately, and kissed her parted lips. For a moment they were unmoving under his, and then they warmed and firmed like ripened fruit. She tasted so sweet, she was so warm and eager, and imperceptibly the embrace intensified. Edward felt his control going; Annunciata had never had any; for a moment he was tempted to give into himself. And then, wearily, he hauled himself back onto the safe side of the barrier. He released her and straightened up, and after a moment she opened her eyes and looked up at him with such a sweet, bruised look that it churned his stomach with longing. He spoke, finding himself unaccountably breathless.

'Someday, little one, you will go too far. What did I predict for you? Ah, sweet cos, you will go far, but it may not be in the direction you expect.'

Abruptly he sat up, pushing himself away from her, feeling her clinging to his senses, softly and inexorably, like marsh mist. It should be a milkmaid he brought up here, not an heiress, and a blood relative at that. The horses had moved to some distance, and he needed an excuse to move, though moving was a little difficult just at first.

'I'll fetch the horses,' he said, 'and we'll ride on a little, shall we?'

He escorted her to within a safe distance of Shawes, and left her there.

'It will be far better for you, believe me, if you pretend to have been out alone all day,' he said. Annunciata frowned. 'The worst you can get up to alone is indecorum,' he added with a smile. 'I remember you used to run off alone when you were a child. Let today stand as a childish prank.' Annunciata surveyed his face, trying to read into his expression more than it would bear, and finally, with a small sigh, she gathered her tired pony's reins to head for home. He called after softly, 'Goodnight, sweetheart. And if ever again I should shew so little respect for your reputation as to invite you out alone with me – refuse me, Nance. Refuse me.'

97

When she was out of sight, he rode in the other direction, to head across Hob Moor to the great south road. His day alone with Annunciata in the great open spaces of the moors had left him feeling lonely and isolated, and as dusk fell he sought out the yellow lamplight that fell from the unshuttered windows of the Hare and Heather. An hour or two of good company and a pint of two of strong Yorkshire ale would warm his cold heart, and would lend colour to the story he would construct to cover his day's absence. He rode into the yard, handed Bayard over to the ostler, and then ducked in under the low lintle into the warm, bright parlour. Though the room was full, it seemed strangely quiet to Edward. He wondered if he would ever get used to the lack of music and singing and dancing in ale-houses and inns: the law that forbade them, and the law that forbade the ringing of churchbells, had probably made more difference to life than anything else the Puritans had done. Well, at least the Hare and Heather had survived: the major-generals had closed many of the inns as being superfluous to the needs of travellers. The two inns on either side of the Hare had been closed, and the Cat and Fiddle was now a private residence; while the Green Man, which was at least three hundred years old, had simply become derelict, and was in the process of disappearing as people took its stones and slates to mend their own houses or barns.

Edward took his firkin and sat down on a wooden settle near the fire. There was a cheerful buzz of conversation going on all around him, and he could sense an air of pleased excitement in the room which suggested some celebration. He turned to his nearest neighbour and said, 'You are looking happy, sir – was it a good harvest?'

'Pretty good, sir, thankee. But you'll find a smile or two in here tonight, and not for the harvest neither.'

'What is it then?'

'Why, sir, haven't you heard? The news from London, sir.'

'Didn't Will shew you the news-sheet?' another man chimed in, leaning across towards Edward, eager to be the first with the news. 'Will had it this fore-noon, straight up the road by fast post-horse. News about Parliament—'

'Now, Sam,' the first man remonstrated, 'it's for me to tell the gentleman. It's me he asked.'

'Ah pray God we might get our good King back at last,' cried an old woman, sitting across from Edward in the chimney corner. Her face was so meshed with wrinkles that her features were almost indistinguishable, and she sucked on a clay pipe, further obscuring herself with clouds of acrid smoke. 'It was never merry in England since we lost our good King.'

There was a murmur of agreement, but it was cautiously spoken, and Sam threw a glance towards her and said, 'Hush, Mother,' and flicked his eyes meaningfully towards Edward.

Edward smiled and said, 'You needn't be afraid of me, sir.'

'Course you needn't, Sam, you 'apless godwit. Don't you know that's Master Morland,' a third man piped up.

'But tell me this news, goodman,' Edward prompted gently.

'Why, sir,' the first man said importantly, 'it's just that the Rump is gone. The Rump is thrown out and gone for good, sir. General Lambert, he marched in with soldiers, so it says, and threw them out, and all the people of London behind him, as are we all.'

'Oh pray God that general calls back our King from over the sea,' the old woman cried again. She rocked herself backwards and forwards in excitement, imagining it. 'The King to come home, and everything to be as it was.'

'The good times come again,' Sam joined in eagerly. 'Remember what it used to be like in here of an evening? With the old fiddler and his bitch in the corner, and dancing outside in the fine weather, and the travelling players—'

'Times were good then. We had no good times once the King left us,' the old woman crooned.

'Is that what Lambert intends,' Edward asked, 'to recall the King?'

'It don't say, sir, in the news-sheet,' the first man admitted reluctantly. 'That's all it says, that General Lambert threw out the Rump.'

'Aye, Lambert threw out the Rump, but who's to throw out Lambert?' A new voice interrupted, a young, strong voice, full of contempt. Edward knew the man, a tall ruddy fellow with a shock of yellow hair. He was Rob Smith, the blacksmith who lived out near Aksham Bogs. 'You're whistling down the wind, my lads, if you think things can be the same again, just like that. We're no better off with the generals in charge than we ever were. Why they can't even control their own men. In the midlands they are plundering villages for their food. No one's paid them, poor devils, and no one means to, not Rump nor Lambert; but without them we've got no government at all.'

'Well, and to the good,' the first man said doggedly. 'If we got no government, the King can come home.'

Rob Smith looked to Edward for help, and seeing he intended only to listen, not speak, went on, 'Don't be a fool, Gil. If the King came back the generals and the Parliament would be on trial for their lives. They won't let the King come back. Nor won't the Puritans, neither.'

'Pah! Pox on the Puritans,' Sam said, and spat juicily into the fire. 'Here, listen up, did you hear the one about the Puritan that went into a bawdy house by mistake, thinking it were a barber-surgeon's?'

Soon they were away, capping each Puritan-story with one even more unlikely, and Edward knew they could go on like that all night. When he had finished his ale he bought his companions all a drink and earned himself much favourable comment, and the conversation turned to the harvests and the price grains were fetching in the markets. A little later Edward slipped out and fetched his horse, now rested and fed, but he did not immediately ride homewards. The mood of the people had interested him, and he decided to visit a couple more ale-houses on his way home and discover whether many people were thinking of the King being called home.

It was late when finally he rode in through the barbican of Morland Place. The yard was empty, and he was glad of it – he wanted to be alone. He jumped down and led Bayard into the stable-building, and when a sleepy lad came tumbling guiltily out of the hay-loft he sent him away, saying he would tend to his own horse. It was dark in the stable, but once he got accustomed to it there was just the faintest gleam of starlight, and Edward needed no more than that to make his horse comfortable.

Edward stepped quietly out into the yard and looked up at the house. There were no lights shewing, and the house seemed to sleep, rearing its parapeted roof against the star-crusted sky. The main door would be locked; he would go in through the buttery. The yard dogs did not even lift their heads as he passed, knowing his scent; he passed in through the small door, through the buttery, and into the hall. The dogs lying in front of the embers in the two great fireplaces moved and sighed in their sleep but didn't wake. He needed no light to find his way about his home and moved as quietly as a cat up the stairs and headed along the passage towards the east bedchamber. Passing the back-stairs, which lay between the north and west bedrooms and led up to the attics where the servants' bedrooms were, he heard a stealthy step coming down them, and instinct made him dart into the shadow of the saloon doorway. Whoever it was, they did not mean to be discovered – there was no glimmer of a light, and no servant would move about the house on legitimate business without a glim.

Edward pressed himself back well into the shadows and, his eyes accustomed to the darkness, saw a pair of legs coming down the spiral stair, legs clad in dark breeches but ending in bare feet. Bare feet make no sound, he thought to himself grimly. And then a sound from the other direction caught his attention: the door to the great bed chamber was opened cautiously, and a faint light, as of a thin rushlight well-shielded, fell across the passage. At once the descending legs froze, and in a blinding flash of revelation Edward understood what was happening. The man on the stairs was the spy, Makthorpe's spy! Who else would creep about the house like that? He must have some hint that there was something going on this night, and the person coming out of the great bed chamber was walking into a trap.

A white bedgown, partly covered by a dark wrap and dark hair, and slender white hands guarding the light, so slender that the light shone through them in a ruby glow of blood. Of course, it was Mary – and of course, she was going to some assignation. Edward's face grew grim. Not a lover's assignation, he knew at once, but a meeting with her priest, to hear the Mass. Violent anger rushed through him that she could so betray her husband's trust, her husband who loved and cherished her. It would break Ralph's heart if he were to find out! And she was endangering the whole house, the whole family, with her folly. The white figure paused, looking about her with what appeared to be uncertainty rather than caution, and then headed towards the staircase. Surely, Edward thought, she would not be going to commit the gross folly of hearing Mass in the chapel? But no, of course, there was no way through the south side of the house at this level; she would have to go down to the lower floor and go through the chapel to the vestry to reach the stairs up to the priest's room. Perhaps she had thought Lambert would come to meet her; perhaps that was why she hesitated. She must have made this arrangement with him, and somehow the spy had come to hear of it.

Edward knew he had to act. Like a silent shadow, he moved swiftly along the passage to catch up with Mary at the top of the stairs, and he reached out and grabbed her by the arm. He did not reckon on her reaction. Mary had had no idea he was there, and as he came out of the darkness, she was already tense and nervous because of the need for secrecy. She dropped the rushlight she was holding and shrieked.

'For God's sake, shut up!' Edward hissed. 'It's me, Edward! You'll wake the house!' He swung her round, and her wide eyes stared into his uncomprehendingly not recognizing him in the darkness. He saw her mouth open to shriek again; was aware, by some extra sense, that the spy had come forward from the staircase to some point of vantage where he could see what was happening. It was important for the spy to think her assignation had been with him; without further words, Edward clamped his mouth down over Mary's in what would appear to be a passionate kiss, and would, incidentally, stop her from making another sound.

Mary was evidently convinced, and she made muted noises of protest under his lips. Her arms were well-pinioned by Edward's, but she was making strong efforts to disengage herself.

Edward slid his mouth round to her ear to whisper urgently, 'Don't struggle! It's me, Edward. We're being watched, you bloody fool. Pretend it was me you were meeting.'

Her struggles hesitated.

'Edward?' she whispered.

'Yes,' he said grimly. 'Kiss me again, for God's sake. We're being watched.'

'Who by?' she whispered.

'Makthorpe's spy,' he breathed soundlessly.

Mary jerked in his arms in sheer fright, and she cried out, 'Makthorpe?'

Edward could have wept with frustration. Even as she spoke, he heard the soft bare feet behind him making their escape, and as the door to the great bedchamber opened again he released her and rushed in futile pursuit back along the passage to the backstairs.

Behind him now he heard Ralph's voice saying, 'What is it? What's happening? Mary, what are you doing?' And then, in a mixture of surprise and anger, 'What were you doing with Edward?'

The figure fleeing ahead of him reached the backstairs, but there stumbled on the first step, giving Edward a chance to catch up. Up the spiral they ran, with no attempt at silence now, though their feet made little enough noise. The fugitive was just out of Edward's reach, his bare feet flashing upwards just beyond Edward's grasp. Edward still had no idea who it was – he had seen nothing but those feet and the back of a fleeing figure. Panting, he reached the top of the stairs and saw the man running away between the rows of store-room doors, and gave chase, wishing he had had a quart less ale that evening. He was shorter than his quarry, but his shoes gave him a better purchase on the smooth wooden floor, and as the man reached the end of the wing Edward was closing on him.

'Don't be a fool,' Edward called breathlessly. 'There's nowhere to run to!' The man hesitated, looked away to his right down the length of the north wing, lined with servants' beds, and then, with an abrupt movement of panic, turned to his left. There was nothing there, Edward knew, nothing but the trapdoor out onto the roof. What was the man doing? Had he simply run in blind panic? But no, Edward realized now, he was hoping to get across the roof and down, by a rainwater pipe, perhaps, onto the stable roof. He wanted to escape, above anything. He must fear what Ralph would do to him, then, for he could not hope to escape detection. A roll-call of the servants would instantly show who was missing.

Edward ran on, turning the corner into the windowed alcove with the roof-trap above. It was open, and the fresh night air blew in. The man had been tall enough, he guessed, simply to jump and scramble up. Edward had to make use of the window-sill, and heaved himself out with an effort. Now he was on the roof, with the smooth grey slates under him and the black, star-pitted sky above him. He looked away to his right, and then left, and saw the dark shape cutting out the stars, scrambling awkwardly down towards the parapet. He was going the other way, to get down by the roof of the old kennels.

'Stop', Edward cried. 'You can't hope to get away. Don't be a fool, man!'

The dark shape ahead resolved itself against the sky as he turned his head to see where his pursuer was, and in that moment, perhaps, his balance was impaired. Edward saw the figure rock, heard and saw the foot slip, and for a breathless, horrible moment, the bare feet scrabbled for hold on the old, slippery slates.

'No!' he cried out, hardly aware he had spoken. The man half slid, half rolled down the yard of slates, hit the parapet and somersaulted over into the well of darkness. Edward's breath went out in a soundless yell; there was one despairing shriek, and then the horrible sound of a body hitting the cobbles.

For a moment there was silence, and Edward, frozen with horror, heard his own breath sobbing in his throat; then all the dogs seemed to begin barking at once. Edward's legs began to shake. He took a firm hold on himself, and turned back towards the roof-trap. It was only a yard away, but when he reached it he gripped it hard as if he had crawled a hundred yards to reach its safety, and when he dropped down onto the floor inside, his legs almost gave way under him.

Mary was standing where he had left her, staring down into the well of the stairs. Ralph was gone – down there, presumably. As Edward reached her she looked at him, mute, terrified, bewildered. Edward paused.

'What did you tell him?' She stared, not understanding. He took her arm and shook her ungently. 'What did you tell him?'

'Nothing!' she cried. 'Nothing! I—'

'Say nothing, do you hear? And for God's sake, go and get your priest. A man is hurt.'

He shook her once again, seeing that she was going rigid with panic, and then ran on down the stairs. By the time he reached the yard there were several servants there, one of them with a light.

Ralph was kneeling in his nightshirt beside the fallen man. He looked up as Edward pushed his way through and said, 'What happened?'

'It's Makthorpe's spy. He slipped. Bare feet. Is he dead?'

'I think so,' Ralph said. He seemed bemused. The dead man was lying sprawled face-downwards, one arm flung out above his head, the palm upwards as if in mute appeal.

'Who is it?' Edward asked. Ralph still did not move, and Edward knelt on the other side and put his hands to the shoulders, and with a clumsy heave turned the man over against his knee. The head rolled over onto his thigh, and the side of it was loosely squashy as no skull should be. Edward tried not to feel sick. The dead face rolled upwards towards the starlight, the unseeing eyes gleaming dully, one side white and unmarked, the other caved in and already reddening with slow, dark blood.

'It's Barnabus,' Ralph whispered. He stared, and reached out a hand as if to assure himself, but his fingers stopped just short of the man's cheek. He looked up at Edward in appeal. 'Barnabus?' he said. 'But he was my own man. I've known him since he was a boy. I can't believe it.' Slowly the hurt sank in, and Ralph's eyes registered the anguish of betrayal. 'I've always been good to him. I promoted him from the stable to be my personal man. How could he do this to me?'

Edward said nothing. There was no comfort he could offer Ralph. He, too, had known Barnabus for years. He had been born at Twelvetrees, the son of one of the stablemen there, and had grown up amongst the Morland brood mares, had tumbled about with their colts in the paddocks. Ralph had picked him out for preferment for his quickness of mind and his way with horses. He had been educated at the free grammar school, St Edward's school, which had been endowed largely by the family, had become a gentleman groom straight from school, and then been chosen by Ralph as his own body-servant.

And now he lay dead in the starlight, his head stoved in by the cobbles of the stable yard, his dead traitor's eyes staring upwards sightlessly as if in stubborn refusal to meet his master's gaze. Edward could not bear those eyes any longer. He placed his fingertips over them and pressed the eyelids closed.

'I don't know, Ralph,' he said. At the sound of his voice, Ralph seemed to recover from his daze. His face hardened.

'And you,' he said suddenly. 'What was your part in this?' Edward said nothing, but carefully set the body back down onto the cobbles, and stood up. Ralph stood too, his eyes not leaving Edward's face. At that moment there was a noise and disturbance and Mary and the priest, Lambert, came out from the house. Mary was as white as her bedgown, and her eyes were huge with panic. Edward thought that at all costs he must get her away from Lambert and away from the corpse, before she said anything incriminating.

He stepped back and caught her elbow, and holding Ralph's eyes said, 'Let's go into the house. Lambert can see to this, and the servants.'

He swung Mary round hard enough to leave her no choice, and Ralph quickly came to her other side and took charge of her.

'Yes, we'll go inside,' he said. 'I want to talk to you. You and Mary.'

Someone had lit one of the torches, and the hall seemed dazzling after the darkness outside. Bran and Fern were lying by the fireside, and they yawned and got up and came over to greet their master, pausing halfway to stretch themselves fore and aft. Ralph walked over to the fire with

Mary, and Edward followed, so that when they turned to face him, he was like an accused facing his judges. They stood side by side, between him and the fire, with the flaring torch behind them, its light falling on his face. Bran stood between Mary and Ralph, licked them alternately with thoughtful affection, while Fern flopped down again across the hearth, her tail whisking the ashes.

'Well,' Ralph said. 'What have you to say?' He was looking at Edward, but the question was addressed to them both impartially. Edward saw Mary's mouth open and then shut again as she tried to nerve herself to tell the story. She would tell the truth, he knew; not for any loving reason, but because she refused to be ashamed of her faith, and because she did not like Edward, and would not want it thought she cared for him. But looking at Ralph's grim, hurt face, Edward knew that the truth would hurt him far more than Mary could ever imagine. He loved Mary so much that her betrayal would wound him to the heart, and he had been wounded once already tonight. Edward's decision was instantaneous. What he was going to say would hurt Ralph, but not half so much; he would be angry, of course, but one day he would forgive him, whereas he would never be able to forgive Mary. Lightly he said.

'It was my fault. You mustn't blame her, really, Ralph. I've been bothering her for weeks – haven't I, Mary? – and I think she agreed to meet me in the end just to be rid of me. Nothing happened, you know.'

'I saw you – embracing,' Ralph faltered.

Edward gave a grim smile. 'I expect you saw her struggling, too. If you hadn't come out then I think I should have had four fine scratches down my cheek. She's a strong girl, your Mary.'

'You – were trying – to take her from me?' Ralph asked, clearly finding it hard to believe.

Edward forced a smile. 'Oh, I never really believed I

could, of course. But I suppose that was the challenge. You know me, Ralphie – anything's fair game!'

Ralph turned slowly to Mary. He looked as bewildered as a man who has seen rain falling upwards.

'Is this true?' he asked her. She hesitated, swallowing nervously, and as her eye went from Ralph to Edward, the latter fixed her with a steely glare. If you tell him now, he thought, I'll *kill* you. She found her voice at last.

'I – I didn't mean anything, Ralph,' she faltered.

'Why didn't you tell me, if he was bothering you?' Ralph asked her gently, then answered himself. 'But of course, you didn't want to turn me against him.' He looked at Edward, his expression cold, and Edward felt the chill of loss enter his soul.

'She was more loyal to you than you deserve,' he said. Edward forced himself to be still, though it hurt him inexpressibly to have Ralph look at him like that.

Finally Ralph shook his head wearily. 'I can't think now. I will have to speak to you in the morning. I don't know – how you could. I don't think I can bear to have you in the house after this. Go now. We'll speak tomorrow. You too, Mary.'

'Ralph, I—' Mary began, but he silenced her with a gesture. Just then a servant came in from outside.

'Master, can you come. Master Lambert wants you.'

Ralph nodded, and with one last, terrible look, followed the servant out. Mary stood staring after him, her fingers twitching nervously at her gown. Then she looked at Edward, puzzled and apprehensive.

'Why?' she said at last.

Edward looked at her with contempt. 'Because I love him,' he said. 'You had better go to bed. You have done enough mischief tonight.'

'And you?' she asked defiantly.

'I have some packing to do. I won't give him the pain of sending me away. When he wakes in the morning, I shall be gone.'

'Where will you go?' she asked in a small voice.

'To London, I suppose.'

The first realization crossed her face. She made a small movement as if to hold him back.

'Oh don't—' she began, and broke off against the hardness of Edward's look. He turned away. Fern, who had been too comfortable in the warmth of the hearth to follow Ralph, smiled up at him and smacked her tail against the flags. He reached down and caressed her head slowly, waiting for the pain in his heart to pass. Then he straightened, and said to Mary, without looking at her:

'You are safe now. Be good to Ralph – he loves you. Try to be what he thinks you are.'

CHAPTER SEVEN

Sam Symonds paused at the edge of the hill to rest his damaged leg, which always ached after any great exertion, and his grey lurcher, which had been ranging ahead of him, ran back to look up impatiently into his face, its breath smoking in the bitter cold. Last night there had been an iron frost, and there had never been enough warmth in the day to ease it, so that all around him the tussocky, sheep-fouled grass was held in its pitiless grip, every blade, every bracken-frond, rigid and white with rime. The light was dying now from the blank grey sky, though up here on the slope of Bell Hill there was a little thin yellow light still in the west. He looked down towards the valley, to the place where Blindburn ran into the River Coquet, to the grey cluster of buildings that was his home.

Down there it was already dark, and the stone walls were a grey blur in the murk, cheerless and silent as if deserted. The hard-edged December wind flattened the thin banner of smoke from the tall chimney and tore it into shreds; behind it the dark bulk of Loft Hill reared up oppressively, menacing the huddled buildings, and beyond that there stretched the bare heights of the Cheviots, featureless and grey in the growing dusk: Woden Law, and Beefstand Hill, Mozie Law and Windy Gyle. It was a hard and pitiless place in winter; soon, he knew, the snows would come, and they would be alone until the spring.

The lurcher whined and jabbed his hand with a hard muzzle, and Sam sighed and rubbed at his aching leg. He had broken it badly at the siege of Leicester, fighting in Prince Rupert's cavalry, and it had never healed sound. It was worse in the cold weather, but today it hardly ached more than the rest of him, for the cold and desolation seemed to have entered into his bones. He looked down at the comfortless grey steading, and then, as he watched, a small yellow point of light winked and then flowered as someone within the house lit the first lamp. At once the darkness around seemed to intensify, and the wind pitched a little higher by contrast. Comfort was down there, light and fire and food and people, while up here was the treacherous darkness. He started forward eagerly, turned himself sideways with his sound leg foremost and began to descend the hill.

When he reached level ground he was able to lift his eyes at last and he saw, at the same moment as his lurcher barked a warning, that there were strange horses in the three-sided byre in the home paddock. Visitors, then, he thought, stepping out more quickly. Visitors at any time were a rarity in the wild lands, but at this time of year doubly unexpected. As he reached the house the door opened and his wife came hurrying out, her face flushed with some emotion.

'Francis is here,' she said. 'I thought you must have met with an accident, you were so long. When it got dark and you had not come back – come in quickly, you must be near starved of cold.'

Sam let her fuss over him, enjoying the sensation. Anne Morland was not normally very demonstrative of her affection for him; she was brisk and efficient and far quicker-witted than Sam, and he had always thought her too good for him. She was beautiful to him still, with her golden curls untouched with grey, though the harsh weathers had lined her face and roughened her cheeks. The sparseness of their life had sharpened her temper, and he was grateful when she did bestow one of her infrequent caresses on him.

Now she sent a servant away for hot wine and herself helped him off with his outer clothes, and rubbed his frozen hands between her own rough palms until they stung with blood. The servant came back with a cup of spiced wine into which a hot poker had been thrust, and Anne stood over him to make him drink it down in one go. It made him cough a little, but at once he felt better as the warm liquid spread a glow inside him.

'Now,' she said, taking the cup from him and giving it to the servant, 'you can come in and speak to Francis. They will bring supper in by and by.' She pulled back the leather curtain that hung over the parlour door – all the doors were curtained in winter – and flinging open the door ushered him into the small winter-parlour. At once a great sense of comfort reinforced that of the hot wine inside him. In the great fireplace, which took up most of one wall, a small mountain of logs was blazing brightly, with that clarity of flame that frosty weather seems to induce. Besides the firelight there were three pairs of candles – unusual luxury – with silver sconces behind them to increase their power; and in all this light the tapestries which lined the walls, which by day appeared old and dusty and brownish, suddenly glowed in richer, warmer colours.

On stools on either side of the fire sat two young men. They were almost of an age, but there could hardly have been a greater contrast between them. The visitor, his nephew Francis Morland, was the son of Anne's half-brother Frank, who had been killed at Marston Moor. Francis was sixteen, but looked older, for the weight of responsibility had been on him for many years. He was tall and broad with the true Morland colouring, bright blue eyes and dark hair which he wore shoulder-length and curling in cavalier style. His rather sombre face was tanned dark brown by wind and weather and darkened further by his black moustache; but as he looked up he smiled a greeting, and his face was lit and made charming by the genuine warmth of heart that shewed in the smile. The life he led was as harsh as any Borderer's. He farmed the Tods Knowe estate in the next valley, kept cattle and a few sheep, and took care of his mother Arabella, who was ailing. In addition he had oversight of the Emblehope estate which Mary Moubray had brought into the family. It was a heavy responsibility and a great deal of work, but he bore it well and uncomplainingly, and was a good and patient master to his people.

On the stool opposite Francis was Sam's son, Crispian. Though he was fifteen, and a man in Northumbrian terms, he was no more than five feet high, and did not look to grow more. He was heavily-built, with a barrel-shaped body and a short neck which added to the impression of smallness he gave, and his liking for his food and drink was already increasing his girth. He had Anne's pale blue eyes and golden hair and her sharp, pretty features, but his hair was thin, and he wore it cropped very short like a Puritan, which made his head look too big for his body. He had been a great favourite with Sam's father, who had made much of him as sole heir to his fortune, and had given him an inflated sense of his own consequence. When Sam's father had died, Crispian had already proved himself lazy and proud, and Sam's attempts to alter his character had had little effect other than to make him sullen.

Yet for all that, Sam could not dislike him. When he was not crossed, Crispian could display great charm, and it was often he who kept the household in good spirits through the dark lonely winter, with his singing and playing and games and morrissing. Anne, he knew, felt it very deeply that all the sons she had borne Sam had died in infancy, and that his only male heir was not a child of his body – Crispian was in fact the posthumous son of Sam's brother, whom he had adopted as his own. The only children of Sam's that had survived were his daughters Frances, who was now eleven, and little Nan who was eight. These two were sitting on the floor now, gazing up at the visitor with fascination – pretty Frances wide-eyed with admiration that amounted almost to hero-worship, and plump little Nan silent and shyly adoring.

Francis stood up and came forward a step to hold out his

hand to Sam. Sam took it and shook it warmly – a broad, warm, dry hand, its palms hard from a lifetime of handling reins.

'Uncle! God keep you. It is good to see you again.'

'Welcome, Frank, welcome. God bless you. I had not thought to see you this side of lambing. How is your mother? Is all well?'

'Mother is just as always, sir – sickly, but no worse, though the cold plagues her.'

'As it does all of us,' Sam said ruefully. 'My game leg aches with the frost.'

'Will you take this seat by the fire, sir?' Frank asked quickly.

Sam smiled pleasantly at his son. 'No, no, Frank, sit ye down. Crispian will give me his seat. You have been travelling and need the warmth.' Crispian stood up with no more than a little reluctance, for he admired his cousin and liked to appear well before him. Sam took the seat and stretched his legs out gratefully before the blaze as his lurcher pushed in between the little girls and flopped down by his side. The girls squeaked a little and pulled their dresses out of the way of the dog.

Frances knelt up, her face flushed with excitement. 'Papa, Frank rode right over Ravens Knowe to come here, think of that!'

'Why, hinny, did he?' Sam said gravely. 'Right over the top?'

Frances nodded. 'Yes, sir, the very top, and he brought me a present.'

Sam caught Frank's eye and smiled. Nan had crept round to his other side and was gently insinuating herself onto his lap, and he picked her up and settled her there with a hug. 'Was that why he came, hinny, to bring you a present?'

Frances hesitated, torn between the probable truth and this very flattering picture of her consequence. 'Well,' she said at last, 'partly, I expect.'

Frank smiled. 'I didn't come right over the top, only round the side, under Windy Crags and past the Roman camps.'

'Still,' Sam said, 'it was a good, hard ride, just to bring a young lady a present. What was it?'

'It was ribbons,' Frances said importantly. 'Blue ribbons, and Mama says they will trim my grey dress.'

'Good,' Sam said, and then bent his head to his younger daughter, who had snuggled into his chest and inserted her thumb into her mouth as a talisman against shyness and strangers. 'And did he bring you a present too, chuck? What did he bring you?'

Nan nodded, but vouchsafed no more, for she would not take her thumb from her mouth.

Frances answered for her. 'He brought her a baby, a wooden baby in a blue dress. It was a very nice one,' she added, her voice wistful, for she was only just beginning to consider herself too old for childish toys, 'and it had a white apron too.'

'Mother made the clothes,' Frank said. 'And I carved the baby.'

'Well the apron won't stay white for long, nor the dress blue,' Anne said. 'In a week's time they will both be near to black. There never was such a little sweep as that child. Lord knows, even Frances was never so bad, though she's only just past the stage of making mud patties.'

Sam saw how the words mortified Frances' new ladylike dignity, and hastened to draw attention away from her. 'Well, Anne, I think this little one is ready for her bed. Come, little suck-a-thumb, kiss me goodnight.'

'Yes, it is time,' Anne said, turning to the maid standing behind her. 'Sally, take Nan and wash her and put her to bed. Frances, you too.'

Sam caught Anne's eye. 'Oh, I think Frances can stay up for a little supper, don't you?' Frances, whose face had fallen, now gazed hopefully from her father to her mother, and when at last her mother nodded agreement, it was all she could do not to fling her arms round her father's neck, and pretend that this was a normal event.

The servants came in with the trays of supper, and in the bustle of drawing the benches up to the table and laying out the food, Sam spoke quietly to Frank.

'It must be something important that brought you here, as I guess.' Frank nodded. 'Well, you cannot go home again tonight, so let it wait until we have eaten. Once the servants have cleared we shall not be disturbed again.'

They sat down to the board and ate their supper, cold beef and hot pease porrage, oaten bread and curd cheese and dried smoked fish, and dried apricots for a relish, in honour of their guest, all washed down with small beer. Their conversation was light and cheerful, about family and farming matters and all the small news of what they had been doing since they last met. Crispian soon grew voluble, teased Frances and clowned for Frank and even made his mother laugh, but Sam could see that even he knew that something important was in the offing.

At length they finished their meal, the servants cleared the table and were dismissed for the night, Frances went off reluctantly to her bed, Crispian fetched his lute, and the four adults settled down before the fire for the last hour of the day. When Sam had lit his pipe and Crispian was picking a quiet, gentle tune that blended into the sounds of the crackling of the fire and the hooning of the wind in the tall chimney, Anne said, 'Well, Francis, suppose you tell us what brought you here on such a bitter day?'

Frank gathered their attention and began. 'You know, of course, that the generals have recalled the Rump?'

'Yes, though God knows why,' Sam said. 'Is it less corrupt than when Lambert dissolved it last?'

'No, sir,' Frank said, 'but to many it is less of an offence than the sole mastery of Lambert, who would make himself Protector if he could. It was not Lambert's idea to recall the Rump.'

'Whose, then?' Sam asked.

'General Monk did it, and General Fleetwood joined him because he would not have Lambert as his leader. And the Rump has made Monk commander in chief over the three kingdoms, and he is even now assembling his army on the Border, ready to march into England.'

Sam almost came to his feet. 'But – good God – you are sounding as though you approve!'

'Of Monk's actions? Yes, sir.'

'You want us to be conquered by an army under a man who was known to be Cromwell's most loyal follower – while you condemn Lambert for wanting the same power?'

'Father, listen to Frank – let him explain,' Crispian said. There was a silence, and even his fingers on the lute strings grew still. Sam slowly subsided, and Francis went on quietly.

'Sir, it is true that Monk was Cromwell's loyal man. It is also true that his army is the only disciplined one in the three kingdoms. True, partly because they have been isolated, up in Scotland, from the infections of disorder that have corrupted the other armies; but also because Monk himself is a man of honour and principle.'

'A man of overweening ambition, it would seem,' Sam growled. 'To march into his own country like a – like a – *Frenchman* – at the head of a conquering army . . .'

'No, sir, I beg your pardon. It is not ambition. He has no ambition for himself. He wants only what is best for the country and the people. He followed Cromwell because he believed Cromwell to be right, and to offer a hope of strong and just government. Now he wishes to be rid of the corrupt and divided rule that Cromwell's death has bequeathed us. He marches with an army to take London from Lambert, and when he has it, to call a free Parliament.'

A free Parliament! The words sounded like a song in the quiet room. How long was it since there had been such a thing in England?

'But can he do it?' Sam asked after a moment. 'Even Cromwell himself, with all his power, did not dare.'

'The times are different now,' Francis said. 'The people are tired of the rule of soldiers. They are tired of fanatics and preachers, red coats and black coats, disorder and misrule. A free Parliament will have to moderate its aims and desires.'

'A free Parliament,' Crispian added quietly, 'might recall the King.'

As if it were a signal, the fire burned up more brightly at that moment, drawn upwards by some fluctuation of the wind. In the golden glow, Sam looked round the faces gathered there, and saw the same wish reflected in each one.

'Is that what Monk wants?' he asked.

Frank shook his head. 'I don't know. He has never said so. I think he wants nothing more than a legitimate government. But if that government declares for the King, I do not think he would go against it.'

'So,' said Sam at last. 'And what is it that you want me to do? Although I think I can guess.'

Frank leaned forward eagerly. 'Sir, General Monk has been consolidating his forces over the Border. He has removed all suspect officers from command, and drilled the men and disciplined them, and he is now gathering an additional regiment at his camp at Coldstream, on the Border itself. It is to be the cream of his army, and he has put out a call for recruits. I am taking as many men as I can spare to join him there. I came to ask you to send men too.'

Sam smiled and nodded. 'Now it is out. I guessed that is what you would say. You know that my men last fought with Montrose, for the King. How should I ask them to go and fight with Monk, for Parliament.'

'But not the same Parliament, Father,' Crispian cried.

Francis added, 'My men, too, fought for the King. Most of their fathers fell at Marston Moor, with my father.'

'And what will you tell them?' Sam asked.

'I have told them already. I have told them that a free Parliament will restore to their seats all those who were ejected because they would not accept a republic. The monarchists will resume their seats.'

Sam looked from Frank's dark, manly face to Crispian's light, eager one. He could see that Crispian was frantic to go, to head the men he hoped his father would send. How would Crispian endure a long march in the depths of winter, Crispian who liked ease and comfort, whose plump body rarely left the fireside when the snow was down? Then he looked at Anne. Her face was closed to him, her eyes were fixed on the dancing flames of the fire. She did not want to reveal her feelings: but so many of her family had died fighting for the King, that she must surely want anything that might further that cause. He came to his decision.

'Well, Frank, I will ask my men – I cannot send them against their will, but if any want to go with you, I will free them.'

'Thank you, sir. And yourself?'

Sam shook his head. 'I am long past my fighting days, and my leg pains me enough here at home. But I could offer you my son as your lieutenant, if he wishes to go.'

Frank grinned broadly, and looked towards Crispian, who jumped to his feet, paling a little. 'You – will let me? I can go? Oh Father, thank you!' He clasped his father's hand and wrung it gratefully, and there was such genuine, unforced delight in his face that Sam loved him more then than at any time since he was a baby. The two young men burst into eager talk about their plans, and Sam watched them with pleasure. He had been so taken up with Crispian's delight that he missed the look of anguish that had crossed his mother's face, to be quickly suppressed and hidden.

General Monk received them in his lodgings in the small grey border town of Coldstream. He was a small, squat man, so short-necked as to appear almost like a hunchback, with a powerful, florid face that had evidently been very handsome in his youth. He looked up as the two young men entered, and regarded them expressionlessly with flat and fathomless dark eyes. He was a man used to keeping his counsel: his face told nothing.

Crispian glanced once, nervously at him, and then stepped backwards, heartily glad that he could look to Frank for leadership. It had taken them, because of the weather, a week to ride up from Tods Knowe, passing up Redesdale and crossing the Cheviots at Carter Bar and then following the Jed and the Teviot down into the Tweed valley, and after that week, Crispian was already a different person. He had found it hard to keep up with the others, hard to endure the long hours in the saddle without complaint, harder still to bear the icy discomfort of camping out at nights and making do with cold rations. After the first day his feet and hands had developed a crop of chilblains which burned and tormented him without cease; after the third day he was so saddle-sore that it was agony to remount after any pause to rest; and his belly seemed to rumble ceaselessly in its demand for the comforts it had known.

But, hard though it was, he had endured, and keeping his eyes fixed on his hardy cousin he had struggled on, suppressing even his involuntary groans in his desire not to let Frank down. His main wish now that they had reached Coldstream was to rest, perhaps to find a bed somewhere and stay in it for the next week, having food brought to him at regular intervals. But they had been intercepted as soon as they reached the town, and Frank had requested an immediate interview with the general; and when he had appeared to assume Crispian would accompany him, the latter could only straighten his aching back and hobble in his wake. Now they were face to face with the man who was in command of the only effective army in the kingdom. Crispian found him terrifying, and his admiration for Frank reached its height when his cousin drew himself up and said calmly, 'General, we have brought you twenty men, good men, loyal Borderers. We wish to join you on your march to London.'

Monk surveyed them both expressionlessly. 'Your name, sir,' he said at last.

Frank drew himself up even more. 'General, I am Francis Morland of Tods Knowe, and my father of the same name was one of Lord Newcastle's Whitecoats. He died at Marston Moor, sir. This is my cousin Crispian Symonds, whose father was in the same regiment.'

If the news surprised or impressed Monk he did not shew it. 'Newcastle's Lambs, eh?' he said. He looked Crispian over briefly, and then returned his gaze to Frank. 'The name of Morland is not unknown to me,' he said. 'I was Lord Cromwell's general. What do your family think of your throwing in with me?'

Frank took a step forward. 'Sir, I do not think there are two sides any more. My family would surely approve of my actions.'

'Your family are royalists,' Monk said flatly.

'General, I have heard – we have heard—'

'Rumour is seldom reliable, Master Morland,' Monk interrupted. 'I march to London to restore a free Parliament, nothing more. I am no royalist. I do not care for succession and legitimacy and the Divine Right. My concern is only for order, peace, and law; my desire is only for a strong and fair government. Believe me, Master Morland, I would place power in the hands of a grey ass if that is what would bring peace and order to England.'

'Yes, sir,' Frank said stiffly. Monk turned a quill over and over in his fingers, watching the movement as if it were not his. He had surprisingly slender and beautiful hands. At length he looked up.

'On that basis, do you still wish to march with me?'

It dawned on Frank that they were accepted, and delight crossed his face.

'Yes, sir. Yes, please, sir.'

'Very well. You are welcome to join us. You and your men will begin training tomorrow. My clerk outside will see to your billeting.'

And with a nod he dismissed them. Outside the two young men clasped hands in delight.

'I thought he was going to turn us away when he said we were royalists,' Crispian said. 'By our Lady, he's a stiff old bird, isn't he?'

'It's my belief,' Frank said happily, 'that underneath it all he's as firm a royalist as we are, but he's too cautious to let it shew until he knows which way the wind is blowing. But anyway, we're in, Crisp, and that's the main thing. Now to get ourselves settled.' He grinned and slapped his cousin's back. 'What would you say to a hot bath? If there's such a thing to be had in Coldstream.'

'By God, if there is I'll sniff it out!' Crispian cried. 'And then—'

'Something to eat!' Frank finished for him. 'You are wasting away, my good cousin, and we can't have that, can we? After all, there's that long march south ahead of us.'

'Don't!' Crispian groaned. 'At the very word "march" every bone in my body aches separately. I am a polyphony of pain!'

The next morning they entered upon an intensive course of training, and on 2 January, 1660, the whole of Monk's army, numbering some seven thousand men, broke camp and crossed the Tweed into England on the first stage of the journey to London.

As they passed through the north lands, through what had once been known as Percy's kingdom, they met no resistance, and in fact new recruits joined them every day. By the time they reached York, where they were met by

Lord Fairfax with a considerable force, it was clear that, whatever Monk himself said, no one believed that he did not mean to recall the King. At every stopping place, the taverns were full of the talk of it. People said that Monk had been in communication with the King for nearly a year, and when the news came that King Charles had moved his exiled court to Breda in the Netherlands, it was said that he had done so on Monk's advice, to be nearer home when the call came. In taverns the people drank the King's health openly, as they had not for over a decade, and in some churches he was prayed for by priest and congregation alike. A number of anonymous inns abruptly revealed themselves to be called the King's Head, and in every village there was sure to be at least one newly painted sign swinging in the breeze, displaying a brightly daubed and wholly idealized portrait of the King none of them had ever seen.

As they neared London the army began to be on its guard, for Lambert's army, though undisciplined, was a large force, and scouts rode out ahead every day in anticipation of opposition. But as they came nearer and nearer the capital it became plain that Lambert hesitated to initiate what might amount to a new civil war. There had been bloodshed enough already, and besides, with every day there came fresh evidence that the people were with Monk and were longing for the return of their King with a fervour that amounted almost to frenzy. Anyone who pitched himself against the idea was likely to come to harm; and so when Monk's army finally reached London on 3 February, it marched in not only unopposed, but attended by considerable rejoicing.

Frank was almost disappointed that there had been no chance to prove himself in arms, Crispian emphatically glad. The march had hardened him and fined him down, but nothing would ever make serious inroads into his love of personal comfort. As soon as they and their men were billeted, the two cousins went down to the wool exchange to enquire after their uncle Richard, Ralph's father, who had been living in London since 1650, acting as the family's agent and factor. Richard Morland was well known, a figure of some consequence in the City, and they were directed at once to Milk Street where he rented a house.

The house was not hard to find, for it was the only one in the dark, narrow street which did not have a shop on the ground floor. A distinct smell of cattle overlaid the normal stink of a London street, and from behind every house came the muted bellowing of cows which were stalled in the backyards to provide milk for the residents of the metropolis. Crispian looked up at the house and wrinkled his nose.

'It doesn't look much,' he said. 'Do you think this can be right?'

Frank shrugged. 'Nothing in London looks much, after the Borderlands. We are used to larger spaces, you and I, that's all. But the house seems good enough to me, compared with any of the others we've seen.'

'I suppose so,' Crispian said, looking up at the tall, narrow building. It was largely made of wood, which gave it a flimsy air to someone used to farmhouses of stone, and its upper floors jutted out over the street, helping to block out the light and block in the smells, which rose in an almost palpable miasma from the open kennel down the middle of the street and the nameless piles of filth all around. Only the topmost gable, which reared up above the rest of the buildings, was in sunlight, and Crispian looked up at it with something like longing.

'Let's knock,' he said. 'I should like to get out of this street.'

Their knock was answered by a maid-servant who took up their names, and a few moments later they were being ushered into a cheerful, comfortable parlour to be greeted by a sandy-haired man with a neat moustache, dressed with severe elegance in black doublet, slashed to shew a white linen shirt beneath, black frilled breeches, black stockings and shoes, a deep collar of white lace providing the only touch of richness. He came towards them, smiling and holding out his hand.

'I should have expected this. You came in with Monk, as I guess? I am Richard Morland – now which of you is which?'

Frank introduced them both, delighted with the cordiality of their welcome. He had never met his uncle before, but had heard plenty about him. Richard Morland had been many things in his time, but the most notorious of his exploits had been his violent adherence to the cause of Puritanism, and Frank had expected to be greeted at least equivocally. Wonderingly, he allowed himself to be introduced to a diminutive, dark-eyed lady, whose greying dark curls were neatly covered with a lace cap, and whose clothes shewed the same severly prosperous elegance as Richard's

'My wife, Lucy,' Richard said, and then indicating two small fair boys of about five and seven years old, whom the lady had evidently been teaching out of the book she held, 'my sons, Clovis and Edward. Will you take some refreshment with us? My dear, would you send for wine and biscuits?'

While Lucy rang for a servant, Richard seated his guests, and concealed his amusement at their air of slight bewilderment. He knew better than anyone how varied had been his career, how ill-assorted his allegiances. From boyhood upwards he had gone from one extreme of behaviour to another all in the cause of rebellion against his father, whom he had, underneath it all, loved and admired. He had made enemies of his entire family when a series of shocks brought him to his senses. First there had been the murder of the King; then the death of his stepmother and his father's consequent grief; then the news of the death of his best, his only true friend, Clovis Byrne, who had been serving with Lord Montrose in Scotland. Richard had come to realize almost too late what he really valued in life, and in order to make up just a little to his family for the wrong he had done, he had left home and gone to live permanently in London, leaving his father and Morland Place with a more suitable heir than he could ever be – his son Ralph.

In London he had met Lucy, Clovis's former mistress, and when the news came of his father's death, he had turned to Lucy for comfort, and had asked her to marry him, and under her gentle, intelligent guidance he had gone the last necessary steps along the road to his redemption. Even though it was too late, he was now, he hoped, everything his father would have wanted. Naturally, little of this was known at home, and while he entertained his young guests he could see that they were finding it difficult to reconcile him with the legendary Puritan fanatic they had been told about.

The refreshments came, and Richard plied the two young men with questions about their homes, asking with half-concealed hunger for news of the family. At length the talk came round to their march to London with General Monk.

'So, as it came about, there was no need for us to fight,' Francis finished their story.

'Are you sorry?' Richard asked, amused.

Francis and Crispian exchanged a glance, and Crispian smiled ruefully. 'Just a little,' he admitted. 'It will be hard to tell the other lads back home that we did nothing but march.'

'I think when you go home you will have things so much more exciting to tell that no one will notice that you have not been blooded in war,' Richard said. The boys gazed at him hopefully.

'Do you mean that there is truth in the rumours?' Crispian asked.

'That depends what rumours you have heard.'

'That the King may come back,' Francis said. 'The general has never said other than that he wishes to re-establish free Parliament, but the talk is that he has been negotiating with the King for many months.'

Richard smiled. 'For once rumour is founded on truth. I see no reason why you should not be a party to the truth,' he added, glancing at Lucy, who nodded faintly, 'though for the moment I must ask you to keep it to yourselves.' The boys agreed eagerly. 'Yes, the general has been in communication with the King. There is a party of men who believe that the best thing for England would be to recall King Charles; a number of us have been working in secret towards that end, and our plans are almost at fruition.'

'You, sir?' Crispian said. 'You have been involved?' And then he reddened, realizing how rude it sounded. Richard, however, merely smiled.

'Oh, yes. It surprises you, of course, after the stories you have heard about me. But I have been reclaimed,' he smiled at Lucy, 'and I assure you I am now as Morland a Morland as any of you could wish. And there is someone else—'

At that moment there were footsteps on the stair, and the door was opened abruptly to reveal a handsome, fair-haired man in riding clothes. His pale hair was awry and his face was flushed from the cold air and the speed of his coming.

'It's done,' he cried as he came in. 'The Rump is to call a free Parliament for April, and then at once to dissolve itself.'

'A free Parliament will call home the King,' Lucy said. 'Thank God.'

'Yes – Hyde is to go and negotiate with him, but Monk believes he will agree to everything.' The fair man cast a glance of polite enquiry towards the two young men, and returned his gaze to Richard to grin and say, 'The Rump to dissolve itself, almost twenty years after its first election. By Our Lady, there'll be some celebrations that night.'

'Without a doubt,' Richard said. 'By the by, Ned, there

are two cousins of ours who marched in with Monk from Northumberland – Francis and Crispian.'

'Of course,' said the fair man. 'I should have known. God greet you.'

The boys murmured a polite response as Richard completed the introduction.

'Another member of our secret society who has been working for the return of the King, and has just now come from Whitehall – my brother Edward.'

'Fresh from Whitehall and looking very pleased with himself,' Lucy added, studying his face shrewdly. 'There is something more he has not told us. What is it, Ned?'

Edward grinned. 'Our Master Hyde is to go to the King in the Low Country to negotiate the terms with him.'

'So you told us – what then?' Richard prompted.

Edward's smile became seraphic. 'I have been chosen to go with him.'

BOOK TWO

Lion Couchant

The Ploughman and Squire, the Erranter Clown,
At home she subdu'd in her Paragon Gown;
But now she adornes the Boxes and Pit,
And the proudest town Gallants are forc'd to submit;
All hearts fall a leaping wherever she comes,
And beat day and night, like my Lord Craven's
    Drums.

Charles Sackville, Earl of Dorset: A Song

CHAPTER EIGHT

Annunciata and Kit rode towards Twelvetrees, Kit on his own horse and Annunciata on a white mule, for her old pony, Nod, had died peacefully in the home paddock a week ago. It was a fresh, blowy spring day, the sky shewing a watery blue between big scudding clouds, bands of pale sunshine chasing shadows across the faint, blurred green of new grass. It was lambing time, and all around them was the perpetual din of lambing, the high voices of the new young and the deep chuckling calls of the ewes in response.

'What exactly did Ralph say when he spoke to you?' Annunciata asked, not for the first time.

'I've told you,' Kit said. 'He just asked me to bring you to meet him at Twelvetrees.'

'But he must have said why.'

'He didn't.'

'And you didn't ask,' Annunciata said scornfully. Kit only smiled. He seemed to have grown taller and broader since Edward went away, for Annunciata, missing her favourite suitor, had fallen back on her old and faithful admirer for company.

'I expect he wanted it kept a secret,' Kit said calmly. Annunciata considered. A secret probably meant a present or a treat, and she liked both very much.

'Oh,' she said, and let it drop. A new hat, perhaps? There was talk of new fashions coming in from abroad, and there had even been one or two brighter garments to be seen on Sunday at the village church. Kit had a new hat, and it was being tugged by the breeze, making him lift his hand nervously to check it every few minutes. He was growing his hair again, too, like many other young men.

'I like you with long curls,' she said aloud, and his blue eyes flickered towards her doubtfully, wondering if she was mocking him. Annunciata kind was still a new experience for him. 'It would be lovely to see the end of horrible dull Puritan clothes and cropped heads. Do you really think the new Parliament will call the King home?'

'Of course – not a doubt of it,' Kit said. The new Parliament, which met for the first time on 20 April, had been elected on the old franchise. 'You know what Crispian said.' Crispian had called in at Morland Place on his way home to Coquetdale; Francis had stayed on in London a while longer as an aide de camp to General Monk.

'Oh, Crispian,' Annunciata said scornfully. 'I wouldn't be surprised if he got everything wrong.'

'You didn't think much of him,' Kit said. 'I wonder why.'

'He was plain and rude,' she said indifferently. The truth was, he had been inclined to pay too much attention to Cathy for her liking. 'He had no notion of etiquette. It is a good thing that he is going back to his farm. He would never do well amongst well-born people.'

Kit suppressed a smile, knowing how quickly his cousin took offence, but he was forced to speak up in Crispian's defence.

'I know you think he should not have given Cathy preference over you, but he had been staying with her father, and he had lots of private messages to give her, and very little time in which to give them.'

Annunciata looked cross, and Kit quickly changed the subject.

'I wish I had been there the night the Rump was dissolved, don't you? With all the bonfires and the sides of beef being roasted. It must have been a wonderful sight. Would you not love to go to London?'

'Of course,' she said, and she thought, one day I shall go. She had not forgotten the prediction Edward had made for her. 'Oh, if the King comes home – when the King comes home – we shall have new fashions again! How wonderful to wear bright new clothes. And there will be balls and plays and music and – and the King will have to marry, too!'

Kit smiled at her. 'Is your ambition riding so high, cos? Would you be queen of England? I think you have been listening to gossip about our absent King.'

Annunciata blushed. The stories about the King were a legion, but they were not such as a well-brought-up young lady would repeat. 'Of course not. I was just thinking that if there is a Queen there will be a queen's court, and many appointments will be made.'

'Appointments?'

'Maids-of-honour, ladies-in-waiting,' Annunciata said. Kit's face fell.

'But if you had a place at Court, you would have to live in London most of the time. You might never come home.'

'You were just saying yourself that you would like to go to London,' Annunciata pointed out.

'To visit, not to live,' Kit said. 'I should have to go, once the King came home, to ask him to restore my land to me. But I would not want to live in London.'

'I should,' Annunciata said dreamily. 'Think of it! The King's Court. The rich and the famous; the noble men and beautiful women. Great public balls and intimate private suppers—'

'When I spoke of your going to London,' Kit interrupted her reverie, 'I thought of you going with me.'

'With you?'

'As my wife,' Kit said, reddening.

Annunciata stared for a moment, and then turned her eyes away and said merely, 'Oh.'

Having begun, Kit felt he must go on.

'Annunciata, don't you think it is time we thought of being married? We have been as good as betrothed all your life, and you are fifteen now, old enough to marry. I know my estate isn't much, but the King will give me back my lands for certain, once he is restored to his throne, and then – well, I could never be completely worthy of you, but it would not be a shameful match. And you know that I love you. No man could love you more.'

'It is to my mother that you must speak,' Annunciata said dismissingly. Kit persisted. He wished he could take her hand, and realized that it would have been better to bring up the subject when they were both stationary. He felt at a disadvantage, looking down on her from the height of his saddle.

'I know, but I want to know what you feel. You know that your mother would not go against your strong wishes.'

Annunciata was not so sure of that. It seemed to her that her mother had been bent on thwarting her since the day she was born. But in any case, she did not want to think about marrying yet, least of all marrying Kit. She liked Kit, and since Edward had gone away, she had found how good a companion Kit could be. It was true that he did not flirt with her so outrageously, nor flatter her so grossly, nor tease her so indiscreetly, as Edward; but he was more intelligent and more learned than his uncle, and his conversation stimulated Annunciata and occupied and exercised her mind.

But she wanted him as a suitor, not as a husband. Once she married him, she would not be able to mix freely with other men; she would not have them pursuing her or bringing her gifts or writing her poems or flirting with her. As soon as she married Kit she would be shut away from the fun with the other matrons, and that would be that. She must keep Kit dangling as long as possible, however, for if she told him she did not want to marry him he might well go and pay court to Cathy.

'I can't talk about it now,' she said. 'When you have got your estates back from the King, then you can ask me. Not now.'

Twelvetrees was an old manor-house which had once been used by the Morland family as their second home, when Morland Place was being sweetened. The family had last lived there in 1630 when Morland Place was being rebuilt, and had found the fifteenth-century building horribly uncomfortable and inconvenient. Since then the family had not used it, and the house was falling more and more rapidly into disrepair. The stables and outbuildings, by contrast, were in continuous use, and were constantly being repaired and enlarged, for it was at Twelvetrees that the favoured Morland activities of horse- and dog-breeding were carried on.

The main stable yard was a ferment of activity when Annunciata and Kit rode in, but they were greeted at once by a groom, who led Annunciata's mule to the mounting-block and called over two boys to take their mounts when Kit had helped Annunciata to dismount.

'The Master's out in the paddock with Kingcup,' the groom told them. 'I'll have a boy take you.'

Kingcup was the young stallion. The old stallion, Prince Hal, the fourth stallion at Twelvetrees to bear that name, was close to retirement now, but through her mother, whose interest in horses was not even second to Ralph's, Annunciata had heard great things of the four-year-old. She and Kit followed the boy through the warren of outer buildings and were brought to a gate beyond which was an enclosed yard formed by the backs of stable-buildings that surrounded it on three and a half sides. The earth of the yard was bare and hard-packed, and around it a circular track had been worn where horses were lunged and exercised daily.

Around this track there now trotted the new stallion. He was big, bigger than his sire, with a development of crest that promised great strength when he came to his full growth. His chestnut coat was much lighter than most of the Morland horses, almost a yellow-gold, which had given him his name. Ralph was standing in the middle of the yard with the lunge rein and whip, calling and chirrupping to the horse as he walked and trotted around the circumference. Ralph acknowledged them with a nod of the head, not wanting to break the horse's concentration, but as he circled on the farther side Kingcup saw them at the gate and at once began to misbehave, curvetting and putting in little bucks and side steps. After a few more uneven circuits, Ralph halted the stallion and brought him into the centre. The horse dipped his head to Ralph's hands and nibbled them like a foal, and then abruptly swung up and made a feint of biting, his teeth snapping together with an audible click half an inch from Ralph's ear. Ralph cuffed him gently, took a turn of the rope about his muzzle, and led him over to the gate where his cousins were waiting.

'Hello! What do you think of this fellow? Don't you think he is looking well?'

'Wonderful,' Annunciata said enthusiastically.

Kit added, 'I'm afraid we distracted him. He was going well until he saw us.'

'No matter,' Ralph said. 'I was thinking of bringing him in anyway. He is too young to concentrate for very long together. Open the gate, boy, and then run and fetch Andrew here,' he added to the child who had brought them thus far. In a moment the groom came to lead Kingcup away, and Ralph was free to attend to his visitors.

'Well, now,' he said, 'I expect you have been wondering why I asked you to come here.'

'Indeed,' Annunciata said. 'Especially when you have not graced us with your presence at Shawes for many a week past.'

'I have had a great deal to do,' Ralph said apologetically. 'I never realized before how much – how much there is to do,' he finished after a brief hesitation. He had been going to say, how much Edward did, and Annunciata guessed it. Ralph missed Edward very much, and blamed himself for his harsh words which he believed had driven his uncle away. He rarely mentioned Edward's name, finding the whole episode too painful to be recalled. 'Still, I think when you see what I have been spending my time on this past week you will excuse me for neglecting you recently. Come and see.'

'What is it?' Annunciata asked, as she and Kit followed Ralph between the buildings. Ralph grinned at Kit, and she felt a stirring of excitement as she saw that whatever it was, Kit was in on the secret.

'You'll see in just a moment,' Ralph said. He led them across another inner yard, between two more buildings, and they were suddenly out in the open, and ahead of them was a small fenced-off paddock containing just one horse. 'There,' Ralph said with pride. 'What do you think of her?' And he chirrupped, and the filly lifted her head from grazing and started towards them.

Annunciata gazed, enchanted, and could find nothing to say. She was a beautiful chestnut filly, whose coat was the bright deep gold of an autumn leaf, unbroken by any markings except a small white star between her eyes. She came towards them with her ears pricked and her eyes alert with kindly intelligence; her forehead was broad, her muzzle delicately tapered, her neck finely arched. Her shoulders sloped cleanly, her chest was deep, her ribs well-sprung; her muscled quarters were high and rounded, her legs clean and strong, her feet fair and round and hard as flint. Her confirmation was perfect, but more than that, she moved with a flowing grace that made it seem as if her hooves barely touched the ground. A few yards away from them she suddenly broke into a canter, in sheer light spirits, and it was like thistledown being blown across the grass.

'She's perfect,' Annunciata said at last.

'I think you're right,' Kit said. 'I've never seen a horse quite so lovely.'

'She's very like her grand-dam,' Ralph said. 'Do you remember Mam's mare, Psyche, Kit?'

He opened the gate and went into the paddock and the filly came over to nuzzle him. He caught her by the forelock and led her forward.

'Come and speak to her, Annunciata,' he said. Annunciata went into the paddock and stroked the golden filly admiringly, and she nuzzled her gently and blew at her hands. 'I think she likes you,' Ralph said, smilingly. The filly regarded Annunciata with great dark gentle eyes in which the sun made a rich tapestry of gold. 'It's just as well, isn't it?'

'What do you mean?' Annunciata asked, running a hand over and over down the silken, arched neck.

'Because she's yours.' He smiled at the expression on Annunciata's face. 'Yes, indeed, I mean it. Her name is Goldeneye, and she's rising four, and the groom is bringing a saddle and bridle for her now so that you can try her. I've broken her myself, and she's as gentle as she is good, and before you ask me, yes, I have spoken to your mother and made it all right with her. She's yours, Annunciata – with my love.' Still she stared at him, unable to find the words to thank him. 'Now at last you can use the bridle-ornaments. It was well time you had a lady's horse.'

The groom came with the tack and saddled Goldeneye, and Ralph lifted Annunciata into the saddle, and in a moment they were cantering round the paddock. It felt like flying to Annunciata, used as she was to Nod's uninspired plodding; Goldeneye seemed to skim the earth like a swallow, making nothing of the task of bearing her new mistress, and her mouth was so light that it felt as though she was reading Annunciata's thoughts. The two men watched smilingly.

'They make a pretty couple,' Ralph said. 'It was high time she had a good horse.'

'The filly's perfect,' Kit said, 'and not a bit too good for her.'

Ralph glanced at him with sympathetic amusement. 'And nor are you,' he said.

Kit shook his head. 'I wish it were true. I wish she thought so.'

'Faint heart—' Ralph said.

Kit smiled ruefully and tried to stiffen his resolve. 'When the King comes home – when I get my estates back—'

'Aye,' Ralph said comfortingly. 'Everything will be well when the King comes home.'

At dawn on 26 May the ship *Naseby*, freshly renamed *Royal Charles*, slipped from her moorings and left the Hague for Dover. On the lower part of her afterdeck two young men leaned on the windward taffrail looking out across the water. It was a clear, sparkling day, with the promise of heat, and the bright sea chuckled under the wooden belly of the ship as she cleared the shelter of the harbour bar and picked up the breeze. Her sails filled and she leaned to her course, springing forward like an eager horse as a volley of commands sent the seamen scurrying to the sheets to bring her closer to the wind. The breeze lifted the hair of the two young men: two very different heads of hair, the one straight and pale, the other dark and irrepressibly curly. The dark-haired man lifted his head and snuffed the breeze like a hound.

'By God and St Patrick, my Ned, but that smells good! I'll swear it's got the scent of England in it, and that's a sweet smell I never thought I'd smell again.'

Edward grinned at his companion. 'Your imagination runs away with you. That breeze is coming off Jutland. If it were coming from England we'd be a week getting there.'

His companion turned blue, innocent eyes on him. 'Is it possible I am wrong? No, not in the least possible. The breeze has come from England and is turning around just over *there*,' he pointed vaguely, 'to bring us home again.

Do you think a foreign wind could smell so fresh, or wing us so swiftly towards Dover? Fie on you for a traitor!'

'Oh Hugo,' Edward laughed. Since he had arrived at the Court of the exiled king, he had become very friendly with Hugo McNeill, Viscount Ballincrea. McNeill was half Irish, half French, one of the many displaced peers who had been wandering from one European court to another in the train of King Charles. His father had died fighting for the Martyr King, and McNeill had lost his land to Cromwell's invading forces, and had been exiled for his religion and his royalist background. As penniless as his master, he had, like his master, covered the bitterness of exile and the shame of beggary with a cynical humour. He had lived largely by gambling, and by the charity of his mistresses, who had been a legion; for Hugo McNeill was handsome, witty and charming. He had a sweet, almost boyish face, tanned very dark by his constant outdoor exercise, luxuriant dark hair, bright blue eyes, and a charming smile of which he made good use. Like the King, he had enormous spirits and energy, and his late nights of heavy drinking and gambling frequently followed by strenuous love-making, never seemed to have any ill-effects on him. He was five years older than Edward, but looked younger than him.

They had their backs now to the sea, leaned comfortably on the taffrail, and turned their eyes to the leeward side of the afterdeck where an enormously tall, lean man was strolling up and down in his shirt-sleeves, the white linen dazzling against the thick black curls of his jet-black hair that hung over his shoulders. King Charles was above two yards tall, with a dark, heavy, lined face, made darker by his black brows and moustache. It was possible to look at the King and think him ugly, for he had thick lips, a long bulbous nose, and the sad dark eyes of a monkey; but he had only to look at you, and you fell under his spell, and if he smiled at you, you wondered how you had ever thought him anything but beautiful.

'It will be his last taste of informality for a long time, I suspect,' Edward said. 'Strolling in his shirt-sleeves will be a thing of the past.'

Hugo smiled. 'Don't wager your purse on it, Ned. Once he's safe at home, he'll go back to all his old, bad habits. Ah, and talking of bad habits, see who is digging pits for him now.' They watched as a beautiful, tawny-haired woman insinuated herself into the King's path so that, in sheer courtesy, he had to offer her the place on his right arm. 'By God, but Mrs Palmer has a hungry look this morning. She hopes to dine on titles and jewels before this day is out.'

'She's very beautiful,' Edward said, regarding the King's mistress critically. 'And yet – I wouldn't be Master Palmer. I should not like to get in her way.'

'Oh, Roger is essential to her,' Hugo said. 'It would not be at all proper for the King to have an unmarried mistress. And he benefits by what she brings him. Don't waste your sympathy on Palmer. Rather pity the poor King – she would eat up rubies like grapes and drink diamonds like water.'

'He can always be rid of her if he wants. He is the King,' Edward said. Hugo shook his head with mock sadness.

'Ah yes, but I fear our sovereign lord suffers from a rare and incurable disease – he can't say no. At least, not to a woman. He finds it hard enough to refuse a man, if he's a friend, or a plausible rogue. That's why there are so many of us, running at his heels like hounds on a spent fox.'

'Will he get you back your estate?' Edward asked.

Hugo raised an eyebrow. 'Who knows? He'd need all the treasure of Eldorado to repay everyone who claims to have lost his all in the King's cause.'

Edward smiled. 'So you stay with him out of affection? Just as I thought. Underneath that hard, world-weary exterior—'

'There is a hard, world-weary interior,' Hugo finished for him. 'No, no, credit me with no virtue, Ned, no altruism. I am a penniless exile, a beggar in ragged velvet. Shining with the King's reflected glory I can make an adequate living for myself with the cards and dice and sweet words for the ladies. The alternative does not bear thinking about.'

Edward Hyde came out on deck from the after-cabin and began to make his way towards the King.

'There goes your master,' Hugo said. 'See how the King inclines to him, hears him out patiently, the fat and stuffy old bore. The King loves him, you see, and Charles Stuart is faithful where he truly loves. You would be wise to stick with your master, if you have favours to ask – as I suppose you must. Which of us nowadays does not?'

'Well,' Edward admitted with a rueful smile, 'there is the little matter of the lost estates – confiscated or sold to pay fines or, like the Scottish lands, simply stolen. If the King would only see fit—'

'Get your request in as early as possible, that is my advice to you,' Hugo said. 'Every man and his dog will flock to Whitehall with the same idea in mind, and those that ask first will be the lucky ones.'

'I have already mentioned it to the King,' Edward said, and Hugo laughed and smacked him heartily between the shoulder blades.

'Well done, Ned Morland! You put us practised beggars to shame! And there I was, thinking you were so shy and humble you would need a great deal of chivvying by an interested friend before you would put aside your unselfishness.'

Edward grinned unwillingly. 'It wasn't like that,' he said, and as Hugo snorted with disbelieving laughter he said, 'no, truly! When I was first presented to the King, he said that the name of Morland was not unknown to him, and asked me if I was any relation to the Morlands of York. So naturally I told him, and he wanted to know what my family had done and—'

'He is his own worst enemy,' Hugo sighed. 'If he goes

on reminding people of his debts like that he will have to start borrowing from Mrs Palmer to pay them.'

The people of England went wild with joy at the return of their King. From Dover all the way to London the roads were lined with cheering crowds, and in every village the church bells rang wild carillons of celebration. The entry into the city was planned for the King's thirtieth birthday, and the procession rested at Blackheath on the night of the twenty-eighth and was joined there by everyone who was to have a place in the ceremonial re-entering of the capital. The day dawned bright and clear, and the sun rose in a cloudless sky like an omen. The procession was not expected to reach London until after noon, but by eight in the morning there was no inch of space to be had anywhere along the processional route. People stood in their best clothes and holiday mood, patiently pressed shoulder to shoulder, while those owning houses along the route did a brisk trade in window space, and crowded themselves and their families perilously along the leads.

The streets were decorated with all the bright flowers of May, and green boughs were formed into decorative arches over the roads. The houses of the rich were decorated with tapestries, nailed to the front beams, glowing in the bright sun, and flags on poles hanging out of the windows. Garlands of plaited ribbons, scarlet and gold and green and azure, were looped along the housefronts and suspended across the streets from torch-brackets. By order of the Lord Mayor, the public fountains ran wine all day, and the church bells rang non-stop from before dawn until after dark. It was two o'clock before the cannon on Tower Hill boomed out the salute to the King and the procession began to wind its way through the narrow streets.

The noise was deafening, from the cheers of the crowds, the clattering of horses' hooves, the clamour of the church bells, and the drums and trumpets of the military and household bands accompanying each section of the brilliant parade; and yet it was as nothing to the roar that arose when the tall figure of the King himself, riding on a white horse, finally came into view. The people cried out in a frenzy of adoration, sinking to their knees, stretching out their arms to him, crying his name, crying: 'God bless your Majesty!' and 'Long live the King!' They threw flowers under his horse's feet, and the scent of crushed roses was added to the multitude of other street smells. The sweating trumpeters and household drummers blared out their music, but it was unheard in the great swell of cheering that filled the narrow streets like the roar of the sea.

Now they were passing out of London and along the Strand, where the elegant palaces of the rich stood with their gardens running down to the river. The procession was so long it took seven hours to pass from beginning to end. There were twenty thousand soldiers, horse and foot, all with their swords unsheathed and held up so that they flashed blindingly in the sun, and they cheered almost as loudly as the crowd as they marched along; the Lord Mayor and his Aldermen were there in their robes of office, their gold chains and swords; then came the livery companies, each in its own livery of bright, medieval colours, carrying their banners and relics; and there were all the lords and nobles and other cavaliers who had followed the King into exile – the whole of Charles' ragamuffin Court, now gaudy with borrowed finery, cloth of silver, scarlet satin, cloth of gold, azure velvet, gold chains about their necks, long feathers in their hats. Edward rode amongst them on Bayard, whom a servant of Richard's had brought down to Blackheath for him. He was better mounted than many of the household who had had hastily to buy or borrow what they could: some of them concealed under bright caparisons the deficiencies of a jennet or plough horse. Bayard was not an ideal horse to ride in a slow-moving procession, surrounded by flapping banners and screaming crowds: he sweated up, flattened his ears, slithered about on the cobbles, and kicked out. As they went down Ludgate Hill he swung his quarters into the crowd and knocked three people over like ninepins, but they simply got up again without even breaking the rhythm of their cheering, almost as if they hadn't noticed.

Hugo, who was riding beside him, grinned up at Edward and shouted, 'That great brute of yours will make you unpopular.'

'They didn't seem to mind,' Edward yelled back.

'Oh, not them! If you want to knock anyone down, make sure it's the common people – they'd think it an honour. Besides, they are so hysterical with joy today you could cut off their arms and legs and they'd still dance you a hornpipe on their stumps. Just make sure your monster doesn't kick anyone else's horse. It's bad enough you having a horse so good when some of us are mounted on mules.'

At last they reached Whitehall, and there Edward finally caught sight of Richard, who was in the welcoming party gathered there to greet the King. There were more soldiers in scarlet and silver cloaks, more bands, more church bells, and another cannonade, as well as the speeches of welcome. The King, with his brothers, the Duke of York and the Duke of Gloucester, General Monk, the Lord Mayor, the Duke of Buckingham and Master Hyde, dismounted and stood bareheaded in the sun to hear them, and then Hyde presented the principal members of the welcoming party to the King. Richard was one who came forward and knelt to kiss the King's hand.

Edward nudged Hugo and said, 'Look, there's my brother, Richard. He's one of the ones I mentioned to the King, who worked to recall him.'

Hugo smiled and said, 'That should do you some good, then, when you come to make your requests. Keeping your name before the royal attention is a very important part of this begging game. Ah, thank God, we are going in. I need to get out of the sun before I faint.'

Edward pressed his fingers to his ears. 'I need to get away from the din, before I lose the power of hearing altogether.'

'If there's any man in London with the full use of his voice tonight, the people will hang him for a republican,' Hugo said. 'Does this man want you?' He gestured to a serving-man who was trying to thrust his way towards them, casting a wary eye at Bayard as if he had previous experience of the striking power of those great hooves. Edward looked and then raised a hand in greeting.

'One of my brother's servants. What ho, Matt?'

'I'm to take your horse, Master. My master particularly wants you to catch up with him, sir.'

Edward glanced at Hugo, who nodded. 'This is the time to do the family some good, I suppose,' Hugo said. 'A pair of Morlands will be more than twice as striking to the eye.'

'Come with me,' Edward said quickly. 'Matt, will you take Lord Ballincrea's horse too?'

'Well sir,' he said doubtfully, 'stabling's hard come by tonight—'

'Good man,' Edward said quickly, swinging down from the saddle and throwing his reins to the man before he could change his mind. 'Holy Mary, I'm stiff! Come on, Hugo, let's hobble in together.'

It was well Richard had thought to send Matt to them, as they soon saw, for everyone was now trying to dismount at once and there was growing chaos in the outer courtyard, which Edward and Hugo were glad to escape. After the main party everyone was now trying to crowd into the great hall where there would be more speeches for the great ceremony of welcome. When they caught up with Richard Edward saw that it would be more than a pair of Morlands to confront the King, for Francis was also with him, representing the Northumberland branch, and Kit, representing his own interests. It was the first time Edward had met anyone from home since he left, and he was a little disconcerted. Kit was far more embarrassed than he, however, which made it easier for Edward to appear calm and unconcerned.

'Richard has been telling me of your part in this happy day,' Kit said shyly as he clasped Edward's hand, 'and I wanted to say how proud – I mean, we all – I mean, I'm sure it—' He stuttered to an embarrassed pause, and Edward finished his sentence for him with a wicked smile.

'It makes up for everything else I've done, is that it?' Kit went scarlet.

'Oh I didn't mean—'

'It's all right. How is Ralph?' Edward asked quickly.

'He's well. Everyone is well at home,' Kit said. This was not the time to ask more, but Edward determined to get Kit on one side at some point and ask for more detailed news. Now he introduced his family to Hugo.

Richard looked at him keenly as they shook hands and then said, 'You must come and stay with me if you have no lodgings yet. I have a house in Milk Street. I know my wife would be honoured to have you.'

'You are very kind, sir,' Hugo said, and Edward could see that it was not just a form of words – he was genuinely touched by the hospitality. 'But I think I must stay here at Whitehall, however uncomfortable it may be. If I do not keep close to the King, I shall lose my advantage.' He said it with a smile, but Richard nodded, seeing the force of the argument.

'Then I hope, sir, that you will be a very frequent visitor at least, and dine with us as often as you may.' They had been walking along all this time, and now at last were passing into the great hall where the ceremony was to continue, and General Monk caught Richard's eye and sent him hurrying to the great man's side on some business. The speeches were very long and elaborate, and at their conclusion the whole party was to walk over to Westminster Abbey for a service of thanksgiving. As the Lord Mayor spoke the words, Edward was close enough to see the King visibly wince before recomposing his expression. He made a gracious speech, but asked that further ceremonies could be postponed to another day, saying that he was very tired, disordered by the journey and with the noise still sounding in his ears. There was a murmur of polite laughter at that last remark, for many of them were suffering the same way. A royal request was the same as a command, and so the Lord Mayor had no alternative but to cancel the rest of the official engagements, and leave the King free to seek the peace of his private apartments, which had been made ready for him.

'Let us hope that Cromwell has not left them in too bad a condition,' Hugo murmured to Edward as they drew back to make a pathway to the door for the King.

'I hear that most of the martyr king's collection of paintings was sold,' Francis said. 'The King will have to start all over again.'

The King and his immediate companions reached them, and the Morlands and Hugo swept their low bows. The King gave them a pleasant, if tired, smile as he passed, and Edward heard him saying to George Villiers in a low voice, 'I think I must have only myself to blame for staying in exile so long. I haven't met a man this past week who hasn't told me he has always desired my return.'

They straightened up as the King passed on, and Hugo, looking after him, said, 'He's off to start that collection of beautiful things. It won't be paintings, however – it will be living beauty that he fills his apartments with.'

'What do you mean?' Francis asked.

Hugo smiled cynically. 'Where do you think he is going? To sleep? To meditate upon God's will in restoring him to his throne? Or to seek the solace of Mrs Palmer's ample bosom?'

Francis looked shocked and said, 'Excuse me, but I think Richard is calling me,' and hurried away, and Kit quickly excused himself and followed. Hugo roared with laughter and flung an arm round Edward's shoulder.

'It worries the poor boy to think that the King, like any

other man, must use a piss-pot. Come now, my Ned, what shall we do? Shall we follow our lord King's noble example?'

'I'm damned hungry,' Edward said.

'So am I. Let us go and bespeak the finest dinner London can provide – and I'm a Dutchman if we have to pay for it, either! What, two loyal cavaliers? We shall be feasted and feted tonight. And what do you say to some female company? London is full of pretty women, if those that were lining the road are anything to go by—'

'And after fifteen years of Puritan rule, they will all be unspoiled,' Edward added. 'Of course, they might all be virtuous.'

'Pigs might fly,' Hugo said. Arm in arm the two handsome young men walked towards the door. 'We shall have our pick of the best. The man who sleeps alone tonight is a fool or a traitor—'

'Or both.'

'A Puritan.'

'A sad dog.'

Laughing, they passed out into the evening sunshine.

CHAPTER NINE

The King, like a monk of old, rose with the sun. In summer, when the sun rose early, he was able to take his walk in the Privy Gardens almost alone, while his courtiers were still sleeping off the effects of the previous night's drinking. Pretty soon, though, their servants would shake the would-be petitioners awake and bundle them off to fall in behind the King, lest someone else gain the favour they had been angling for.

Hugo, being blessed with a strong physique and a lively intelligence, soon made an arrangement with one of the King's chamberers who, for a small consideration, would pass the word to his servant, Gilles, as soon as the King stirred. Gilles would then wake his master, fetch hot water, and have him washed, shaved and dressed in time to be at the garden wicket along with His Majesty's spaniels.

'I'll swear,' he told Edward, 'that I don't actually open my eyes until I hear the damn dogs. Gilles dresses me like a mother dresses an infant, in my sleep. Then he says, '*Votre coup de matin, 'sieu*' and holds my nose and pours it down.'

'What's in it, that morning draught of yours?' Edward asked, amused. 'It must be a powerful nostrum to revive you at that time of the morning.'

Hugo shuddered delicately.

'A little notion of my own. Lemon juice in hot water, unsweetened. It would wake the dead, my child, and it certainly does the trick for me. My tongue shrivels at the touch, springs back into my throat and forces me to my feet, and away I go, one-two, one-two, one-two, down the back stairs and across King Street to fetch up against the Privy wicket like a dutiful piece of flotsam pressing itself affectionately against the piers of London Bridge, all ready to bow and flourish and cry 'Good morning, Your Majesty' in a fresh and ringing tone as if I had been up and scrivening since Prime. And Charles Stuart smiles at me with a nice mixture of admiration and disbelief, and when the rest of the barnyard come tumbling down the path, sticky-eyed and yawning, I am already deep in conversation. Grand slam!'

Edward laughed, and said, 'But does it do you any good? Has he given you back your lands yet?'

Hugo wagged a finger at him. 'In time, my child, in time. You cannot rush these delicate negotiations.' He lowered his voice and stepped closer. 'To tell the truth, Ned, I am in no great hurry to get back to Ireland. Ballincrea is the very devil of a place, except for the hunting. No, all I want is for it to be well known that I will, eventually, have my estate again, so that I can get credit at the 'Change. For the rest, Whitehall suits me, and I suit Whitehall, so I am content.'

One Sunday in July the whole Court, and a great number of hangers-on, were crowded into the gardens enjoying the sun after a spell of dull, cold weather. Hugo was there, chatting to a young woman whose inexpert application of face-paint suggested she had not long come up to London from the country, and whose eager flirting glances towards every young man who passed her suggested she was anxious either to lose her virtue or find a husband. The whole barnyard, as Hugo called the courtiers, had been in the garden above two hours, but he had not yet caught sight of Edward, though Kit and Francis and Richard had all greeted him as they passed. Then at last he saw his friend coming in from the direction of the Tilt Yard, and excusing himself to his companion, who was beginning to bore him, he sauntered over to meet him.

'God's day to you, Master Morland. That last cup of metheglin last night must have been too much for you. The Morlands have been flapping in the King's wake like seagulls after a herring-boat these two hours, but never a sign of you.'

'I've been working, not sleeping,' Edward said indignantly, and then a frown crossed his face. 'Lord, how the river smells when the tide's down.'

'That's why they call this the Privy Garden,' Hugo said imperturbably. He came close to Edward and peered at his neck, pulling his doublet this way and that.

'What are you doing?' Edward asked, almost impatiently.

'Looking for your collar,' Hugo said. 'The Chancellor's dog ought to wear the Chancellor's collar, or someone might steal him, and he's such a good, hard-working little fellow.'

'Better than being like these curs, begging for scraps,' Edward said, gesturing towards the hangers-on.

'Ned, my dear, you are in grave danger of becoming virtuous. It's associating with virtuous old men that does it. Master Hyde will ruin you.'

'He's very good to me,' Edward said shortly. Hugo slipped an arm through his and forced him to stroll slowly towards a quieter part of the garden.

'Hush, now, don't be fractious. Come with me and smell the roses. I want to talk to you seriously.'

Edward allowed himself to be drawn, and smiled reluctantly. 'I want to talk to you, too, Hugo. You've been running up the most enormous debts.'

'But what else can I do, *mon vieux*? I haven't the money to pay.' His face was the picture of troubled innocence, and Edward was amused despite himself.

'Has it not occurred to you to live less expensively?'

'Of course not,' Hugo said at once. 'What a foolish thing to suggest. I must have my food and wine, and my servant's keep, and one or two little trifles to amuse me—'

'One or two little trifles, you call them? What about all the new clothes? And the paintings, and the marbles, and the furniture? I swear your apartment looks like a thieves' storehouse! And the money you lose at cards and dice—'

'Ah, now there I have you. The money I lose at cards and dice is my own, money I have won at cards and dice on more fortunate occasions.'

'On less drunken occasions,' Edward corrected sternly. 'Do you really think it is a good idea to be drunk every single night?'

Hugo's face became suddenly serious. 'Yes, my Ned, I do. I think it is quite, quite essential. Why do you think I do it? Why do you think we all do it? For I am not alone. When you have lived in exile, when you have given everything for a cause and lost it all, and lost the cause too, then you have a great emptiness inside which is intolerable to live with. The wine helps us to forget the emptiness.'

Edward's grey eyes grew greyer, like an autumn sky before rain. He looked into Hugo's eyes, like to like. Hugo said gently, 'Yes, you know, my Ned. You have an emptiness, too. You fill yours with work, I with wine, and gambling, and women, and pretty pictures. It is the same thing.'

'But it isn't enough!' Edward cried, as if the admission had been wrenched out of him. Hugo looked sad, and for the first time Edward saw that he was older, much older in spirit, than he appeared.

'No, it is never enough. Everyone needs something to love, and love is the only thing that will fill that great dark hole inside a man.' He turned his face away at last, contemplating the fresh blue sky. Edward looked too, and Hugo went on, almost to himself, 'All the time I was abroad, I dreamed of home. Papa and I gave up everything for England, for home, for the way of life we treasured, for the King, for honour, for loyalty. And we lost, and I wandered reviled and unloved from country to country, knowing that my enemies were living in my home and not appreciating the beauty of it. And all the time I dreamed of the gentle northern skies, the tender blues, the subtle greys, the long, haunting twilights of summer, the fragile dawns of spring. For a time I thought that one day I might come back to them, that I might regain what I had lost. But when we came back, I found I had lost more than my country. I had lost myself.' He looked at Edward. 'I cannot any longer believe in honour, and loyalty, and virtue.'

They walked on in silence for a while, and then Hugo laughed, and said, 'Ah, but love, I could believe in love! Have you no sister, niece, cousin to send me, my Ned? I ask for nothing, except that she be beautiful, sweet, virtuous, and very, very rich!'

Edward shook his head and laughed. 'Never a one, Lord Ballincrea, and so I beg your pardon.'

'And if you had one, you would not give her into the wicked clutches of your reprobate friend, would you? Never mind, I love you still, Ned – so much that I am willing to forgive you for finding Court life not to your taste. Ah, yes, there is no need to look surprised. I have seen you grow more and more restless these past weeks. I have seen you look with distaste upon our revels.'

'I'm sorry,' Edward said. 'I don't mean to sneer. But it is not for me, you know, though I like drinking and dancing and gambling and women—'

'But not all the time.'

'That's right. I loved London when I first came here, but I'm tired of it. I'm tired of noise and stink and people crowding around all the time. I feel closed in, trapped. I want the open air and fields of my home. And I want a job to do. I am not used to being idle. I cannot enjoy my leisure if I have no work to compare it with.'

'I knew it,' Hugo laughed. 'Master Hyde has corrupted you!'

'And he that wounded me shall make me whole,' Edward smiled. 'The Chancellor has found the perfect thing for me, and is making it my reward for good service.'

'What then? Nothing to take you too far away, I hope?'

'He is to make me one of his Charity Commissioners.

He has given me the area around Leeds, so I shall be close to my home. It is perfect, quite perfect. I shall ride about the country and investigate the local charities. I shall be a man of power and influence. People will respect me, and invite me to dine with them, and introduce me to their daughters. And when I am tired of the provincial life, I shall come to London to make my report to the Chancellery, sample the delights of the city, and ride away again before I can tire of them.'

Hugo sighed. 'Well, so you are content,' he said. 'And at least I shall see you from time to time.'

'Often, I hope,' Edward said, clasping his friend's hand. 'I should never want to lose you, Hugo. Say we shall always know each other.'

'I swear it,' Hugo said, closing his other hand over Edward's. Their eyes were very bright as they looked at each other, and then they turned at the end of their walk and strolled back towards the crowds.

Chancellor Hyde looked across his work-table at the young man standing before him – a tall young man, with a handsome, high-cheekboned face, wide blue eyes, dark love-locks. A Morland face, he could call it, for the similarity with Richard Morland's other nephew, Francis, was very marked, and emphasized by the two young men's being always together. They were good young men, he thought, very different from the gaggle of amoral, French-speaking rakes who had come back with the King from Europe, and for that reason alone he would have wished he could do more, even had they not been the nephews of a man Hyde was already finding very useful.

'I am sorry,' he said. 'I wish I could give you better news, but there is nothing I can do.'

'But—' Kit began, ready to explain all over again, but Hyde held up his hand.

'I know, and believe me, you have my sympathy. But

you must understand that every day we receive hundreds of petitions of exactly the same kind. Hundreds of people all over the country have lost their land, and want it back. Many of them have given all they had for the King's cause. Their fathers, their brothers, their sons died in battle. Your own father, I know, died at Marston, and the King is not forgetful of these things. But we cannot give back all the land that has changed hands. If we were to do so, we should be committing a grave injustice to those who purchased lands in good faith. Put yourself in the place of someone who bought lands openly and honestly in a public sale, and now had it confiscated. Quite apart from that, in some cases the land has changed hands many times, has been broken up into parcels, boundaries changed – the confusion, Master Morland, the confusion would be nothing short of chaos.'

Kit's blue eyes burned and his lip jutted in a way which signified he felt that that was Hyde's problem, not his. He was concerned only with his own land. He knew where it was, and he wanted it back. Hyde looked at him wearily, reading his thoughts without difficulty. Whatever he and the King did, they would make enemies. There was no entirely fair or entirely right answer to the problem, but it would never be possible to make others see that. Kit braced himself to begin arguing again.

'Sir, in my own case,' he began, and the Chancellor cut across him firmly and smoothly, wanting to end this tedious interview as quickly as possible.

'You must not think the King is unaware of the problem. We have discussed it very fully before coming to a decision. It has not been officially announced, but I will tell you in order to relieve your mind of any doubts, that we have decided on a policy which, while not perfect, will mete out a kind of rough justice in this matter. Those lands which were confiscated by the late rebel government will be restored to their former owners; those lands which were sold, whether to pay fines or to provide arms for the King, or for any other reason, will not. The sales, made legally, will be upheld. Your own lands were sold, and I am afraid there is nothing more that I can do for you. Good day to you now.'

Dismissed so firmly, Kit had no alternative but to bow and leave. Outside, he fumed. Watermill, destroyed by the Scots, then sold to pay fines raised against him by the rebel government because his father had died defending the King, was not to be given back! Thus the new King rewarded loyalty to the old! He passed out into the public corridor, and Francis came hurrying towards him, linked arms with him and drew him away to talk privately.

'What happened?' he asked anxiously, seeing Kit's lowering brow. 'What did he say?'

Kit told him. 'All I have left is a few houses in York, and the one warehouse on Queen's Staith. It does not pay to be faithful to kings, that it doesn't!'

Francis looked shocked. 'You mustn't say so,' he said. 'Kit, remember you are a Morland. *Fidelitas—*'

'I remember I am a Morland. The King does not.'

'But, see,' Francis said, anxious to comfort his cousin, 'the confiscated lands will be returned. So Ralph will get his estate back. He is not forgotten. You must see that it is fair to him.'

'What use is that to me?' Kit cried in frustration. 'How can I marry Annunciata if I have no estate? How can I marry anyone?'

'But what about the Scottish estates? What did he say about them?'

'He said that was not a case for his intervention. He said that as they had simply been seized, I must go and claim them back, and if they would not yield them to me, I must go through the normal processes of law to have them evicted.'

'Well, that's all right then,' Francis said.

Kit looked at him bitterly. 'You think so? Do you think those Presbyters will simply give my land back to me? And if I have to go to law it will take years, and even then they may not find for me.'

'Of course they will, you have clear title. But look—' he thought furiously, 'I think we may do better. You know that the army is to be paid off in September? That will mean a great number of men coming back home, many of them Borderers. There are a number of Tods Knowe men serving, and some of the Bell Hill men. Why should we not make up an army, and go up there and force them out? I'd help you, and I'm sure Crispian would. I shan't be paid off – the Coldstream regiment is being kept on, and I am staying in my commission until spring, but I can help you organize things. Or if you want to wait until spring, I'll march with you.'

'Would you? Would you really?'

Francis grinned. 'Of course. I joined the army for a fight, and I never had it. My blood has never had a chance to cool. Don't despair, Kit, we'll get your land back for you, and have a deal of fun in the process!'

In the rose-garden at Morland Place, the scent of the roses in the hot July sunshine was almost unbearable. Mary was sitting in a sheltered spot where the heat was trapped by a hedge of roses almost ten feet high; it towered above her, a cumulus of creamy blooms, deepening at their throats to a tender shell-pink, heartbreakingly fragrant, humming with bees. One festoon hung almost to her shoulder, and without moving her head she could look into the open face of a huge flower. A bee flew down and landed on its flushed petals, so close to her eye that she could see it as if magnified. She saw its legs with their tiny hooked feet, its sacs so stuffed with golden pollen that it looked as though it was wearing bright yellow pantaloons. Its eyes were golden, and its pelt was gold and dark-honey and black in stripes. If I reached out my finger very gently, she thought,

I could stroke its back, and it would feel like thick fur, like a cat in winter.

Suddenly her loneliness welled up in her, rising in such a swift flood that even as she closed her eyes she felt tears seeping out from under her lids in an astonishing flow. She remembered a day from her childhood: she had been about nine years old, and she had run out from the house onto Emblehope Moor. Their house, square grey stone, like a small fortress, had stood right on the moor, so that it seemed to roll like a brown and purple sea to lap against the very walls. When the wind blew, it whispered in the tall bracken and the high pine trees with a sound like the sea. So she had told her father once, and he had laughed and said, 'But you have never seen the sea, hinny.' No more had she, and yet she could have told him, it is a sound one is born knowing.

But there had been no wind that day. It had been still and hot, and the land lay baking under a great cornflower of a sky, so blue that the zenith looked dark when you stared into it. She had gone by the sheep trods, and the small black flies had risen in clouds from the bracken on either side as she passed. Her feet were bare, and the crumbly earth was warm under her toes. Here and there in the bracken the sheep grazed like small fallen clouds; they raised their surprised black faces as she passed, Y-shaped against the green shade, with yellow eyes like gold coins, and the nearer ones flounced away, flaunting their ridiculous tails.

Out of the bracken onto higher ground, and finally to the highest place, where there were grey outcrops, gilded with lichen, and all around a sea of rose-purple heather. And there she had laid down on her stomach to stare out over her kingdom. Gorse and broom burned yellow like Moses' burning bushes, and far off she could see the squat grey of her house with a wisp of smoke rising straight up in the windless sky. Bees had been busy in the heather all around her, and she had rested her head on her bare forearms to watch them. The Mary in the rose garden felt a tug of pity in her heart for that Mary of long ago. With her eyes closed, the sound of the bees took her back across the years to that day; she could remember so clearly the hot, delicious smell of her sun-baked skin, the peaty smell of the earth, and the little furry bees grazing in the heather. Then she had lifted her head and seen, far off, horses cantering along the track to her house: her father had come home!

She had jumped up and run back along the trods, winged with joy, for she had loved her father dearly, and his rare visits home were a special delight. Yet even then she had felt some kind of foreboding, some sense that this happiness was especially precious, because it was the last time she would ever know it. She had entered the house, calling for Papa. The inside of the house was so much cooler that it struck chill to her bare arms, raising goose-flesh; the stone-flagged floor cold to her dusty feet. He was in the parlour, and turned as she came in, held out his arms, spoke her name. She flung herself on him in a hug, and felt, transmitted through her small bony body, the quality of his sorrow. He had spoken love to her, but when she stood back and looked up at him, she had seen grief, despair, hopelessness in his face.

She had learned later that the cause was lost, the King captured, and so he had come home, suddenly an old man. He had gone on fighting even after that, until he met his death in the last battle of all, outside Carlisle, but he had never again believed that the cause could be won or the world he loved saved. His hope and his joy had died, and something of Mary died with it.

He had brought her a puppy, something she had wanted for a long time. It grew apace, a yellow hound pup, and was her constant companion for the rest of its short life. It had caught its leg in a deer-trap, some four years later, the year they killed the King, and Mary had had to kill it to end its agony. She had never had another dog, though Ralph had offered her one again and again.

The thought of Ralph brought her slowly back to the present, and she became aware again of the smell of the roses, and the sound of murmuring voices as well as the bees. A blanket was spread on the grass in front of her, and her two youngest children were playing there, while Pal, the nursery maid, and her own maid Audrey looked on, peacefully threading beads and talking in low voices to each other.

Mary opened her eyes. The baby, Mary Marguerite, was almost a year old now, and was going to be another golden giant like most of her siblings. Her hair was as straight as water, despite all Pal's efforts to make it curl, and was bleached silver-white by the summer sun. She was big and strong for her age, and was able to crawl so briskly it was hard for Pal to keep up with her, and already she was pulling herself upright in preparation for walking.

For the moment she was sitting quietly, however. She was dressed only in a sleeveless shift, for Ralph felt that sunshine and fresh air was good for all growing things, and insisted that the bairn should not be bundled up in clothes in the heat of the day and kept out of the sun. Leah was scandalized, but Ralph overruled her, and Mary was not interested enough to take sides. Daisy seemed to enjoy it, and crawled around the garden half-naked, her limbs growing shockingly brown and her hair whiter and whiter. The thing that was holding her attention at the moment was a brown furry caterpillar, walking ambitiously along the finger that Martin was extending under the baby's nose. He was telling her a story about it in the strange language that he used and that the baby seemed to understand, a mixture of proper English, Yorkshire dialect, French, and wholly invented words. Martin adored the baby, and would have spent all his time with her if he had been allowed. He chattered to her all the time, played with her, sang her to sleep when her teething made her fractious.

He could soothe her colic as not even Leah could, and when, as she often did, being an adventurous bairn, she fell and grazed herself or bumped her head or got her inquisitive fingers stung by bees, Martin would rush to her and gather her into his arms and croon over her in their own secret language.

Leah had remonstrated about it, and Lambert had complained that Martin was often late or absent from his lessons because 'Baby had needed him', but Ralph had only laughed and said that it was never too early for a man to grow a tender heart, and that it was right for a boy to love and cherish his sisters.

'After all, it's not possible for anyone to cherish Sabine,' Ralph added, laughing. Sabine was a hoyden, and bullied all her brothers, except Edmund who, feeling chivalry was inappropriate in her case, returned her blows with interest.

Pal looked up from her work and saw the mistress watching the bairns, caught her eye and smiled, and Mary smiled back automatically, but it was a smile that touched only her lips. Why did she feel so lonely, so shut off from everything? She was mistress of Morland Place, an honourable and responsible position, she had a husband who loved her and was kind to her, and a large family of healthy children, and she was pregnant again. She ought to be happy; she knew it, and she knew that her discontent was a sin; but she did not love her husband, nor care for her children, and the only thing she could think of that she wanted was to go home.

There was a sudden scrambling of movement from the maids as they caught their work together in their aprons and got to their feet, and Mary looked up to see Ralph coming through the hedge.

'Ah there you are, my lady. You have found a pleasant spot,' he greeted her, stooping to put his lips against her cheek. He was hot and smelled, as he always did, of grass and horses. He was wearing britches and boots and a shirt and there was dust on his face; she guessed he had been over at Twelvetrees. Now he smiled at the maids and swooped down on his two children, taking them up one in each arm and lifting them shoulder-high as though they were weightless. 'And how are my least bairns? No lessons today, Martin?'

'No, Papa,' he said, looking solemnly into his father's face.

'He has had a headache, sir,' Pal said, 'and Master Lambert thought it were reading in such heat, and sent him off.'

'Good. Your health is more important than booklearning – you can always catch up on your lessons another time. And how is my sunny-faced little Daisy?' He nuzzled his face into her neck and made her gurgle with laughter. She seized a handful of his hair and tugged hard, and he yelped and blew into her ear and she laughed the more, and pulled even harder. Ralph glanced at Mary to see if she was enjoying the joke, but at the sight of her unmoving face, he put the children down and went to sit beside her.

'How is my lady?' he asked gently, taking her hand. Despite the heat of the day, her hands were cold and damp. 'Have you a pain? Do you feel sick?'

Mary shook her head. She had always carried easily, but this pregnancy had been different. She had suffered from nausea, not just in the mornings, but intermittently all day; she had had little appetite, and sometimes after a meal she would feel tightness and discomfort in her stomach, and would vomit. Ralph looked at her anxiously, for she looked so pale and thin, not even shewing her condition though her fluxes had stopped four months ago.

'Did you have something to eat, as I told you? You ate no breakfast.'

'I was not hungry,' Mary said.

'But you should be – how will the bairn grow if you do not eat? Oh Mary, what ails you, my heart?' He took both her hands and pressed them to him, and she looked at him, wondering if she could ask the question that was in her mind.

He saw the question in her face and prompted her gently. 'Is there something that you want? Something that I could do for you?' She nodded slowly. 'What is it, Mary? Anything in the world that you want I will get for you, if I can.'

'I want to go home,' she said abruptly, as if the words had forced their way past her reluctant lips. 'Oh Ralph, I want to see my home again.'

Loving her as he did, he did not say this is your home, nor let his hurt shew on his face. Instead he smiled a little and said, 'Is that all? Then you shall go. As soon as the hay is in, I will take you myself. The roads should be safe enough now, if we travel by daylight. There now, is that good enough?'

She only nodded, but the relief in her eyes was enough repayment for him. At that moment someone else came into the garden, an elderly servant, looking for him. It was Parry, the bailey from Shawes.

'Sir, my mistress sent me,' he said, bowing to Ralph.

'Yes, Parry, what is it?'

'Master Kit has come home from London, and will come over to see you this evening and tell you the news.'

'Kit home!' Ralph said eagerly. 'Why, I will not give him the trouble of waiting so long and riding so far. Tell your mistress I will come over at once.'

Ralph had come and gone in his energetic way, heard the good news as it related to himself, commiserated with Kit over his own bad news, invited them all to come to Morland Place for supper, and gone home to his dinner. Now Kit was left alone with Ruth in the small parlour. She was standing near the window, staring reflectively at a piece of broken harness which she was pulling again and again through her fingers. Where other women, within doors,

166

generally had a bit of sewing or embroidery about them, Ruth's hands were busy with mending harness, whipping rope, whittling pegs or polishing brasses.

Kit watched her, his mouth dry. He wanted to bring up the subject of Annunciata, but didn't know how to go about it, and half hoped and half feared she would broach the matter herself. But at last she did look up at him.

'I think Ralph will find it less easy than he thinks to part Makthorpe and his land. Chancery may grant it to him, but if he expects Makthorpe to give it to him he will soon find his mistake.'

'It may not be easy,' Kit said, 'But it will be easier than my task when I go to Scotland.'

'You go in the spring?'

'Yes.'

'And return when?'

'I don't know. That depends—' He could not quite say, on whether there is anything to return for. He said instead, 'That depends on how long the business takes. I should not like to leave with the matter unresolved.'

'If you do not get them out,' Ruth said briskly, 'it will always be unresolved. But you can come back here, if that's what you want to know. There will always be a home here for you.'

She said it without warmth, without a smile, matter-of-factly, as if she were telling him that it was raining outside.

Kit reddened. 'It is good of you. I have lived here so long on your charity—'

Ruth met his eyes expressionlessly. 'You work for your keep,' she said.

'I have often wondered—' Kit said awkwardly.

'Why I took you in, you and your mother?' she finished for him. He nodded. 'Because I promised your father that I would look after you both, and a promise made to the dying cannot be broken.'

'You saw my father when he was dying?' Kit said in

surprise. The story had always been told that he was dead when Hamil Hamilton brought him home, killed in battle.

'Your father came home the night before Marston Moor. He was here above two hours before he had to go back and join his regiment. He was dying then. He had been dying for a long time. There are some plants that flourish in the warmth and shelter of a garden, but plant them out on the moor and they wither and perish. Your father was like that. It was not the Scotsman's sword that killed him.' She was looking at him, but her eyes were far away, and there was a sadness in her face that made her look so much gentler than normal that he dared to speak.

'Ruth, I love Annunciata. I want to marry her. If I get back the Scottish estate—'

Her eyes snapped back to the present, and the softness was gone.

'No,' she said. He opened his mouth and shut it again, and she went on, 'I can do better for Annunciata than that. She is a considerable heiress.'

'You are ambitious for her, of course,' Kit began.

Ruth raised an eyebrow. 'Has it never occurred to you that I love her?'

Kit was embarrassed. 'Of course,' he said, but it was not of course at all. Proud of her, yes, ambitious for her, he could believe that, but it had never occurred to him to associate Ruth with love, except perhaps love of her horses, whom she treated with a tenderness she never lavished on human beings.

'I want the best for Annunciata. I am ambitious for her, but also I want her to be happy. I have had little enough happiness in my life. If Annunciata really wanted you, I would not stand in the way, though you were penniless. But she would not be happy with you – and you, though you won't believe it now, you wouldn't be happy with her.'

'I love her,' Kit cried.

Ruth looked at him steadily. 'Forget her,' she said. 'You

168

will be going to Scotland in the spring, but she'll be gone before that.'

'Gone? Gone where?'

'I am sending her to London. She will live with Richard and Lucy, and they will present her at Court, and there she will find opportunities enough to make the best of her abilities. And she'll find a husband there sooner or later. Knowing her, I'm inclined to expect it to be sooner rather than later, but I trust in her basic common sense. And Richard and Lucy will prevent her from making too gross a mistake. So you see,' she added, looking more kindly at Kit, 'she will be out of temptation's way as far as you are concerned, and out of sight is out of mind.'

'I'll never forget her,' Kit said. 'I'll always love her.'

'Just as you please,' Ruth said, and left him alone.

CHAPTER TEN

Ralph rode home thoughtfully, and went to seek out Mary. It was almost dinner time and she had gone in from the garden, she and the children, so he went to the nurseries, thinking she would have gone there to see the older ones as they dressed for dinner – for as they had breakfasted in the nursery and gone straight to their lessons, neither Ralph nor Mary had seen them yet that day. But a maid at the door told him she was not there. He went to their bed chamber and looked in, and finding it empty was going away to seek elsewhere when the door of the closet opened and Mary came through into the room. She started guiltily when she saw Ralph, and put a hand to her lips as if to wipe them, as a child will caught stealing jam.

'Oh, Ralph, you startled me,' she said. Her other hand was losing itself in the folds of her gown.

'Are you all right, Mary? You look pale,' Ralph said.

She looked at him strangely, as if wondering what to tell him, and then she said in a normal voice, 'The sunshine gave me a headache, that is all.'

'Have you been taking physic for it?'

The hand by her side lifted involuntarily, and he saw that it was clasped around something before she dropped it back to its hiding place. 'No – I – it was nothing much. It has almost gone,' she said, and then, determinedly changing the subject, 'Did you see Kit? What did he tell you?'

Ralph, puzzled, let the subject be changed, and told her the news of the Chancellor's decision. If she did not want to admit she was taking physic, he would not force her to, and yet he wondered why she should be ashamed of it.

'So it looks as though we shall get our land back by and by,' he finished.

'Poor Kit,' Mary said thoughtfully. 'It is hard to be punished for virtue, and to see those who did not fight for the King sitting back at their ease on cavalier land.'

'There was something else he told me, too,' Ralph went on, looking steadily at Mary. 'It concerns Edward, my uncle Edward.' Mary coloured and looked confused, and Ralph took a half step towards her, reaching out his hand imploringly.

'Hear me out, Mary, please. Kit says that Edward has been appointed Commissioner for Charities in the Leeds area. That means he will be travelling around within a few miles of here for some months. Mary, I want to see him again. I want to ask him to come home.'

'Oh,' Mary said, and some tension went out of her expression and she looked down at the floor.

Ralph went on, hurriedly, as if she might stop him before he had said all he wanted. 'I mean for a visit, that's all. I understand his commission would prevent his staying here anyway, but, oh Mary, I miss him so much. I grew up with him, he was closer than a brother to me. I know what he did to you, and I know how dreadful it was for you, but, please, won't you do this for me? Just receive him. You need't have anything to do with him once he's here, but receive him into the house so that I can—' he hesitated. 'If I say, apologize to him, it is not meant as a slight to you. I truly believe that he meant no harm, that it was only high spirits, and I believe I was too harsh in sending him away. I want to be reconciled to him. Will you do this for me? Of your generosity.'

He paused, and for a moment he thought she was not going to answer, for her head remained bent for so long. Then at last she looked up, and her face was expressionless, as if she had been composing it in the preceding silence.

'Invite him if you wish,' she said. 'It doesn't matter.'

'But will you receive him?' Ralph pressed eagerly. She

nodded, and he seized her hands in gratitude. 'Thank you, my darling. Thank you. God bless you for your generous mind.' An indefinable expression of distaste flitted across Mary's wan face and she withdrew her hands almost roughly and turned away.

'I must dress – it is almost time for dinner. Where is Audrey? She should be here. Will you call for her for me, Ralph?' she said.

Annunciata spread the skirts of her new travelling habit and looked down at them approvingly. It was made of the best French-blue broadcloth, sent up from the west-country to the market in York, and Ralph's tailor had combined forces with Ruth's usual dress-maker to decide on the style and cut. The result was, to Annunciata, quite thrilling. It was the first time she had had any garment so fine, and there was so much material in the skirt that it made her feel positively wicked.

'After the skimpy dresses I have been wearing,' she cried delightedly to Ellen, 'I feel so rich with all this to trail around me.' And she twirled on the spot again to feel the heavy cloth swish against the stone floor of her little chamber. 'Hetty, hold the mirror up more,' she commanded the maid, and she turned this way and that to admire the cut. The bodice was very tight at the waist and fitted snugly over her breasts, and was shaped and trimmed like a man's doublet, with a double row of small silver buttons down the front. It was the fashion, the tailor had assured them, for women to dress in imitation of men when they went riding. To that end there was also a black felt hat with a broad, curly brim which Ellen, muttering doubtfully, had trimmed with feathers. Annunciata held out her hand for it now, and with the help of the other maid, Meg, put it on and adjusted its angle.

'Eh, but tha looks a right Jezebel, and no mistake,' Ellen said, pushing out her lip. 'How tha can coom to dress like a man, with all thy beauty, I don't know. But no good will come of it. I've told the mistress, and told her, but will she listen?'

Annunciata adjusted the angle of the hat again. 'It's just perfect! Oh London must be such a place, if the women all dress like this. Oh this hat! I love it so, I shall take it to bed with me every night.'

'Aye, tha mayest well act like a harlot, if tha looks like one,' Ellen said sourly. Annunciata turned from the mirror and smiled radiantly at her nurse. She knew why Ellen was so disapproving, and it was nothing to do with the clothes. It was because Ruth had refused to let her accompany Annunciata to the wicked city.

'Ellen, don't be so cross,' she said, smiling winningly. 'You wouldn't have liked it anyway, and the journey would have been too much for you – Mother was right. And I shall be all right, don't worry about me.'

'Worry about you? Nay, but I shouldn't waste my breath on it, Miss. The Dark Gentleman looks after his own, they say, and tha'rt galloping this minute down his path as fast as tha can lay legs to the ground. Nothing but vanity and sin, evil talking, and bawdry, that's what tha'll find in London, and the way th'art framing now, it'll suit thee to the ground. Eh, but I've told the mistress—'

'But Ellen, what can I possibly get up to in London, with Richard and Lucy looking after me?'

Ellen looked at her shrewdly. 'They may be good folks for all I know, but there was never anyone but me and your mother could prevent you from doing what you wanted.'

'Well,' Annunciata said, trying to look hurt, 'and don't you think I have enough good sense and enough virtue to keep myself honest.'

Ellen's eyes opened wider. 'Nay, I'm not so worried about your virtue, Miss. You've got the mistress's sound head when it comes to business.'

'Well, what then?' Annunciata said, exasperated.

'You might marry a Protestant,' Ellen said, voicing her fears at last, and Annunciata burst out laughing and flung her arms round her. The door opened just then, and Ruth came in.

'Well, I am glad to find you in such spirits,' she said. 'Does the dress please you? Turn around and let me see.'

Annunciata jumped away and twirled again, laughing, holding her skirts out and up a little to show her soft leather riding boots underneath, and a little lace-edged petticoat. Ruth looked, her expression softening at the sight of her pretty daughter, her pink cheeks, her laughing, sparkling eyes, her curls and feathers.

'You look very fine,' she said. 'Come with me now to my room. I have something for you.' She turned abruptly and went out, and Annunciata followed her, blowing a kiss at Ellen, who merely growled and turned on the maids.

'Why are you standing there as if you were mazed? Come Hetty, Meggie, have you no work to do? There's all that linen to be marked yet.'

Ruth's chamber was small and very dark. The walls were panelled with linen-fold, darkened with age and smoke; the windows were set deep in the two-foot-thick walls, and were so small they let in little light. The bed had dark red damask hangings and its tester was lost in the shadows of the ceiling beams. There was no fireplace – in winter it was warmed in the old manner with braziers – but in a large niche in the end wall was a statue of St Anne, the mother of the Blessed Virgin, who was Ruth's birth-saint, and a vase that was always filled with flowers or, in winter, leaves and berries. That was the only spot of brightness in the room.

Annunciata was sobered simply by being here. She stood quietly, her hands folded, and watched as her mother went across to the low end beam of the ceiling. It was massive – one of the main supports of the roof – nearly three feet thick, and many small niches had been carved in it for the convenient keeping of small articles in a room with no cupboards or shelves. Ruth put her hand into one of these hiding places and drew out a small box and turned with it to the light of the window. Annunciata, watching her, noticed for the first time with a pang that her mother was no longer young. Ruth's face, always thin, was almost gaunt now, and lined with weather and responsibility. There were deep frown marks between her brows, and her eyes looked tired. The great mass of fox-red hair, which Ruth had always worn wound into a crown round her head, was streaked and speckled with grey, and the sight of those silver hairs springing from that head touched Annunciata unbearably. She had always fought her mother and rebelled against her, but she was aware in that moment of how much she loved her and respected her, and how little she would like to lose her.

Ruth came back to her now, and looked at her curiously, as if she were seeing her for the first time, and Annunciata felt strangely shy. Her mother's eyes were brown, not dark brown like her own, but a light, tawny brown, like a jar of honey held up to the light, and her eyelashes were quite golden. She had beautiful eyes, Annunciata thought suddenly. Why had she never married? Surely someone must have loved her sometime?

'I want you to have this,' Ruth said, holding out her hand, and when Annunciata extended her own palm, Ruth placed upon it a gold cross. It was large and heavy, an old-fashioned piece, the sort of cross that Annunciata had seen adorning the bodices of Tudor ladies in old paintings. The cross was of filigree, and set with amethysts of a very dark purple, and from each arm of the cross hung a small drop pearl.

'It's very old, isn't it?' Annunciata said.

'Yes. Nanette Morland gave it to my grandmother Jane when she married my grandfather. I was saving it for your wedding, but I want you to have it now. Wear it, and let it remind you of home, and of me, and of everything I have tried to teach you. You will be going to a place where temptations are many, and various and brightly coloured. Use your common sense, and consult your religion if you are in doubt. I want you to do well for yourself, but I also want you to be happy.'

Annunciata felt tears stinging her eyes, and she nodded, unable to speak for a moment. Ruth's eyes looked at her, kindly for once.

'You are very beautiful, my daughter, do you know that?' she said gently. 'It is well to know it. Beauty is a gift from God, but it is also a burden and a responsibility. Men will want to own your beauty. Don't give it away lightly.' Annunciata nodded again, her eyes fixed on her mother's. Ruth grew more brisk. 'Now, to more practical things. You have your travelling dress. The rest of your clothes must wait until you get to London. There is little point in having them made here and getting them wrong. Lucy will advise you. The money I am sending with you, you must give to Richard as soon as you arrive. He will give you your allowance and pay for your clothes and anything else you need. And Lucy will help you find a maid. None of mine are suitable. Hetty and Meg will travel with you to attend you on your journey, and you will send them back with the men once you arrive. Richard will see to the stabling of your horse.'

'Yes, Mother,' Annunciata said.

'You will be under the charge of Richard and Lucy, so heed them and do what they tell you.'

'Yes, Mother.'

'Do not neglect your religion. Say your prayers night and morning, read your lessons, take the sacrament every day. Be mindful always that each day could be your last on earth.'

'Yes, Mother.'

'Wear the cross and remember what I have told you. And write to me as often as you can.'

'Yes, Mother. Oh, I will. I shall miss you.' She wanted

to embrace her mother, but Ruth's bearing was too stiff and formal to allow it.

Ruth looked at her oddly. 'I think perhaps you will,' she said. 'I am proud of you, Annunciata. I don't know if I've ever told you that. Be proud of yourself. You know why I am sending you to London.'

'To get a husband,' Annunciata said mischievously.

Ruth did not smile, she merely nodded. 'You are beautiful, and you will be very wealthy. You must rise in the world, and to do that you must get a husband. There is no honour in the single state for women of our rank. In London you will do better for yourself than you can do here. Choose wisely, and I shall support your choice.'

'Thank you, Mother,' Annunciata said more soberly. It was a heavy responsibility that Ruth was laying on her shoulders – *find a master for Shawes*. She wondered suddenly if Ruth was tired of running the estate alone. She looked up at her mother earnestly.

'Who was my father?' she asked abruptly.

For a trembling moment she thought Ruth was going to tell her, but in the end she said, 'He was a gentleman. That is all you need to know.'

Edward sat in the parlour of the rector of St Stephen's, Windikirk, taking notes from the slow speech of the Scriven, the churchwarden. He was aware of a feeling of great well-being. Outside the September sunshine was warm and yellow on the grey stones of the church and on the leaves of the great horse-chestnut tree as they began to turn to gold. Inside the parlour it was pleasant and peaceful. Edward had the best chair the house could provide, which had been recently upholstered in red velvet. He had also been provided with the best bed in the house on which he had slept the sound sleep of the blameless last night between the best linen sheets. He was aware of the sensation inside him of one of the best beef puddings he had ever tasted nestling happily in his stomach whence it had been gently coaxed by a pint of excellent Rhenish wine, which the rector had provided for his dinner. Outside in the rector's excellent stables Byard was eating his head off on sweet upland oats, beans, and clover hay.

Edward sighed happily. The life of a Charity Commissioner was a good one. He tweaked his velvet doublet straight and shook the lace at his sleeve end out of the way of the ink before he carried on writing. He was well dressed, well fed, well lodged, and well respected, and he was doing a job which was worthy the doing, and which was unexceptionable to every man, and which, if he did it faithfully and well, should reward him accordingly.

'Now then, Master Scriven, tell me about Lewis's Bread.'

'Well sir, Lewis, he was a gentleman what owned the park,' Scriven began in his slow, careful voice. Churchwarden was an important office in the parish, and Scriven discharged his duties with painstaking care, and as soon as he heard that the Commissioner had come to Windikirk, he had presented himself almost before the gentleman was dismounted to tell about those charities that were under his care.

'The park over yonder? Where the big house is?'

'That's right, sir. Well, he left it in his will when he died that there was to be two pounds twelve and sixpence to be given every year to the poor in bread.'

'When would that be? When did he die?'

'Oh, let me see now – rector'd tell you bett'r'n me, but it were in the time of the old King. Thirty year come Michaelmas I've been churchwarden, and old Ben Hoskins that was warden before me, he was the first to give out Lewis's bread.'

'Very well. Carry on – where does the money come from?'

'Well, sir, Master Lewis gave it as a charge on two closes, about seven acres in all, just out on the road towards

Sherborn. His daughter sold them to Will Masterman along with some other land twenty years back.'

'And does Masterman pay the money regularly?'

'Oh yes, sir, every Quarter day, prompt as you please. I go up there to the house and he hands it over to me, and I comes straight back here and I gives it to rector, and he keeps it for me, and every Sunday he gives me a shilling, and Tom – that's Tom Smith, the other warden, sir – Tom and me buys the penny loaves, and then after the morning service we hands them out to the poor families as we see fit, sir.'

'How many loaves a person?'

'One, sir, or sometimes two, if we see cause. Mrs Clegthorpe, sometimes we give her two, on account of all her children, but never more than two to a family.'

'And you decide who gets them?'

'Yes sir, me and Tom, sir. We know everyone, you see.'

'Yes, of course. So let me see, a shilling every Lord's day. Fifty-two weeks to a year – that's two pounds and twelve shillings. And the gift was two pounds twelve shillings and sixpence? What happens to the other six-pence?'

'Rector keeps that, sir, because every second year there comes an extra Lord's day in the year, sir, because of there being not exactly four weeks in the month. So then the two sixpences—'

'Quite, quite,' Edward said, making notes. 'Are there any other charities given out after Divine Service?'

'Oh yes, sir, there's Rector's Dole, and Percy's Pence, and the widows' pence—' Scriven said eagerly.

'Tell me about Rector's Dole,' Edward said, drawing a new sheet towards him.

When the sun began westering and Scriven had gone home to his gardening and his supper, and the rooks were making a din in the tall elms in the churchyard, Edward slipped out to the stable and saddled Bayard and took him out into the open fields for a ride. There was still very little enclosed land in Yorkshire, though further south there was a considerable amount, and once he had cleared the village fields, heading towards Wetherby, he was on open land, half moor, half grazing, and there was nothing to prevent him galloping, it seemed, to the world's end. Bayard, restless after a long day inside, pulled eagerly at his bit, and smiling, Edward eased his hands and pressed with his heels and the big horse sprang out under him into full gallop, his long stride eating up the land. The air smelled good, and the warm wind whipped through his hair, and Edward was happy.

He rode as far as Wetherby, where there was an inn called the White Rose which was famed for its good ale. There he tied up Bayard in the yard, took a quart of the best ale the house had, refused an offer of supper, and chatted for a while to the landlord, who had heard of him and was anxious that he should stay at the White Rose when he came to investigate Wetherby's charities. Edward caught a whiff of the supper he had refused and a glimpse of the landlord's eldest daughter and promised that he would stay there, before riding Bayard back to Windikirk through the blue-gold dusk.

When he reached the rectory, he saw the rector's servant, Mary, standing in the front garden where she had evidently been looking out for him up and down the road.

'Why, sir, there you are! Rector's been that worried about you. Nobody knew where you had gone, and there's a visitor here for you, been here above an hour.'

'A visitor?' Edward said, and then recollected his position. Probably some local landlord come to tell him about a rent-charge. A strange time to choose, but then the rector's table was famed throughout the district, and a man arriving at supper time would expect to be asked to stay to supper. 'Is John about, Mary?'

'Oh no, sir, he's gone with the cows.'

'Then I'll just put Bayard up, and I'll go in. Is supper ready?'

'Waiting for you, sir.'

'Give me a quarter-hour then.'

He led Bayard round to the stables, loosening the girth as he walked. The rector's mealy-muzzled, fat bay cob looked over its shoulder as they passed the end of its stall and into Bayard's stall next door. Bayard knuckered suddenly and put his nose up to the bars at the top of the stable partition, and another horse whinneyed in reply from the next stall. The visitor's horse, of course. Edward untacked Bayard and fastened his headcollar on, and then, with saddle and bridle over his arm, slapped Bayard affectionately on the rump and went out. As he was about to turn towards the harness room, something made him pause, and go back to the farther stall and look in. A big, handsome red chestnut gelding turned its head and looked at him. A beautiful horse, as beautiful as Bayard, maybe even finer; it had a familiar look about it.

'Red Fox?' Edward said. At the sound of his voice the visitor's horse whickered softly. With a thoughtful frown Edward went to the tack-room, dumped the harness, and made his way through the back passage to the house. There was the sound of voices from the parlour, and the smell of peat-smoke drifting on the air and mingling with the smell of roasting meat told him that the rector had thought it worthwhile to have a fire lit in there. In the two weeks he had been here, Edward had grown very fond of the parlour, and the rector. He pushed the door open, and the voices stopped. The room was in gloaming, filled only with the flickering light from the fire and the dying dayglow from the window. Edward stood in the doorway, and two massive brindled dogs came sloping up to him to jab their hard muzzles into his hand and smile up at him with wolf-yellow eyes. The tall, fair man by the fire turned to look at him, nervously slapping his riding boot with his crop, and the rector smiled expansively and came bustling forward, holding a glass – one of his best Venetian glasses – in one hand and a pewter claret-jug in the other.

'Ah there you are, my dear Edward! Home at last. How we have been worried about you! But there, Mary said you would be back for your supper as sure as a bell, and so you are, so you are. Some claret, my son? And look, here is a visitor for you, your brother come to visit you, such a pleasant surprise. I have asked him to stay to supper since it is so late, and he has agreed to honour us. A little more claret, my dear Master Morland?'

'Not my brother, though we look so alike. In fact, he is my nephew,' Edward said.

'Hello, Ned,' Ralph said.

The rector looked from one to the other and said, 'Well, well, what a great pleasure to have friends and family about one. If you would excuse me for a moment only, I will go and see how Mary is progressing with the supper.' And he hurried out, leaving them alone together. Edward turned the glass in his hand round and round so that the firelight shone through the claret like the sun through a stained glass window.

'A good old boy,' Ralph said at last. 'He is leaving us alone of a purpose.'

Edward looked up. Ralph's expression was hesitant, like a dog that does not know whether to expect to be kicked or caressed. 'How did you know I was here?'

'Kit told me of your commission. It was not hard to find you after that. The whole county is talking about the new Commissioner. The last one was over fifty and had a poor digestion.' Ralph smiled, offering the pleasantry as an opening.

Edward said, 'Nothing is too good for the Commissioner, as you see. The best claret, the best glasses, a fire. In the inns they will not charge me for my ale . . . Why have you come?'

Ralph turned to face him fully, and the firelight behind him made a nimbus around his fair head, turning his moon-pale hair to rose-gold. The long grey eyes were wide with appeal. 'To make friends,' he said simply. 'I miss you, Ned. When you went away, I was so sorry. I had spoken in anger. If you had waited until the next day, I never should have asked you to leave.'

'*You* have come to apologize to *me*?' Edward said.

'I do not think you meant any harm. You always were high spirited.' Edward raised an eyebrow in query, and Ralph made an impatient gesture with his hand. He spilled a few drops of claret on the hearth-stone, and both dogs pushed up to him to lick them up. 'Ned, what does it matter now? The thing is in the past; why bring it up again? I've missed you, and I want to make friends again. Won't you meet me halfway?'

Edward stared at him, not knowing what to say. He was torn by the generosity of Ralph's heart which, believing him to have been wronged, still enabled him to apologize to the wrong-doer. He deserves better than Mary, he thought. He deserves, at least, my silence.

Edward was silent still, not knowing what to say, and Ralph looked at him, puzzled. A lesser man would have been offended at such a cautious acceptance of generosity, but not Ralph. He smiled, and held out his hand. 'I love you, Ned,' he said. 'I can't do without your friendship.'

And still the words would not come, but there was no need of them now. Edward came forward and took the offered hand. The palm was warm and hard against his own, the long, strong fingers squeezed his affectionately, and tears stung Edward's eyes. Ralph laughed suddenly, in relief.

'Thank the Lord,' he said. 'I thought you were going to refuse me! That would have been—'

'Mighty awkward, since we are going to have to sup together at all events,' Edward finished for him. They toasted each other silently and drank, and then Edward asked quietly, 'How is Mary?'

'Not well,' Ralph said, his face falling. 'She is with child again, and the pregnancy does not go well. She is very pale and thin. I had planned to take her home to Northumberland for a visit this month, but the doctor thinks she is not well enough to travel, and so it must wait until next month. She says she is homesick.'

'And what does the doctor say?'

Ralph shrugged. 'He says she is not eating enough, and truly, she ought to be much bigger than she is at this stage. But when she eats she gets sick, and so I don't know what to do. Leah makes her broth and gruel and calves'-foot jelly, and that seems to be all she can keep down. I'm worried, I can tell you.'

Edward nodded. 'And what of the rest of the family?' he asked after a moment.

'Oh, everyone else is well. Annunciata has gone to London, did you know? Richard and Lucy are going to present her at Court.'

'God's breath!' Edward exclaimed. Both men began to smile. 'She'll shake the Court by the ears,' Edward went on.

'She'll make her mark,' Ralph said, 'and come back a countess, as sure as a gun. I admire Ruth for sending her. Not every mother would have the courage to let a daughter like that out of her sight.'

'But then, Ruth is no ordinary mother, and Annunciata no ordinary daughter,' Edward said. And he thought, I shall see her when I go to London to make my reports. Just then the rector came back into the room, and smiled to see them standing together in such evident accord.

'Well, well, I hope you have not been kept waiting for too long,' he said, reaching for the jug again. 'Let me refill your glasses. What do you think to this wine, sir? A very fine wine, don't you think. Supper is ready now, and the servants are coming to lay the table. A simple supper, sir, I hope not too simple for your taste, but we do not pretend to great style out here in the country.'

'Whatever you have, sir, I'm sure it will be good enough for me,' Ralph said.

The rector looked pleased.

'I think you will enjoy it, sir. We have some very fine trout from our own stews here in the village, and Mary has made one of her excellent pies. Oh what treasures lie beneath the crust! Venison, and ham, and forcemeat, and hard-boiled eggs, and oysters and I'm not sure what else besides. And then we have a little cold fowl, and some sallets, and a dish of eels, fit, though I say it, for the King himself! Ah, here comes the cloth. A little more wine, gentlemen? Let me fill your glasses.'

Ralph arrived home the following afternoon, having spent the morning riding with Edward, and having taken an early dinner with the rector, and having with great difficulty refused a longer stay, for the hospitable old gentleman was loath to part with his unexpected guest. One of the grooms came up to him in the yard to take Fox, and as Ralph swung down from the saddle Clement appeared at the main door of the house to greet him.

'Did you see Master Edward, sir?' Clement asked, taking his hat from him and absently brushing the brim on his sleeve. His hands shook, for Clement was over sixty now and suffered from the palsy, but he would not retire from his duties, though his son Clem did most of them without his noticing.

'Yes, and he is well, and he is to come and visit us this day week,' Ralph said.

'Why, that's good news, Master,' Clement said.

'Yes, and we must have a fine dinner that day, so tell Jakes to look out all his best recipes, and make sure he has everything he needs. Where is the Mistress?'

'Why, in her chamber, sir. With the doctor.'

'Oh, yes, I had forgotten he was coming today. Send him to me in the Steward's Room when he has finished, will you?'

'Yes, Master.'

Ralph spent the waiting time polishing and oiling his

fowling-piece, and when the doctor came in he put it aside and said, 'Come in, come in, sir. I cannot shake hands with you, oily as I am. Well, sir, how is my wife?'

Brocklehurst, the doctor, closed the door behind him, walked to the exact centre of the room, folded his hands precisely over the top of his long, gold-headed stick, and said, 'Master Morland, I will not conceal it from you, that your wife is very sick.'

Ralph paled. 'You mean – will she lose the babe?'

'Mistress Morland is not with child,' Brocklehurst said.

'Not with child? What are you talking about? She is six months gone with child. Why—'

'She believes that she is pregnant, sir, and I believed so, but I examined her today because I have been puzzled about her condition, and that which is growing inside her is not a child. It is a tumour.'

Ralph stared at him, unable to make sense of the words. At last he said, 'But – the symptoms – her pregnancy—'

'She has had the symptoms of pregnancy, but these have been caused by the tumour. The sickness, her inability to take nourishment, has been caused by the pressure of the growing tumour on her stomach.'

'Will she get well again?' Ralph asked. His mouth was dry, and the words were hard to form. He knew the answer before the doctor spoke.

'I believe that the tumour is blocking the passage of food to the stomach; she is already weak from lack of nourishment, and she will grow weaker. In other words, she will die of hunger.'

'But there must be something you can do!' Ralph cried out. 'You can't let her starve to death. Good God, man, have you a heart of stone?'

'Master Morland, I wish there was something I could do, but there is nothing.' He paused for a moment, as Ralph stared wildly round the room as if seeking an escape from the situation. 'She is not in pain at the moment, merely some discomfort. Later, if the pain grows worse, I can give you something to ease it. But I do not believe she will suffer much. It will be like – falling asleep.'

'Oh God!' Ralph put his face in his hands, but the relentless voice went on.

'She does not know at the moment, I thought you would wish to tell her yourself. She has been taking physic for indigestion, and I have let her continue with that treatment. It does no harm, and gives her some comfort, I believe. You must decide what and when to tell her.'

'How long has she – will she—?'

'Not very long,' Brocklehurst said gently. 'A month, more or less.'

Ralph drew his shattered world around him, desperately steadying himself.

'And she does not know, you say?'

'She still believes she is pregnant.'

'Thank you,' Ralph said. His eyes grew distant, thoughtful, and he barely noticed when Brocklehurst left. After a while he composed his face into something like its normal expression of cheerfulness and ease and went up the stairs to the bedchamber. Mary was lying on the bed in her shift, her eyes closed. For a moment Ralph could look at her without her knowing he was there. She was so thin that he thought he could see her pulse beat through the skin. She was pale, and around her closed eyes were delicate blue shadows, and her eyelids fluttered with her quiet breathing. He thought for no apparent reason of the tiny blue butterflies that lived on the dry chalky uplands. Then her eyes fluttered open, and the blue was bluer than ever.

She looked up at him, seeming confused, and her face looked young in its vulnerability. She was only twenty-four, he realized; so young.

'Ralph – I must have fallen asleep.'

'I've just got back. How are you feeling, Mary?'

'Better, much better today. What did the doctor say?'

'That you were feeling better.'

'Did you see Edward?'

'Yes. I invited him to visit us. He is to come this day week.'

'Oh.'

'Do you mind? If you mind it very much, I'll—'

'No, no. It's all right. I won't spoil it for you.' She made a great effort. 'We must order a really good dinner.'

'Yes,' Ralph said, struggling with tears. She was trying her best to please him. 'Mary, I wanted to tell you something,' he began, and then stopped. Dear God, how to tell it? Why didn't Brocklehurst tell her? It was his business. How could he, Ralph, find the words. He sat down on the edge of the bed and took Mary's hand, and she looked at him a little apprehensively.

'What is it?' she prompted, and then, 'Don't worry, Ralph, I'll be nice to Edward, truly.'

'It wasn't that,' Ralph said. She continued to look into his face, waiting, half apprehensive, half trusting, and he knew then that he could not do it. 'I just wanted to tell you that I love you, Mary. Perhaps I have not always shown it as I should. I know you have not always been happy—'

'It was not your fault,' she said in a low voice, as if ashamed. 'You have been very kind to me, Ralph, and I am grateful. It was very wrong of me to be unhappy. The truth is, I never wanted to leave home, that's all. I have been homesick. You will take me home, won't you?'

'When you are better. You cannot travel when you are sick.'

'I will be better soon. I feel much better today. Can we go next month?'

'If you are well enough. But – it might have to be – some other time.'

'Some other time?'

'In the spring.' He licked his lips. 'After the babe is born.'

She met his eyes for a long moment, and he thought that perhaps she knew, but in the end she said, 'I don't want to wait that long. Promise me we'll go next month. I'll be well by then.'

Ralph nodded. He did not trust himself to speak.

CHAPTER ELEVEN

Edward arrived for his visit to Morland Place in a mood of caution, but as he rode in through the barbican to the familiar yard he could not prevent his heart from rising. He loved his home, and had found it hard to live with the thought of never seeing it again. Now he looked up at the sun-warmed bricks, the wisteria that his mother had planted beginning to encroach on the windows, the stone panel over the door from which time was beginning to erode the leaping hare, and he felt that any sacrifice was worthwhile to be able to return from time to time.

Brian, his servant, jumped down and led Bayard to the mounting block before the groom could reach him, and it took a sharp glance from Edward before Brian would yield up the reins of both horses to the stranger; he was a young lad who had been in service before to a simple squire from near Huddersfield, and he was slowly having to acquire the fine manners of a gentleman's man. Edward occasionally found his rusticities irritating, but felt Brian made up for it by his fierce loyalty. Clem was at the door as Edward reached it, and greeted him impassively, as was appropriate to an offender come to be forgiven; but as he took Edward's hat he gave him one swift glancing smile, enough to tell Edward that he was welcome. Clement joined them, having taken some time to reach the door, for his infirmities were growing apace, and he greeted Edward less equivocally.

'Master Edward! It is good to see you home again, sir. I hope you will be staying for a while. We have heard so much about your good fortune. Everyone is talking about it. The master and mistress are in the winter-parlour, sir. Clem, take care of Master Edward's man.'

Clement had never liked Mary, though he had always

accorded her the respect due to the mistress of Morland Place, and in any dispute he would always have supported Edward. Clem led Brian away and Clement hobbled surprisingly briskly towards the drawing room, which he, like many of the older servants, still called the winter-parlour.

'How are you, Clement? Is the palsy worse?'

'Why no, Master, it is as it was. It comes and goes, but there's many fare worse a lot sooner. It's the rheumatism that troubles me these days – makes me slow and clumsy. But you, Master, you are looking well.'

'Oh nothing troubles me, as you well remember.'

'Aye, Master, never a day's sickness in all your child-hood. If ever fortune smiled on a child—' Clement smiled and nodded, and reaching the door to the drawing room threw it open and led him in with something of his old flourish. Ralph was on his feet and came forward to grasp Edward's hand before Clement had a chance to say anything.

'Welcome, welcome, my dear Ned. I am so glad nothing prevented your coming. Clement, fetch refreshments.'

It was warm in the winter-parlour, and Edward saw that despite the mildness of the weather there was a good fire in the hearth. Ralph saw the direction of his glance and said in a low voice, 'I hope you won't find it too hot. Mary feels the cold so.'

'It's a pretty sight,' Edward said hastily. And so it was, the great fire burning in the old-fashioned fireplace, above which was the painted panel showing the Morland achieve-ment of arms and the old, dim portraits of Nanette and French Paul Morland. The winter-parlour was the oldest part of the house, hardly changed since it was built. It was panelled in honey-coloured linen-fold, and the bay window which looked out over the rose-garden across the moat had delicately beautiful fan-vaulting to its ceiling. A new painting occupied the place at the other end of the room, opposite the fireplace, a portrait of Mary Moubray, dressed in pale blue silk, seated, with her hand resting on a shield on which were blazoned her father's arms which she had brought into the family: azure, on a bend argent three crosses moline gules. Young Edward would wear them quartered with the Morland arms when he became Master.

The children were all gathered in the room, and had stood politely when Edward came in – young Edward, Edmund, Ralph, Sabine, James Martin, and the bairn Daisy, all gathered to greet him in honour. But first he must perform the difficult task and greet Mary. She was sitting in the shadowy chimney-corner, close to the fire. Ralph said, 'Come and speak to Mary. She is longing to welcome you.'

Edward stepped forward at the same moment as Mary leaned forward out of the shadow into the light. The shock was so terrible that despite himself Edward stopped still, his hand frozen at his side. He had never seen such a change in a person. A gaunt, white shadow sat there, draped in Mary's clothes. By a pitiful irony, she was wearing a dress of pale blue silk, similar to the one in the portrait, and Edward, as he struggled desperately with his expression, forced his eyes not to go back to the picture which presented such a horrible contrast. The blue dress hung loosely as if on a dressing-frame; Mary's forearms, in the portrait so agreeably plump, protruded like peeled sticks from the lace gathers at the sleeve-ends, her hands lying in her lap like a random collection of bones, too big for the fleshless wrists. She was wearing the fabulous black pearls, and where, in the portrait, they closely encircled the white column of a neck, in real life they hung loosely on Mary's collar-bones, and her neck rose gaunt and sinewy, looking too weak to hold up her head. Only the hair was the same: she had worn it loose for the portrait, though in normal life she had had it plaited up and wound around her head. Now in the extremity of her illness, she wore it loose again, for the weight of it pinned up was too much for her in her weakness.

Mary looked at Edward's face, and bitterness swept over her. She saw in his expression how ill she appeared. She knew that the servants were whispering about her illness, that they expected her to die, that many of them wished her dead. Some, she had heard, had even whispered that she was not pregnant, but suffering from a malign growth. Had Edward heard these things too? Had he come to gloat? Or had he come to shatter her life by revealing the truth about that night when Barnabus had died? How much had he told Ralph? It was typical of Ralph, she thought, to ask him to come back. Ralph, who wanted to be loyal to everyone. She lifted one of her hands from her lap and held it out to Edward. She must greet him, whatever it cost her, whatever it meant. Edward, controlling himself, stepped forward, took her hand, and bowed over it very low, his lips hovering above her hand but not actually touching it. His hand felt very warm; hers was cold and clammy by contrast.

'You are very welcome here,' she heard herself saying. 'You have been away a long time.'

'Madam, I – I am honoured to be received by you,' Edward said. Ralph looked on, smiling with satisfaction. It was all right, he thought; Edward is restored to the family, and Mary has behaved very well. Now at his nod the children came forward, and were soon crowding round Edward, whom they had always loved. By the time Clement came back with the servants, carrying China ale and hypocras by way of refreshment, Edward was sitting near Mary with the children round him playing a game of crambo, with plump little Daisy in his lap and Martin stationed between Edward and his mother where he could keep an eye on her and on his baby.

A while later Ralph took Edward for a walk around the gardens, for exercise before dinner, leaving the children to their governor and governess, and Mary to the peace of the fireside. Ralph went first to the stable yard to let out Bran and Fern who had been shut in a stable, and with the hounds frisking happily ahead of them the two men crossed the moat and walked along the broad path beside the rose-garden.

'I have to shut the dogs up now,' he said. 'They will follow me, and they make Mary nervous: she is afraid they will jump up at her and knock her down.'

Finding the subject introduced, Edward said cautiously, 'I was – surprised at the change in Mary.'

Ralph turned to him, his face naked with pain. 'How does she look to you?' Edward hesitated to answer, and Ralph went on, 'Oh, I know, I know. When I came back from visiting you – well, I suppose I had got used to it, but seeing her again after being away only for one day – and since then she has seemed to waste daily.'

'But what is wrong with her? I thought you said she was with child.'

'So I thought. So she thought – and does still. The doctor told me differently.' He told Edward what Brocklehurst had said. 'But she does not know. I couldn't tell her. She still believes there is a bairn. Does she seem – very sick to you?'

Edward, unable to find words, could only nod. Ralph stopped and stood staring at the slow waters of the moat with unseeing eyes. The dogs came running back and nudged him with their hard muzzles, and he stroked their heads absently.

'Yes,' he said. 'I know it really. She's dying, Ned. Brocklehurst said a month, but I cannot see how she can last another week. She eats nothing. She is starving to death. It's horrible.' Suddenly he looked up at Edward. 'You know that Mary is a Catholic? I have been wondering whether it is wrong of me not to tell her. Ought she to have time to prepare herself in her own way? Lambert is an ordained priest of her church. Ought I to tell him, to let him tell her, so that he can give her what comfort there is?'

Edward held his gaze steady, sweating lightly under his velvet clothes. Did Ralph know? Had he guessed? Was this his way of finding out? But no, Ralph had never been so indirect. He would have asked straight out if he had suspected something – that would have been his way. And he loved Mary, loved her still. It was that love which Edward had gone to such lengths to protect.

'It is for her to seek that comfort if she wants it. But she has given up her church for you, and it would seem like – mistrust, if you sent Lambert to her.'

'But I should give her the opportunity, shouldn't I? I should tell her. But I can't. Oh Ned, will you do it for me?'

'Me?' Ralph looked embarrassed.

'It would be easier coming from you,' he said. Edward could see, in a strange, twisted way, that, even if things were as Ralph supposed them to be, it would be easier coming from him. But, dear God, what a task!

'I don't know, I don't know if I could,' he said frankly. 'When we go back in, let me speak to her alone. But I can't promise you anything.'

Ralph pressed his hand in silent gratitude and they walked on. Leaves planed down on the still air to rest on their reflections in the moat, red-gold and gold-brown, the jewels of autumn.

The interview took place in the winter-parlour, where Mary spent more and more of her time. Ralph had gone up to dress for dinner, and Mary was waiting for her women to come and take her up to dress. Edward went out with Ralph, waited a moment, and slipped back in. Mary looked up in surprise, and with a nod dismissed the maid who had remained with her.

'I have done my duty,' she said before he could speak. 'He asked me to receive you, and I have done so. What have you come for? To destroy me? I have given him no cause to grieve since that day. I will swear it if you wish.'

'There is no need. I believe you. He loves you.'

'Then why have you come? Do you hate me so much?'

'I bear you no malice. Indeed I pity you from my heart,' Edward said.

Mary's mouth tightened. 'I do not need your pity.'

'It shocked me to see you looking so ill. And Ralph – he suffers with you.'

'You have been listening to servants' gossip. I am perfectly well. I know what they say, how they wish me dead. But I'll show them – I'll show you all!' She tried to rise to her feet, and fell back into her chair again, exhausted. Her eyes met Edward's and she stared up at him with a mixture of defiance and terror, like a cornered animal. *She knows*, he thought, and pity moved him. There was no need to tell her.

'Why are you so afraid?' he asked her gently. Her eyes searched his face, looking for something she could trust.

'I am afraid of Hell,' she whispered. Edward did not know what to say. She closed her eyes briefly, as if shutting out an unendurable vision, and then forced them open again.

'Will you tell him?'

'Not if you don't want me to.'

'*Tell him nothing*,' she whispered, and fell back in her chair, looking really ill now. 'Send for my maids,' she said, closing her eyes.

It was much later, after Mary had been got to bed and the doctor sent for, that Ralph managed to have a few words alone with Edward.

'Did you tell her?' Ralph asked.

'No. I think perhaps she knew, but would not admit it.'

'Brocklehurst says it's the end. She is sinking fast. Will you stay with me – until the end?'

'Of course. I can send my servant with a message. I won't leave you.'

The candles had been lit in the great bedchamber, dozens of them, for the darkness frightened Mary. They had been burning since dusk and the room was warm and stuffy with them. Mary lay propped up against the pillows of the Butts bed, struggling with death, her hand fast in the hand of Ralph, who sat beside her. She stared into his eyes, but she did not see him. Behind him Edward stood quietly, ready to do anything that was required. Lambert had come into the chamber once or twice, but she had sent him away, crying hysterically.

One of the candles began sputtering, and Edward went quietly to trim the wick. Mary's eyes followed the movement. She had not spoken for a long time, and now she said, 'Ralph, you promised to take me home.'

'Yes,' he said, pressing her hand. Her eyes came back to him.

'Keep your promise. Don't let me be buried here. I should never have left Northumberland. Take me home, Ralph, promise me.'

'I will, I promise,' he said. It was the first time she had spoken of dying, and the tears that sprang to his eyes were tears of relief as well as pain.

'I'm sorry,' she said in a small, sighing voice. He did not know what she was sorry for, but the pain in his throat prevented him from asking. 'I shall never see it again – Emblehope, Blackman's Law and Hindhope Law, and the ravens circling, and the wind from the north, and the rain on the wind. I want to go home. Oh, I want to go home.' There was naked longing in her voice, and she began to cry. 'It isn't fair. I don't want to die. Ralph, don't let me die. I want to go out under the sky and feel the rain on my face. Don't put me in a dark coffin and bury me under the earth. Don't leave me in the dark.' She began to sob, her voice rising hysterically. 'I'm afraid! I don't want to die! I'm afraid!'

Ralph tried to soothe her, tried to put his arms round her to comfort her, but she cried the more, and pushed him away with what little strength she had left.

'You brought me here! I left the Church for you!' she

cried. He let himself be pushed, and looked helplessly towards Edward, and Edward with a small shrug came to take his place. He took her hands in his, and she looked into his face, still sobbing, but waiting to hear what he had to say.

'What are you afraid of?' he asked her softly.

'*You* know,' she whispered.

'Tell me.'

'I left the Church. I'll go to Hell.'

'Listen to me, Mary: there is no Hell.' She stared, her sobs faltering. 'There is no Hell,' he said again, quietly, calmly. 'It's a tale the priests invent to frighten their children, just as our nurses used to scare us into being good by telling us Old Nol was coming for us, do you remember? Hell is here on earth, and we make if for ourselves. There's nothing more to fear than this.'

Her eyes were wide in her white, drawn face. She pulled Edward closer to her, and he smelled the strange, sweet-pungent smell of her sickness. 'You lied for me,' she whispered. 'I must tell him. I cannot – leave – with that unsaid.'

'Be easy,' Edward said. 'He has forgiven what he thought was done. The rest doesn't matter. Let him love you. You can still do that for him.'

She closed her eyes as if in exhaustion, and he did not know if she had understood or accepted what he said; but when he drew his hands gently away, she let him go, and when Ralph resumed his place, she let him hold them. The silence grew about them like a flower opening, and time moved slowly onwards, as the candles burned low. From time to time Mary opened her eyes and looked towards the windows; she held Ralph's hands, and once or twice when he made to withdraw them she snatched them back, gripping them with surprising strength. Edward watched, and thought of the day to come some time in the future when he would lie on his own death bed, contemplating the lonely darkness of the grave, and his pity for her kept him there, and awake, through the vigil. At last the sky outside began to lighten and the candle flames paled to primrose, and from the pre-dawn greyness a blackbird spoke, tentatively, sang a short phrase, and then another, as if trying out a new skill. After the long night, it was like the first blackbird on the first dawn.

Mary opened her eyes at the sound, and turned her face towards the windows keeping her eyes fixed on them instead of on the candles. The grey faded, became flushed with gold; the blackbird sang more urgently, was joined by others, as if their song was what would bring the sun back to the world. Mary's grip on Ralph's hand relaxed.

'It is morning,' she whispered.

'Yes, my dearest,' Ralph said.

'I did not want to die in the dark,' she said.

A little while later Edward left his place to blow out the candles. Their pale flames were almost transparent in the strong morning light.

Annunciata loved everything that happened to her from the moment she left home. All the servants turned out to wave her goodbye as she set off mounted on Goldeneye and dressed in her blue broadcloth habit and feathered hat. When they reached the bend in the track she halted and turned back to wave her gloved hand and to take a last look at the squat grey bulk of Shawes, chill and gloomy in the grey light of before dawn. When next I see you, she thought, I wonder what will have happened to me? When next I see you, I may be a married woman. And she remembered Edward's mocking prediction. *A duchess? Well, a countess perhaps*. Then she turned her eyes firmly forward and touched her heel to Goldeneye's side, and she sprang into a hand-canter, the coral ornaments swinging against her cheeks.

She was soon beyond her knowledge, for she had never ridden far from home, and even with Edward had ridden northwards, not south. She was accompanied by the two maids, who were to attend her on her journey, Parry, the steward, who was taking charge of her bourse of gold, and four menservants, who were there for her protection on the road, and to take care of the horses and baggage. It made her feel very important to have so many servants dedicated to her care, and nothing that happened on the journey lessened that feeling of importance, for they kept close to her the whole time, and whenever they stopped, or if anyone approached them, they crowded round her as if prepared to defend her with their nails and teeth.

Sleeping at inns was wonderful too, for she had never slept away from home, except at Morland Place, which hardly counted. When it came time to stop each day, Parry would stop some decent-looking person and ask for the name of a reputable inn in the vicinity. When they reached the inn, they would remain mounted out in the street while Parry went in to look around him and inspect the rooms they were offered. Then, if it seemed a good place, he would come back and lead Annunciata's horse into the yard. One of the men would see the horses attended to while the others would carry Annunciata's luggage up to her rooms, and there the two maids would unpack her sheets and make up the bed, while Parry went downstairs to bespeak dinner.

The inns varied in detail, but were all much the same in the large, some cleaner, some dirtier, some bigger, some smaller, some quieter, some very noisy indeed. The food was always good, and was a great novelty to Annunciata, who had not eaten abroad before. Each place they stopped had its own specialities, and she enjoyed sampling them, and tasting the different wines and ales and ciders and perries that were offered. In most places the landlord himself, or the landlady, would bring up her meal, for everywhere she went she aroused great curiosity. Before long her reputation was travelling before her, and when she stopped at night she would find people were already aware that Mistress Morland was a young lady of great beauty and immense fortune, travelling to London to be presented at Court, and were hanging over their balconies and out of their windows to catch a glimpse of her.

'Oh Miss, you'll cause such a stir when you get to London,' Hetty said one night when they were making up the bed.

'I wouldn't be surprised if the King himself didn't come out to meet you,' Meggie said, and they both giggled.

'They say he's the tallest man in the world,' Hetty said dreamily, 'and the handsomest.'

'And he's not married yet, Miss,' Meggie added, 'so you've a good chance.'

'Oh hush, Meg,' Annunciata said quickly, seeing Parry coming along the balcony.

'If you can persuade Mrs Palmer to leave the country,' Meg went on irrepressibly. Parry came in in time to hear the last words, and he dealt Meg a light but telling slap on the ear.

'Mind your language, you wicked girl. Mentioning that woman's name before your mistress!' Meg reddened and went back to her bedmaking, and Parry turned to Annunciata with a stately air. 'Your dinner will be up in half an hour, Mistress. And I've spoken for a smith, but there isn't one to be had until the morning, and so we may be late in starting tomorrow.' One of the horses had sprung a nail that day.

'Very well, Parry,' Annunciata said, and was arrested by a noise out in the yard, a sound of voices and laughter and music. The door was open, and she went out onto the balcony to look down into the yard before Parry could stop her. There below two young men had ridden in to the yard, followed by a group of servants and musicians on foot. The young men were dressed in a rich and extravagant style which made Annunciata stare. Their short-waisted doublets were decorated with bunches of ribbons hanging from the shoulder; their wide satin breeches, tied at the knees, were overhung with loops of ribbon, and there were ribbons dangling from their waists, where their shirts shewed between the bottom of the doublet and the top of the breeches. Most amazing of all, every ribbon was a different colour, and none the same colour as breeches and doublet. The young men wore their hair long and curling, and their wide hats were much befeathered.

It was impossible not to recognize them for what they were, men of fashion. It was also impossible not to realize that they were, despite the early hour of the evening, extremely drunk. Annunciata, though fascinated, was about to withdraw, when one of them looked up and cried out.

'There she is! There she is!'

The other looked up too, and waved his hat above his head, almost lost his balance, and only saved himself from pitching over backwards by grabbing at his horse's mane.

'Damn' right, Jack, that's her all right. The beautiful and mysterious heiress. Your servant, Ma'am!' He tried to bow in the saddle, and pitched forward this time, bringing himself up short with his nose on the pommel. Annunciata repressed a smile, looked haughty, and was backing off just as Parry, scandalized, dashed out to drag her back in.

'Damme, she has her father with her,' the first man muttered audibly, while the second cried forlornly, 'Don't go in, Madam! I am longing to be your servant, Madam! We are both aching to be your servant.'

'The impudence!' Parry exclaimed, giving Annunciata's arm a little shake. 'Stay within, Mistress, and do not tempt impudent scoundrels to make a spectacle of you.' Then he went back onto the balcony and called down, 'Be off, you impudent young rakes, before I send for the watch! How dare you address a young woman of quality in such a way?'

'Damme, the old boy's got a tongue like a rasp,' the second man cried.

The first man, who was not so drunk, shook his arm and said, 'Be quiet, Dick, and come away. He's right. We'd better not make a fuss.' Then, raising his voice, 'Peace, old man, we meant no harm to your pretty daughter.'

Parry grew red at this and bellowed, 'My *mistress*, sir! How dare you!' At which the two young men stared, and then began to roar with laughter.

'Well done, old greybeard!' the first man cried. 'I hope I may do as well when I reach your years.' And they rode away before Parry could correct their misapprehension. When he came back into the chamber, Annunciata bit her lip hard so as not to laugh, for she did not want to hurt Parry's feelings.

'Is London going to be like that?' she asked.

'Very much worse, I am afraid, Mistress,' Parry said, shaking his head. Oh good, Annunciata thought, and she felt that at last she had found out where she belonged.

Town by town they moved southwards, and places that had been merely names to Annunciata became realities: Nottingham, Leicester, Northampton, Aylesbury. The roads grew more crowded, the inns noisier, and then at last they were in a village called Hampstead, and London lay below them, looking beautiful and peaceful, a forest of church spires, a faint haze of chimney-smoke, and the River Thames a broad silver snake winding away to the sea. Annunciata felt her excitement rising. She had never seen so many churches, even in York, and the thought of how many people there must be in London to need so many churches took her breath away. A little later they were riding into the city past St Giles's Fields and along Fleet Street and her breath was taken away in reality, for though York was renowned for its foul air, she had never smelled anything so strong as the stink of London.

She quickly forgot it, however, in the excitement of the crowded, noisy, exciting streets. Her menservants looked anxious as they tried to steer her safely through the tangle of carriages, carts, riding-horses, cattle, chairs, pedestrians, pedlars, sweepers, street sellers, beggars, soldiers and loungers, and guide her round the worst of the piles of rubbish and ordure. The maids frankly gawped, too astonished to pretend the sophistication they did not have, and kept as close as they could to their mistress for fear of being separated. Annunciata had to concentrate on guiding and controlling Goldeneye who, despite her long journey, was nervous and pawky at the strange smells and noises, but she was still able to notice that no one she passed had as fine a horse as hers, and that, though the women she caught a glimpse of in carriages and chairs had what appeared to be breathtakingly lovely clothes, they were not as handsome as she knew herself to be, and they looked at her with interest and some dislike.

She was not sorry, however, when, after seeking directions several times, they found themselves at the door of Richard's house in Milk Street, for she was beginning to feel exhausted by the battery of new sensations, and longed to be safe within, to have a hot bath to ease her aching muscles, and a little silence to soothe her nerves. One of the men lifted her from the saddle while Parry knocked, and the door was opened by a trim maidservant, who was pushed aside almost at once by a small, elegant, kind-faced lady who took Annunciata's hands.

'My dear, come in, come in, you must be exhausted. I am your cousin Lucy. I am so glad to see you. I have been looking forward to your visit so much. Come up to the parlour. Richard is still at Whitehall, where he sups today, so we shall have a quiet meal together with the children.'

Annunciata followed her up the stairs, feeling an instant liking for her. She liked the way Lucy did her hair, and though her clothes were plain, Annunciata appreciated their elegant cut and fine material. She would not have been a Morland if she did not value good cloth above fripperies. The parlour was small, but neat and elegant, and there she was met by two small fair boys, Lucy's children, who greeted her with wide-eyed respectfulness. Lucy offered her the most comfortable chair, settled her in it, gave her a footstool, and in a few minutes was handing her a silver goblet from a tray which a maid brought in.

'It's lambswool,' Lucy said, smiling. 'I thought it would comfort you after your long journey. We shall have supper soon, and then perhaps you would like to have a bath.'

Annunciata sipped the lambswool, relishing its taste of childhood and comfort, and then smiled up at Lucy.

'You are very kind,' she said. 'You seem to know exactly what I want, exactly what will make me feel at home.'

'I am very glad, my dear,' Lucy said, and leaning closer said, 'To tell you the truth, I have long felt the lack of a companion of my own sex. I had a younger sister when I was a child, and we were close companions. Since she died, I have missed having a woman to talk to. I cannot tell you how much I have hoped that you would be – well, someone I could like.'

She waited for Annunciata to finish her drink and then sent the maid away with the empty goblet. 'Supper will be in almost directly,' she said. 'Do you wish to use the privy?'

Annunciata nodded, and Lucy led her out onto the landing, up another flight of stairs, and into a tiny closet where there was an elaborately carved chair with a hole in the seat. Annunciata had never seen a close-stool before, and her inquiring mind could not forbear to ask how it worked. Lucy, evidently amused, opened the door at the front of the chair to reveal the metal container within. 'The servants empty it twice a day into the outside privy down in the yard, and that in turn is emptied by the night carts. What they do with the . . . debris, I cannot say. All I know is that they come in from the country at night and go back there.'

Annunciata nodded, and Lucy in her turn became curious. 'How do you manage at home?' she asked. 'If you will pardon my curiosity.'

'We have garderobes, both at home and in Morland Place, and I have never stayed anywhere else.'

Lucy left her alone, and when Annunciata came back down into the parlour, she said, 'We are going to be great friends, you and I, I can tell. When I was younger, I was frequently punished for asking questions on what were thought to be indelicate or unladylike subjects. But I never could bear not to know things. My first husband, God keep his soul, was a wonderful man, for he loved to answer my questions, and believed that any mind that could think up a question deserved to have the answer without prejudice. And Richard has learned to accept that a woman may have an intelligent mind without being the less womanly for it.'

'My mother is like that,' Annunciata said. 'She always insisted that it was important for me to be educated just as if I were a boy. I didn't like it when I was a child, though,' she admitted.

'I have had some correspondence with your mother,' Lucy said, 'and I think I should like her if I met her. And oh my dear,' she clasped her hands in pleasure, 'I was so delighted when she asked me to supervise the making of your gowns, and when reputation had you to be a beauty. Well, for once reputation has not said the half of it – you will have London by the ears, and I shall have such a wonderful time dressing you, and taking you about! Tomorrow, we shall have my dressmaker in, and Richard shall send us in some bales of cloth to choose from. And in the afternoon we shall ride down to the New Exchange and buy ribbons and see what everyone is wearing. How *sensible* of your mother to have you a riding habit made, and such an elegant one! You may go abroad in that without comment, until your gowns are ready. And how sensible of her to leave your clothes until you got here. York may be a very fine place, my dear, I am sure it is, but to dress *for* a place, *at* a place, is so much the best rule.'

The door opened and three maids came in bearing the supper trays. The food smelled savoury and good, and at first glance there were two dishes that Annuciata did not recognize. Her mouth began to run water in anticipation.

'And then,' Lucy said, watching the maids set out the table with quiet, efficient movements, 'when we have you dressed to perfection, we shall present you at Court, and *then* the fun will start!' She met Annunciata's eyes with an expression of innocent mischief, and they both began to laugh in sheer lightheartedness.

CHAPTER TWELVE

Annunciata's first day in London was a busy one. Richard's household rose at five, and Richard, Lucy, Annunciata and the two boys breakfasted together in the parlour on bread, small beer and fresh herrings, bought from a street-seller whose cry of 'Here's fine herrings, eight a groat; come buy my whitings, fine and new' under her window had been the first thing Annunciata heard on waking. By the time Hetty had come in to dress her she had begun to wonder if she would ever get used to the noise of London. At home in Shawes the dawn was attended by the singing of birds and, further off, other animal noises, cattle lowing, dogs barking, cockerels challenging the sun. There was certainly a sound of cows lowing here in Milk Street, but even that was accompanied by the clashing of milk pails and a gruff-voiced man bellowing astonishing profanities. From the street came a medley of wooden and iron wheels on cobbles, loud voices, and street cries: 'Any milk here, mistress?'; 'Small coals a shilling!'; 'Custards, pippins, pies and tarts!'; muted at first, but growing with the daylight.

Richard and Lucy did not seem to notice it. They breakfasted all unconcerned, and then Richard jumped up, tugging at his neckerchief.

'It will be hot today, ladies, I can feel it in the air. I must be away, or I shall miss the tide, and I am due at Whitehall at six.'

'You have sent word for the cloth to be brought up?' Lucy asked.

Richard came round the table to kiss her brow. 'Yes, dearest, now do you lack anything? Then I shall be about my business. I must send off the Yorkshire servants before

I go. Goodbye, cousin. Enjoy your first view of London. Clovis, Edmund—' The two boys stood up and bowed their heads for their father's blessing, and a moment later Richard was gone.

Lucy and Annunciata exchanged a glance. 'Is it always like this?' Annunciata asked.

'Not always. He does not go up to Whitehall every day, of course, and when the tide is making it takes only five minutes. But today – by the by, if you have any word you wish to send home, you had better prepare your letters now. Your mother asked that the servants be sent back at once.'

'I'll go and write a letter now,' Annunciata said. She went to her room and wrote a letter to her mother, and she had just finished when Lucy came in.

'All ready? Come and bid your maids goodbye, then, for they are off directly. We shall have to see about finding a suitable woman for you. By the by, you need not be afraid to write home when you wish, for Richard franks our letters for us at the Treasury. The earl is very good about that.'

'The earl?'

'The Earl of Southampton. He is Lord Treasurer, and a very useful person for Richard to know.'

Hetty and Meggie cried most gratifyingly to be saying goodbye to Annunciata, and she gave them the last of her journey-money in thanks. She shook hands solemnly with Parry and the footmen, and felt both sorry and excited when they had gone, for they were her last link with home. Now she felt the adventure was really beginning. Hardly had they gone than there was a tremendous rapping at the door below, and soon a procession of men were staggering in carrying bales of cloth, and hard on their heels came a tiny dark woman with very thick face-paint followed by a child carrying a basket. This was Lucy's dressmaker, and she and Lucy fell at once into animated conversation about the number and style of gowns that Annunciata was to have.

The dressmaker, whose name was Mrs Drake, eyed Annunciata with a professional and impersonal appreciation, and said, 'Yes, yes, it will be a pleasure to dress her, you are quite right, Madam. A very handsome girl indeed, and a good figure, tall but not too tall. Turn about, Mistress,' she directed. Annunciata found it impossible to resent the order and dutifully rotated on the spot. 'Excellent colouring, whatever Madam Palmer may say. Dark hair with a clear complexion suits so many more colours, and red-heads are so often red-skinned, and blondes can be so pasty. Now, Madam, shall we start with a walking-dress? What do you say to this green taffeta?'

Annunciata had little to do but stand and be draped with different lengths of cloth and turn around when she was bid and be prodded and pinned, for it was all decided for her. She did not mind, however, for both Lucy and Mrs Drake were so elegantly dressed that she had no fear their taste would let her down, and they were evidently in a better position to choose clothes for London society than she was. The materials were lovely – bright clear colours that she knew would look wonderful against her clear skin and dark hair and eyes, and delicate textures that would feel good as well as look good. After the long years of the Commonwealth it was wonderful to be able to dress excitingly.

Mrs Drake went at last with a promise to send the clothes as soon as possible, and before the bales of cloth were sent away a shoemaker came in to see what had been chosen and measure Annunciata's foot so that shoes could be made to match each gown. Then another sempstress came in, a more humble woman, a round, fat, shy mouse of a creature who had been waiting without while the more exalted people took their custom. She was to make Annunciata's underwear, her smocks and shifts and her boned busks, and she had brought with her samples of linen and lace. It was strange to Annunciata to have a woman in from outside the household to make undergarments: at home it had been done, with all the other household sewing, by Ellen and the maids and even by Ruth and Annunciata herself.

'London is very different,' she said to Lucy when Mrs Caplin had gone. 'I suppose that here you must be able to buy anything – anything in the world.'

'Indeed you can,' Lucy said with a smile, 'and after dinner we shall go to one of the best places for doing it – the New Exchange. There we shall buy your gloves and stockings and ribbons.'

'Buy? With money?' Annunciata asked, wide-eyed.

'Why no, of course not. The things will be sent upon credit as always,' Lucy said, amused, and then, as Annunciata looked disappointed, 'Why, what is it?'

'Oh, nothing. It's just that I have never bought anything before. I thought it might be fun.'

Lucy smiled. 'Then we shall take some coins with us, and you shall buy what you want,' she said.

'But I haven't any money.'

Lucy's smile broadened. 'My dear, your mother sent a great bag of gold with you from Yorkshire. I know Richard had it taken to his goldsmith last night, but he always leaves me a little money each day for the things that have to be paid for, like milk and fruit. We shall spend that.'

Their dinner came up at eleven – a fried breast of mutton, a dish of white cabbage, and a dish of prawns and cheese. The ale was new, but to Annunciata, used to Yorkshire ale, was very weak and thin; but Lucy had forks upon the table, which was a great novelty. Annunciata had, of course, brought her own set of knives and spoons with her. She had seen forks before, for Morland Place had six, which were used by the guests of honour at great feasts; but Lucy handled hers with an ease and indifference which shewed she took it for granted that dinner would be eaten thus. Not to be outdone, Annunciata made no comment upon it and watched out of the corner of her eye how to use hers.

After dinner Lucy ordered the coach, and she and Annunciata went up to their rooms to dress, and Lucy sent Pal, her maid, to help Annunciata once her own hair had been done. Then Matt announced that the coach was at the door, and in a few minutes the two women and the maid were bowling along Cheapside. As Richard had said, it was a hot day, but they had to keep the windows up against dust and smells and worse splashings. Their progress was slow and erratic, for the streets were narrow and much thronged, and there seemed to be no right of way other than that won by contest of voice.

'It is of the first importance to have a good coachman,' Lucy said as a drayman entered upon a vociferous quarrel with her own man as to who should take the corner from Cheapside into Paternoster Row first. 'My man Ben is wonderful. He holds his breath so that his face goes red as fire, and there are few men who will stand up against him.' A moment later they were jolting on again in support of Lucy's claim. Annunciata did not at all mind the slow progress, for it gave her a chance to look about her. Paternoster Row was the street of booksellers and binders, as she could see from the signs swinging above the doorways, and clerics and lawyers seemed to number largely amongst the sauntering pedestrians. Then the coach eased its way round the perilous corner into Paternoster Lane, and Annunciata got her first good look at St Paul's cathedral, the greatest church, after St Peter's at Rome, in Europe.

'It has fallen into sad disrepair,' Lucy told her. 'Cromwell used it to stable his soldiers' horses, and it was never cared for under the Commonwealth. When the spire fell down, it damaged part of the nave, and as you can see it has never been repaired. They even sold off some of the stones to Jews to build a synagogue.' Annunciata craned her neck to stare up at the great building, noble and beautiful still with its square tower rising from the centre of the four arms of its cross-shape. 'I wish you could have seen it as it was when I was a girl,' Lucy said, 'before the war.'

They turned into Ludgate Hill, passed by Lud-gate itself, one of the seven great gates of the city, and thus out of London proper and into the no-man's-land between London and Westminster that was more and more being thought of as simply an extension of the city. They drove along Fleet Street, past the pleasant houses of the wealthy and fashionable, and Lucy had the coach stopped outside St Dunstan's church to watch the wooden figures come out on their oiled tracks and strike the hour on the bell with their wooden mallets. Annunciata was fascinated, and wanted to know how it worked. Lucy shrugged, and said that she must ask Richard.

They passed the church of St Clement Dane, standing like an island in a sea of traffic which washed it on all sides, and swung to the left down the Strand. Here were the great houses of the nobility – Essex House and Arundel House and Somerset House and the Savoy Palace – standing in their large and beautiful grounds, with gardens that ran all the way down to the river.

'They have their own landing stages and water-gates,' Lucy said with a touch of envy. 'It must make it so convenient for getting about London.' The carriages around them now were conveyances of people of fashion, and they moved slowly so that their occupants could be seen. Many of them were going to the New Exchange, which was just beyond the Savoy Palace, and Lucy and Annunciata had to wait in a long queue of vehicles before they could be driven up to the entrance and set down. Then, with Pal at their heels, they stolled forward into the double galleries of black stone, lined with stalls, while the coachman drove their coach away to make room for the next comer.

Annunciata was almost breathless with excitement, and

she had to force herself to breathe and walk slowly and not to gawp like a country-girl. It was plain that the purpose of visiting the galleries was not just to buy, but to saunter and gossip and be seen. Many of the people thronging the 'Change were common folk and country folk up in London for a visit, and they were the spectators to a moving parade of elegantly dressed women and elaborately dressed fops. On either side of the walks the stalls were heaped with beautiful goods that almost made Annunciata's mouth water – ribbons and laces and shoes and gloves and stockings and cravats and handkerchiefs and scarfs – and were attended by young women of great elegance and beauty. It was said that a 'Change woman could marry whom she pleased; many of them were reputed to be the mistresses of the greatest in the land, and by their demeanour they evidently held themselves high.

Lucy was obviously well known by the number of people who greeted her, or nodded to her, or curtseyed to her. Annunciata soon realized that no one else was dressed quite as she was, but because of her striking looks she drew glances of surprise and admiration rather than contempt. Her clothes were expensive and well-cut, and she held her head high and looked her haughtiest; there were many nudges and murmurs as people asked each other who she was. Lucy looked at her with amusement out of the corner of her eye, and drew Annunciata's arm through hers.

'I would lay you half of Lombard Street to a China orange that no few of these chatterers will go home to bespeak themselves an outfit like yours. You will set a new fashion. Look, there's Lady Denham over there, with Lady Shrewsbury. Two of the wickedest women in the world. Don't stare at them, or I'll be obliged to curtsey. We've been introduced, you see. Ah, now here is someone you may look at – the Chancellor's daughter, Mistress Hyde. Poor thing, how fat she is growing. I'll introduce you. Curtsey, my dear, but not too deep.'

Anne Hyde drew level with them. She was a woman in her twenties, no great beauty, with her wide mouth and sallow skin and heavy chin, but her dark eyes were intelligent and kind, though at the moment she looked rather harrassed and nervous. Lucy curtseyed to her, and she curtseyed in return, and then the two women kissed lightly.

'Lucy, my dear, how nice to see you,' she said. 'It is too long since you have dined with Papa and me. I must speak to him. How is your good husband?'

'Very well, I thank you. He is with your father this moment, I believe, doing some business. May I introduce my husband's cousin, Mistress Annunciata Morland.'

Anne Hyde looked at Annunciata with calm, speculative eyes, and she curtseyed as she had been told and returned the look evenly. Then Anne Hyde smiled, and her face seemed not so plain after all.

'Another Morland,' she said. 'We have so much to thank your family for, Mistress. I hope we shall see you at Court soon.'

'Thank you, Ma'am,' Annunciata said.

Lucy added, 'Richard hopes to present her next week.'

The women spoke a few more sentences and parted, Anne Hyde moving off quickly, her anxiety resuming its dominance of her expression.

Lucy took Annunciata's arm and whispered, 'That is why people dislike her and her father so much – the assumption that Hyde and England are indivisible terms. "We have so much to thank you for" – when the Chancellor says that kind of thing, ambitious men begin to fret and count the steps up to the throne. Ah well – she's a good-hearted thing, and her father has been very kind to us. I wonder – tush, here comes Mistress Palmer. Draw aside a little, my dear. She passes through here like a hundred-gun ship.'

Now Annunciata, unable to prevent herself from goggling a little, was to get her first close view of the King's

215

notorious mistress. Her approach made a great deal of stir, for she was accompanied not only by her serving woman, a footman, two negro boys and a number of dogs, but also by a group of admiring young men; and as she passed the rest of the crowd parted and fell back for her and her retinue, so that she was like the wind bending aside the corn. She was certainly a striking-looking woman, a fraction less tall than Annunciata, but tall enough to be imposing, with a well-developed figure. Her eyes were blue, her skin very white, her nose thin and with an arching nostril that gave her a disdainful look, her mouth full and red, her chin rounded and very determined. Her hair was dark auburn, and fell in profusion of curls down her back and round her face. Annunciata drank in every detail of her dress, which was of pale lilac silk, and noted the profusion of jewels about her neck, wrists and fingers. Mrs Palmer gave Lucy a cool nod as she passed, and Annunciata a very hard, though brief look, and Lucy returned the nod with a slight inclination of the body which could just about be classed as a curtsey.

'You know her?' Annunciata said when she had gone.

'Anyone who is at Court at all often knows Mrs Palmer. One is introduced and therefore cannot avoid the acquaintance. Ah now, my dear, here is my favourite stall for gloves. Would you like to have a pair? What about these? Or those with the fringes?'

The goods now occupied Annunciata's attention; the quality and variety thrilled her, though the prices shocked her, for she had never known before how expensive small items of dress could be. Fine fringed gloves fifteen shillings a pair; stockings eleven shillings; cork-soled shoes four shillings a pair; a lace palatine three pounds; a silver hat-band fifteen shillings. She and Lucy strolled up and down the galleries examining the fine wares, and stopping to chat with Lucy's large acquaintance, many of whom she introduced to Annunciata, and all of whom were interested in the stranger. One or two gentlemen were introduced too, though they were the staid and respectable married kind who were accompanying their wives; but Annunciata could not but be aware that she was being eyed with some interest by the fashionable young men who hung around the 'Change women or flirted with the strolling ladies from the Court. Lucy told her that many of the houses nearby were let out as small lodgings to bachelors and members of the Court for whom lodgings in Whitehall could not be found, and that many of them had nothing better to do all day than wander about the 'Change pestering women, or sit in ale-houses and smoke and drink and gossip.

Annunciata eventually bought two pairs of gloves and three of silk stockings, and then it was time for them to go back to their coach. They were walking back towards the entrance when a group of young men passed them going in the same direction, and one of them, turning back to look, stopped and came back, smiling at Lucy broadly and holding out his hands in a gesture of expansive affection.

'Mistress Lucy, what do you here? God's day to you! Tell me you have left that husband of yours at last, so that I can take you away on my white horse.'

Lucy placed her hands in his and smiled at the greeting: this was evidently someone she knew well and liked. Annunciata tried not to stare, but he fascinated her. His voice was dark and caressive, with a strange accent that she could not quite place, part French and part something else. He was not tall, but very handsome and very elegant; his brown face expressed the sweetest of good-temper, and his blue eyes were alight with amusement and vivacity. Somehow Annunciata felt she knew him already, had known him for a long time.

'Hugo,' Lucy was saying, 'how lovely to see you. I thought you were abroad.'

'I came back with Prince Rupert a week ago. It was the briefest visit, to take a message from the King to his aunt. I had intended to call upon you, but not seeing Richard at Court, I thought you must be in the country.'

'Richard has been at Whitehall, but mostly in Master Hyde's offices. But, let me introduce my cousin Annunciata. My dear,' turning to Annunciata, 'this is Lord Ballincrea, who was your cousin Edward's closest friend, and now, I hope, numbers himself amongst mine.'

Hugo McNeill smiled at the compliment, and then turned to bow to the young woman he had been trying, from good manners, not to stare at. He bowed very low, and she curtseyed gracefully, and as they both straightened up their eyes met and they looked at each other with a frank curiosity, and both smiled at the same moment. Almost without knowing he had done it, Hugo extended his hand and, improper though it was, Annunciata had placed hers in it. It was as if they had known each other all their lives; Hugo had the maddest urge to take her away somewhere and talk to her – just that – and only the awareness of people looking on made him behave himself, and convert their *faux pas* into a piece of gallantry by bending over her hand and kissing it in his most French manner.

'Your servant, Madam,' he said, releasing her hand reluctantly. Then, to Lucy, 'May I dare to hope that this acquaintance, so unexpectedly begun, will ripen? Will you be presenting Mistress Morland at Court?'

'Yes, indeed. She has come here for that very purpose. But Hugo, now you are back, you must not neglect us. Will you dine with us?'

'With the greatest pleasure. When shall I attend you?'

Lucy had regard to the state of Annunciata's wardrobe, and said, 'On Saturday? Annunciata may be prevailed upon to play for us. I understand she is a talented musician.'

'I have no doubt of it. Until Saturday then. My good wishes to your husband, in case I do not see him at Whitehall.'

He bowed again and withdrew to join his waiting companions, and Lucy and Annunciata walked on. Lucy told her a little more about Hugo, and exclaimed over the pleasant chance of seeing him, and Annunciata smiled and wondered why she felt so happy at the prospect of seeing him again in just a few days.

Ralph kept his promise to take Mary home. She was buried in the burying ground above Tods Knowe, by the little turf-roofed church, where the moor lapped against the low stone wall like a purple-brown sea, close by the double grave of Mary Percy and Big John Morland. Everyone agreed that it was very handsomely done, and that nothing was stinted in the procession from the house to the church. There were twenty poor women in the mourning gowns and kerchiefs that Ralph had provided, and then the household servants, drawn from the three houses, all in mourning gloves and scarves. Then came two young men leading black horses caparisoned in black, with tall black plumes nodding on their headstalls; and finally the coffin, draped in cloths shewing her father's and her husband's arms, borne by six gentlemen, led by Crispian and Francis. The pall, embroidered with her father's badge, a lion couchant, was held by six ladies, led by Cathy and Elizabeth. Then came the mourners, with Ralph, Edward, Sam Symonds and Anne being the chief amongst them, all in long black cloaks; next thirty mutes, twenty of them children, and then the rest of the friends and villagers not in mourning.

The procession went to the church at dusk so that it was dark by the time the Mass was finished, and the procession back to the house was torchlit and so bright that it could be seen as far away as Rochester. At the house the funeral feast was laid out, with macaroons and biscuits and cold meats and white wine and claret and burnt ale, and the poor from up and down Redesdale gathered at the gates while food and drink and coins were distributed amongst them in Mary Moubray's honour.

The family had not been back home a week when another death occurred. Leah was supervising the children's prayers at their bedtime one evening when she suddenly felt very tired. Pal fetched her a stool and sent Beatrice to find Clement to send up a drop of aquavit to revive her; Leah sat down on the stool, sighed, and died. It was only after her death that Ralph discovered what the servants had known for a long time: that Mary Moubray had been mistress in name, but that the real mistress of Morland Place was Leah. She had nursed Mary Esther and Mary Esther's children, and Ralph and Ralph's children, and in later years she had fulfilled a role between governess and housekeeper and mother-of-the-maids which was impossible for any one other person to fill.

'I don't know what to do to replace her,' Ralph said to Cathy one evening shortly afterwards. 'Every day a servant comes to me with another question, and I discover one more thing that Leah was used to decide upon. And as far as the children are concerned – Pal and Beatrice are very reliable, but neither of them is fit to be governess, even if I find a new governor—' For Lambert, finding no joy at Morland Place with Mary gone, had moved on, much to Edward's private satisfaction.

'No one could replace her,' Elizabeth said quietly. Leah had been kind to her, for her mother's sake.

'No *one* person at least,' Cathy said.

'What do you mean?' Ralph asked.

'It is plain to me that Leah had many tasks that she acquired as time went by, that should not strictly have been hers. Now she is gone, we must divide all her tasks up again, and give them to different people to perform. Many of the things she did should have been Clement's province, for instance. The rest could be divided quite easily into a housekeeper's duties and a governess's duties.'

'How clearly you put it all,' Ralph said admiringly. 'Have you been thinking about all this for long?'

Cathy smiled ruefully. 'Oh yes,' she said. 'Long enough

to be able to propose to you that I take over her duties as housekeeper.'

'You?' Ralph said in surprise.

'Do not sound so doubtful. I have lived long enough in Leah's shadow to know how she did things. I have helped her every day of my life, just as I used to help Mam when she was alive. I dare say no woman in this house knows better how it is run.'

'Of course – I was not doubting your ability,' Ralph said hastily. 'But, dear Caterpillar, would you *want* to do it?'

'I am not beautiful, so I had best be useful,' Cathy said.

Ralph looked at his plain little sister compassionately. 'You may marry, Cathy. You are only sixteen. You will marry and then I shall have to find a housekeeper anyway.'

'Who would marry me?' Cathy asked. 'Even if you provided me with a dowry—'

'I have been remiss,' Ralph said, shamedly. 'I should have had your welfare more at heart. I will find you a husband, little sister, and a good one at that. I will give you such a good dowry that—'

'Don't, Ralph,' Cathy said quickly. 'I know you mean it kindly, but—'

'I have not been kind enough,' Ralph said.

'I don't want to marry,' Cathy said. 'And even with a dowry—Ralph, you know perfectly well what my mother was, and how people hereabouts hated her. Our father left you here, and you have avoided the taint, with Mam and Grandfather bringing you up. But for me – why else did our father leave here?'

'But he is different now,' Ralph said, puzzled.

'I know that, and you know it. He is well-loved by us, and well respected at Court, but the people hereabouts will never forget that he brought home the Puritan, and gave Morland Place to the Roundheads, and they will never forget, as they have for you, that I was his child. And my mother – what was she? The foreigner, the fanatic, the heretic. I am her child.' Ralph opened his mouth to protest and she cut him off again. 'And there are those who believe he was not truly married to her. And perhaps they are right.'

There was a silence, and Ralph said at last, 'Oh Caterpillar, things aren't as bad as you imagine them. But—' seeing she was about to argue with him, '—we won't talk about it any more now. You shall be housekeeper, if that is what you want, and I shall treat you with all honour, as mistress of the house in all but name. But what shall we do for a governess?'

Cathy smiled and turned towards Elizabeth, quietly sewing a shirt for the baby, sitting as always on the edge of the family circle, one of them but not quite one of them.

'Elizabeth loves the children, and they love her, and she is a gentlewoman, well-born and accomplished. Who better than she to bring up your bairns?'

Elizabeth looked up, caught Ralph's eye upon her, and blushed deeply. Compliments had not often come her way. Ralph looked at her with new eyes, aware that he had not done right by her either, for she was the daughter of his aunt Hetta whom he had loved, and he had let her be slighted by the servants. Well, he would make amends now.

'None better – until she marries. Elizabeth, will you do this for me?'

Elizabeth nodded gratefully, and Cathy smiled a little sardonically and said, 'You have your rewards here on earth, Ralph. You are kind to poor female relations, and they serve you well in return.'

'If you weren't my sister, I would spank you,' Ralph said severely. 'I won't have you speak so of members of my family. Come, Elizabeth, will you give us some music? I must experience these talents of yours before I let you loose amongst my children.'

A cold easterly wind brought rain sweeping in, confining

222

Ruth to the house, making the kitchen chimneys smoke sullenly, and putting Ellen in a bad humour so that at last Ruth, goaded beyond endurance, slapped her and sent her away to brood and sulk elsewhere. Alone in the solar she stood by the window, staring out at the grey sodden country, feeling restless, confined, dissatisfied, wondering how Annuciata was faring, searching amongst her memories for comfort, though she knew there was none there.

Down below her there was a sound of horse's hooves, and craning her neck she saw Kit pass, coming in from the city where he had been to inspect his four houses on North Street, the property that had been his mother's dowry. As if he knew she was there, he turned his face up, making the rain run off the broad brim of his hat down the stretched tent of his cloak. She saw his white face and the black gash of his moustache, blurred by the rain. He did not see her, with the light against the window, and dipped his head and rode on. Young Kit, he was always Young Kit to her, though she called him by his name, though he wore the Morland arms with the crescent in chief, head of his own cadet branch, though his father was dead and there was none to dispute his name with him.

It was sixteen years since he had died. She turned the number over in her mind, wonderingly, finding it had no real meaning to her in that context. Sixteen years since he died, but for her it was yesterday. She had loved him from her own childhood, that Kit who was Young Kit's father. She remembered him coming home, fresh from Oxford in the fashionable Court clothes that Oxford men wore then. He had kissed her hand and smiled at her, remembering her from before he went away, and she had fallen in love with him, never to be cured. That memory was clear, and her last memory of him, the day he died, and in between there was only a blur, for in between he had been Hero's, not hers.

But on the day he died he had belonged to her again. She had held his horse for him to mount before he rode

223

away, and he had kissed her. His last words had been hers, and hers the last mouth he had kissed, hers the last woman's face he saw before he rode away to die. 'Look after Hero and the child, until I come again,' he had said, and looked at her with death in his eyes. They had shared that last secret, keeping it from Hero, the secret knowledge of his death. The next day he had come home, hanging limply across the saddle of a foundered horse, his cold, dead hands swinging with the horse's weary steps, and she had washed him and buried him, and taken up the burden he had left her.

Young Kit, the Haltling's bairn, the child of Kit that she should have borne. Looking like his father, so like: how she could have loved him, if she had not defended her heart against him. Well, she had brought up Kit's child, and cared for Kit's widow, who was little use to anyone after Kit died, growing more and more childlike and dependent until her early death. Young Kit was hers and not hers, just as Kit had been.

Of the incident that brought Annunciata to be, she remembered little: a shadowy, dreamlike episode, taking place in the dark lap of sorrow and grief, unreal, half forgotten. She remembered his strong, lean body, how warm it had been, how sweet his skin smelled, despite the exertions of the day, a warm, wholesome smell like something good baking; she remembered how silky his dark curls were – Annunciata had his hair; she remembered his tears, a child's tears for a man's grief, a man's tears from a child's body. In the morning his eyes had been already distant, looking towards the next problem, the next responsibility, the next grief; great, dark eyes, indescribably beautiful – Annunciata had his eyes.

But the incident itself, dreamlike, at once relegated to the back of her mind as a fantastic tale of long ago, had given rise to a reality. She had borne, at the age of thirty, her first and last child, and for fifteen years she had worked and contrived and laboured to make that child everything she would have liked to be. Now, at last, she had launched her on the world, a proud and beautiful ship on her maiden voyage, all pennants flying and guns thundering the salute, and it had left her feeling restless and useless. Thrown back onto the old relationship of being half-mother, half-brother to the Haltling's bairn was like being returned to the past. It had not been easy, but it had been simple, to be Annunciata's mother. Now she was having to be aware of how unhappy she and Annunciata between them had made Young Kit.

When Annunciata was born, it had been her dear wish that one day she and Young Kit would marry, and it had delighted her that Young Kit had fallen in with the scheme so readily. He had been fascinated by Annunciata from the moment she was born, and as she grew up the fascination came to look so like love that it had become a universal assumption that they would marry. Annunciata and Young Kit: a child of theirs would be the child that Ruth had wanted all her life, a child of her blood and Kit's. In that way, she had felt, she would re-write history the way it ought to have gone; in that way, she and Kit would be joined for ever as they should have been.

But she had reckoned without Annunciata. Annunciata was not Ruth, and Ruth had too much basic honesty not to admit it to herself, though it was painful, though it took a long time. And Annunciata was entitled to something better than her mother's second-hand dreams. She grew up loving Kit but, as Ruth soon saw, it was more a sisterly love. Besides, she was a considerable heiress and very beautiful, and either of those qualities alone would have entitled her to a better husband than the Haltling's bairn, penniless as he was after the depredations of the war and the Republic. Even if he got back his Scottish estates, he was not good enough for Annunciata, and Ruth knew it, and she knew also that Annunciata knew it.

But it left, metaphorically and literally, the problem of Young Kit's unhappiness on Ruth's hands. She began to long for the time when he would go to Scotland, even to hope that he would not come back, though she loved him and would miss him. The door opened and he came in, stripped of his outer clothes, bringing with him a smell of wet wool. His inner garments were no more than damp, but his hair was soaked, clinging in wet coils to his skull and dripping onto his nose and collar.

'How did you get so wet?' she exclaimed as he came in.

'The wind is very strong. It blew my hat off, and I had much ado to get it back,' he said. He had a towel in his hands, and as he spoke she took it from him and began to dry his hair. His ducked his head to her and closed his eyes in pleasure at the comfort of her rough towelling as she pulled his head towards her and buffeted it unmercifully.

'Did you get your business done?' she asked. His voice came out jerkily from under the towel.

'Oh yes – I have seen all four tenants, but there is much to be done. The roof of number one is leaking, and all of them need work on their chimneys. But on the whole they had kept them up well.'

'And so they should. What else did you do?'

'I called in at Morland Place on my way home.' She released him and he emerged red-faced and towelled and straightened up. 'Cathy and Elizabeth are to replace Leah. Cathy is to be housekeeper and Elizabeth governess.'

Ruth nodded. 'That will do well enough. But what when they marry?'

'I suppose Ralph will have to think again. But there is no likelihood that they will marry soon. Neither of them has a dowry, and after all—'

Ruth raised an eyebrow. 'They will marry, and I dare say sooner than you think. Either of them would be a good match for a man without much property.'

Young Kit did not recognize this description of himself. 'But Elizabeth is penniless and Cathy is so plain,' he said dismissively.

'Cathy is very accomplished, very learned, and of good

226

family, and Ralph will give her a dowry that will not shame him, or I do not know Ralph. Added to that she is well versed in the running of a great household, and that alone is an accomplishment that no man would be wise to underrate.'

Kit smiled – smiling, he looked more like his father than ever – and put his arms round Ruth's rigid shoulders.

'I do not underrate you,' he said, misunderstanding her, 'nor ever have. Could I have lived with you all my life and not know your great good qualities? I owe you everything, Ruth, and I never forget that.' He drew her to him and kissed her cheek, and for a moment she unbent enough for him to hold her close, so that his rain-cold cheek was against hers, his moustache prickling her, and his breath warm in her ear. Old feelings, long forgotten, long shut-away, stirred in her, and for a moment she rested against him, delighting in the hard, strong shape of his man's body, pleasantly close. She had never had the luxury of being cared for, never known the delight of strong, capable hands that said, rest a while, I will take care of you, carry your burdens. *Kit*, her heart said; but it lasted only a second, before her mind said, *Young Kit*, and she straightened up and pulled away from him.

'You had better change out of your doublet and breeches, and give them to Parry to have dried,' she said. It was a good thing that he was going away, she thought. She would be better off alone.

CHAPTER THIRTEEN

As a result of the dinner with Lord Ballincrea on Saturday, it was decided that Annunciata should be presented to the King on Sunday, and Hugo requested the honour of being allowed to perform the ceremony himself. Annunciata was delighted at the implied compliment, but would have felt obliged to refuse, out of loyalty to Richard. Lucy, seeing this, nudged Richard hastily into accepting.

'That would be most kind of you,' Richard said. It would reflect well on Annunciata to be introduced by a viscount, and one, moreover, who was a close personal friend of His Majesty.

'Then let it be tomorrow,' Hugo said eagerly, 'and, if you please, after chapel. The King likes to walk in the gardens after the service, and he is always refreshed by his little nap during the sermon, which puts him in the best possible humour.'

Annunciata looked a little shocked at the idea of the King sleeping in church, and then decided that Hugo was joking.

'And how shall it be done?' Richard was asking.

'Oh, it will be the easiest thing in the world. I shall come out a little ahead of His Majesty. If you will station yourselves where you may see us all leaving, then as soon as you see me, come towards me and I shall introduce you, and then you may stroll with the King's party as long as you like.'

Lucy sent her personal maid, Pal, to dress Annunciata for the important occasion the next morning, and came up herself a little later to supervise the dressing of her hair. She found Annunciata pale and silent with nervousness, and sympathetically sat her down and rubbed her hands while Pal plied the curling-irons.

'It is very natural for you to be nervous, natural and quite proper,' she said, 'but there is nothing to be afraid of. The King loves all beautiful things, and he will be delighted with you. He will smile and be gracious, just you wait and see.'

'I shan't know what to say,' Annunciata said.

'You won't have to say anything. The King will say "Welcome to the Court" or something like that, and you will say, "Thank you, Your Majesty" and he will walk on and it will all be over. Now then, let me see you. Stand up and turn around.'

Annunciata stood up and revolved obediently, and Lucy smiled. 'You look perfect. That colour is exactly right.' Annunciata's manteau was of midnight blue velvet, her petticoat of a blue silk just a shade lighter and with a hint of turquoise about it, and her long collar and cuffs of the finest lace. Pal had curled her hair all round, leaving it smooth and flat on top, and lifting the mass at the back so that it fell like a dark waterfall from the crown of her head to just below her shoulders.

'Should I paint her, Madam?' Pal asked. Lucy shook her head.

'No, no, she is perfect as she is. Paint would only hide her beauty. Pinch your cheeks, my darling, you are too pale. And just before you are presented, bite your lips once or twice to redden them. Now, have you your handkerchief? And your gloves? You will not need a muff today, I think – it is pleasantly warm. Now are you ready? Then we shall go down.'

Richard did not say much when he saw his young cousin, but he smiled and his eyes were warm and approving. Annunciata lifted her skirts carefully and climbed into the coach to sit with her back to the horses, and was very quiet during the journey through the town to Whitehall. Whatever Lucy said, she could not help being afraid, for the

King was the King, God's Annointed, His representative on earth, and she – she was the humblest of mortals, and a woman, and, though she kept the knowledge locked so deep that she hardly admitted it to herself, and *a bastard*. She was excited and pleased at the prospect of being presented, but she knew she would not be happy again until it was all over.

They took up their station in the gardens where they had a clear view of the chapel door, and Annunciata forced herself to stop fiddling nervously with the fringes of her gloves but stand tall and quietly. The wait seemed to go on a very long time, but in fact it was not more than five minutes before there was a flurry of movement and the chapel doors opened and the King's party came out. She saw Hugo at once, her eye being drawn irresistibly to him even though he was one amongst a crowd of dozens; then there was someone else to look at, someone who could even draw her attention from Hugo.

The King was just as she had expected him, towering over his subjects, and having about him the same kind of presence that she had known before in great stallions, a mixture of beauty and majesty and sexuality. Her critical eye told her that he was not handsome – his face, in fact, was heavy, dark, downright ugly – and yet he was beautiful, and the ambivalence puzzled her. It must be the grace of God inside him, shining through his outward flesh, she thought, and the idea pleased her.

'There he is,' Lucy was whispering at that moment. 'You can always tell the King even in a crowd – he is the only one with a hat on.'

'Who is that beside him?' Annunciata asked.

'The Duke of York, of course. You can see the family resemblance.' The Duke of York was as tall as his brother, but lighter in build. His hair was finer, and brown rather than black, and his face was romantically handsome. Yet he was not beautiful, Annunciata thought. 'He is very close with Master Hyde,' Lucy went on. 'They are talking like conspirators.'

'Come, Lucy, Annunciata, we must go to meet them,' Richard said, starting forward. Annunciata was still surveying the King's party. Now she saw another tall, dark-haired man, coming out behind the King and the duke. As she watched, the duke turned back and drew him into his conversation with Hyde, and he frowned as if concentrating on a difficult problem they were setting him. He was as tall as the royal brothers, and his hair was as dark as the King's, and his eyes were the dark, Stuart eyes, but his face was altogether finer, more handsome, more noble. If she had not seen the King first, she would have thought this man was king, for his face had the dignity of authority in it, as well as a kind of purity that she would have associated with kingship. She asked Lucy who he was.

'That's Prince Rupert, the King's cousin. We saw a lot of him at Oxford during the war, though I doubt if he'd remember me now. He left England in '46, and is only just returned.'

Prince Rupert! But of course, it had to be. Annunciata stared at him, thrilled and amazed, for he was such a legendary figure, it was as if she had been told she was looking at Theseus or Odysseus. He was a great hero out of history, Prince Rupert of the Rhine, who had fought for the Martyr King, leading his dashing cavalry from one end of the country to the other. More than that, she would not have been a Morland if she had not thrilled at his name. Kit's father and his uncle Hamil had both fought and died in Prince Rupert's own regiment, as had Ruth's nephew Malachi, whose death had left Annunciata heiress-apparent to the Shawes estate.

'And behind him,' Lucy went on hastily as they walked forward to where Hugo waited for them, 'is Lord Ormonde, Steward of the Household, and the little man behind him is Master Nicholas, and he's Secretary of State and a great friend of Prince Rupert's—'

But there was no time for more. Hugo was before them, making his bows, and now the King was approaching, and Hugo was smiling at him, and the King was raising a polite eyebrow, knowing very well that a presentation was at hand.

'Your Majesty,' Lord Ballincrea began. The King halted courteously, and behind him the great crowd of courtiers and hangers-on halted too. Annunciata's mouth dried at the size of the audience. 'May I be permitted to present to you the latest member of the Morland family to come to Court? A cousin of Richard's, Your Majesty – Mistress Annunciata Morland, of Shawes.'

A discreet push in the back from Lucy unfroze Annunciata's feet, and she found herself taking the required step forward and going down into a deep and graceful curtsey. She was glad of the opportunity to keep her eyes down, and she remained at the bottom of her curtsey, her eyes fixed on the King's shoes, her mind whirling with confused excitement, until she heard a deep, pleasant voice saying, 'Rise up, my dear.'

Then she lifted her eyes cautiously and found the King smiling at her and offering her his hand. She knew that she was supposed to kiss his ring, but his hand was held out to her palm upwards, and for a second she panicked, not knowing what to do. Then her mind cleared, her heart slowed from its irregular thudding, and as if she had been at Court all her life she place the tips of her fingers onto those of the Annointed of God and allowed him to raise her to her feet, and she looked up into his face and smiled back at him.

An almost inaudible murmur ran round the onlookers at that moment. Annunciata was aware of it, though she did not yet understand it, as she stood, as cool and unflustered as any *grande dame*, her hand and the King's touching, their eyes surveying each others' faces with intelligent interest, as if they were equals. One other impression remained there to be sorted out later at her leisure: that as

Hugo spoke the word *Shawes*, someone had turned their head abruptly towards her as if the name meant something.

But she had no time to think of that now. The King was speaking.

'It is very good of you, Richard, to keep bringing us beautiful women to grace our Court. You are very welcome here, my dear, and I hope we shall see a great deal of you. The name of Morland is one that we hold very dear. Come tell me about yourself. You are from Yorkshire, of course – one day I must visit it again. It is very beautiful, I have no doubt.'

The King began walking on as he spoke, and Annunciata saw that he expected her to fall in beside him, and she quivered at the enormity of the honour. But the Duke of York, with a pleasant nod of the head, made room for her, falling back to walk between Hyde and Prince Rupert, and Hugo hastened to take up station on the King's other side, while the King moderated his long stride to fit in with Annunciata's smaller steps. Out of the corner of her eye she saw Richard and Lucy smiling complaisantly, but she had little attention for anything but the King, who was wanting to know about the part of Yorkshire she came from. She answered him, and in a moment he had discovered her love of horses, and they were chatting pleasantly about them like old friends. When they reached the end of the walk she was telling him about Goldeneye, but as they turned, she saw the quality of his attention change, and she knew that her time with him for the moment was over and that she must fall back and allow him to go on to some other business.

He said to her, bowing slightly, 'I hope very soon to have the pleasure of seeing you ride your excellent mare. St James's Park is lovely for riding early in the day, before the crowds gather.'

And then, in the nicest possible way, she found herself dismissed, and the King's attention was claimed by someone else. Annunciata stood almost stunned, pink and breathless from the encounter, but she had no time to think over what was said, for Hugo at once took the arm that the King had vacated, and was looking at her with a rather speculative interest. Richard's presence had been claimed by Hyde and the duke and prince, and so Lucy came up on Hugo's other side and he at once gave her his other arm.

'Well, my dear, that went off well, much better than I expected for the first meeting,' Lucy said. 'What was he saying to you?'

'Oh, he was asking me about Yorkshire, and then we spoke about horses a little,' Annunciata said vaguely, her eyes still on the retreating royal back. Lucy, bright-eyed, was looking around her at the other courtiers.

'You have certainly caused a sensation,' she said. 'Just look at them stare and point. My darling, they will talk of nothing else until they have seen you at a formal function.'

'It should not be long, Madam,' Hugo said, still with that thoughtful air. 'The King spoke of wishing to see Mistress Morland ride in St James's Park.'

Annunciata glanced at him, and a sudden idea darted through her mind that made her blush deeply. 'Oh, he didn't mean it,' she said hastily. 'He was only being polite.'

'Madam, though I hate to appear to contradict you,' Hugo said with a mock formality that concealed some genuine emotion, 'the King may often say things he does not mean – indeed he is famous for it – but one is never in doubt when he really does mean something. If I am not greatly mistaken, there will be a formal invitation soon.'

Lucy smiled and tugged his arm. 'I think you are not mistaken, my Lord. Look who goes there.'

Hugo looked where she pointed, and saw a small, neat, dark-haired man drawing Richard's attention away from the business he was so seriously discussing.

'Yes, indeed, it is Henry Bennet. That will be your invitation.'

They were not long left in suspense. They had done no more than two turns of the path when Richard broke away from his companions and came across to them.

'Lucy my dear, Annunciata, Henry Bennet has just brought an invitation from His Majesty to a small private dance and supper tonight. I hope I did right in accepting on your behalf as well as on mine.'

The smiles he received were answer enough. 'And now,' he went on, 'Master Hyde and their Highnesses have need of me in the Old Palace. Would you mind very much going home unescorted? You will be quite safe with Ben.'

Lucy was about to acquiesce when Hugo interrupted. 'Sir, I have finished my business here this morning. Perhaps I might be permitted to escort the ladies home.'

'Why Hugo, that would be delightful,' Lucy said quickly. 'Will you have the leisure to stay to dinner?'

'With great pleasure,' Hugo said.

'I shall not be home,' Richard said. 'I shall dine with Master Hyde, while we work.'

'Be sure to be home in plenty of time to dress for tonight,' Lucy said.

'Of course, my dear. Shall we have the pleasure of seeing you tonight, my Lord? Perhaps we could travel together?'

Hugo gave a strange little shrug and grimace. 'I was not invited,' he said.

Lucy insisted that Annunciata rest during the afternoon so that she might be fresh for the supper dance that evening, and she was not sorry to have a little time alone to consider quietly the events of the morning. The largest part of her thoughts was devoted to the King. That he should have been so gracious, so kindly, that he could have invited her so quickly to a private function, the sort of private supper that young noblewomen and their fathers would give a fortune to attend, suggested some rare kind of favour. Some of it might be due to her family and the loyalty they had shown the crown, but Annunciata knew her own attractions too well, and had heard too much about the King's private life not to suspect that there was some more immediate reason for his kindness.

And if that was true, what then? She trembled to think. Barbara Palmer was his mistress, and no one at Court seemed to think the worse of her, she reasoned. *Not true*, said the voice of her conscience, *Lucy thinks very much the worse*. In France, she told herself, Kings' mistresses were treated like Queens, were honoured and given titles and lands. *But this is not France*, said her other self. Then she shook herself briskly. She was supposing far too much. The King was only being kind, nothing more. But Hugo thought he meant more, she remembered, thinking of Hugo's expression. What would her mother say? But then, what had her mother sent her here for?

She forced her mind away from those issues to consider the other thing that had been nagging at the back of her mind: the person who had been alerted by the name of Shawes. Searching through her memories, she finally discovered that it had been Prince Rupert whose eyes had been drawn to the King at that point. She remembered that there was a story amongst the servants at Shawes that he had once stayed there during the war; this incident seemed to confirm it, and she was pleased. The Duke of York had nodded politely to her too, she remembered; and everyone had looked and wondered who she might be. She remembered Lucy's voice saying 'You have caused a sensation'. It was pleasant to make such a stir, she thought drowsily, and wondering what sort of a stir she would make that evening she drifted off to sleep in a confused whirl of memories in which dark eyes and long white hands figured largely.

She was woken by a great commotion downstairs, and as she struggled up onto her elbow, dazed with sleep, Pal came into the room with an expression of suppressed excitement.

'What is it?' Annunciata asked sleepily. 'What's happened?'

'That master's come home, Miss, and such news! Oh Miss! But it's sad for you, for they've cancelled the supper-party that you was to go to.'

'But what is the news?'

'They'll tell you downstairs, I dare say,' Pal said, bustling about picking up clothes. 'Missus sent me up to say there'll be a little supper here instead, and she has sent word to one or two people to come, so I'm to dress you for it. Come along now, Miss, the hot water'll be here directly.'

Annunciata saw that she would not get more out of Pal, so she got up obediently and allowed herself to be washed and dressed. Perhaps Pal had deliberately not told her the news, for wondering what it could be distracted her mind from the disappointment of missing her first royal party. Pal dressed her in a pretty and modest gown of apple-green watered silk with a deep lace palatine, and dressed her hair behind with dark green ribbons, and then stepped back to survey her handiwork.

'There now, Miss, you look as pretty as a picture. Go on down with you.'

The news was startling enough, justifying the commotion. Annunciata found Richard still striding about looking grave and worried, and Lucy, though sitting composedly enough, looked excited, scandalized, disappointed and anxious by turns.

'Oh, Annunciata, what a pity for you,' were her first words. 'Your very first party! But never mind, my dear, there is sure to be another very soon. And oh, pity that poor lady! I always liked her. But what could she have been thinking about to do such a thing? And I thought she looked worried when we met her in the 'Change, did you not think so, Annunciata? I was telling Richard how we met her—'

237

The news was soon told. Anne Hyde, the Chancellor's daughter, had contracted a secret marriage with the Duke of York, which had been going on for months. She was now far gone with child, so that the secret could not be kept any longer, and she had prodded the duke into revealing it. He had blurted it out that day at the Old Palace when he was in conference with Master Hyde and Richard and the Prince.

Hyde's reaction was typical of him, though not what anyone would have expected who did not know him well. He had been furious and disgusted, and had sworn he would sooner see his daughter a whore at Madam Bennet's house than disgracing the royal blood with an unworthy marriage.

'No one, of course, will give him credit for meaning it,' Lucy said. 'They will merely think him quick-witted to wriggle out of the blame.'

'But he does mean it,' Richard said sadly. 'He may be stubborn and bullheaded and interfering and infuriating, but his loyalty to the King has never been in question. The trouble is that his attitude encourages the duke's wavering. He is already regretting his rashness, and now is seeking to deny the whole thing.'

'Perhaps it would be best if it was denied,' Lucy said doubtfully. 'Though I feel for the poor creature, the duke *is* the heir apparent, and she is only a commoner—'

'But it's too late now. Everyone in Court knows about it, and even if Anne Hyde can be brought to accept a denial – which I doubt because she's as stubborn as a goat, just like her father – there'll be the babe which, if it is a boy, will always find those to say he should be the next King. Lord, why does the duke have to be such a fool! Of all the people to choose for a mistress, he has to pick upon Anne Hyde! It isn't even as if she was handsome.'

'Oh, she's well enough,' Lucy said. 'I just can't understand her lapsing so far. I have always thought her virtuous.'

'All virtue has its price,' Richard said drily. 'Hers was marriage.'

Annunciata listened to all this in silence, and at last they seemed to remember her presence and looked a little awkward.

Richard said, 'I'm afraid this is not a very good beginning to your stay here. You must think you have come to a very strange place.'

Annunciata smiled and shook her head. 'You forget we hear the news in Yorkshire almost as soon as it happens in London. I am not completely unaware of the reputation the exiled Court had.'

Richard nodded. 'That, of course, is the root of the trouble – they have all been spoiled by wandering about Europe penniless and homeless. It has made them all shiftless and unthinking.'

'The King must have been upset about it, if he cancelled the party this evening,' Annunciata suggested.

'He had to be told at once, of course,' Richard said. 'He was closeted a long time with the duke, and then he called Hyde in, and by that time it was all over the Court. When I left he was preparing to see the young woman. But I think the thing that really upset him was that the duke was not prepared to see it through.'

'Even if he likes Anne Hyde, which I believe he does,' Lucy said reasonably, 'he couldn't much relish the thought of her as a sister. She was his own sister Mary's maid, after all.'

'The King is right-thinking, even if he isn't always right-acting,' Richard said. 'And before I left, Berkeley and Jermyn had come in to say that Anne was not honest and had laid with them, and Killigrew hurried in with the same story and claimed the child was his.'

Lucy shot him a warning glance and nodded towards Annunciata, and Richard shook his head.

'I think she ought to know what kind of a Court it is. I would not have her face it unprepared. The duke pretended to believe them, but the King sent them about their business.'

'It might be a way out,' Lucy said thoughtfully, 'if she could be persuaded—'

'No one would ever believe it,' Richard said. 'Those three are renowned scoundrels, and the duke's best friends. The speed with which they hurried up with their stories proves that. No, it's my belief that the King will persuade the duke to stand by his obligations, but it's a bad business. And, of course,' he went on, smiling at Annunciata, 'it has spoiled your evening's entertainment. But we shall have a little private supper-party here, and we have invited one or two people along. Your cousin Frank will be here, and William Morrice, who's a friend of General Monk, and Second Secretary of State, and William Coventry, he's Secretary to the Lord High Admiral, and another army captain, Robert Ferrers, so we shall have a deal of good talk. Oh, and of course Lucy asked her great favourite, Lord Ballincrea, so he'll be able to tell us what's being said around the Privy Chambers.'

'And luckily I was able to bespeak three brace of fat ducks, and a barrel of oysters, so we shan't lack for dainty fare,' Lucy said, 'though it won't be what you would have had at the Palace. But Richard keeps an excellent cellar, and the young men will all want to dance with you.' She spoke lightly, but her eyes were on Annunciata, and she saw, as she expected, the fine blush of pleasure that was aroused by the mention of Hugo's name. It was a situation, she thought, that would bear watching, for Hugo was a charming rogue, and Annunciata, for all her airs, was little more than an innocent.

The house on North Street, on the corner of the passage that ran down beside All Saints Church, was the one with the bad roof, and having made a stand about the duties of tenants, Kit felt he had to shew he understood the duties of a landlord and have it mended before winter. It was a tricky job, and he had borrowed Dickon, the estate carpenter, from Ralph to lead his workmen; but even so, he felt it necessary to ride in from time to time to see how the work was coming on. He was balancing at the top of a ladder one day arguing with Dickon when the latter broke off to look down over his shoulder.

'Why isn't that our Miss Cathy below? What may she be doing here?'

Kit looked down and saw his cousin on horseback with Audrey attending her, reining in their mounts and looking up at him. He hastened down the ladder and in a moment was standing before Cathy, holding her pony's bridle, and asking the same question.

'I came in to order some things for the feast tomorrow,' Cathy said. The following day was Little Ralph's sixth birthday, and he was to be breeched ceremonially and with a party. 'You are coming, are you not?'

'Of course,' Kit said. 'But couldn't you have sent a servant for the things?'

'I wanted to come myself, to be sure of picking the best,' Cathy said quickly, 'and then as I was on my way home, I saw you and stopped to speak.'

She blushed deeply as she said this, and had Kit's mind been more on what she was saying he would have realized that it was quite a step out of her way for her to be there on North Street. But he was not quick to notice such things. He did not even notice, as Cathy had hoped he might, that she was wearing a new wine-red manteau which suited her better than anything she had ever worn before.

'You are looking forward to the party?' Kit asked politely.

'Of course,' Cathy said, 'though it is as much work as pleasure to me. I discover every day how much Leah used to do about the house. But it will be pleasant to dance – if anyone asks me.'

'Do you not lead off with Ralph?' Kit said, puzzled. As

honorary mistress of the house, it would be for her to open the dancing, unless there was a lady guest of honour.

'Oh yes, I dance the first with Ralph,' Cathy said, and paused, and Kit at last recollected his manners.

'I would be honoured if you would reserve the next dance for me,' he said, 'if you do not think it dull to dance with such a close relative.'

'I don't think of you as a relative,' Cathy said, but the implication seemed to pass Kit, and she went on, 'Thank you. I should like to dance with you. Things are going well here?' She glanced up at the workers on the roof.

'Slowly,' Kit said. 'It is one of the trials of owning property.'

'Then perhaps you should not try to own any more,' Cathy smiled. 'Will you not change your mind about going to Scotland?'

Kit raised an eyebrow in surprise. 'Would you have me penniless?'

'You have enough to live modestly in comfort,' Cathy said. 'And happiness does not depend on property.'

Kit smiled. 'What does it depend on, then?'

'On living a godly life, in good company. If a man has the right wife—'

'Ah yes, if he does,' Kit said, his face darkening.

Cathy sighed inwardly and changed tack. 'Have you seen Ralph this morning? He was coming in to town.'

'No, I haven't seen him. Is it more trouble with Makthorpe?'

Cathy nodded. 'He has managed to delay the hearing again, on the question of the land. Ralph is furious, but there is nothing he can do. Makthorpe has more money than Ralph, and since he was once Justice of the Peace, he has influence too. He has boasted to Ralph that he can have the hearing put off month after month for the rest of his life. How I hate that man! He came to the house again the day before yesterday, just to gloat and leer. He stares at me in such a way, it makes my skin crawl.'

'If only Edward were home,' Kit said. 'Edward would think of something. But he is not far off – Huddersfield, is it not? Cannot Ralph send to him, to ask his advice?'

'There is nothing anyone can do about Makthorpe,' Cathy said. 'Unless my father gains more influence at Court. Or –' with a touch of malice – 'unless Annunciata becomes the King's mistress.'

Kit looked pained and wistful and shocked all together. Cathy gave another inward sigh and said, 'I do but jest. I must be on my way. God's day to you, Kit. I will see you tomorrow.'

'God's day, cousin,' Kit said, and then, rousing himself to courtesy, 'Do not forget you have promised me a dance.'

'Oh no, I would not be likely to forget that,' Cathy said sadly, and rode on.

Annunciata cantered Goldeneye along the path in St James's Park and relished the freedom. Since neither Lucy nor Richard owned a riding horse they could not accompany her, and so it had been decided that she would go to the park in the coach with a servant, while a groom rode Goldeneye along behind, and then the coach would wait for her while she rode and take her back again in the same manner. But once she was on horseback, the coach and the maid could be left behind, and she could enjoy being as alone as she had been since she first came to London.

It was a sparkling day, still cold from the night, though it was dew that glittered on the grass, not frost, the clear pale sky flushed gold by the rising sun, and she had the park to herself except for the birds. Goldeneye was fresh, having lacked exercise for some days, and she knew by the feel of her that she was looking for an excuse to pretend fear and buck or bolt. Every now and then she would put in an extra step in the attempt to unseat her, and Annunciata smiled with the pleasure of outwitting her. Her mouth was strong but flexible against the spring of

Annunciata's wrists, and as the mare flicked her head from side to side, testing her hands, the gold-and-coral bridle ornaments danced and clinked and caught the sun.

She came to the edge of the lake, and reined Goldeneye in for a moment to look at the strange water-fowl that the King was collecting there. As she watched the King himself came into view round the end of the lake, tall, bare-headed, and alone except for a swirling wake of spaniels. He saw her at once, smiled, and came towards her. Goldeneye tucked her chin well in and moved her forefeet, her ears flickering back and forth as she wondered whether the dogs would provide excuse to snatch the bit and gallop off. The little brown and white dogs saw her too, and ran forward, tails waving, and as the leaders ran up to her forelegs and yapped, Goldeneye went up into a slow and showy half-rear which did not in the least discommode Annunciata, for she had been watching the ears, and knew it was coming. It did, however, give her the opportunity to display her fine horsemanship, and as she brought her down again and turned her on the spot to face the troublesome dogs, she knew that she was looking at her very best.

The King called the dogs off and stepped in to catch hold of Goldeneye's reins.

'My apologies, madam,' he said. 'My dogs are more unruly even than my courtiers. You are not alone, I imagine?' He looked round for her escort.

'A coach waits for me at the gate, Your Majesty, but I was the only one with a riding-horse.'

'All too few of the Court ladies ride,' the King said. 'You look so pretty and so graceful – and you have such a healthy colour in your cheek – that I could wish you may be starting a new fashion.'

Annunciata bowed her head to the compliment, and said, 'And you, Your Majesty – are you alone?'

The King grinned an almost boyish grin. 'I have outwalked them all for the moment. They will catch me up all too soon. How are you enjoying life in London, Mistress Morland? You find it a little confining, I imagine?'

'It is very exciting, Your Majesty, though I have not had the opportunity to ride as often as I do at home.'

'Yes, I know what you mean,' the King said, his eyes growing thoughtful. 'I should like to ride with you at Windsor, Mistress Morland. I have a beautiful park there, and the hunting is very fine. Next summer when we move, I hope you will be with us, and permit me to show you the best rides.'

Annunciata, her cheeks glowing with the compliment, could only smile. The King was still looking at her thoughtfully, his great dark eyes fixed on her face, and the world seemed to grow very still around them. Even Goldeneye stopped throwing her head up and down and nibbled quietly at the King's sleeve, and the dogs stopped their running to and fro and sat down panting at their master's feet. Annunciata gazed at the King, and knew that they would be disturbed at any moment, when the rest of the early morning walkers caught him up.

As if he had read her thought, the King said, 'How peaceful it is, and now I wish it could go on being so. I should like to ride alone with you in the early morning, and see that fine glow of health in your cheek. A very English colour, Mistress Morland, did you know that? The ladies of France have not such skin.' Dark eyes gazed into dark eyes. 'We shall be disturbed at any moment. I want to see you again. You are too far away, living in the city. Should you like to come to Court? A Court should have as much beauty in it as possible. Shall I find you a place at Court? Would you like that?'

'Yes, Your Majesty,' Annunciata said, finding that he wanted an answer. It seemed strange that he should ask, for surely everyone wanted to be at Court?

'My sisters and my mother will be coming to Court soon. I should like you to meet my sister Henrietta. You remind me of her greatly – there is something of the look of her in

245

you when you look at me, as now, with that—' He broke off abruptly, flicking his head round as the first of the courtiers rounded the end of the pond. 'Damn,' he said softly, and became brisk and businesslike, smiling still, but with a different smile, a more public, less tender smile. 'The new Duchess of York needs a household,' he said. 'And I believe she is a friend of your cousin and guardian. I shall appoint you to her household for the time being. And,' he added, looking into her eyes for one last time, 'I shall tell Albemarle that there is to be room found for your horse. One day there will be time to ride with you.'

He inclined his head and walked on, more slowly now, not trying to escape his train. Annunciata looked after him for a moment, her eyes shiny with delight and adoration, and then, realizing that she did not want to have to speak to anyone else, she turned Goldeneye and cantered away from both the King and the courtiers.

She reminded him of his favourite sister. He wanted her at Court. He had called her beautiful. His words whirled in her mind, and she tried to steady her thoughts, for fear she would forget some of them. She was to go to Court, and take her horse – a rare privilege – and surely that could only mean one thing? A bird rattled up from under Goldeneye's hooves, and she made a breenge that almost unseated her and drew her mind back to what she was doing. The most important thing, she thought more sensibly, was that she had made the first important step in her career upwards, and much sooner than anyone would have expected. Lucy and Richard would be delighted, and Mother would be so proud.

She turned into the main path and rode towards the waiting coach. Now why, at that moment of all moments, did she suddenly think of Lord Ballincrea? And why did she imagine his face with a disapproving expression?

CHAPTER FOURTEEN

'Maid of honour to the Duchess of York,' Lucy said, spreading the stiff, crackling paper with her fingers. 'Well—'

'It is only the beginning,' Annunciata said. 'After all, what other household could he send me to?'

'True. And when he marries he will probably transfer you. And to allow you to take your horse – that is a great honour.' She looked at Annunciata curiously. 'Your mother will be very pleased. And Ralph, no doubt – especially if you put in a good word for him with the King.'

Annunciata's eyes sharpened, and she and Lucy looked at each other for a moment with perfect comprehension. Finally Lucy said, 'Your mother trusts, as do I, that you will always act with honour, as you have been brought up. But, of course, only you can decide in the end where honour lies.'

Annunciata nodded, and that was all that was said on the difficult subject; but she had already decided that if the king asked her, she would say yes. It did not, now, seem a difficult decision to make – she, like almost everyone who had ever met him, was in love with him.

The only remaining difficulty was the finding of a maid, for Annunciata could not move into lodgings in Whitehall without a suitable serving-woman. It was difficult to find a good maid in a London crowded with returning exiles and provincial families hoping for favours or grants of land. Lucy and Annunciata interviewed a dozen in one day, and none of them was even possible. Eventually they engaged an older woman, a sharp-eyed, sallow-faced Londoner called Jane Birch, whom Annunciata did not at all like, but who appeared to be clean and efficient. Footmen were easier to find, and they quickly hired a young man of sixteen called Tom Willet who had not long come to London from Kent, and was willing to act as groom to Goldeneye as well as footman to her mistress.

On the evening before Annunciata was to take up residence at Whitehall Richard and Lucy gave a supper-party in her honour as a kind of farewell, and invited their closest friends. It was the kind of party Lucy liked best, small, intimate and gay, with herself and Annunciata the only women, the other guests being intelligent, talking, influential men. She had never been over-fond of female company, and had spent so much of her early life in the company of students, dons, lawyers and courtiers that conversation of that sort was the breath of life to her. But she sat Hugo between herself and Annunciata, for a little light relief.

Hugo seemed in a strange mood, at times joking, at times serious, as though he had something on his mind that was troubling him.

'You have not gone entirely to the best position in Court,' he said to Annunciata at one point. 'There are still some who seem in doubt as to whether to curtsey to the new duchess or snub her.'

'The King has no doubts on that score,' Lucy said sharply.

Hugo lolled one elbow on the table and conveyed a fragment of bread to his mouth with his long elegant fingers. 'Even the King may not relish the unpleasantness that is to come,' he smiled. 'Princess Mary will be here before the end of the week, and the word is that she has sworn to refuse to receive the duchess. She says she will not call her own former maid "sister".'

Lucy looked wise. 'If she is to live here for the rest of her life as she plans, she will need a pension from His Majesty, and if His Majesty tells her to receive the duchess—'

'Well, be that as it may, Queen Henrietta is expected

hot on Mary's heels, and you cannot imagine that she will accept Anne Hyde as a daughter?'

'Why is the Queen coming?' Lucy asked.

Richard overheard the question, and answered for Hugo. 'The matter, I believe, is the marriage of the Princess Henrietta. The King and Prince Rupert are to carry out the negotiations.'

'That may be what is said, but the real reason is that she has sworn to part York and his duchess,' Hugo said.

Richard smiled. 'She will not do it. What the King sets his mind on, he is not shaken from, the the marriage is too well known to be hushed up. He will make the Queen receive the duchess, and that will be an end to all resistance. Do not worry, Annunciata, your career at Court will not be prematurely terminated.'

'When the King takes a personal interest in a young woman, her career at Court is likely to advance rapidly,' Hugo said.

Lucy and Richard exchanged a glance at his remark, and then Richard said as if apropos of nothing in particular, 'Annunciata will be moving with a very staid and respectable set, by the look of it. Chancellor Hyde and Secretary Morrice and Master-of-Horse Albemarle and Prince Rupert—'

Lucy smiled. 'All the Morland connections at Court are impeccable,' she said.

Hugo added, as if he had thought of something pleasant, 'With only Lord Ballincrea to represent the other, dissolute side of Whitehall life. Well, Madam, if you will permit me I shall do my best to redress the balance and be as frivolous as my sober nature allows me.' And he bowed towards Annunciata, looking at her from under his eyelashes with a wicked smile. The servants came in with the next course, and he changed the subject. 'God 's' me, Mistress Lucy, can it be ices you are serving? How glad I am that the autumn has been hot enough to warrant their being fashionable. Have you heard that the King is to build an ice-house in St James's Park? It will be a great service to us all if he does, for then we shall be able to have ices all summer long. It will be another reason for gentlemen of taste to haunt the park, though I daresay they will go more towards noon than dawn.' A glance at Annunciata's pink cheeks was enough to restore his good humour completely, and the conversation continued on the inexhaustible topic of food.

The presence chamber was brilliantly lit with candles and torches and hot and stuffy with the heat of many bodies. Annunciata advanced along the strip of carpet from the door to the dais, her eyes fixed on the backs of her new master and mistress, her own back very straight and her head held high under the gaze of what seemed like hundreds of curious eyes to either side of her. The Duchess of York was wearing a new green satin gown which became her very well, and her light-brown hair was clean and fluffy, hanging loose down her back just in front of Annunciata's face; but there were big wet circles on the green satin at the armpits, for the duchess was sweating with nervousness as well as with the heat. Would the Queen accept her, or snub her? That was the question in everyone's eyes.

Queen Henrietta, widow of the Martyr-King, sat ramrod straight on the chair on the dais looking straight ahead of her but not at the duke and duchess. She was a tiny woman with a thin, pinched face that had been pretty once, in her youth, but was now merely old. Her black hair was much crimped after the fashion of France in her youth; her clothes were all black, for she kept perpetual mourning for her husband, but very rich and much bejewelled. Her eyes were small and black and bright like a monkey's and her little wizened hands were rather like a monkey's too, as they clutched in her lap at her chatelaine. Behind her on one side stood Princess Mary, the widow of the Prince of

Orange, the King's eldest sister. She had the long, dark, sallow face of the Stuarts, dark hair in long ringlets, and her dark eyes were bright with disapproval. It was towards these two silent judges that the new Duchess of York walked with reluctant steps.

The duke bowed to his mother, who nodded coldly in acknowledgement, and then presented his wife. The duchess went down into a deep curtsey, and for a long moment she remained there, stranded in the down position while everyone wondered with horrified, bated breath whether the Queen would leave her there for ever. But after what seemed like a very long time, she extended her hand and Anne Hyde touched it gratefully and began to rise.

'My daughter,' Queen Henrietta said graciously, 'let me kiss you.' Anne Hyde blinked in surprise for a moment, and then inclined herself towards the Queen, who placed her hands on her daughter-in-law's shoulders and kissed her on the forehead. There was a murmur of surprise and applause around the room, and as the duchess straightened again the Queen shot a look of private triumph at King Charles, who returned it with one of grim amusement. Princess Mary then greeted her former maid with much less kindness, but unimpeachable correctness, and the company relaxed.

Annunciata made her deep curtseys to the Queen and Princess Mary, and was moving away to take up her position behind the Duchess of York when the King beckoned to her. Surprised, she looked round at first to see if it could be her he meant, and then, aware that many eyes had also remarked the gesture, she went forward towards him. She was glad to know, at least, that she looked well enough to meet any gaze: her Court dress was of pale violet satin, deeply décolleté, with huge puffed sleeves to the elbow, from under which the lace-trimmed sleeves of her under-bodice were drawn. The lacings of the over-bodice were hidden by a pearl-trimmed plastron, and fastened to the top of it she wore the pearl-and-amethyst cross which her mother had given her. Her hair was drawn back from her face to the crown of her head with a half hoop of pearls, from which it cascaded down her back in dark natural curls, and around the base of her throat she wore a thin strand of amethysts set in gold, which Lucy had lent her for the occasion. Despite the fact that she wore no face-paint, and despite her lack of jewels, she knew that she looked more beautiful and elegant than most of the Court women who were staring at her with critical eyes.

The King had been standing behind the Queen on the other side from Princess Mary, and with him, almost crouching in his shadow as if for protection, was his youngest sister, the Princess Henrietta Anne, whom the King called Minette. She was as tiny as her mother, whom she much resembled at first glance. She wore her hair crimped after the French fashion, and her bejewelled dress was in the French style, but looking more closely Annunciata saw that the plain, pleasant face of the Princess more closely resembled the Stuart than the French side. Princess Henrietta had no great beauty, but she had great charm, and her sweetness and goodness shone out from her face so that it became no wonder that she was the King's avowed favourite.

She smiled as Annunciata approached, and the King stepped forward, took Annunciata's hand and himself presented her to his sister. Annunciata curtseyed, confused and delighted by the distinction, and heard the murmurs of the onlookers as a background to the King's voice as he spoke.

'You are just the same age, I believe. I am sure you will be friends. Minette, Mistress Morland has kept your image before me these last few weeks. There is something in her face which so strongly reminds me of you, though I cannot quite put my finger on it.'

Minette's voice was soft, hesitant, charmingly husky,

strongly accented. She smiled at Annunciata and then looked up at her brother.

'But Charles, she is so much more beautiful than I. I never was a beauty, you know.'

The King looked down with great tenderness at his sister, and said, 'I do not think Mistress Morland will think it anything but a compliment when I say that she reminds me of you. To look like you must be the highest a woman can attain to.'

Minette smiled adoringly at him, and then returned her attention to Annunciata. 'I hope we shall be able to see something of each other while I am here,' she said. 'If Charles says we should be friends, then we must be.'

The King nodded pleasantly to her, dismissing her, and Annunciata curtseyed again and glided backwards into her more retired place behind Anne Hyde, her heart beating so hard with excitement that it felt like a trapped bird under her tight busk.

When the rest of the introductions had been made, the music began, and the King and the Duke of York began the ball by dancing with Princess Mary and Princess Henrietta, while the Queen graciously called for a chair so that the Duchess of York could sit beside her. Having given in, it seemed, she was prepared to do so gracefully. When the first dance was over and the second was struck up, the rest of the courtiers were able to join in, and at once there was a polite scramble for hands. Annunciata half hoped that the King would dance with her, but he led out Princess Henrietta, and in a moment Prince James's friend Berkeley was beside her, bowing, and she let him lead her into the set.

'Lord, look at Tom Killigrew fret,' Berkeley said as soon as they had taken their places. 'When the King spoke to you he swore he'd get you for the first dance and find out what His Majesty said to you. And now I've beaten him to both prizes. I've got the first dance, and I already know what the King said. At least, I know what everyone is going to think he said, though if you wish you may give me the true version. I promise never to tell anyone.'

Annunciata laughed. 'Perhaps you had better tell me. It would not do to be less well informed about my own conversations than everyone else.'

Berkeley gave her a nod of approval. 'Wit as well as beauty. Well, it seems that the King said you reminded him of Princess Henrietta. It's a good job that Barbara Palmer is not here tonight – she's a woman you would do well not to stir up. Not that I think Mrs Palmer would care to remind anyone of anyone other than herself, and Minette is no beauty either, but it's well known that the King dotes on her, and so everyone is supposing that you will be putting Barbara's nose out of joint. Unless, of course—' He stared at her with interest.

'Unless what?' Annunciata asked, still amused.

Berkeley surveyed her speculatively. 'Yes, there is no denying that there is something of a family resemblance,' he said. 'I can see why the King would be reminded of his sister. Now I wonder – of course, you must be at least fifteen.'

'And a half,' Annunciata said drily.

'Yes. So it would be unlikely that you could be a natural daughter of His Majesty.'

Annunciata tried to look shocked but couldn't quite manage it.

'We must just put it down to coincidence, I suppose,' Berkeley concluded. 'You dance very well,' he went on. 'I hear that you also ride well. I would not be surprised if you were not to start a new fashion. Once it is known how much the King admires a trim figure upon horseback, the saddlers will be rushed with orders for sidesaddles.'

'Is nothing secret?' Annunciata asked, raising her eyebrows.

'In Whitehall?' Berkeley said, raising his. 'But our ladies will not be able quite to imitate your style, which will be a relief for you, no doubt. After all, you are of an old

254

family, extremely well-connected amongst the old guard, and well endowed, it seems, with family heirlooms. My groom tells me your horse's bridle bears some pretty decorations, and then there is this—' His hand brushed the cross at her breast very lightly, and the gesture was not quite innocent. She drew back from him a little, not liking him so well now, and he smiled as an adult might smile at a precocious child.

'This is one of the few places in England where a little discreet display of Catholicism can be quite fashionable. It will not stand against you with the King, at all events. And if I might give you a word of advice – be modest in your demands, but firm. The King promises much but parts with little. A woman in your position would do well to imitate him.'

The music had ended as he spoke, and he bowed to her and led her back to her place, where half a dozen of the young men of the Court were already waiting to ask for the hand of the newest beauty at the Court. Annunciata accepted the first offer she received almost without noticing, for Berkeley's conversation needed quite a little thinking about.

The last dance before supper was announced, and Annunciata's hand was very firmly taken by one whose touch she was beginning to recognize, and Hugo McNeill led her away from the crowd of young bucks amongst whom she had been about to take her choice.

'My pardon, lady, for leaving it until now to address you,' he said as he led her to the set, 'but I wanted to be sure of being able to ask to take you to supper. Are you enjoying yourself? You have certainly been the centre of attention tonight. Had I not been an expert at cutting-out expeditions, I should have had no confidence of being able to speak to you at all.'

'I hope I should never be indifferent to old friends,' Annunciata said.

Hugo looked as though he would smile if he were more sure of himself. 'Do you think of me as an old friend?'

'You were one of the first people I met in London,' she said. 'And the first I danced with.'

'And that, of course, is a very important distinction amongst civilized societies,' he said with mock solemnity. 'Might I be permitted to remark on how very beautiful you are looking this evening? And if the King had been using his eyes instead of his heart, he would never have thought you liker to the princess than to an angel.'

Annunciata give a smile that was half exasperated. 'Does everyone hear everything that is said?'

'But of course. This is Whitehall. Does it trouble you? Are you finding this public life not so much to your taste as you thought.'

'Of course not,' Annunciata said quickly, not wishing to seem unsophisticated. 'I love it. It is the most exciting—'

'Oh, Princess,' Hugo said shaking his head sadly, 'have you been corrupted already? Now come, tell the truth, and shame the dark gentleman. Did you not find the gossiping of all those young men of fashion a little distasteful?'

'Distasteful? Why should I? I am not a child,' she said haughtily. He pressed her hand.

'Not good enough. I have been watching you all evening, and I saw you draw away from Berkeley as a cat draws away from spilled wine. Come now, confess.'

'Well—'

'You have been used to better company, have you not? To the company of gentlemen? You have been used to rather more formal and gentle manners from your admirers?'

'Well—'

Hugo smiled approvingly. 'That is good. Now we have the truth. And in return for your confession, I shall tell you two things that will interest you. When you have been at Court as long as I have, you will know there is nothing so valuable one person may give another than to be interested, amused or diverted for a few moments.' Annunciata laughed unwillingly. 'Now then – firstly, I knew that you were as beautiful as an angel long before you came to Court, and had you not come to London I should have found occasion to go to Yorkshire and seek you out. Don't you want to know how I knew?'

'Not at all,' Annunciata said with an effort. 'I am not so vain as to—'

'Nonsense again, Mistress Morland,' Hugo grinned. 'Your vanity is in excellent order, and you, like me, like nothing so well as being talked about, which is as it should be. So I shall tell you – your cousin Edward told me about you.'

Annunciata, aware that he was watching her closely, managed not to blush or look conscious, and Hugo smiled in such a particular way that she hastened to speak.

'Well, for the first thing – and what was the second thing you were to tell me?'

'The second thing is not about you. Shall I go on?'

'Yes, do. I do not want to talk about myself.'

'Ah, nobility itself! Well, the second thing is about Princess Henrietta. She is betrothed, as you may know, to Philippe d'Orleans, who is King Louis' brother, and the King is to make the match. That is why the Queen has come. But Prince Rupert who knows Philippe very well, and who loves Minette almost as much as the King does, is outraged at the betrothal, and wants to arrange a different and much better match for his young cousin.'

'Why does he not like the match with Philippe d'Orleans?' Annunciata asked.

Hugo gave a grim little smile. 'If you were a little older, or a little less innocent, I would tell you. Suffice it to say, he is not – a gentleman. In fact, I think he is not human at all. I know Philippe too – and I would say he is a beast, except that all the beasts I have met in my life have been pleasant and gentle creatures compared with Orleans.'

'So why does the King want to wed his favourite sister to this – beast?'

'For reasons of policy, *chère Madame*. Also, I think Henriette does not mind so much, as long as she can live in France, and the King will always do what is the least trouble to him. But Prince·Rupert – there is a different man.'

'What is he like, Prince Rupert?' Annunciata asked curiously. 'I have heard so much about him. Many of my family, you know, served with him.'

Hugo nodded. 'That also I know,' he said. 'Well, the Prince is – all gentleness, all courage, all honour. I think he will find himself a little out of step with the times in this gay new England of ours. But he always loved England. He will be happy enough, I guess, to make his home here, and live quietly on the pension the King gives him.' The music ended. 'There,' Hugo said, taking her hand again, 'I have amused you for the whole length of a dance. Does not such a service merit a reward?'

'Of course,' Annunciata laughed. 'What reward would you like?'

For a moment he looked very seriously into her face, and she trembled a little, wondering what he was going to say. And then he seemed to change his mind, and he bowed and said lightly, 'I wish to be allowed to take you in to supper. Dare I hope?'

'Of·course, sir. I should be honoured,' Annunciata said, and curtseyed.

Although he was still in mourning, Ralph determined to make that Christmas a cheerful one at Morland Place, for it was his nature always to struggle against misfortune. Besides, he reasoned, he had his troubles, but there was much to be thankful for. His children were all remarkably healthy, not even suffering from the usual childish ailments, except for little Martin who seemed always to be hurting himself, tumbling down or bumping into things or cutting his fingers. Also the arrangement with Cathy and Elizabeth was working very well indeed. Cathy was a perfect mistress for Morland Place, and had everything running even more smoothly than when Leah was in charge. 'As nice as milk from a cow' Clem said; and Ralph said that Cathy had grown at least three inches since taking up the reins of the household. Elizabeth, though young, was an excellent governess for the children, being both energetic and patient, and the problem of a governor or tutor had been shelved for the moment by sending the older children to St Edward's school.

Another thing to be thankful for was the resumption of a normal relationship with Edward. Nothing had been said on either side about their former quarrel, and Mary's death had wiped it out as a cause of dissent between them. Ralph had turned to Edward so needily, and Edward had responded so generously, that it had made all well again. Edward had promised to spend Christmas with them at Morland Place; Ruth and Kit would, of course, come over; and Crispian was to come down from Coquetdale, bringing his young sisters with him, though Anne was ailing and could not travel, and Sam had declined to leave her. So all in all, it should be a lively season.

Ralph was out on Red Fox, accompanied by Arthur who was gradually replacing Barnabus both in duties and in Ralph's affections, a few days before Christmas, looking over the coverts and deer runs.

'We shall have plenty of hunting while our guests are here,' he said, 'and we want to make sure for the ladies' sakes that it all goes smoothly. Cathy gets bored and poor Elizabeth gets cold if they have to sit around much.' They were riding towards the Ten Thorns, and Ralph checked Fox and sighed and said, 'I suppose we'll have to harbour this side of the Gap. It is such a nuisance not being able to use the Whin. When I think of Master Makthorpe turning us out, I could—'

Arthur coughed nervously, being a little too far away to nudge his master.

'Over there, Master,' he hissed. 'He's over there. Have a care he don't hear you.'

Ralph's head whipped round, and as he stared he drew rein. It was Makthorpe, coming down towards Ten Thorn Gap from the direction of his own house, and he had evidently seen Ralph and was hurrying to a meeting with him – but the strange thing was that he was smiling. At least, Ralph assumed that that was what he was doing, but it was evidently an exercise in which he had had little practice.

They reached the Gap at the same time, and Ralph, seeing Makthorpe draw rein, went through. There was a public road here to Rufforth, and Makthorpe could not prevent him from using it; but Makthorpe had no intention of preventing anything. Still smiling his terrifying smile, he called out to Ralph.

'Ah, Morland, I thought it was you. I wanted to speak to you. Will you step aside a while and have a private word with me?'

'I cannot think of anything I have to say to you that I do not wish to say publicly and in court,' Ralph said sternly.

Makthorpe spread a hand. 'It is about our – quarrel, shall we say – that I want to speak. Step aside a moment, will you not? Perhaps your man would hold our horses.'

Puzzled but intrigued, Ralph dismounted and gave the reins to Arthur. Makthorpe followed suit, and in a moment they were walking away along the line of thorns, Ralph keeping on the open side of his companion just in case. Makthorpe seemed to be having difficulty beginning what he had to say, but Ralph did not help him, and walked in silence, until at last Makthorpe stopped and turned to face him. 'You are having quite a party at Christmastide,' he said. 'I've been told about some of the preparations.'

'What's that to you?'

'I've not been invited.'

Ralph stared in astonishment. 'Is this a new crime on the calendar?' he said. 'How will you bribe a jury to convict me on that score?'

'No, no, you don't understand. Look,' Makthorpe paused for a moment, thinking hard. 'Look, what's the difference between us?' Ralph forbore to answer. 'I'm a landowner, you're a landowner. What's the difference? I've got a lot of land hereabouts now—'

'You've got a lot of my land,' Ralph said.

'Did I steal it from you?' Makthorpe said. 'I bought it, in good faith. Why should I give it back for nothing?'

'You'd get compensation.'

'And what would I buy with that compensation? Where do you think I'd get land like it?' Ralph shrugged. That was not his problem. 'Why do you think I wanted it in the first place? Why do you think I once swore I'd have Morland Place?' Ralph again kept his reply to himself, and Makthorpe nodded as if he had heard the unspoken words. 'I know what you think, and perhaps you're not entirely wrong. But people hereabouts aren't fair to me.' Ralph raised an eyebrow. This was a new complaint. Makthorpe clenched a fist and the words burst out of him. 'You give a party, and everyone wants to come. But no one wants to come to my house, or invites me to theirs. They won't ever forget that my father was a butcher, and that yours was a gentleman. And if I owned all of your land, and lived at Morland Place, they'd still hold it against me.'

He stopped, and Ralph stared at him curiously. Was this the dark secret behind Makthorpe, that he longed to be a gentleman? Or was it a trick? In a way he hoped it was a trick: this new Makthorpe was not worthy of serious opposition.

'Well, so what can I do about it?' he said.

Makthorpe seemed to make up his mind. His eyes narrowed and he fixed Ralph with his glare, more like his old self. 'I want to marry your sister,' he said. Ralph was so taken aback he could not speak. Makthorpe went on.

'You want the north fields back – well, I'll make them her marriage portion, and write it in my will that they're to revert to your heirs after my death. In return, I marry your sister and become part of your family, respectable, and respected. It's a fair bargain.'

Ralph recovered his power of speech, but forbore to use it to its full advantage. 'Why should I do this, to get back what is mine under the law?' was all he said.

Makthorpe's eyes grew narrower still. 'Because I have the means and power to prevent your ever having what is yours under the law. I'll never give up, Morland. I've got money and influence. The north fields will never come back into Morland hands any way but this.' He watched Ralph's face like a cat watching a mousehole. 'Come on, what have you to lose by saying yes? I'm not a bad match, you know. I'm rich, and my estate is unencumbered, which is more than you can say for yours. I'll not ask any dowry. And I'll treat her well – she'll want for nothing. What do you say?'

Ralph was gathering his forces of speech when he suddenly noticed something that had been vaguely troubling his senses since this interview began. Makthorpe had bathed; Ralph was standing downwind of him, and he didn't smell. It was that sudden realization that disarmed him, and instead of delivering the verbal broadside he had prepared, he said only in a cold voice, 'It is not for me to say anything. My sister will marry whom she chooses. I would not force her to marry where her inclination did not lie.'

Makthorpe blinked at that. It was not the answer he had expected, either way.

'Very well,' he said abruptly, and strode away so rapidly that he was on his horse and riding off before Ralph had got back to Arthur.

Ralph thought that that was the end of the matter, but there he had miscalculated. He did not return home all day, taking his dinner at an inn as he rode about his business, and when he did get back in time for supper, Makthorpe had paid a visit and gone. Clem told him so as he came in through the door.

'He came in a quiet, gentlemanlike way, sir, and asked to speak to Miss Cathy. I went to her and she said she'd see him, so I brought him to her in the parlour, and stayed outside myself, in case she should need me. But it was all quiet, sir. He stayed about the quarter of an hour, and then he left, and Miss Cathy said nothing to me, sir, about why he came.'

'It's all right, Clem, I know why he came,' Ralph said. 'Where is Miss Cathy now?'

'She was dressing for supper, sir, but I think I saw her going into the long saloon a bit since.'

Ralph ran up the stairs. Cathy was alone in the saloon, walking back and forth. She had dressed for supper in a plain black gown which, though neat, was not in the least pretty or becoming, and she had pinned up her rather fuzzy hair into a tidy coil on the back of her head. She turned to face him as he came in, folding her hands across her stomach like a nun.

'Cathy,' he began, wondering if she was very distressed; but her face was serene, almost expressionless.

'Makthorpe was here,' she said. 'He came to ask me—'

'I know what he wanted. He spoke to me out in the fields today. I didn't know he would come here.'

'What did you tell him?' she asked.

Ralph hesitated, thinking now that he should have been more forceful, that he should have said the words to Makthorpe that had sprung to mind. The disarming aspect of the man was impossible to describe, seemed incredible at a distance. 'I told him that I would never force you to marry where you did not want.'

Cathy looked at him steadily, and then gave a little sigh, so faint a sigh that afterwards Ralph thought he had imagined it. 'He made me an offer, a very correct offer of marriage,' she said calmly. 'North fields as my portion, to go to your heirs after his death. Everything else to pass to the heirs of my body. No dowry to be asked for. A very generous establishment for my lifetime.'

Ralph made a helpless gesture with his hands. Cathy looked at him steadily.

'I told him I would give him his answer tomorrow. I wanted to know what you said first.'

'Why didn't you just refuse him?' Ralph asked.

'You want north fields back?'

'I'll get them back, through the processes of the law.'

'But the law is expensive, and very slow. Makthorpe says you won't get your land that way.'

Ralph shrugged. 'It may take time—' he said. Cathy turned away and walked once up and down the room. When she came back, her face was set like a mask.

'I'll accept him,' she said.

'But – but Caterpillar,' Ralph cried, appealing with her old name, which seemed to rouse her to something like anger.

'Caterpillar! Catalina Eruca,' she said bitterly. 'I remember the old joke, as perhaps you do not. I am your housekeeper, Ralph, and though that is not unpleasant to me, I should like to have an establishment of my own.'

'You will,' Ralph said. 'You will marry—'

'Marry whom? There are precious few young men, after the war, and those have their pick of the rich and the beautiful. I am neither. I may never have another offer.'

'But *Makthorpe*?'

'He is willing to make me a proper settlement, an establishment as good as Mary had here. Women cannot expect always to marry where their hearts lie. He will treat me well enough.' She looked Ralph in the eye with a mixture of bitter humour and pity that made him want to cry out. 'He loves me, you see.'

Ralph had nothing to say to that. 'If it's what you want,' he said slowly.

'I shall tell him tomorrow,' Cathy said briskly. 'Now,

you had better go and get dressed. Supper will be ready soon.'

Alone again she walked to the end of the room and stared at the leaping flames in the chimney-place, her face thoughtful and distant. She thought of Mary, of Annunciata, of Kit, of Elizabeth, and she could not quarrel with her decision. Love could not endure, but money and property and respectability did, and it was only weakness that necessitated the wiping away of a tear as she heard footsteps in the passage outside.

BOOK THREE

Lion Rampant

When wearied with a world of Woe
To thy safe Bosom I retire
Where Love and Peace and Truth does flow,
May I contented there expire.

Lest once more wandring from that Heav'n
I fall on some base heart unblest;
Faithless to thee, false, unforgiv'n,
And lose my Everlasting rest.

John Wilmot, Earl of Rochester: *A Song*

CHAPTER FIFTEEN

Christmas was very quiet at Whitehall, for Princess Mary died of the smallpox on Christmas Eve. That left only three of the children of Charles I alive – Charles, James, and Henrietta – and the King soon had to say goodbye to his favourite sister, for the Queen cut short her visit and left soon after Christmas, afraid to stay longer with Princess Henrietta, since the latter had never been strong and the infection was rife in London. Plans for her marriage to Phillipe d'Orleans had been completed, despite Prince Rupert's objections, just as Hugo had predicted, and though the Princess seemed quite content with the arrangements, the thought of sending her to such an ungentle husband seemed to make the King even more unhappy at parting with her.

Annunciata was sorry to see her go too: in the short time that she had been at Court, she had spent quite some time in the company of the Princess, and had found a great deal in common with her. It had also made her much closer to the King, who had encouraged the friendship, and had often been seen in the Galleries with an arm round each of 'his two little sisters' as he called them. When he came back from seeing his mother and sister on their way, he said to Annunciata in the hearing of enough people for it to be all round the Court in no time, 'You must comfort me for the loss of Minette by reminding me of her every day, Mistress Morland. You must be my Minette-in-England.'

Those who did not like Barbara Palmer – and they were a legion – repeated the words gleefully, predicting an end to her reign and a swift promotion for the beautiful Yorkshire heiress. Annunciata heard the rumours, and enjoyed the scandal, even when it grew more lively. Wagging tongues seized on her illegitimacy and the mystery of her father, the King's affection for her and the likeness many perceived between her and Princess Minette, and for a few weeks the Galleries and the 'Change bred a series of scandals about her which grew more and more absurd, culminating in her being the natural child of the Martyr King, despite that fact that he had left York three years before she was born.

Annunciata enjoyed it all and did nothing to scotch the rumours. Birch, her maid, looked down her nose at her, and complained to Lucy's maid, and Lucy remonstrated gently with Annunciata, who merely laughed.

'It is not a thing over which I have any control. I cannot stop them talking about me. Besides, it will all be forgotten as soon as the next scandal comes along. You yourself have told me that, that no story lasts more than a week at Whitehall.'

The King appeared not to notice, although it may have been partly to appease his mistress on that score that shortly afterwards he created Roger Palmer Earl of Castlemain, the honour to devolve upon his heirs got upon the body of his wife Barbara. Annunciata was out of circulation at that time, for Anne Hyde had been brought to bed of the Duke of York's child. It was a son, and was Christened Edward, and until the King married the infant was heir apparent to the throne. When Annunciata returned to society from the confinement chamber she discovered that her absence had ended the currency of her scandals, and that she had been replaced by the Castlemain creation.

'The King seems to have lands to give away in Ireland,' Hugo complained as they played at dice together at one of the King's little intimate parties. 'If he can give Roger Palmer a piece of Ireland that big, why can't he give me back my little piece?'

'You don't ask often enough or firmly enough,' Annunciata said. 'And you don't really want it back anyway.

What would you do in Ireland? You'd pine away in the country.'

'That's true,' Hugo said. 'Still, it would be pleasant to have an income, and not to have to make my living from playing at dice and cards.'

'Cheating at dice and cards you mean,' Annunciata said, and threw a venus.

'Now who's cheating?' Hugo said. The King paused behind her chair at that moment, and Hugo appealed to him. 'Your Majesty, you must be the judge. Did you ever see a woman throw the venus as often as Mistress Morland?'

'Not without some help,' the King smiled. 'But then, Mistress Morland is an angel, I firmly believe. What more help does she need?'

'There'll be another scandal if she goes on winning so often,' Hugo grumbled. The King rested his hands lightly on Annunciata's shoulders.

'Another scandal about Mistress Morland? We can't have that.' He approached his mouth to her ear and said, 'Really, the greatest scandal is that someone so beautiful should still be unmarried. We must see about finding a suitable husband for you.' His warm breath tickled her ear for a moment, and then he straightened up and moved on. Annunciata thought it all a joke, and was surprised when she glanced at Hugo again to see that his face was dark with anger. As soon as she looked at him, he transformed his expression into a smile, and she forgot the incident in the pleasures of the gambling, feasting and dancing, but when Jane Birch came to light her to her room, Hugo waylaid her on an empty stairway.

'I must speak to you,' he said, and flicked a glance at Birch.

Jane Birch stood her ground and glared disapprovingly, and Annunciata was annoyed enough to say, 'Stand further off, Birch, and wait for me.'

The maid moved reluctantly a yard or two back, and in the gloom Annunciata turned to Hugo and said in a low voice, 'What can you want with me that won't wait until the morning? There will be another scandal if we are seen talking alone like this.'

Hugo snapped his fingers. 'Scandal, pooh! You are hoping to be a much greater topic of conversation than that. I heard what the King said to you tonight.'

Annunciata was genuinely puzzled. 'He didn't say anything to me that anyone might not hear.'

'He said that he would find you a husband,' Hugo said.

'But what is wrong with that?'

Hugo stared. 'Don't you know? Don't you really know? No, I see that you don't. The King, my dear Mistress Morland, is French enough to have some of the habits of French kings. And a French king never makes an unmarried girl his mistress. It wouldn't be proper.'

Annunciata opened her mouth to protest, and then coloured deeply. Hugo saw it even in the half darkness of the passage, and said, 'So you understand me. All this innocence was just a pose. He is to make you his mistress – if you are not already.'

Annunciata could not understand why Hugo was so angry, and she tried haughtiness on him. 'The King has behaved to me with the kindness of a brother, nothing more,' she said loftily. 'But even if I were to become his mistress, what would be wrong with that?'

'How can you speak like that?' Hugo cried.

Annunciata glanced round at her maid and said, 'Hush! She will hear. Hugo, you have lived at Court a long time, and you have been in foreign courts too. How can you be shocked at the idea of the King taking a mistress?'

'The King may have a thousand mistresses, and I should only applaud him. But not *you*.'

'Why not?' Annunciata cried, frustrated. 'What is wrong with that?'

Hugo bared his teeth in what was almost a grin. 'There are two things wrong with it, lady. One is that I love you.' Annunciata stared in amazement, not having expected this. He took a step nearer, and lifted her hand to his lips. 'And the other,' he said, 'is that you love me.'

Annunciata tried not to smile. 'What are you proposing, my Lord?'

'I propose nothing. I tell you, Madam, that you are to marry me. I cannot wait any longer for you to understand your own heart.'

She put her head up and looked under her eyelids at him like a queen looking at a churl. 'I, sir, am extremely rich, and you are penniless. Is that a match?' Hugo gave a piratical smile, and drew her by her captive hand towards him.

'Ah, lady, you have the money, true, but I have the title, and that, as even the King would tell you, is a very fair match.' And despite the watching servant, he kissed her, and despite the watching servant, she let him.

Ralph was grooming Kingcup with long, hard strokes, and the big yellow stallion was leaning blissfully to the pressure. He believed it important that even a stud stallion should be used to being handled, and gentling the horse himself was a pleasure to him. Also it gave him time to think, and he was much puzzled now. Edward was sitting on a straw bale, well out of range of Kingcup's hooves, just in case, and enjoying watching him as much as Ralph was enjoying the work.

'If it is what she wants,' Edward said, 'and no one is forcing her—'

'Of course I'm not forcing her,' Ralph said, the cadences of his voice moving with the rhythm of his strokes. 'But I wonder if I ought to override her – step in and forbid her – I just don't know. What should I do, Ned?'

'What you must do first, my Ralph, is to make up your mind,' Edward said, smiling a little. 'If you feel you have the right to play the Master and interfere, then you do not also have the right to ask someone else to make up your mind for you.'

Ralph paused and thought about this. 'Yes, you're right, of course.' He rested his elbow on Kingcup's withers while he thought, and the horse looked round curiously and fidgeted because the delicious grooming had stopped.

'Look, Ralph,' Edward said at last, 'Cathy knows what she is doing.'

'But does she?' Ralph said, resuming his work. 'She's very young.'

'My dear, she's seventeen, and a grown woman. She has been running your house for you long enough for you to see that she has a very practical nature. No doubt love and courtship are less important to her than a good establishment. She is very level-headed, and sensible enough to judge the situation and choose what's best for her.'

'But a man like that – a man she doesn't like—?'

Edward shrugged. 'I am very willing to believe he appears differently to her than to us. Are you sure your scruples are not on your own behalf – because you do not want him in the family?'

'Oh, as to that,' Ralph said, 'I think he will not get the bargain he has spoken for. People will not think him more respectable because he has married my sister.'

'Unless your sister makes him more respectable,' Edward said.

Ralph straightened up and slapped Kingcup on the rump to move him over, and came out from the stall. 'I hadn't thought of that,' he said.

The wedding was not to take place until May, to give Cathy a chance to find and train a replacement for herself as housekeeper, a difficult task in which Ruth offered to help her. Ruth, alone of the family, understood what Cathy was about, but typically would not interfere even to the extent of giving an opinion. Opinion amongst the servants was fairly equally divided: between those who thought it was a good thing because Makthorpe was so rich, and those who thought it a bad thing because he was not a gentleman. Makthorpe wisely made few and very formal visits to Morland Place, where it was remarked that his appearance was much improved, and his manners less offensive than everyone remembered.

The housekeeper problem was solved in an unexpected way when Francis arrived at Shawes to consolidate his plans with Kit for the expedition to Birnie. He had exhanged letters with his mother all through the winter and had been worried by her isolation at Tods Knowe.

'I wish she could come and live down here,' he said. 'I wonder would Ruth give her a home at Shawes.' Ruth, when applied to, saw the solution immediately – Arabella was the ideal person to take over the running of Morland Place. It was soon and speedily arranged, and the escort that was to ride with Frank and Kit to Northumberland was to bring Arabella back. It was also arranged that Sabine, who was growing wild from lack of discipline, should go to Coquetdale to live with Anne and Sam for a year or two, which meant that, with the older boys at school, Elizabeth had only Martin and Daisy to look after, which eased matters considerably.

The news of Annunciata's betrothal to Lord Ballincrea and the stir made by Kit's approaching departure completed the rout of Cathy's betrothal as subject of dissent, and only Kit went on feeling vaguely outraged. The evening before his departure he went to Morland Place to say his adieux, and when Cathy came to wish him luck in his venture he drew her to one side and said;

'I suppose by the time I come back again you will be wed to this man.'

'Yes. Unless—' Cathy said, and stopped.

'Unless what?' Kit said, and he sounded almost angry.

'Unless – you come back very quickly,' Cathy finished.

He had the feeling that was not what she had been going to say, but he could not think of any other 'unless'.

'Look, Cathy,' he began, and she raised her eyes to him quickly. He didn't know how to go on. 'Do you really want to marry him?'

'What is the alternative?' she asked quietly.

Kit frowned. The alternative was, of course, not to marry him, but Kit knew she didn't mean that. At last he said, 'But you don't love him.'

'Few women are lucky enough to marry where they love,' she said. She paused for a moment, looking at him, and then when it became obvious that he was not going to say anything else, she said, 'Good luck with your venture, Kit. I hope you get everything you want.' And she turned away abruptly, leaving Kit feeling vaguely dissatisfied. But Cathy's face when he looked at her again was so closed that it would have taken a determined man to reopen a conversation with her. A little later he rode back to Shawes, and comforted himself with the thought that she wouldn't really go through with it. He could not imagine coming back to Shawes and finding Cathy married to Makthorpe, and so he chose to believe that it would not, could not happen.

The King give his permission for her marriage to Lord Ballincrea so readily that Annunciata decided there was nothing in his attitude to her but the elder-brotherly kindness she saw him display towards Princess Henrietta. Ruth was asked for her consent, and after consulting Richard, Lucy and Edward as to what sort of a man Hugo McNeill was, she gave it, and even, to Ellen's disgust, agreed to the wedding's taking place at Whitehall.

'My young miss to be wed away from home?' Ellen complained.

Ruth was unmoved. 'She has more to gain there than here. Shawes will always be waiting for her.' It mystified

Ellen even more that Ruth did not want to go to London for the wedding, but to Annunciata it did not even need explaining. It was as if Shawes and her mother were a different life, on a different planet. She could not imagine taking Hugo to Yorkshire any more than she could imagine her mother at Whitehall.

The King's kindness towards Annunciata continued. He offered to give her away in the absence of any close male relative, to allow her to be married in the Chapel Royal, and by the Bishop of London; he had new apartments allotted to Annunciata and Hugo, promoted her to Lady-in-Waiting, and promised her a position in the Queen's household when his marriage negotiations, which had been going on since February, were completed. He also made Hugo Gentleman of the Privy Chamber and Keeper of the King's Sweet Coffer, and gave him an honorary commission as a colonel of the Life Guards which gave him a small but welcome income; and he gave Annunciata a magnificent wedding-present of a string of pearls, which she wore on her wedding-day, and six gold plates.

He also made Richard's two sons choristers of the Chapel Royal, a position which would be likely to lead to appointments as Gentlemen of the Chapel when they were older, and promised to give Richard a knighthood in the coronation honours in April. Lucy stoutly maintained that these two things were an acknowledgement of Richard's services to the crown; but though Richard had no doubt that the King valued him, he was also sure that his value would not have been acknowledged without the catalyst of the King's fondness for Annunciata. The coronation honours also included the Earldom of Clarendon for Hyde, which pleased Richard, and comforted the Lord Chancellor and his daughter and son-in-law a little for the loss of Anne's son, who had lived only a few weeks.

The wedding took place at the end of March, and because of the King's well-known interest, and his presence at the ceremony, it was the best-attended function of the spring besides the coronation itself. The King, Prince Rupert, the Duke and Duchess of York, Chancellor Hyde, the Earl and Countess of Castlemaine, the Duke of Albemarle, Sir Henry and Lady Bennet, Coventry, Mildmay, Herbert, Killigrew, Talbot, Nicholas – all were there, and all brought presents for the most popular couple of the moment, some from affection, some from expedience, and some because it seemed they were the rising stars. After the ceremony there was a party in the Ballincreas' new apartments, and during the feast a messenger came in with a letter of congratulations from Princess Henrietta, accompanied by a parcel containing her wedding-gift to Annunciata. With tears in her eyes Annunciata opened the parcel. In a small gold box was a gold-and-ivory oval on which was painted an exquisite miniature of the Princess herself. The King, looking over her shoulder, took the thing gently from her hands and examined it, and when he met Annunciata's eyes, his too were wet.

'It is the most precious of all my wedding gifts,' she said softly. 'I shall wear it always.'

The King's smile was tender. 'Your love for my sister is the most precious gift you can give me,' he said.

When the dancing began, the King led off with the bride, and Hugo had to wait until Prince Rupert and the Duke of York had danced with her before he could take her hand.

'Never mind,' he said, 'once they have put us to bed, you will be mine entirely, and they will be able to do nothing but imagine my bliss.' Annunciata's eyes shone so brightly as she looked up into his that it brought a lump to his throat which made further speech impossible.

Much, much later she lay in his arms in the big bed in their new apartments and listened to the revellers crossing the courtyard below. Hugo stroked the loose hair from her damp forehead and she shifted herself more comfortably in his arms, her head on his shoulder, and kissed the base of his throat, the only part of him her lips could reach.

'Are you happy, my lady?' he murmured. She sighed from the depths of her soul for answer, and Hugo smiled. 'The bliss they imagine cannot come anywhere near to the truth,' he said.

'Why do you sound surprised?' Annunciata asked. He kissed her brow.

'You notice too much, heart of my heart. Why am I surprised? Because – because the sinner cannot imagine heaven, can he? Would not the homeless wanderer be surprised at coming home?'

'I don't know what you're talking about,' she murmured contentedly, kissing his throat again. 'How delicious your skin smells. Like grass.'

Hugo laughed. 'If you are my heaven, I shall be yours. I shall shew you things you have never even dreamed of. Look at you, lodged under my side like a gull in the side of a wave. Bird that you are, never fly from me, Annunciata. Promise me.'

'Why should I go?' she murmured, growing sleepy now. 'Where should I go?'

'Nowhere,' he said, holding her tighter. 'That's right, sleep now. Sleep in my arms.' He looked down at her, the relaxation of her lovely face, her lips softly parted, the dark fans of her lashes trembling on her cheek as she drifted into sleep, and loving her was so much and so new that his soul did not know how to manage it, was restless with it as if with a pain from which there was no ease. He went on speaking softly, though he knew she was asleep now and could not hear. 'You do not love me as I love you, I know that; but I can make you love me too much ever to leave me. Sleep, I will protect you, I will keep you. From your own innocent courage I will protect you. Bold, bright and fearless, who would not want you. He shall not have you, lady. I have come home in you – I shall be your home, too.'

For Annunciata, it was an idyllic summer. The Court moved with the hot weather to Richmond, to Hampton, to Windsor, and where the King went, Hugo and Annunciata went, drifting gradually from the staid and respectable society she had been used to keep to the wilder company of the new young people, for whom pleasure was the be-all and end-all of life. As a favourite of the King, she was much feted, and yet she occupied an unusual position in the Court, at once fashionable and unfashionable. Nothing could ever be hidden for long in that closed society, and so it was well known that though Annunciata rode and hunted, supped and danced with the King, she did not lie with him. He gave her gifts, honoured her family, sought her company, and did not take her to his bed, and so, the Court reasoned, there must be something else at the root of it. Rumours of her parentage were revived, and once more it became the fashion to gossip about Lady Ballincrea.

Annunciata only laughed at it. She was in love with the King, in love with Hugo, in love with life. It was not the fashion for a husband and wife to make much of each other, and so in a society where most scandals concerned the discovery of adulteries, the Ballincreas were a scandal for the opposite reason. They went everywhere together, rode together, played cards together, dined together, and it was soon said that they were more like twin brothers than husband and wife. No sooner was it said than fresh stories were invented. One of the Duchess of York's women, a Mistress Hobart, was known to enjoy dressing in men's clothing and performing unnatural acts with members of her own sex, and it was soon known for fact that Lady Ballincrea had been Mistress Hobart's first victim. But the story, like other stories, slid off Annunciata like water from a duck's feathers. Scandal seemed to have no power to stick to her that summer.

She and Hugo were invited everywhere, to every party, dance, supper, ball, picnic, hunt, water-pleasure; it became fashionable to admire her beauty and wonder over her unfashionable attachment to her husband. Ladies copied her riding habits, and those who had been wont to follow the hunt in carriages took to the saddle again. Her hairstyles and gowns were copied with more or less success, and face-paint was applied *à la vicomtesse* in an attempt to reproduce her fresh-cheeked, unpainted look. She wore the Princess Henrietta's miniature and the pearl and amethyst cross on her Court gowns, and miniatures and crosses became the rage and were sold in various forms in the galleries and 'Changes. The only thing about Annunciata that was not copied was her marital fidelity, and the same ladies who admired and copied her fluttered around Hugo at every opportunity, hoping for the distinction of being the first to lure him into infidelity, even while their husbands danced attendance on Annunciata and wrote poems to her chastity.

The Court was in London in May for the opening of the first Parliament of the reign, and a few days later to receive Elizabeth of Bohemia, known as the Winter Queen – she was King Charles' aunt, and Prince Rupert's mother, sister of King Charles I. She had been very beautiful in her youth, and even now, after a lifetime of sadness and trouble, she retained her gaiety and spirit, so that people saw in her what she had been rather than what she was. She took up residence in the house of Lord Craven, her lifelong correspondent and friend. Prince Rupert had gone abroad immediately after the coronation on business for the King, and was not there to greet her; but the King treated her kindly, and the staider elements at Court paid her respect. Annunciata was struck by the family resemblance between her and the King. She had the Stuart dark eyes and charming smile. Had the King looked more like his father's family and less like his mother's, he would have been handsome indeed.

In June Annunciata discovered that she was pregnant, was vaguely pleased, and was touched and surprised at how deeply the news seemed to affect her husband. The King, too, was delighted – he loved children, and acknowledged a number of bastards of his own, including the one that Lady Castlemaine was in the process of gestating. The quality of his pleasure in Annunciata's pregnancy was such that the outer circle of Court began to whisper that he was the father of her baby, though the inner circle knew better. Annunciata took pregnancy very much for granted, and was surprised when, in August, after much prompting by Jane Birch, Hugo told her that she must not ride any more, and suggested that they moved back to London. Annunciata resisted that suggestion, and for the rest of the month sulked furiously about the summer palaces, fretting to be out on horseback. But in September when the whole Court moved back to Whitehall she recovered her temper, and set about enjoying her retirement by redecorating their apartments and having her portrait painted by Peter Lely, the newly-arrived Court painter.

She had herself painted in a loose, flowing robe which hid her growing bulge, her hair hanging unconfined over her shoulders and down her back. The King gave her a puppy to amuse her and compensate her for the loss of Goldeneye's company, and Annunciata called it Charlemagne and asked Lely to include it in the picture. She also insisted that he paint in the miniature of Princess Henrietta, and when he objected that it would not look right on an informal robe, she decided that it, and the pearl-and-amethyst cross, should be depicted lying on a small table at her elbow, to which the artist agreed.

Despite the redecoration and the portrait and the puppy, she began to find herself feeling lonely, for she was too big to go out much, and pregnancy made her sleepy in the evenings. She insisted that Hugo did not miss parties on her account, and he made only a perfunctory protest. The King called in to see her when he could, as did one or two others, but after six months of being the most feted beauty at Court, she found herself suddenly dropped in a backwater, watching the main stream of life passing her at a distance. She wished very much for some female company, but the only person she could think of that she would have liked to see was Lucy, and she was not in London. Richard had been sent on an embassy to Cleves, where he was to meet up eventually with Prince Rupert, and Lucy had gone with him. For the first time since coming to London, she thought longingly of home, of Shawes and Mother and Ellen and even of Cathy and Elizabeth. Then, one morning when Hugo had gone off to play tennis with the King, a visitor was announced.

'Who is it?' Annunciata said crossly. 'I don't want to see anyone if all they can do is tell me how much I am missing. That cat Bellenden yesterday had nothing to say but how everyone that used to call is flocking about Bess Hamilton.'

'It's a gentleman, my lady,' Birch said with massive disapproval. 'He asked for my Lord, and when I said you were alone he said he would speak with you. He *said*,' her tone of voice implied the highest degree of disbelief, 'he *said* that his name was Morland.'

Annunciata jumped up. 'Ralph!' she cried. 'It must be Ralph. Is he a fair-haired man, tall, with grey eyes?'

'I couldn't say, my lady,' Birch said dismissively.

'Oh never mind, send him in, do. It must be my cousin Ralph.' She ran over to the looking glass in the corner and rearranged the folds of her robe, and pinched her cheeks to make them glow, and then picked up Charlemagne and arranged herself on a little gilt chair with the puppy on her lap. Birch reappeared in the doorway, stepped back, and reluctantly allowed the visitor in. He took a step into the room, gave a wickedly ironic grin, and went into a low bow that was so subtle a parody even Annunciata was not sure whether it was meant to be real or not.

'My dear Lady Ballincrea,' Edward said. 'How delighted I am to see you looking so well!'

'Now, let me look at you,' Edward said when Birch had brought wine and reluctantly left them. Annunciata laughed and put her hands in his, and he stepped back and then twirled her around. 'You know,' he said, 'I have never been an admirer of *la femme enceinte* – in fact, I have often thought women should lock themselves away from conception to confinement – but I must say, my dear Viscountess, that you quite reconcile me to the condition.'

'Oh nonsense – I look quite gross, and you know it,' Annunciata said.

'But your cheek is pink, your eye is bright, your smile is radiant. If it is not your pregnancy, then it must be my presence that makes you glow. Think now, my Nancy, to what would you like it attributed?'

Annunciata felt her running heart trip. 'No one but you ever called me that,' she said. They looked into each other's eyes, and she remembered, dangerously, the many times she had flirted with him in the past. Abruptly she drew her hands from his and went to the little table where the wine-tray stood. 'Will you take some wine, Commissioner?' Her hand shook a little as she poured, but she soon steadied it. 'There—' she turned and held out the goblet to him, and he was standing exactly as he was, his eyes fixed on hers unwaveringly. 'Don't, Edward, don't look at me like that,' she said breathlessly.

'Do you remember the time we ran away for the day, and rode out onto the moors?' he said. She did not answer, but her expression told him she did. He advanced and took the goblet, his hands covering hers so that she could not let it go. 'Do you remember what I predicted for you?' She nodded. 'This is the beginning, my Nance, only the beginning. Great days are ahead for you. I have been hearing about you – the darling of the Court.'

'Not so much the darling now,' she said with a little rueful smile. 'You see me here, alone, deserted.'

'Oh, that will pass. Once you have had the brat, all will be well. They say, dearest, that the King is mightily in love with you?'

'He is very kind,' Annunciata said, 'but there is nothing improper.'

'So they say,' Edward said. His eyes were searching her face as if for the answer to some unspoken question. 'They say also that Lady Ballincrea is the only virtuous woman at Court?' There was the faintest breath of a question in the statement.

Annunciata said, 'Hugo and I are very much in love.'

'Ah,' said Edward, and he released her hands, took the goblet, and toasted her. 'To the only happily married couple at Whitehall,' he said, and then he smiled and cocked his head at her. 'But my dear, you know, don't you, that you cannot further your career until you have rid yourself of these old-fashioned scruples?'

Annunciata laughed. 'You talk like a courtier, Edward,' she said. 'But come now, tell me all the news. I have heard nothing from home for so long. And tell me about your life as a Commissioner. Mother writes that you are mightily well thought of in Yorkshire.'

Edward led her to a chair, and drew another up close to her, and began to tell her all the news, and Annunciata abandoned herself to the bliss of a long and uninterrupted chat with someone whose interests were closely identified with her own, who had known her all her life, and who understood her. It was better, in some ways, than being with Hugo, for Hugo had not known her as a child, and there was nothing quite as powerful to charm away unhappiness as 'do you remember'. Yet as she listened and chattered and laughed she had the feeling that something had gone on in their first interchange that she had not thoroughly grasped. Some question had been asked or answered, some warning delivered, some information imparted which she had not understood.

Edward told her of his own life, his job and how respectable he now was; about Morland Place, and how Arabella, Frank's mother, had taken up residence; of Cathy's unexpected marriage to Makthorpe; of Kit's departure for Scotland. She told him all that he did not already know about her life at Court, shewed him her half-finished portrait, described the work she was having done on the rooms, and how she and the King had very similar taste in decoration. Birch came in twice with various excuses, and looked disapproving at how relaxed her mistress was, sprawling in the window-seat with her bare ankles shewing where her gown had fallen open, and with a most indecent colour in her cheeks, while the so-called 'Master Morland' held her hand and made her laugh in a most abandoned way.

'How comfortable it is to have you here!' Annunciata exclaimed to Edward at one point, and did not notice that he looked a little strangely at her. When dinner-time came, Hugo did not return, but instead sent a message to say that he would not be back until supper-time, and Annunciata discovered she was not at all disappointed.

'I'll send Tom out to bring us some dinner in, and we shall eat together here, just the two of us,' she said.

'That would be delightful,' Edward said gravely.

Annunciata laughed. 'How formal you are! Oh, but I'm glad Hugo is not coming back, for we shall be able to have a comfortable chat together, and if you are going away again tomorrow we shall need all afternoon to get all our talking done!'

'Should we ever be done talking, Nancy? I doubt it,' Edward said, smiling. 'But I, too, am glad Hugo is not coming back though never tell him I said so.'

'Oh, Hugo would not mind,' Annunciata said. 'He loves you.'

'I'm glad you know it,' Edward said. 'I hope you know that he loves you too.'

'Well, of course,' she said. 'Now what shall we have for dinner? Oh Edward, it's so lovely to have you here. I wish you didn't have to go away again.'

'I don't have to,' Edward said. 'But I want to. Shall I ring for your servant?'

CHAPTER SIXTEEN

It was a strange winter: in December it was as warm as
May, and the spring flowers, confused, came through the
earth and withered amongst the fallen autumn leaves.
Cathy gathered some crocuses and brought them indoors
and put them in water in a little stone jam-jar – Makthorpe's
house did not run to such frippery as glass bowls. They
smelled warm and damp; perhaps because they were out of
place, out of their time, they smelled of loneliness. That
was the hardest thing about being married to him – not
him, not the house, not her social position, but the
loneliness. She had grown up in a houseful of people, and
now she was alone all day except for the servants. Even her
husband, poor company though he was, would have been
welcome to her, but he spent all day out about his business.

She was still standing in the parlour with the crocuses to
her nose when one of the servants came in – a draggle-
tailed slut, like most of them, for the respectable servants
would not work for Makthorpe – and said, 'There's a lady
here, Missus, come to see you.'

Cathy stared, hardly taking it in. A lady? 'A visitor?' she
said aloud. The servant stared at her with helpless, near-
idiot eyes. 'Shew her in. Bring her in here to me.' The girl
went away, and came back a moment later followed by
Ruth.

'I was passing nearby, and thought I should see how you
are,' Ruth said in lieu of greeting. She was in riding habit
and boots, her stiff reddish hair escaping from under an
old-fashioned black hood, and she looked about her with
a frank curiosity which made Cathy smile.

The slut had vanished again, and Cathy said, 'I am glad
to see you. I would offer you refreshment, but I'm afraid

it would be more trouble than it is worth to try. It has taken me all this time to get the servants to understand their daily duties, and a request out of the ordinary would confuse them.'

Ruth waved a hand, peeling off one of her gloves the while. 'I require nothing. I cannot stay long – I have a young colt out there who will not stand being tied. But how do you fare? You look pale.'

'I am not so often out as I was,' Cathy said.

Ruth glanced around her. 'It is better here than I imagined.'

'I want for nothing,' Cathy said a little stiffly. 'And the servants are only pathetic and stupid, not wicked. Have you come to report back? Or to see if I have learned to regret my actions?'

Ruth almost smiled, and her eyes were understanding. 'I have not yet learned to condemn you,' she said. 'Perhaps I understand why you did it.'

'He is kind to me,' Cathy said defiantly. 'He loves me.'

Ruth studied her a moment. 'Well enough,' she said. 'If you want a place to go to, you can come to me. Remember that.'

'I'll remember it. But I will not come.' There was an awkward silence. 'Tell me the news of home,' she said.

Ruth's eyebrow went up. 'Home?' she said. 'Oh, things are much as they were. I have a letter from Annunciata, who is very large, and expects the child at Christmas. She speaks mostly of Court matters. The King's bride is expected in spring, and there is much preparation. She will have to move out to a house when the bairn is born, and she and her husband have been looking for a suitable place. She asks for more money, but that is nothing unusual.'

'And what of Morland Place?' Cathy asked, not meeting Ruth's eye.

'Arabella's rheumatism is better. Ralph was bitten in the shoulder by Kingcup, and it won't heal, even though

Arabella sewed the wound up with black thread. Edmund has a bad cough, and little Ralph led a band of boys from the school on a honey-stealing raid and was the only one not to get stung, which is what you would expect of that young man. And Elizabeth misses you.' She fixed Cathy with her gaze. 'Will you not visit? Come for Christmas. Why should you cut yourself off?'

Cathy did not answer. The reason was that she would not have her husband slighted by her family, but to admit that was as bad as letting it happen. Instead she said, 'And what news of Kit and his venture?'

'He has his land again – did you not hear?'

'How should I hear? Who is to tell me?'

Ruth ignored this. 'Poor Frank,' she said. 'He wanted so much to have a good fight on his hands, after the taking of London was so easy. He and Kit and Crispian got their men together and pitched near the castle and worked out their campaign like Prince Rupert trying to take Austria! And then when finally they marched up to deliver their demand, the Scots simply slipped away and scattered.'

'That does not sound like the Scots,' Cathy said.

'It seems they were just a band of gypsies. The people who had taken the place at first had left it because it was too uncomfortable and too big to care for without a large number of servants. They left the place half-derelict, and the gypsies moved in. Kit said it was in a dreadful state, and the smell fit to kill a Christian, so the only battle his army had was the battle against the dirt and squalor. Frank and Crispian have gone home long since, of course, but Kit will be there for some months yet, until it is all in order again and he has found a fit steward to take charge in his absence. But from his letters, I don't think he will stay away from there very long. I think it will be his home from now on, and he will only visit us here.'

Cathy nodded, keeping her eyes fixed on the crocuses as if they alone interested her.

'And now,' Ruth said, 'I must be going, or my youngster will break his reins. Am I to tell them you are well, then?'

'Yes,' Cathy said. There seemed nothing else to say, except, as Ruth reached the door, 'Thank you for coming.'

Ruth made a strange kind of grimace, and was gone without further comment.

She knew that Makthorpe had heard about the visit when he came in that evening by the wariness of his demeanour. She did not trouble him to ask, but said at once, 'I have had a visitor. My cousin Ruth, from Shawes.'

'And what did she want?' he asked, his voice rough. He hunched his shoulders defensively, and to Cathy it made him look like a cold bird on a bare branch.

'She wanted to see if I was all right, and to offer me a home if I wanted to leave you,' Cathy said, her tone indifferent.

He hunched still further. 'And what did you tell her?' he said surlily. 'That you would go?'

Cathy looked at him. 'I never lie to you, not even the politic lies that are between husband and wife. Why then do you trust me so little? If I wanted to go, I would have gone.'

'If you wanted to go, you have good enough cause,' he said, and his voice grew small despite him, and the eyes that met hers were defiant and afraid.

'I see no cause,' she said gently.

'A marriage unconsummated is no marriage,' he said. 'You could leave me and get an annulment.'

'I don't want to leave you,' she said. 'I am your wife.'

'Not properly—'

'Only you and I know. Do you think I would tell anyone? And as far as I am concerned, I am your wife, and there's an end.'

He came a step towards her now, his big frame still hunched, his eyes humble. It hurt her to see it; she hated his love for her and his dependence on her, not for itself, nor because of who he was or even what he was, but because she could not return it, and it angered her that any creature should love unloved, should be grateful for kindness. She had spent her life thus; she wanted everything that lived to be proud and invulnerable.

'Cathy,' he said shyly. As he drew near her she could smell him, but it was no longer an unpleasant smell, though still strong. He smelled of the day's sweat and the open air and horses and tobacco. He would bathe, either that night or the next day. He would never forget again, since the time, quietly and casually, she had reminded him. 'Cathy,' he said, 'you know I can't help it.'

'I know,' she said.

'With other girls – other *women* – you know what I mean – but with you – it's because—'

'I know,' she said. She knew. It was because he had never had a decent woman. He could tumble a slut or a whore or a servant-girl, but Cathy, plain faced, flat chested Cathy, unmanned him; he loved her. She wanted to shut her eyes as the memories of their nights flooded her mind – the sweating and fumbling in the dark, the repeated attempts, the repeated failure, the smell of his humiliation, eventually his tears. Her own body, the desired and unattainable, lying cool and passive between them like a barrier; she wanted to shut her eyes to shut out the memories, but she could not for she knew he would know what she was thinking, so she looked into his face, not seeing him.

'Cathy,' he began again, and then a paroxysm of coughing seized him, and stopped him. It was one of those coughs that went on and on, and she was able to step back with good excuse. In the end he hawked and spat into the fire, and was instantly contrite.

'Oh – I forgot—' he said.

'Your cough is worse?' she said.

He shrugged. 'It is no better. But everyone is coughing. In the city today—'

'I will get you some honey to soothe your throat, and

tonight I will rub goosegrease into your chest for you,' she said briskly. He did not smile, but his eyes accepted the kindness. Since he could not be a lover to her, they seemed to be slipping more into the relationship of father and daughter. It made him seem older than his years.

Annunciata woke and found the bed empty again. So he had not come back. She was too big to go to parties any more, but she insisted he went, and he sometimes came back very late. Once he had not come back at all, but had sauntered in the next morning when she was eating a plateful of stewed gooseberries to say that he had slept with Kynaston rather than disturb her so late. She missed him, missed his warmth in the bed beside her, missed his lovemaking. But all would be well when the bairn was born. She could not expect him to sit every night in the apartment doing nothing. She was so big now that even going about in daylight was embarrassing, and Hugo had continued the house-hunt alone, and had chosen a small house in King Street and was having it furnished. It meant he was often away during the day too. She was disappointed that she could not share in the business but, as he reasoned, they must have the house ready to move into as soon as the baby was born. 'And you know we have the same taste in things,' he said. 'You will like everything I have done, I promise.'

The house was turning out to be very expensive, and there was everything for the laying-in to be bought as well. Ruth had never refused money when Annunciata asked, but she hated to be continually asking, and with Hugo's extravagance and her dislike of living on credit, she was always exceeding her income. The King was being very kind, however, and made her frequent discreet gifts. He had promised Hugo an earldom very soon to make up for not being able to give him back his Irish lands, and when the baby was born he had said he would rent Annunciata a large part of Northumberland at a peppercorn rent so that she could lease it out at a profit.

It was almost impossible to get comfortable in bed, and she had been sleeping sitting up, propped by bolsters and pillows. She felt as if there was something very sharp in amongst the pillows, pressing into the small of her back. She shifted restlessly, and then heard the noises in the anteroom. For a moment she went cold with fear, thinking it was a robber, but then she recognized Gilles' voice murmuring something. She called out to him. The second time she called he called back.

'*Un instant*, milady.' In a moment he came through into the bed chamber, looking rather ruffled. He carried no light, but was backlit from candles in the next room. Annunciata leaned through the bedcurtains.

'What is it?' she said softly. 'I heard the noise in the next room.' Gilles gave a very graphic shrug, illustrative of regret at having woken her and reassurance that it was a matter of no importance that caused the noise. 'It is your master?' she asked.

'Yes, milady. I am helping him to sleep on the chaise-longue *là-bas*, just for tonight. He thought it better. Rather than disturb you when you sleep so ill. *Mais alors*, we have disturbed you *tout de meme*.' He gave a charmingly comic bow of gentlemanly regret. Annunciata read through it to a more serious sympathy beneath.

'How is he?' she asked softly.

Gilles' eyes were suddenly sharp, as though he contemplated saying something and then rejected it reluctantly at the last moment. 'A little disguised, as the gallants say, milady.'

'Disguised?' She did not know the expression. Gilles became very down-to-earth.

'Foxed,' he said blankly. 'He drink, he puke, he drink again. Now he sleep. By and by, maybe puke again. I am sorry, milady. I thought he should not come back here so, but he would come, and then it seemed better not to make

293

un spectacle dans les corridors. I shall sleep there with him, he will not disturb you.'

Annunciata sighed. 'I was not asleep anyway. I have a pain in my back. Gilles, if you can leave him for a moment, could you bring me something to drink?'

'But of course, milady. But if you have a *mal*, should I not call your woman?'

Annunciata considered Jane Birch's ministrations and shook her head. 'It is only backache. If you could bring me some ale, that may make me sleepy.'

'I will bring it, milady. And I shall be by the door here, awake. If you need me, call softly, I will hear.'

'Thank you, Gilles,' she said, and they exchanged a look of sympathetic understanding before he left her.

She did not see Hugo the next morning. Gilles hustled him away to bathe and shave as soon as he woke, and by the time he was to visit his wife, she was in labour and shut away from the world of men. For a long time the doctors and midwives argued about whether or not she was in labour, for she had no contractions, just a continuous, broad, knife-like pain in the back, but she was only two weeks off her time, and they had no reason not to play safe. So while Annunciata hobbled round the room between two strong girls, the rest of the servants stripped the bed chamber and refurbished it as the lying-in chamber. By the end of the day the chamber was fully equipped, the pain was just the same, and Annunciata, who had vomited continuously all day, had retired to the great bed, too weak to walk any more, despite the midwives' scoldings.

That was Monday. By Tuesday morning the situation had not changed, except that Annunciata was lapsing for short periods into unconsciousness. The King sent his own doctor to her, who said she should be given broth and wine to strengthen her, and they duly fed her, and she duly vomited it up again. A raging thirst took hold of her, but she could keep nothing down. Even tiny sips of milk that she took to moisten her mouth and throat would come up again in half an hour or so.

She was in a delirium most of the time. The pain was no longer inside her: it had become too big, and now she was inside the pain, and through its transparent walls she saw the normal life of the world going on. She saw the light change as the sun moved across the room, saw people come and go, saw faces loom over her and retreat, saw their lips moving, sometimes even heard the words: the King was frantic with worry for her, they assured her; her husband was in an apartment nearby, and it was all Gilles could do to stop him rushing in to her. *Foxed*, she murmured. She suddenly seemed to see everything very clearly, she understood things without needing explanations, she read people's thoughts without needing their words. Night fell, darkness seeped into the room, and Birch came with candles, looking as neat and disapproving and unflurried as ever. The pain was growing thicker, still transparent, but a denser barrier between her and the world. She could not hear much now, and her lapses of consciousness were no different to her from wakefulness. From time to time the doctors examined her and talked together and went away again. Then Birch came near and looked down at her and she knew that she was dying.

A priest, I must see a priest, she said, and she could feel her lips moving, but she did not know if she was making any sound. She repeated it, kept on repeating it. The faces that looked at her did not seem to notice. Birch swam through her vision and she reached out to grab her arm and attract her attention, but to her amazement her arm did not move, would not respond to her command. Perhaps it is too late, perhaps I am dead already. She found Birch's eyes and looked the urgency, and Birch leaned down to her and said, 'What?'

A priest, she whispered, and when Birch nodded understanding and straightened up she was so grateful and relieved that she would have wept if there had been enough moisture left in her body. The priest came, and then the King sent four of his own chaplains, and they knelt beside the bed and prayed in relays. At midnight they gave her the last rites, and she sank back gratefully into the arms of the pain. And that was Tuesday.

She woke at dawn, surprised still to be alive. Birch was there, and as soon as she opened her eyes the servant brought wine and wet her lips, and then as Annunciata struggled to lick them, she lifted her head and supported it gently and fed her little sips of wine. The pain was different now, not grinding and all-over, but griping and in one place. The wine did not come back, and Jane Birch smiled a grim little smile – the first Annunciata had ever seen on her face – and fed her a couple of spoonsful of broth laced with brandy. The room seemed quiet – all the onlookers that had crowded around her had retreated to the other end of the room. Only one priest and one doctor were at the bedside. Annunciata asked questions with her eyes, and Jane Birch answered them.

'I sent them all away. They were troubling you,' she said. 'You were crying in your sleep. They used up the air,' she said, and it didn't make sense to Annunciata. 'It is seven of the clock on Wednesday. Can you take a little more broth? You are too weak to labour.' Annunciata managed to press her hand. 'What is it? The pain? Different? Like a hand squeezing?' She closed her eyes for a moment. 'God be praised. Doctor, come here.'

The new pain was easier to bear. Birch fed her sips of broth, and soon she was drunk enough not to mind the pain. 'Foxed,' she said quite clearly. Then there was a gush of hot wetness. 'I'm bleeding,' was her thought. She was frightened. There seemed to have been so much wetness, she must be bleeding to death. 'The waters,' the doctor said, and she remembered Mary Moubray in the hayfield saying, 'The waters have broken.'

'Not long now,' Birch said, pressing her hand.

'The pain has gone,' Annunciata whispered. Was it over? Was the baby dead? She clutched Birch's hand, the only surety in the world. Was it dead? Had she killed her child with the pain? But then something inside her seemed to open up like a flower, and she felt a live thing, a live, moving, wriggling thing, forcing its way without her volition down through her body towards the world. Her eyes met Birch's and she knew that she knew. The baby! 'The baby!' she cried. There was a murmur from the watching crowds, and they all involuntarily stepped forward a little, the better to see, but Annunciata was no longer aware of them, or of anything save only herself, her baby, and Birch, her new-found friend.

There was no more pain after that, and everything was very quick. At half past eight on Wednesday morning it was all over, and Birch straightened her aching back with a sense of relief and triumph. Annunciata smiled at her sleepily, the pain forgotten, sinking into an exhausted sleep too deep to hold thoughts or dreams. Birch looked at her for a moment and then turned away, ushering the onlookers out. Outside in the anteroom she found Gilles, his brow furrowed.

'How is milady?' he asked fearfully. It had been going on so long he thought she must be dead, and he didn't want to hear the words. Birch looked exhausted, as if she herself had laboured those two-and-a-half days.

'Asleep,' she said. 'She will be all right. Strong as a horse, those up-country gentry-women.'

'And the baby?' Gilles said eagerly. He had a soft place for little ones.

'Twins,' Birch said with grim satisfaction. 'A boy and a girl. Both healthy. And big – Our Lord alone knows how she ever got them to birth. Where is he? He must be told.'

And Gilles wriggled, unwilling to be a party to the shame. 'All day Monday he wait,' he said. 'But it was too much for him. Monday night—' He shrugged. 'And since

297

then—' He met Birch's eyes reluctantly. 'Must one tell her?'

'She'll find out, soon enough,' Birch said. 'But I won't tell her. Try and find him, will you? You must have some idea where he is.'

'Oh I have the good idea,' Gilles said gloomily, and went away, head-down.

Annunciata slept until three, and woke feeling so well that she tried to sit up and was pained and astonished to discover she was too weak. Apart from soreness there was nothing wrong with her. She might never have been in labour.

'Did I dream it all?' she asked Birch.

'No, my lady. You have two fine babies. I'll bring them to you in a moment. Let me wash you first, and change your bed-gown. We changed the sheets while you were asleep, and tidied the room. Then I will get you something to eat. Once you have got your strength back, you will be as good as new.'

'Having babies makes you talkative, Birch,' Annunciata said mischievously. Birch did not smile. Annunciata guessed she would rarely see that smile again, but it did not matter. She understood now. 'Are they nice babies?'

'The very best,' Birch said.

'And where is my Lord?'

'He was here while you were asleep and went away again. He will come back when he knows you are awake,' Birch said without hesitation, and as Annunciata was about to speak again she drew her nightgown over her head and muffled her. She washed her, dressed her in a fresh gown, and brushed her hair for her, and propped her on the pillows with their new covers of lace and ribbon – the lying-in linen, for her to receive visitors. 'There are close to a hundred people outside waiting to see you. You have caused quite a sensation,' Birch said. 'But first some food. You must eat and drink in quiet.'

'I am so thirsty I could drink the moat at Morland Place,' Annunciata said. Birch went to the door and called, and presently Tom came in with a great silver tray from which savoury aromas rose. 'Oh good, bring it here,' she cried, and as he placed the tray on the bed and smiled shyly at her, she said, 'Birch, am I not to see these prodigies of mine? Strange to think I have lived with them all these months, and I would not even recognize them in a crowd.'

Tom chuckled at her joke and backed off, and Birch went to fetch the bairns while Annunciata investigated what was under the covers of the dishes. All her favourite things, good rich nourishing food to build up her strength again – stewed oysters, lobster-and-cream-broth, chicken breasts fried with asparagus tips and mushrooms, a dish of spinach with garlic and chopped nuts – by the time Birch came back Annunciata had her mouth full and a spoon in each hand.

Birch stood beside the bed, a white bundle in each arm, and a strange expression on her face as tenderness warred with her habitual dourness.

'Here you are, my lady. No, don't you stop eating, I'll hold them for you. Here you are – Baron Rathkeale, my lady, and her young ladyship. The prettiest children I have ever seen.'

And Annunciata stared, feeling strangely shy; how *odd*, she thought, not to recognize your own children, but indeed it could be any babies Birch offered her. She wondered if they ever got mixed up, and the mistake never noticed. But they were beautiful, she thought. The birth-redness had gone from their faces while she slept, and they were delicately pink like river-washed pearls, thoughtfully sleeping, their tiny, perfect fists composed under their chins; all new and unspoiled, unused, like dawn, like daybreak, like the dew silver and unmarked on spring meadows. My son, my daughter, she thought, but the words did not yet mean anything. They were new souls, perfect new beings that God had sent into the world, and until the world marked them they were God's little ones yet. She felt a profound and holy wonder, that she knew she would never forget, even if she never recaptured it. Then one of them yawned, hugely and humanly, and she laughed aloud in delight.

'Which is which, Birch? I can't tell.'

'This is his lordship, Madam. The girl is a little bigger. And they are both the image of you. Wait until you see them awake. Oh, and my Lady, the King has been and seen them, and he has sent a present. You, Tom, fetch that box.'

Under Birch's guidance Tom opened the box and held up for Annunciata's inspection two Christening robes of the purest, finest white silk, deeply yoked and trimmed with exquisite lace, and scattered with tiny seed-pearls.

'He said he would come and see you as soon as you sent word you were well enough, my Lady,' Birch said with evident satisfaction. It reflected on a lady's woman, when a lady was a friend of a King. And then the boy-child woke, and opened his eyes, and stared at Annunciata blankly, and she said the first thing that jumped into her head.

'He looks like His Majesty!'

The hard work was over and the sweets began. Another cradle was hastily procured and the babies were installed under their coverlets of richly embroidered satin at the side of the bed, which was furnished with its lace-covered pillows and silk sheets and a counterpane of yellow satin embroidered with birds and butterflies and flowers in bright colours, after the Chinese style. There were silver ewers and jugs and goblets prominently displayed on the dressers around the room, and the centrepiece of all was Annunciata, Lady Ballincrea, in a succession of delicately beautiful robes, her hair flowing over her shoulders, sitting up in bed and receiving visitors and gifts.

Hugo had been and gone about his business, and Annunciata was satisfied. His eyes had glowed when he looked at the babies, and he had been unable to speak when he kissed her. Any words would have been inadequate, and Annunciata was glad his rapture had made him dumb. He sent her delicacies and flowers most hours of the day, and meanwhile, he said, was hurrying to finish fitting out the house so that she could move in as soon as she was up.

'You have certainly fooled us all, my Lady,' he said, 'having two at once. The nursery is only half furnished. I shall have to order another of everything, including nursery maids. Lucky that I chose a house big enough in the first place.'

Lucy and Richard had been amongst the first visitors, newly back from their travels, and with promises of returned-travellers' tales as soon as she was up. They had brought things from abroad for her and for the children. 'They will have to share them, I'm afraid. We never thought of its being twins. Get well soon, darling, and we will have a huge party for the Christening.'

The King came, and held her hands for a long time and said, 'We were all afraid – but here you are, well and strong. Thank God.' Then he shewed her the things he had brought for her and the babies, and told her that she must ask him for anything she lacked, and then asked to see the bairns. He held them with the skill of accustomedness and with the tenderness of a big, strong man for helpless things. 'They look like you,' he said at last. 'I am glad. I think they will have your dark eyes, Annunciata, and your – you know, you have such a look about you – I have said before, have I not—'

'The first thing I said when I saw the boy, Your Majesty,' Annunciata said with a smile, 'was "He looks like the King".'

The King roared with laughter. 'I hope you were alone when you said it.'

'Birch is to be trusted,' she said.

He looked down at the sleeping bairns again and said, 'There is talk enough about us already – I suppose you must know that? I am sorry that it should be so, but—' He shrugged.

Annunciata smiled. 'I know. It doesn't matter.'

'But I think as these two grow the talk will not grow less.' He looked at her with a faint frown, and said, 'Every so often I think that I must imagine it. Yet others see it too, don't they? You do have a strong resemblance to members of my family. If it weren't that I know better, I could almost imagine that you were a daughter of mine.'

'I would sooner be your sister,' Annunciata said. She felt so comfortable with this big man, for all that he was the annointed of God. It was like being with – say, with Ralph.

He smiled at her, lighting his heavy, ugly face into beauty. 'Then you shall be, my dear. And now – will you receive some more visitors? James and Rupert are without, and would like to pay their respects.'

'I should be honoured,' Annunciata said, and it was more than a form of words. Notice from the King was one kind of honour, but notice from his family, in such a respectable way, was even more. Prince Rupert and the Duke of York were admitted, and paid their respects, each in his own way – the duke with stiff formality that masked his basic shyness and awkwardness, the Prince with a serious gentleness that masked nothing. Before they went away, the King said, 'Lord Ballincrea has not yet asked, but I think he would not be displeased to have James and Rupert as sponsors to the children? What do you think?'

Annunciata's eyes were like stars. 'That would be wonderful, Your Majesty,' she said. The three Stuarts smiled, and bowed, and made their way out.

★

They opened the floodgates for other visitors. Annunciata had caused a sensation by almost dying, by having twins, by having twins that were reputed to look suspiciously like the King, and by being visited by the King, his brother and his cousin. No one wanted to be the last to visit Lady Ballincrea, no one wanted to bring the meanest gift, no one wanted to slight the babies when the fashion was to praise them, no one wanted to miss out on gossiping afterwards that they were the image of His Majesty. Everyone came, from Lady Castlemaine downwards, all brought gifts, all sat around the bed chamber, nibbling cakes and sweetmeats, sipping wine and caudles, their eyes raking the room to assess the worth of its furnishings, their ears and tongues busy with gossip. Some were more welcome than others to Annunciata, but even those she did not like personally she received graciously, for just as they knew the value of her silver ewers and the pearl bracelet the King had brought her, she knew the value of their attention and their goodwill.

Lady Castlemaine brought her a set of silver forks with inlaid ivory handles and had the grace not to explain to her what they were for. She sat a while and was more friendly than Annunciata had expected, especially once she had seen the babies.

'People are talking, as people will, Madam,' she said. 'It does not do to worry about gossip, though it does not do to ignore it. But I have seen enough of His Majesty's children to be able very firmly to quash any such tattle if it is mentioned in my presence.'

'I am very grateful to your Ladyship,' Annunciata said, and Lady Castlemaine bowed slightly in her chair, and then sat back, resting her hand casually on her lap to emphasise the bulge of her advancing pregnancy. Everyone knew she was with child to the King, and everyone knew she had sworn to lie-in at Hampton Court. It was the kind of desperate boldness for which she was renowned, and Annunciata felt a little sorry for her, that she had to struggle all the time to keep up her position. She did not let any pity shew, however, for that would have been a gross insult to the Countess. Nevertheless she had the feeling that Barbara was glad enough that Annunciata had no designs on the King, and had no intention even of pretending the babies were his.

Not far behind Lady Castlemaine came Lady Shrewsbury and Lady Carnegie, two of the most fashionable and most scandalous Court beauties. They were both dressed in the height of fashion, and painted with a boldness that startled Annunciata a little, for it was daytime and there were no men about. But then of course they were very likely going on to a play and supper somewhere. They came, she assumed, because it was fashionable to have been, and it was dull to do what was not the fashion. She had never been particularly friendly with them, mainly because she did not move in their circle.

They examined the gifts brought by their friends, shewed their own gifts and were thanked, and looked at the babies.

'Very handsome,' they said, and exchanged glances of satisfaction. 'The image of their father, would not you say?'

Annunciata felt wicked. 'The King thinks them the image of their mother,' she said. 'For myself – I think they look much like themselves. Do not all babies look alike to you, *mesdames*?'

'Oh Lord, yes, intolerable little monkeys. Once they grow a little they can be pleasant enough. You will be packing them off to the country somewhere as I guess? Or perhaps you will be going with them?'

'I have no plans to leave Court at the moment,' Annunciata said quietly.

'And what does his Lordship think of his progeny? Has he been in to see them yet?'

'Of course,' Annunciata said. 'He was with me almost at once.'

Carnegie raised an eyebrow. 'Was he, then? I must say I am surprised. I would not have thought he would be in any condition, after the party.'

'What party?' Annunciata said, puzzled. Shrewsbury exchanged a glance with her friend, and then said with heavy emphasis as if covering up an indiscretion.

'Why, his poor Lordship was so worried while you were in labour – God's faith, Madam, we all thought you were like to die–'

'The poor man was fretted to a string, and so his good friends made him take a little drink – quite against his will of course–'

'And one thing led to another,' Shrewsbury took it up again. 'The result was the poor man didn't draw a sober breath the whole time you were in labour, and the last I heard he was sound asleep and didn't even know he was a father yet.'

'The best thing really,' Carnegie said comfortingly. 'After all, what use for him to suffer too?'

'You were there? At the – party?' Annunciata asked in a small voice, wondering how much to believe. It seemed, she recollected, all too likely. Shrewsbury gave a smile in which contempt, pity and malice all had their share.

'Lord, no. Hamilton and I are not friends at the moment. Besides–'

'Hamilton?' Annunciata asked.

'Bess Hamilton,' Carnegie said, and the two women watched her, their masks of affability off.

'Bess Hamilton?' Annunciata repeated. 'But why–'

'Come, child,' Shrewsbury said briskly, 'you can't pretend you didn't know something was going on. Not that it's been Hamilton for long. Before her it was–'

'Stop!' Annunciata cried. 'What are you saying? My husband – his Lordship–'

Shrewsbury smiled. 'All men are the same, child. All anyone can do is to beat them at their own game. The woman who does not is a fool.'

'Besides,' Carnegie said with a smile that was not at all pleasant, 'why should you begrudge poor Hugo a little pleasant company, a female friend, when you are so *famously* friendly with His Majesty?'

Annunciata said nothing, staring at them as if dazed. They looked at each other and then got up to go. As they were about to leave, Shrewsbury looked back with an odd access of pity, and leaned over the bed to say; 'It isn't to be expected, Madam. But you know, I firmly believe he was faithful to you for several months. We all used to remark on it. You should be glad of that.'

Then she picked up her skirts, and the two Court beauties swept out.

CHAPTER SEVENTEEN

In the drawing-room of the new house on King Street, Annunciata received the guests for the Christening feast. The room was beautiful, and it was as much to shew it off as anything that they had delayed the Christening until they had moved into the house. The long room was light and airy, with tall windows that looked towards the river. The walls were panelled in gold and green brocade, and curtains of gold and green striped sarcenet hung at the windows, so different from the heavy drapes and tapestries Annunciata had been used to at home. The floor was of a light-coloured polished wood, and thick pale China carpets covered much of it. There were two huge mirrors, four feet wide and reaching the whole height of the room, their frames gilded, and in them was reflected the furniture which Hugo had chosen or brought from his own apartments – beautiful ebon and japan, sandalwood and spicklewood, light and delicate, and little spindle-legged French chairs of mahogany with their seats upholstered in striped brocade to match the walls and curtains.

It was a charming room, everyone agreed, and a fitting background to the precious things Hugo had collected and now deployed lovingly on dressers and tables – marbles and statues, silver, glass, gilt, porcelain, mother-of-pearl, Indian shell. Above the fireplace hung the portrait of Annunciata, finished in time for the moving-in – she gazed down at the company with great, dark, bright eyes, her slender neck and shoulders rising from a loose robe of vivid, deep, midnight blue, her hair loose down her back. In her lap Charlemagne sat, raising one paw to her wrist as if to attract her attention; one white hand rested in her lap, the other gestured casually towards the small round table

307

beside her on which lay an open book, the gold cross, and the miniature of Princess Henrietta. It was a marvellous piece of work, and a very good likeness, and the guests praised it openly and murmured quietly amongst themselves about how like it was not only to Lady Ballincrea but to certain other important persons.

Annunciata received her carefully-selected guests with a poise that hid the nervous uncertainty underneath. She had not spoken to Hugo about the accusations – or were they revelations? – made by Lady Shrewsbury and her friend. Hugo himself had behaved no differently towards her, seemed as affectionate and loving, admired the babies, praised her and laughed with her and talked to her, but she felt different. When he left her on business or to play tennis or to see a man who had a new marble to sell, she always wondered if that was only an excuse. When he came back she wondered if he was coming fresh from another woman's bed. Jealousy was new to her – she had been used to arouse it, not suffer it – and she found it painful both to her heart and to her pride. She could not broach the subject with him, and it created a barrier between them. The fact that he did not seem to notice the barrier only made the hurt worse for her.

She took refuge, as many a one before her, in the enjoyment of social success. She had taken great trouble with her dress – Mrs Blake had proved a genius when given the best fabrics and unlimited money to work with, and Annunciata was often pressed to reveal the name of her dressmaker, but never would. Her gown for this occasion was of cloth-of-silver over a petticoat of stiff lilac taffeta, the bodice and sleeves trimmed with silver lace; she wore the King's pearl bracelet and the pearl-and-amethyst necklace which was Hugo's present to her, and her hair was dressed behind in a Roman knot wound about loosely with pearls that glowed beautifully amongst her dark curls. She looked statuesque, remote and beautiful – a kind of beauty that the other Court women could not and would not wish to copy. That was what she wanted, an individuality.

The babies, dressed in the Christening robes the King had given them, were brought in for the toast by the new nursery-maids that Birch had selected. The King himself gave the toast, and Hugo and Annunciata stood side by side, smiling at each other and the company, the proud parents of two babes who promised to have more than their fair share of luck, for they were not only handsome, healthy and well-born, but they also had some very eminent and influential people for their sponsors: the Duke and Duchess of York, Prince Rupert, Lady Clarendon, the Duke of Albemarle, and, by proxy, Princess Henrietta, Duchesse d'Orleans. The toast was drunk to loud acclaim, the babies woke and began to cry and were hurried away, and the party broke up into little groups to enjoy the excellent food and drink the Ballincreas had provided, and to gossip under cover of the music provided by a group of musicians on a small dais at one end of the room.

The King and Prince Rupert chatted a little to Annunciata and Hugo, for they were soon to leave. The Prince looked grave and abstracted – his mother, Queen Elizabeth, was ill, and he and the King were going from the Christening party to visit her.

'I pray she may soon be well, Your Grace,' Annunciata said.

Prince Rupert looked down at her from his great height, and his dark eyes were momentarily warm. 'Thank you, Madam, but I confess I am greatly worried. She is very old and very tired, and she has been much troubled by a cold which nothing seems to rid her of.'

'Everyone has colds this winter,' the King said, trying to be more cheerful. 'It is this strange weather, I believe. She will shake it off, Rupert, never fear. I have sent Fraser some of my own physic, and he has promised to make her take it.'

The ghost of a smile touched Rupert's lips. 'You know my mother believes in nothing but blood-letting.'

'Well, Fraser will not bleed her, Rupert, you know that. And rightly too—' the King broke off, smiled at Annunciata, and gave a little bow. 'I am forgetting my manners. Pray forgive me, Lady Ballincrea, all this must be very tedious listening.'

'I know how interested you are in medical matters, Your Majesty,' Annunciata said demurely. 'It did pass through my mind to ask your advice for my own family in Yorkshire. Their last letter says they all have troublesome coughs and colds—'

'She teases you, Charles,' Prince Rupert said smiling.

Charles looked down at her tenderly. 'She may tease me all she wishes. We must go now, I am afraid, for there is much to do. The Portuguese ambassador has been following me like a shadow these three days and I cannot put him off much longer.'

'How are the negotiations proceeding, Majesty?' Hugo asked.

Charles made a wry face. 'Slowly. I hope she may be here by Easter, but I think May or even June more likely. Still, it gives me more time to have the Queen's apartments made ready. There have been some very curious alterations made to them by the previous tenant.'

They all laughed at that, for during the Commonwealth Cromwell's wife had been famous – or perhaps notorious – for her household economies and strange contrivances.

'Perhaps they may be of use, Sir,' Hugo said, 'if the present landlord is as penniless as he claims.'

'But he cannot get credit without a little show of riches,' Charles said pleasantly. 'But enough of this – Rupert grows restless. I take my leave of you, with thanks. My lady, will you hunt with me tomorrow morning? We shall chase the deer at Epping.'

'With great pleasure, Your Majesty,' Annunciata curt-seyed.

'Rupert – you come too. You spend too much time working. We will go very early – may I send a coach for you, my lady? Good. Tomorrow then.'

By the time the last guest had gone, Annunciata was very tired. She had not long been up from her childbed, and the long standing had wearied her. When they were alone she yawned and stretched her aching back, and turned to Hugo, who was examining an imagined blemish on one of his small marbles.

'It went very well, I thought, did not you, Hugo? But Lord, I am tired. Will you call for my bath? I ordered a simple supper, as we are alone. I thought we could have it in the bed chamber, and have the fire lit there. It gets damp in these rooms after sundown, even though the days are so warm. And then I thought—'

Hugo turned to her, and he looked strangely. 'Why, I thought you knew,' he said. 'I have arranged to sup with the Clarendons.'

'No, I didn't know,' Annunciata said, and felt a seed of anger inside her. 'Why did they not mention it when they were here? It does not give me much time to bathe and change. Where are we to sup? At Clarendon House?'

'No, my dear, not *we* – I am asked alone.' Annunciata stared at him, and he shrugged. 'It is in the way of business. There is much to do with—'

'I don't believe you,' Annunciata said, and Hugo broke off. He looked at her patiently, not as if he was at all worried or surprised, and it made her even more angry. 'You can't use my condition as an excuse to get away from me any more, can you? So you call it business. But I know what business it is that you have, and it isn't at Clarendon House, it is at Whitehall.'

'You do not know all my business,' Hugo said quietly, still ready to be reasonable.

Annunciata clenched her hands into fists, remembering all the evenings she had spent alone during the late stages of her pregnancy. 'I know more than you think. I know, for instance, what business it is you do with Bess Hamilton.'

Hugo raised one eyebrow, and he gave a wry, half amused smile. 'Oh, you know about Bess, do you?' he said.

Annunciata was shocked and angry. 'Is that all you have to say? Don't you even want to deny it?'

'Deny it? Why should I?' Annunciata made an inarticulate sound of rage, and stepped towards him, lifting her hands, and he caught her fists easily in his own and held her at arm's length. 'Why should I deny it, if you already know?' he said. 'Control yourself, my lady, you are not a squire's daughter now. You are a lord's wife—'

'You don't need to remind me of that,' she cried. 'You forget it yourself.'

'You are my wife and I have never forgotten that.'

'You forget yourself with Bess Hamilton – and I dare swear there are others.'

'Of course there are,' Hugo said.

Annunciata, shocked, cried, 'Oh!' and fell back from him, and stood trembling, staring at him, white-faced.

'How dare you use me thus,' she said at last in a low voice.

Hugo shook his head. 'Lord, you are acting very strangely, my lady. What matters it that I lie with another woman from time to time? What did you expect? No man is faithful to his wife, least of all a courtier. You must accept the rules if you want to play the game, and benefit by the play.'

'It is not playing to me,' she said.

Hugo took half a step towards her. 'Annunciata, it means nothing. It does not alter our marriage.'

But she stepped back, away from him. 'Don't touch me,' she said coldly. He shrugged and turned away.

When he reached the door she cried out, 'Where are you going?'

'To Bess's,' he said without turning. 'I dare say she will

not tell me not to touch her. I hope when I return you will be in a more reasonable state of mind.'

And he was gone. Annunciata stared at the closed door disbelievingly, and she raised her quivering fists slowly to her chest, for she thought she could feel her heart breaking. She wanted to weep, but her anger was so great it prevented her. Charlemagne came sniffing around her slippers and whined softly, and she sat down and picked him up to cuddle him. But after a moment he wriggled away from her, and she put him down and continued to sit, her hands idle in her lap.

When Birch came in an hour later she was still sitting thus, immobile, in the dark, for the candles had not been lit.

'Why, my lady, are you still here?' Birch said, coming across to her. Annunciata did not answer, and when Birch touched her tentatively, she found she was shivering lightly all over, like a terrified and cornered animal. 'You are cold, my lady,' she said briskly. 'I'll send for hot water – your bath will warm you. And I think it is cold enough for a fire in the bed chamber. Come, let me help you to your room.'

Annunciata stood up and let Birch usher her into the bed chamber, moving awkwardly as if her limbs were not under her control. Birch looked at her with sharp sympathy, and chose to attribute her weakness to other things.

'It was too much for you, so soon after your confinement,' she said. 'When you have bathed I think you should get into bed, and I will have your supper sent to you there. I will send word to his lordship that you will sup alone.'

At the mention of her husband, Annunciata seemed to revive. She turned slowly to Birch, and her eyes were burning as brightly as if she was fevered.

'Accept the rules, he said. We'll see. He'll have to swallow the same physic, and we'll see how it chokes him.'

It was not long before the coldness between them became

public property. They behaved perfectly correctly towards each other, and in public no one even so much as hinted that anything had changed. But the ladies and gentlemen of the Court watched them, gleefully, bright-eyed with amusement and malice, and privately laid bets on what would happen next. Ballincrea would take a public mistress, they thought, and one or two daring souls wagered on Castlemaine, who had never been faithful to the King. And Lady Ballincrea – the innocent, untouchable, unpainted, aloof Lady Ballincrea – what would she do? The leading gallants of the Court began to preen themselves, wondering which of them was going to lay successful seige to that walled garden.

All that happened at first was that her ladyship became feverishly gay. With the brief interruption when Queen Elizabeth died in February, the winter season at Court gained pace, and the Ballincreas were invited everywhere, and were seen everywhere, sometimes together and sometimes separately; and they gave parties, balls, suppers, entertainments of all kinds. At first out of curiosity, and later simply because they were the best parties, no one refused an invitation. The Ballincreas spent money lavishly, their food was the best, their wine flowed from a seemingly inexhaustible cellar, and their masques and plays and ballets were imaginative and gorgeously costumed. But though everyone watched minutely, no one could detect that Lady Ballincrea had taken a lover – even those who had once believed the King to be her lover had now reluctantly to give up the idea, for he continued to treat her with the same brotherly tenderness he had always shewn. In May the King's bride, the Princess Catherine of Braganza, finally arrived in England, and the King and Prince Rupert rode down to Portsmouth to meet her. When she came back to London, the Court paid homage, and there were a series of entertainments staged by the noble and wealthy to fete the new Queen, in which each new host and hostess tried hard to outdo the last.

Lady Ballincrea, newly appointed Lady of the Bedchamber to the Queen, was not laggardly, and the Court waited with amusement to see how she would put on something more lavish and spectacular even than Buckingham's. But they should have known from past experience that what she aimed at was never more of the same, but something different. Instead of yet another ball or dinner, she arranged a performance of William Morland's *Missa Solemnis* in St Paul's Cathedral, where, according to family legend, it was conceived. The King was well-known to love music, and to wish the great Church music that the Commonwealth had banned to be revived, and so he was certain to accept the invitation. It would be something seemly, gracious, and beautiful, to which all the best people could go; and then, in the evening, she planned a very select and intimate party at Ballincrea House, where there was to be a delicious informal buffet supper and a private performance of William Morland's ballet, *Theseus and Ariadne*, for which the costumes were reputed to be going to cost a thousand pounds or more.

'Well, lady, you have done it this time,' Hugo said when the acceptances for the supper came in from the Yorks. 'No one in the Court can ever outdo you in this, for who else has an ancestor who wrote an Anglican mass? Your fame is fixed for ever. The rest of them are scrabbling through their family vaults, looking for a painter or a poet – I hear that Carnegie is going to have a reading of her great-grandmother's laundry-lists, with forty fiddles and a ballet of eunuchs in gold tissue.'

Annunciata laughed – he always had the power to make her laugh – and he looked at her curiously. Recently she had behaved towards him with every appearance of normal polite affection, but he knew that she was different, and he wondered what she was planning. She was a pretty sight, sitting at her little escritoire opening the letters, the sunlight from the open windows touching the white rosebuds she had pinned in her hair, the little breeze blowing the delicate white muslin of her morning dress, and rustling the papers so that she had to set Charlemagne on top of them for a paperweight. The little dog sighed and dropped his nose on his paws and dozed in the May warmth.

'What is it you plan, Annunciata?' he asked suddenly. 'What are your ambitions now?'

She looked at him with innocent surprise. 'Why, what everyone plans – to get wealth, to advance myself and my family. Richard would like to be an ambassador. He has his knighthood, but what about a baronetcy for him? And something for Ralph – I am in the best position of any of us to help. The King is fond of me.'

Hugo scowled. 'Yes, I know. It has long been a scandal. And all this for your family?'

Annunciata smiled sweetly. 'That old scandal is long dead, my dear. And of course, you would not understand the pull of family, having none yourself, would you? But forgive me, I have much to do, and I have to attend the Queen at noon.' And she jumped up, scooped Charlemagne into her arms, and went away with a swishing of skirts to the bed chamber, calling Birch as she went to come and dress her.

Hugo stood by the desk, frowning, for a moment, and then he picked up the last letter she had opened and glanced at it idly. It was from Edward, a brief note to say that he would be coming to London to make his report to the Chancellor, and would do himself the honour of calling on her. Hugo's face cleared. Edward! He hadn't seen him for so long! It would be wonderful to see his friend again – it would compensate him for his uneasiness about his wife.

Annunciata was a frequent correspondent, and Ruth always took her letters over to Morland Place to read to Ralph and Arabella and Elizabeth, who awaited each one

316

eagerly. Ralph listened with amusement and pride to the unfolding tale of Annunciata's progress in the world, and often said he must go up to London some time to see her and her husband. 'Though I know I shall find he is not good enough for her,' he would add. Arabella and Elizabeth listened with wonder to the stories of another world which seemed as remote a fantasy from the realities of Morland Place and sheep and cloth and farming.

Ralph was much in need of cheering up that spring, and Annunciata's letters were a brief respite from his worries. The strangely warm winter had been followed by a long spell of heavy rain, which had meant that the ploughing was late, which in turn would mean a smaller harvest; and the wetness coinciding with lambing meant a great many dead lambs, and an increased incidence of footrot. But those things were as nothing compared with his worry over his son, Edward.

The children had all had colds during the winter, but long after the others had shaken them off, Edward went on coughing, a racking, spasmodic cough that seemed to leave him temporarily breathless and exhausted. Arabella dosed him and physicked him, gave him honey to soothe his throat, painted his tongue with treacle – an old Borderlands trick, that – to stop him coughing, but he remained pale and thin, and had little appetite. His ninth birthday fell in January of 1662, and Ralph had planned a great surprise for him. On the morning of the day he was led blindfold out into the yard, and when the blindfold was whipped off, there before him stood Edmund holding the halter of a three-year-old chestnut gelding.

Edward's eyes shone, and he stared speechlessly first at the horse and then his father. Ralph smiled, happy at the boy's excitement. 'It's time you had a man's horse, not a pony,' he said. 'His name's Torchlight. He's backed and mouthed, but it will be for you to school him and bring him on just as you wish.'

'Oh Papa!' was all that Edward could say. Edmund was

more vocal, and was hopping up and down on one foot in a way that would have had Fox halfway across Yorkshire. Torchlight was of a more placid temperament, however, and after one surprised glance he merely reached out a tentative muzzle to chew at the strange human's pale hair – which in the sunlight did look remarkably like straw.

'Come on, Druid, don't just stand staring like a dummy!' Edmund cried. Druid was his nickname for his brother, whom he said was as dull as a dolmen, and whom he felt it his continuing task to liven up. 'Do try him. He looks so fine – I want to see how he moves! Papa, did you get a saddle?'

'Gideon has one,' Ralph said, with a nod at the head groom, who went into the harness room and came back out with a soft new saddle and bridle. 'Now you must be sure to be tender with his mouth, Edward, and be patient with him, for he's young and has much to learn.'

Edmund jerked his hair away from the exploring teeth and said, 'As patient as Master Lambert was with us, Papa? That means he must only beat him once every five minutes.'

The two boys spent all their time from then on training the young horse, sharing him, as they shared everything, on completely equal terms. When the school term began again, they were frequently in trouble for playing truant in order to carry on with the important work. Though Ralph made a show of chastising them, he was glad for them to be out in the open air all day, for he still believed in the properties of the outdoor life and hoped that it would improve Edward's appetite and make him brown and strong again. But he grew thinner day by day, and by February, when the wet weather set in, it was generally Edmund who could be seen on the horse's back, while Edward stood and watched from the shelter of a tree.

Arabella complained about the boys' wet clothes, and told Ralph that he must forbid them to wander out in the rain and get soaked through. 'How will Edward ever get rid of that cough if you let him walk about drenched all day?' she said, rubbing the offenders' wet heads so briskly with a rough towel that it was all they could do not to cry out. So their activities were curtailed, and they longed for the infrequent fine periods, while Gideon exercised the young master's precious horse along with the others.

In March the new grass came through, and Edmund went reluctantly to his father to say that Druid lay awake most of the night, tossing and turning, and coughing rackingly. In the mornings he was lethargic, with dark rings under his eyes from the sleepless nights, and Ralph would worry about him, but by the evening he would seem better, lively, even excitable, with a good colour in his cheeks. So Ralph went on hoping for the best. But as Easter approached it became clear to everyone but Ralph what was wrong with the boy. After Easter Arabella broached the terrible subject.

'He must not go back to school,' she said.

'Why not?' Ralph asked.

She looked at him pityingly. 'Ralph, he is very sick. He can hardly get on his horse now. At school Edmund says he dozes most of the time.'

'He always was a lazy boy,' Ralph said with an effort, but his lips were white. 'But he'll pick up as the warm weather comes.'

'You know what's wrong with him,' Arabella said.

'No!' said Ralph. 'It's just a cough. A cold.'

'He can't go back to school,' she said again, inexorably.

'Very well,' Ralph said faintly. 'He can stay home until he's better.'

On the first morning back Edmund and Young Ralph set off together for the school, but by dinner time Edmund was home again and sitting with his brother in the rose-garden, and after that no one sent him away again, and Ralph went to school alone. Martin and the baby were kept apart, seeing Edward only at supper when all the family gathered together, but Edmund was never apart from his brother.

At first Ralph was triumphant, seeing his theories proved right. Without the daily trip into school, Edward seemed to revive a little. He sat out in the gardens, walked about with Edmund, played with Fern's latest puppies, read, played cards with Edmund, even played the lute in the evenings. He still ate nothing, but with the sunshine his skin browned so that he looked healthier, and though in the mornings he was lethargic and weak, in the evenings when the family was together he was lively, almost normal, joining in the games and music that were their evening's fare.

But as April advanced, the temporary respite ended. It was plain that the evening liveliness was fevered, hectic; he was wasting away before their eyes, and soon there came a time when they did not even speak of his getting well again. He and Edmund spent every moment of every day together, but now mostly in silence, clinging together as if they feared to be forcibly parted. Edward asked Edmund to exercise Torchlight for him, but Edmund would not leave his side, and so it was left still to Gideon. One day late in April Clem carried him out into the yard and sat him on a stool in a small patch of sunshine in the corner of the yard, his back to the sunwarmed bricks, to watch the comings and goings of the servants. Fern, still occasionally pursued by her fat, woolly pups, came and flopped down at his feet. A pair of pigeons croodled in the gutter above him, and Edmund sat on the ground and rested his elbow on Edward's knee. After a while, Edward spoke.

'Do you believe in heaven, Edmund? I mean, really, that there is such a place?'

'Of course,' Edmund said, shocked. 'Why do you ask? Do you doubt it?'

'I don't know. Sometimes, it seems so lovely here, I can't imagine anything being better.' He looked down at his hand, resting on his knee near to Edmund's. His own hand was white, thin, almost transparent, like a shadow of twigs cast by the sun. Beside it, his brother's was brown and strong, the sun catching the fine golden hairs on the back of it. He closed his eyes for a moment, to stop the tears seeping out. Fern sighed and rolled over on her side, and two pups, seeing her thus exposed, waddled in to try and nurse from her again. Edward opened his eyes, and Edmund looked up at him.

'Edmund, I want you to have Torchlight when I am dead,' he said. Edmund didn't answer, but his lip began to tremble, and he caught it between his teeth to stop it. 'I wish Father Lambert was still here,' Edward said. 'He could always explain things. He always spoke as if he *knew*.'

Edmund knew what his brother was thinking. He said, 'Of course you'll go to heaven, Druid. And you'll be with Mama then, and—' He could not go on. Edward nodded.

'Would you do something for me? Would you ask Gideon if you can bring Torchlight out into the yard? I'd like to see him.'

'Of course,' Edmund said, jumping up. 'I'll lead him right up to you, and you can give him some salt.' He ran across the yard, and the puppies bounced after him, thinking a game was beginning. Gideon gave him a palmful of salt and untied Torchlight and put the halter rope into his hand, and he led the gelding carefully out of the dark stable and across the yard to Edward's corner. The gelding's hooves rang loudly on the cobbles, and his shadow fell short between his forefeet. Edmund stopped in front of Edward and held out the palmful of salt.

'Here, Druid,' he said, 'you give it to him. He'll lick and lick and stand quietly for ages. Here, hold out your hand.'

Edward didn't move, and though his eyes were open, he didn't seem to be looking at anything. Edmund stared at him in perplexity for a moment, and then his legs began to tremble, and his mouth opened in a soundless wail. At

Edward's feet Fern went on sleeping, her flank twitching as flies landed on it, and Torchlight, bored, butted Edmund with his muzzle and pawed at the cobbles.

For a long time Annunciata lay still feeling dazed, almost dazzled; and then Edward rolled carefully over, taking his weight from her. He drew her onto his shoulder, and kissed her forehead tenderly, and pushed the damp hair from her brow with a gesture that was almost like a mother's. She drew a trembling sigh, and Edward pressed her a little closer.

'You are lovely.'

'It was so – different,' she said at last.

'Different from what?' he asked with a smile in his voice. 'Different from what you imagined? *Did* you imagine it, Nance, all those years ago, when you flirted with me all over Yorkshire?'

'Not really,' she said. 'I didn't know. I never thought further than—'

'I know,' he said. 'But I did. And it is exactly as I imagined. Not different at all. Except, perhaps, a little more wonderful in reality.' He felt her try to turn her head, and moved his own to look down at her. She was looking up at him timidly, as if not sure what her own reaction should be, and he smiled reassuringly.

'So, different from what?'

She looked away, shyly. Different, she meant, from being made love to by Hugo. It was different, she discovered, to be loved by a man who was skilled in it. She had loved Hugo, and he had loved her, and it had been wonderful. This had been wonderful for quite different reasons. Now she said, instead of answering him, 'Do you love me, Edward?'

He laughed softly – she felt his chest move. 'That, my dear, is a very womanly question. What do you think?'

'I don't know. If it were anyone else, I would. But you

– I don't know. Once I thought you did love me, when you kept taking me away from Kit. But now—'

'You and I probably mean very different things by love,' he said. 'I would say that I have only ever loved one woman in my life.'

'Who?' she asked, thinking it would be her. Then, 'Not Mary?'

'Mary? Sweet saints, what put that idea in your head? No, Nance, my pretty bird, not Mary. Someone you don't know. Someone you don't remember.'

'Did I meet her?'

He nodded. 'A long time ago, when you were little.'

She frowned. 'Not your mother?'

He nodded.

'But that's a different thing, surely?'

'Oh yes, very different,' he said. 'And now, my hinny, I must get up, and be gone before Hugo comes back.' He kissed her brow again and climbed out of bed, and she watched him languidly as he moved about collecting his scattered clothes. His body was good to look at, she thought, small and compact and very strong, with smooth skin, hairless and silky. Hugo was dark and hairy, very different. It was pleasant to run one's fingers over smooth skin, she thought.

'Edward?'

'Yes, my Nance?'

'Hugo is your best friend, is he not? You love him?'

'Yes.' He stopped dressing and watched her, amused, as if he knew what she was going to think before she thought it.

'Then why—? I mean, don't you mind? Wouldn't he mind?'

'Of course he would mind – but you aren't going to tell him, and I certainly won't.'

'But why don't you mind doing something you know is wrong?'

'What you mean is, why does he lie with other women

323

if he loves you?' Edward said. She nodded. He came back to her, sat on the edge of the bed and took up her hands and kissed them one by one. His grey eyes looked very clear, like spring water.

'I don't think he does it to spite you, dearest,' he said. 'To him, such things don't matter. It was the way he grew up. And perhaps no sort of love can be entirely wrong. What, after all, are you doing here with me? Are you doing it to spite him?'

'No,' she said, frowning. 'Well, at first I thought so, but even then not entirely, and now—'

Edward smiled. 'You are disarmingly honest,' he said. 'That is one of the things I love about you. And, yes, little one, I do love you. And now I shall prove it by getting gone before anyone finds us.' He got up and dressed quickly, coming back to kiss her goodbye and say, 'I shall be here for a week more, Nance. May I see you again?'

'Yes, please do. Come tomorrow. Hugo will be playing tennis in the morning and he dines in his mess. Come tomorrow.'

'I shall,' he said. 'And may I hope to wait upon you next time I am in London, my lady?'

She laughed for answer, and he swept her a parody of a bow, and went away with Charlemagne yapping at his heels.

They met every day for the week of his visit, and twice he supped with Annunciata and Hugo, and Annunciata discovered the excitement of dissembling as she sat at the small table, her knee almost touching her lover's, pretending there was nothing more between them than met the eye. She began to understand a little why the Court ladies all had intrigues and lovers. At the end of the week Edward went away, back to his duties in Yorkshire; and at the end of June she discovered she was pregnant again.

CHAPTER EIGHTEEN

Annunciata had expected Hugo to be coldly amused, cynically indifferent. What she was not prepared for was his rage.

'Whose is it?' he shouted at her. 'Whose child is it?'

'Why, whose should it be?' she shrugged, turning away from him. 'You are my husband.'

He grabbed her shoulders and turned her back to him, and shook her as he spoke. 'You know damned well that it couldn't be mine!'

'You are my husband. Under the law the child is yours,' she said, forcing herself not to flinch.

'You want me to give my name to some other man's brat?' he shouted.

She tried to pull away from him, and as his fingers bit into her shoulders she said, 'Let me go. You're hurting me.' She stared him out, and he relaxed his grip, but did not let her go. 'Why, my lord, I thought it was the custom amongst you gallants of the Court – to get each other's brats.'

'You damned bitch, I should strangle you for this,' he whispered.

Her own anger flared up, and she wrenched herself free from him violently. 'Strangle me for what? For what you do yourself, and think nothing of? Strange justice that, my lord! If a man could be pregnant, you'd have given me a dozen bastard brats by now!'

He was confused – she saw it in his face. He screwed up his eyes as he did when he could not think readily of a word in English, and said, 'What? What do you mean? You are talking nonsense, and you know it.'

She used her advantage to get away from him, and sat

down at the dresser and began idly to sort through her jewels. 'You think it nonsense? It seems sense to me. You betrayed me with another woman, even while I was giving birth to your children.'

'So that's why you did it – to spite me! Well, I hope you had poor sport of it. And don't think I will acknowledge this child either.'

'You will have no choice,' she said coldly.

His rage flared up again. 'I'll find out, you damned bitch, I'll find out who it was – and when I do—!' He stamped to the door.

'Where are you going?' she asked coldly. 'You have to dress for their Majesties' supper.'

'Find some other man to go with you,' he said. 'Your brat's father perhaps – if you know who he is!' And he went out, slamming the door. Annunciata watched the closed door until she was sure he was not coming back, and then she was able to relax, and the shuddering she had held back took her over.

Hugo had meant, when he stormed out, to go straight to one of his women, but when he came out onto the street he began walking fast to try to shake off his thoughts, and presently he found that he did not want the society of women at all. I wish to God Edward was here, he thought; why did he have to live so far away from the Court? Presently Hugo found himself at the Hercules Pillars, and on an impulse he went inside. The ale was famous there, but his mood was too firey for ale. He ordered brandy, and the quick burning as it went down inside him helped, for it inflamed his anger and hid the pain that was underneath.

He felt betrayed. How could she do such a thing to him? He loved her, and she had taken his love and trampled on it carelessly. He had known all along that she did not love him as much as he loved her, and the awareness had always made him nervous. He had never been able to feel secure in her love, even in that idyllic summer when they had gone everywhere together, like brothers. That had been a perfect time, and of it had been born the perfect children: a boy and a girl, sharing one birth, grown together at one time in one womb, the living symbol of the love that had been between Hugo and Annunciata. And then she had betrayed him, and to make it worse had tried to justify it by equating it with his own taking of a mistress.

Restlessness drove him up again, and he walked out and began to make his way towards the City, stopping from time to time at a tavern and drinking until he grew too restless to sit still any longer and moved on. In this way he came at last to the King's Head in Drury Lane.

He was known there, for it was the tavern he sometimes visited when he was going to the play at His Majesty's, and though it was crowded, the landlord noted his condition and was worried. For Lord Ballincrea to be drunk was nothing unusual, but for him to reel in alone and not properly dressed was evidence of some trouble, he thought.

'Well now, me lord, what can I do for you? The play was done some while back – you didn't come to see me then?'

'Bob, give me some brandy,' Hugo said, swaying a little.

'Brandy, me lord? When I've just tapped the best barrel of ale you will ever be likely to have the chance of tasting? Why, me lord, I wouldn't be able to look meself in the face again, if I was to let you miss this one. Like liquid gold, it is, me lord, and—'

'I want brandy, not ale,' Hugo said fiercely.

'Why, me lord, have you had a shock?' the landlord said sympathetically. Hugo gave a short, hard laugh. A shock, yes, he'd had a shock! The landlord noted it. 'Well, me lord, there's a lot of friends of yours in the back room, there. Why don't you go in a set a while, and I'll bring you something. Have you supped yet? The ordinary's good tonight – a nice bit of lamb with spinach and almonds, or a bit of fish—'

Hugo did not wait to listen, but turned and walked as

best he could towards the back room. The landlord watched him go, and then turned to call behind him into the tap-room for one of the boys.

'Lookee here, Jack,' he said, 'you run as fast as you can lay legs to the ground to his lordship's, and find his man Gilles, and get him here. Tell him his lordship's taken ill. Off you go now – fast as you like!' The boy gave one stare and darted out, and the landlord shook his head and took a bottle and some tankards and put them on a tray and set off towards the back room.

To fail a King's invitation was a very gross breach of etiquette, and Annunciata was in some trembling when she arrived at their Majesties' supper party. She excused Hugo by saying he had been taken violently ill – something he had eaten, without a doubt. The assembled party, either from genuine sympathy or malice, demanded more and more circumstantial detail, and Annunciata had to provide it, growing more and more agitated until at last the King intervened firmly to change the subject. The Queen could only turn her head this way and that like a spectator at a game, for her English was not yet good enough to follow the quick-talking courtiers. She had at last, Annunciata was glad to note, abandoned the ugly, heavy, uncomfort-able clothes of her native country, and was wearing a very pretty dress of rose-pink silk with lace at the neckline. Her eyes followed her husband everywhere with an expression of half-comprehending adoration that made her the butt of the cruel laughter of the faster Court ladies.

They must have laughed at me like that, Annunciata thought, last summer when we were in love. The thought made her sick and sad. How things had changed – how she had changed. From a thoughtless, happy flirt, she had become an innocent adoring wife, much like the poor Queen. The Queen seemed to be the only person in the world who did not know about the King's sexual proclivities. Just, Annunciata thought, as I was the last one to know what Hugo was doing while I was in labour. A woman who loves and trusts is a fool. All the same, she wondered where Hugo was, and she worried a little. He had seemed so violent. Suppose he did find out about Edward – would he really do something rash? But he could not find out. No one knew. All the same . . .

'You are very thoughtful, my lady. I hope your husband's indisposition is not alarming?' It was the King's soft voice beside her. She started back to reality, and looking up at him saw that he knew it was not a bad anchovy that had caused Hugo's absence. She opened and shut her mouth, not knowing quite what to say. He smiled gently. 'Come, Annunciata, you know me well enough by now to trust me. What has he done? Let me help you.'

'Oh, your Majesty, we had a – a quarrel, and he ran out of the house, and I don't know where he has gone,' she said, speaking quickly and quietly so that no one else could hear. 'He spoke violently, and I am afraid he may do himself – or someone else – some hurt.'

The King's eyes were understanding. 'Was his man with him?'

Annunciata shook her head. 'Not when he left. He may have caught up with him outside.'

'I will send someone discreet to look for him. Try not to worry – Hugo can look after himself. We all had to, in the old days.'

Annunciata forced herself to smile, and the King patted her shoulder gently, and went away and spoke a quiet word to one of his servants, who presently disappeared.

Gilles had been in the pantry smoking a pipe and watching one of the maids clean silver when his master left the house. It was not long before Tom found him with the message from Birch that the master and mistress had had words and that the master had dashed out without even picking up his hat. Gilles had not wasted time. He whipped off his apron and flung on his jacket, but even so he was too far behind-hand to catch up with Hugo.

London was a great and sprawling city of perhaps half a million people; but of the courtiers there was, comparatively, but a handful, and they were well-known to all Londoners. The Londoner's greatest entertainment was to observe and talk about the antics of the courtiers, and so it was not hard after some judicious guessing to pick up his master's trail and then to follow it across London. The landlord's boy Jack missed him going, but coming back he met Gilles in the Strand at the corner of Bow Street, and hastened to give his message, and the two of them went on together, cutting through the back alleys for speed.

When he entered the King's Head, the landlord looked up at him with some relief.

'Ah, there you are, sir!' He hurried over and lowered his voice discreetly, nodding towards the back room. 'Your master's in there, sir, in my back room, and mighty foxed! He would not eat anything, and he's been drinking brandy, and it's firing up his temper, if you follow me, sir. There are one or two others with him, but if you can contrive to persuade your master away, you may trust me for the rest.'

Gilles raised his eyebrows. 'You are worried, master landlord, by a drunken gentleman?'

'Mordee, master Gilles, I seen enough gentlemen foxed in my time, I warrant you, but your master is mighty upset about something. When I went in there a bit since with another bottle he was cursing fit to burst, his face as red as my neckerchief. For his own safety, master, I wish you may get him home.'

Gilles clapped the landlord on the shoulder. 'I will do my best, good man. You will be ready to help me if I call you?'

The landlord nodded. 'Let me alone for that, Master Gilles. His lordship's a favourite of mine, and I'm sorry he's not feeling himself.'

As Gilles approached the door of the back room a roar rose up which could either have been merriment or anger. If they were all drunk within, he thought, it was probably a little of each. He opened the door, and saw his master sitting on a settle looking much disarrayed, his face red, a tankard in his hand, and a belligerent expression on his face as he leaned forward to make some point in argument to the man opposite. No one in the room, Gilles judged expertly, was as drunk as his lord, though all were well advanced; they seemed to be watching and baiting him, keeping the argument going for the sake of the fun, while his lord was arguing, albeit drunkenly, from the soul.

Gilles stood inside the door and tried to catch his master's attention, but though Hugo looked across at him briefly, he did not seem to register his presence. The two gentlemen nearest the door, Charles Sackville and Henry Hamilton, glanced up with bleary amusement at Gilles, and Sackville said:

'You had better take your master home, man, before he gets himself into a fight.' Then he raised his voice and bellowed at Hugo, 'Hey, Ballincrea, your nurse-maid is here for you. It's long past your supper time. Run along now!' Hamilton and some of the others roared with laughter, but Hugo merely waved a vague hand at them like someone swatting at a fly, and carried on arguing. The man facing him, Lord Tramore, seemed to be growing angry himself.

'I tell you it's a different matter,' Hugo shouted. 'A different matter. It's the blood that counts. That horse of yours—'

'You can talk all you like about breeding,' Tramore shouted back. 'What do you know about it anyway?'

'I've bred more horses than any man here. I've bred—'

'He's bred more bastards than any man here!' Sackville shouted, and the company roared with laughter, all except Ballincrea and Tramore. Gilles fidgeted uneasily.

'My lord,' he called softly but penetratingly. '*Il faut en aller*. My lord—'

'Bastards, now, bastards, there's the lie to your argument,' Tramore said. 'What about the precious blood transmitted through bastards. Does it make 'em any better?'

Hugo ran a distracted hand through his hair. 'What are you talking about, you damned fool? A horse can't be a bastard.'

'Who d'you think you're calling a damned fool?' Tramore shouted. 'You may know plenty about bastards, but you know nothing about horses.'

'What do you mean I know plenty about bastards?' Hugo said dangerously. 'What have you heard? I'll slit your nose if you spread gossip about bastards.' Had it leaked out already? Did every man here know already, and laugh at him? 'What are you saying about bastards?' He half rose to his feet. The company hushed a little, tense, seeing the moment of entertainment coming close.

Tramore who had meant nothing in particular, smiled maliciously, roused by Hugo's threat. 'You ought to know about bastards, seeing that you married one. What about blood lines now, eh? Your son bred from a bastard line – even if it is a royal bastard.'

Hugo was on his feet now, and towering over Tramore. Gilles' stomach was quaking, but he could not get through the packed bodies to his master, even had he dared. The atmosphere in the room was fairly crackling, like a summer storm.

'Are you talking about my wife, you tavern rat? Do you dare to sully my wife's name with your filthy half-bred mountain-robber's tongue?'

'Your wife!' Tramore said contemptuously. 'No one even knows who her father was, though many can guess.'

'I won't take that from an O'Connell!' Hugo yelled, and flung himself at Tramore's throat. At once the company gave tongue excitedly, cheering and babbling. Two or three jumped on the protagonists, holding them apart, while those nearest the door joined arms and held the doors shut against intruders with their shoulders.

'A fight! A fight!'

'Not in here!' 'The garden out at the back!' 'Get them outside.'

'Challenge him!' 'Let's see it done now. Why wait?' 'Come on, Ballincrea, see him off!' 'McNeill, McNeill!' 'I'll give you five to one on Tramore, damn it!'

Howling and laughing and cheering, the half drunken gallants surged forward carrying the two angry men into the garden out at the back of the inn. Gilles was carried forward helplessly, his face white and sweating, for he knew that now it had been suggested, neither of the men would be able to avoid fighting the duel without losing face. Sackville and Hamilton, considerably less drunk than the others, stayed behind to jam the door to the tavern with trestles, and then hurried out to see the sport.

'Let's have it done properly, gentlemen – we are not animals,' Sackville cried as he hurried out. 'Clear a space – we'll form a ring for them. My lords, are you ready? The honour of your tribes is at stake here. A McNeill or an O'Connell: we shall find out at last the truth of the matter, which has the pure blood, the brave men, the virtuous women, the—'

'Oh shut up, Sackville. Let 'em get on with it, before the constables come,' someone shouted. The two lords, shirtsleeved and rather dazed to find themselves in this situation, drew their swords, saluted, and took guard. They made a few passes at each other, and then fell to. It was a short, sharp fight: Ballincrea was the better swordsman, fighting in the elegant French style, learned in his long exile; but Tramore was the bigger, heavier man, a grim, dogged fighter, and he was much less drunk. A well-placed slash drew blood from his upper arm, and inflamed his temper again, and he came forward with a flurry of sword strokes.

333

Then it was all over. The clamouring crowd did not even see the stroke, it was so fast. Afterwards Gilles tried and tried to remember what happened, but all he could recall was the light reflecting from the sword-blades, and Hugo crumpling up and falling.

At once the noises were cut off and an eerie silence fell for a moment. Then Sackville said quietly, 'We had better make ourselves scarce, Henry.' The words seemed to echo round the walled garden, and in a matter of seconds the gentlemen had melted away into the shadows of the alleys, taking the flares with them, leaving only Gilles and Tramore staring down at the crumpled body of Lord Ballincrea.

Then a quiet, well-dressed man stepped out of the shadows, gave one look around, and said to Tramore, 'Better rub off, sir. Catch the tide. You must leave the country at once.'

Tramore stared at him, shook his head as if dazed, and then trotted off into the darkness, fumbling to sheathe his sword as he went. The newcomer did not watch him go, but bent down over Hugo, examining him. He looked up and shook his head.

'Run clean through. This is the devil of a business. You are his servant?'

Gilles nodded, and then, licking his lips, 'Who are you?'

'A servant of His Majesty. I got here too late. There will be the devil to pay over this. Here you, go in to mine host, and ask him to find something – a hurdle or a trestle – and a blanket, to bring the body in. Run now.' The man he had addressed dashed off. People were gathering slowly from the houses and alleys round about, drawing near the gate to the garden, watching in silence or whispering quietly amongst themselves. Word passed back like running fire and would not be long in reaching Whitehall. Gilles knelt down beside his master, the tears beginning to flow. His hands trembled as he smoothed Hugo's hair back from his brow. His face looked quite peaceful, already relaxing in death.

'Such a waste,' said the stranger. 'I wish to God I could have got here faster, but I had no directions where he had gone.'

'I couldn't stop it,' Gilles said, the tears dripping off his chin now, sobs beginning to shake his chest. 'I couldn't make them stop.'

'It was not your fault,' the stranger said kindly. 'There was nothing you could do. It is the times we live in. Such a waste, poor young man. And pity his poor lady, too.' Somewhere in the darkness nearby a nightingale began to sing, and Gilles' tears fell on Hugo's brown face, and glistened there in the faint light.

Annunciata sat in a darkened room alone, too shocked even to cry. The quiet stranger dealt with everything, with the help of Birch – Gilles was no more use than Annunciata in those first days – and Birch virtually ran the household, as well as looking after her mistress. She washed and fed Annunciata, and otherwise left her alone, coming in from time to time to check that she was all right, taking Charlemagne out for walks, and noting with satisfaction that she was sleeping a great deal, from a combination of shock and early pregnancy.

Calls of sympathy, genuine and otherwise, were made, but Birch would let no one in. Lucy and Richard were the only people she would have allowed, but they were out of the country; but when the King called, she let him by.

'She has seen no one yet. I don't know if she has properly come to understand it. Be gentle with her, Your Majesty.'

'Don't worry, good woman, I will be,' the King said. 'Is she eating?'

'A little, from time to time. Like a baby bird, she opens her mouth, and swallows.'

'Leave us alone for a little while, then come in,' the

King said, and went in. Annunciata, in her black mourning gown, was sitting on one of the spindly-legged chairs by the bedside, her hands in her lap, staring at nothing. Her face was pale, and her hair had been brushed back and held by a piece of ribbon out of her way, and this, combined with her undecorated clothes and lack of jewels, made her look as if she had been ill.

The King sat down beside her and took her hands, and she looked at him questioningly.

'Everything has been taken care of,' he said quietly. 'It could not be hushed up – there were too many witnesses – but no one is very clear about the cause of the quarrel. Tramore is in France and will stay there. The funeral is to be tomorrow. It will be very quiet. You need not attend – a proxy can go for you. Everyone thinks you are ill, so it will not seem strange.'

'I must go,' she said, the first words she had spoken for two days. 'I owe it to him.'

'If you wish,' the King said, knowing better than to press it. 'But everything has been arranged. There is no need for you to trouble. You could go home for a visit – take the children – would not that be a good idea?'

'Not quite everything,' Annunciata said, not seeming to hear the last part. 'There is one thing more.'

'What is it, dear child?'

'I am with child.' The King met her eyes, and she looked a little defiantly. 'It was not Hugo's. He knew. That was why – but in any case—'

'I see,' the King said, and he looked sad. Annunciata's hand, resting in his, tensed.

'Don't blame me,' she whispered. 'Please – not you too.'

The King almost smiled. 'Blame you, my dear? Of all people, that I should blame you! No, no, I am only sad at the loss—'

'I must be married again,' Annunciata broke in. 'Too many people know that Hugo and I – that we – at any rate,

I must be married again, quickly. Oh please, won't you help me?'

The King considered. 'Do you really think it necessary? It will look very unseemly.'

Annunciata gave a grim smile. 'What could be more unseemly than the situation now?'

The King nodded. 'You may be right. Well, I will see what can be done. I am so sorry, my dear, that it went this way for you.'

Annunciata shrugged, looking stronger already, the force of life flowing again through her veins.

'It is the way of things. But I have my babies to think of now, and the new little one that is on its way.'

The King stood up. 'I will see what is to be done. The least I can do, I suppose, is give you the title I meant you to have. It will afford a great deal of protection.' He turned to leave and then turned back. 'Will you go home for a holiday? It would do you good.'

Annunciata thought with longing of Shawes and Morland Place and her mother, but she shook her head. To face them now, with this scandal hanging over her, would be intolerable. Besides, until the future of the child in her womb was assured, she could not be away from the capital. 'No,' she said, 'my life is here now. Perhaps later, perhaps next year. Not now.'

At the end of July the King and Queen were at Hampton Court again, and Annunciata was married there, in the Queen's Closet. The bridegroom was another landless cavalier, a baron of ancient lineage whose Catholicism and loyalty had lost him everything during the Commonwealth. His name was George Cavendish, Lord Meldon; he was forty-five, a small, balding man whose little remaining hair was grey, almost white, with the worry he had sustained. But his blue eyes were kindly, and his smile was pleasant, and he thoroughly understood the situation that led to his

337

marriage to the dazzling and faintly notorious Lady Ballincrea. He was newly created the Earl of Chelmsford, and the title carried with it a grant of land in Essex. It was not a large grant, but it was good fertile land which was being well-farmed by tenants, and would give him a sufficient income not to be an embarrassment to his wife.

The manor-house that had belonged to the estate had been sold to another purchaser with the rest of the land, so there was nowhere for the earl and countess to retreat to. In any case Annunciata preferred to keep Ballincrea House as her home and to live in London for the present, and the earl was happy enough to move in there. It was better by far than the cramped lodgings in St Martin's Lane he had been occupying while he laid siege to the King's generosity.

In August the Court moved to Windsor for the grease season, and Annunciata hunted vigorously with the King every day and danced late into every night. October was the earliest she wished to announce her pregnancy. The baby was due in February, but she would have to entertain right up until then in order for it to seem that the bairn was premature. It was strange being married to someone on such a business-like basis, but it suited her at the time, for she was sore inside still from Hugo's behaviour and his death, and did not want to be troubled by love. George was kind to her, considerate, and willing to play his part in public and to be father to the baby that was not his, and so Annunciata felt it was only fair that in private he should receive some kindness from her. He was very much in love with her, and so she let him make love to her from time to time.

The odd thing about it was that she grew to like it. He was not inexperienced, and his gentleness and great desire to please her warmed her lonely heart. She always slept better when he was there, and when she woke weeping, or the nightmare about Hugo came again, it was good to be able to turn to him, and have his comfortable arms encircle her in the dark. Birch approved of the earl, and the children would always stop crying if he picked them up, and so it was a contented household that moved back into London in October. Birch went ahead with some of the servants to open up Ballincrea House, and on the last day of October, a little behind the rest of the Court, the Countess of Chelmsford arrived in London to open what she intended would be the most brilliant season of her life.

Kit came down from Stirling in the autumn of '62, having at last created enough order in his new kingdom to be able to leave it for a while. He came through Redesdale, spending some time with Francis at Tods Knowe, where his cousin was having a new house built with the material from the now derelict house at Emblehope. The two young men rode over the tops to Bell Hill and spent a few days there with the Symonds family, and Crispian and Frances rode with Kit as far as Hexham when he finally came on south.

He came charged with messages and bearing letters, from Francis to Arabella, from Sabine to her father, and from Anne to everyone, and looked eagerly for news in return.

'Tell me everything, then,' he said to Ruth when they settled down after supper on the first evening. 'What has been happening while I have been away?'

Ruth's news was mostly about horses, the farm, and servants. Clement had died during the summer, and Clem was now firmly installed in all his glory as steward of the household, his own eldest son being trained up in his wake. A new chaplain had been found for Morland Place, but he had lasted only a few months, before being dismissed for debauching the maids, and his place had not yet been filled. Ruth told him of the sad death of young Edward and, somewhat hesitantly, of Annunciata's progress. Kit listened to this latter news gravely, and fortunately for Ruth was too affected by it to ask many questions, for

Annunciata was a subject she did not care to discuss with Kit. All he said was, 'A countess now, then? She has done very well. Will she come home?'

'She has no plans for it. I expect when the children get a little bigger she will bring them here. It would not be good for them to be brought up in London when they get old enough to run about.' She changed the subject. 'Talking of running about, how is Sabine getting on? Is she improved at all? She was getting quite out of hand before she went away.'

'I did not see much of her, but I think she is,' Kit said. 'Of course, she has no one to bully up there, and so she has to mind her manners. Frances is more than a match for her, and when she tried to bully Nan, Frances soon stopped her. They get on happily enough now. Anne teaches them together most energetically, and their father takes them out hawking, and Crispian takes them out riding.'

'Crispian? From what I heard of him he was not a young man to relish the company of small girls,' Ruth said in surprise.

Kit chuckled. 'Oh, Crispian is a changed man,' he said. 'His experiences down south have made him so superior to everyone else that he can afford to be generous and kind and patient. Sam looks sometimes as if he would smack his head for him, but the little girls listen with bated breath to his tales of the gorgeous Court. He will make a good man when he has got the measure of himself; and meanwhile he amuses his mother and Francis, if not his father.' He looked around him contentedly. 'It is good to be back here, though. It is still home to me, though I dare say I shall have to spend most of my time at Birnie from now on.'

'And have you found yourself a wife up there? Some good Scottish girl to keep house for you?' Ruth asked

Kit tried to make light of it. 'It is no more likely than that you should have found a good man to keep house for you,' he said.

Ruth frowned. 'There is no point in wasting your life, Kit, just because the first girl you took a fancy for has wed someone else.'

'Took a fancy for?' Kit said with a hollow laugh. 'Is that how you think of it? If it were no more than a fancy, how could it last so long?'

'Simply through your own perversity,' Ruth said. Then, seeing another change of subject was necessary, she said, 'Tomorrow we must ride over to Morland Place and deliver your letters, and have a good long visit there.'

'And Cathy?' Kit asked. 'Will she come there? Or do we visit her?'

Ruth looked blank. 'Cathy does not visit,' she said. 'And we do not visit her.'

Kit was shocked. 'No one?'

'I have been twice, but it is not easy. She will not come to us, and I think we disturb her. It is better to let her alone.'

'I can hardly believe that all her family has abandoned her like that. Surely Ralph—' and seeing Ruth's face, 'well, perhaps not Ralph, but someone—'

'Arabella does not ride, and cannot walk so far. She did not welcome me when I went, and she has never asked me to come again.'

'Still, I think it is – barbarous, so to leave her to her fate. I will certainly visit her. Will you not come with me?'

Ruth gave a grimace. 'If you will. I hope you may not make trouble for her. But I dare say she will be glad to hear your news. She always had a great affection for you.'

'Did she?' Kit said, surprised. 'I never noticed.' Ruth only smiled at this. 'But then it was a cousinly affection, I am sure. But come, what else is there to tell? Give me all the news.'

341

CHAPTER NINETEEN

The next morning Ruth and Kit set out to ride over to Morland Place, and when they were halfway there they saw two riders coming along the path towards them. Kit at once recognized Red Fox, and a moment or two brought them close enough to recognize Ralph on his back. The other was a handsome chestnut with a white race, ridden by a tall thin young man.

'Here's Ralph come to meet us,' Ruth said a moment later.

'Yes, I see, but who is that with him?' Kit asked.

'Why, that's Edmund of course.'

'I didn't recognize him. He has grown so tall!' Kit exclaimed. They were nearer now and he saw how more than thin, how bone-thin the boy was. 'He is not looking well, either,' he added quietly. Ruth gave him a quick glance.

'Do not speak of it. He has been growing thinner as he grows taller, and we are all worried for him. Arabella says he is growing too fast for his strength, but though Ralph tries to deny it, we are all afraid he is going the same way as his brother. He started a cough on the day of the funeral, and he has never been quite free of it ever since, though it was a dry summer and everyone coughed a little, with the dust. Perhaps Arabella is right. I pray so. Poor Ralph—' But they were too close now, and Ruth broke off for fear he should hear. Bran and Fern ran forward, barking, and sniffed eagerly round the unknown horse, and Kit's mount laid its ears back nervously as the great hounds pushed their grinning muzzles up towards Kit's hands.

'We heard you had come, so we decided to pay the first

visit,' Ralph was saying. 'But see, we were forestalled. How is it with you, Kit? It is good to see you back.'

He heeled Fox closer and the two men clasped hands. Kit looked Ralph over keenly, and saw the marks of sadness in his face. Ralph was thirty-one now, and though he had always looked younger than his age, no one would ever again mistake him for a careless boy. Then he turned his attention to Edmund. The boy's face had a transparent look under its summer tan, and there were delicate blue smudges under his eyes. His eyes were bright and he had an eager smile, and it would have been possible for Kit to believe that he had merely grown too fast for his strength, had he not been forewarned, and had he not noted how quickly and shallowly the boy breathed. Of course, that could be excitement; but when Kit complimented the boy on his mount, and Edmund hastened with pride to explain how excellently Torchlight went, he began to cough. He stifled it hastily with his fingers, and glanced guiltily at his father, and Ralph looked faintly reproachful, as if he had let him down.

Ralph and Edmund turned their horses and the four of them rode together to Morland Place, where the rest of the family was waiting for them. There was Arabella, looking much older than her years but, against the comfortable backcloth of Yorkshire instead of the bleakness of Northumberland, much less frail. She was all in black, in mourning for her husband which she never intended to put off, and her white linen cuffs and collar and cap made her look pleasingly trim and neat, very much the one who ordered the household. There was Elizabeth, just as plump and sweet-faced as ever, but quite markedly a woman now. Kit wondered idly if Ralph had considered making a marriage for her. It might not be a bad idea if Ralph married her himself, he thought, for she made a good mother for his children.

And there were the children – little Ralph, looking sturdy enough, though quieter than Kit had remembered

him, perhaps, he thought, because he was missing his
brother; and Martin, at five still in petticoats, still small
and dark and alien-looking beside his blonde brothers.
Martin was holding fast by the hand his sister Mary
Marguerite, and Kit was astonished at how much Daisy
had grown. She was so big and strong that at three she was
already as tall as Martin and looked much heavier. She was
already possessed of considerable beauty – she had Ralph's
fine features and grey-gold eyes, and her hair was so fair it
was almost silver – and she looked at the visitors with a
frank boldness that seemed to stem from an unafraid
interest in everything that went on around her; yet it was
evidently still Martin who protected her, and not vice-
versa, and Kit wondered how long it would remain like
that, before the balance altered, perhaps so gradually that
they never noticed it.

The next day Kit paid his visit to Cathy. He asked Ruth
to come with him, but she thought about it and then
refused. 'Tell her I will come another day, if she wishes it.
She should send a message by you.' As he rode towards the
house he reflected again on what he thought of as cruel
indifference on the part of the family, and the closer he got
to the house the more indignant he became on Cathy's
behalf. He remembered her own patient kindness, the way
she had always protected Elizabeth, how uncomplainingly
she had helped Leah to run the house, how kindly she had
listened to him when he had been unhappy over Annunciata. It was monstrous that she should be so neglected
when she had wed herself to a beast of a man entirely for
the family's sake.

The house seemed very quiet – too quiet, as if deserted,
and it made him uneasy. He slowed his horse to a walk and
scanned the windows for a sign of life, expecting at any
minute that someone would come out from the front door
to meet him, but there was no movement. Somewhere
within a dog barked, but even that did not provoke any
reaction. Puzzled and wary he dismounted and tethered

his horse to a ring in the outer wall, and walked towards the door, testing that his sword was loose in its sheath, remembering that Makthorpe had nursed a long-held resentment against the Morlands.

He pulled the iron ring and heard the house bell clang hollowly inside, dying away into silence. After a while he rang again, and then stepped back from the walls to look up again at the windows. He thought he saw a flash of white at one of them – a hand or a face just disappearing perhaps – and then at long last there was the sound of bolts being drawn back on the iron-studded door. The door had evidently also been barred – he could hear someone struggling to lift the heavy oaken slat from its rests – and he was puzzled that they should take so many precautions at a time of peace. Then the door swung slowly open, and Cathy stood before him.

She was never less than neat, but there was about her an air of faint dishevelment, as if she had dressed some days before and had not been out of her clothes since. She was thinner than she had been, and her plain, bony face was so pale that the freckles on it stood out like a rash. Her eyes hardly seemed to take him in before they were scanning the open space behind him.

'Kit,' she said vaguely, then, 'Come in, quickly.' He stepped across the threshold and she shut the door behind him and began to bolt it again.

'Cathy, what's the matter? Why are you all locked up for a siege? Why are you opening the door yourself? Have you no servants?'

'Are you alone?' she aked.

'Yes – Ruth said she would come another time if you wanted her. But what's the matter?'

She finished bolting the door and then seemed to remember her duties as mistress of the house, and forced herself to smile and hold out her hand to him. 'How kind of you to come,' she said. 'It is good to see you. Are you

345

home for good? Has your business been successful?'

He would not be sidetracked, and took both her hands in his. 'Where are your servants?' he asked gently but insistently. Her face became bleak.

'There are only two left. Some were sent away, the rest ran away.' She shivered violently, and then swayed on her feet.

'Are you faint?' he asked anxiously.

'I think I am hungry,' she said. 'I haven't had time to eat—'

'Some wine, and some bread,' he said. 'Where are your kitchens?'

'I must get back to my husband,' she said, pulling away from him. 'If you can find Tib, she will get you some wine.'

'Not for me – for you. For God's sake, Cathy, what's happening here?'

'John – my husband – is ill,' she said. 'He is dying – of consumption. He has been dying for a long time. His steward and some of the others who hate me – hate all Morlands – thought I was poisoning him. They tried to kill me, but John got to me in time, and sent them out of the house. But we have been afraid they will come back, so we bolted the doors. Then the rest of the servants – all but Tib and Mary – ran away. They were afraid.'

'What are you afraid of, if they come back?'

Cathy shivered again. 'They swore they would fire the house, and me in it.'

Kit was alarmed. 'In the name of God, we must get you away! I'll take you to Morland Place – you'll be safe there. They would never dare follow you, and even if they did—'

'I cannot leave my husband,' Cathy said.

Kit looked at her set, white face and ached with pity. 'Then we'll take him too. If Ralph won't take him in, I'm sure Ruth—'

'No,' she cried, facing him with a stubborn and angry determination. 'No, I will not take him where he is

346

despised and hated. He is my husband, you all wish to forget that!'

'I don't forget it,' Kit said, 'but surely you see—'

'He is dying, I tell you,' she said desperately. 'In a day or two, maybe less, he will be dead. Nothing can change that. I will not have him end his days with strangers, hostile strangers. Let him die in peace, here in his own house. It is all I can do for him now.'

'But Cathy,' Kit said pleadingly, 'what do you owe him that you should risk your life for him?'

'He is my husband,' she said, and turned away and walked towards the stairs. Kit watched her go with a mixture of pity and exasperation, and then made up his mind. He went along the passage to the left, and after some wrong turns found the kitchen. It was dirty and untidy, as if it had been left in a hurry by servants who had never been very clean. The fire was out, unwashed utensils lay about everywhere, and there seemed to be no food. He searched the pantries, and guessed by the debris lying around that they had been ransacked. After a while he found some clap-bread and a heel of cheese which was well enough when he scraped the mould from it and, evidently hidden by someone who meant to come back for it, a bottle of aquavit. There was also a sack of oatmeal half full, into which the mice had been making inroads. He took the bread and cheese and brandy and went up the stairs. Halfway up he heard a scuffling sound, and whipping back a hanging from a corner he found a slatternly maid crouching there, staring at him with near-idiot eyes, so terrified she could not even scream.

'It's all right,' Kit said, 'I'm not going to hurt you.' He took her by the arm and pulled her up, shaking her gently. 'I'm your mistress's cousin, I've come to help you. Don't be afraid. Stand up, that's right. What's your name?' She stared, unable still to answer. 'Are you Tib?' She shook her head. 'You're Mary, then?'

'Yessir,' she whispered, and relief surged through him.

If she could answer, she could be instructed. 'Right, Mary, you needn't be afraid any more, because I am here and I will look after your mistress and you and no one shall harm you. Do you understand?'

'Yessir.'

'Now then, down in the kitchen there is a sack of oatmeal. I want you to light a fire in the grate, draw some fresh water, and take the oatmeal and make some porrage. You all need some hot food of some kind. Do you know how to make porrage?' She nodded. 'Good girl. Off you go, now. Make a good deal of it, and when it's ready bring some up for your master and mistress, and then you and Tib can have some. Now, where is your master's room?'

It was almost dark in the bedroom, for the windows were tiny, and the furniture was all old-fashioned, heavy and dark, with heavy dark-red hangings. The smell was of sickness and death, and he forced himself not to shrink back. Cathy was there, sitting beside the bed, holding the hand of the man who lay propped up on the bolsters. Makthorpe had been a big man, but sickness and starvation had shrunk him so that his skin hung loose about him like someone else's clothes. His face was green-white and shiny with sweat, his eyes, bright with fever, looked out from shadows like bruises, and his breathing was perfectly audible in the silent room, a hoarse labouring sound. His right hand was held between both of Cathy's, and his eyes were fixed on her face with such intensity that it was as if he feared to look away, as if she could hold him back from the cold grave he knew was at his back.

Cathy glanced once at Kit as he approached, and he said, 'I have found a little food for you. I sent Mary to make some porrage – that's all there is. But I have found some brandy.' He placed the food near her, and she took the brandy-bottle from his hand and, standing up, she slid her hand under her husband's head and tipped a few drops of the aquavit into his mouth. He swallowed, coughing a little, and she gave him some more, and then drank some herself. It was hard to untangle her hands from his, for he clung to her with weak desperation; but she freed herself gently and ate the bread and the cheese ravenously.

Kit wondered why she did not give some to Makthorpe, and catching his glance she said softly, 'He could not eat it. He might eat porrage, if Mary manages to make it. You see how it is, Kit, I cannot leave him.' Makthorpe's eyes were fixed on her, following every slight movement of her head.

'Does he know I'm here?' Kit asked softly.

Cathy shook her head. 'I don't think so. He is very feverish, and I don't think he is much aware of anything, only that I am here. It can't be long now.' She swallowed the last of the bread and resumed her place, giving her hands back to her husband, who clutched them thankfully. She looked back at Kit as he stood, irresolute, behind her. She licked her lips, and hesitated.

'I'm glad you came, Kit. I would be grateful – if – if you would stay with me until it is over. I don't think it will be long now.'

'I'll stay,' Kit said, with a quick rush of warmth. Her face seemed to him, thin and pale as it was, a flame of beauty, a source in the room of light and goodness that seemed to push back the shadows. 'I'll stay with you, Cathy. I won't ever leave you, unless you send me away.'

For one moment longer she looked at him, and though she did not smile, there was something in her eyes that told him she would not ask him to go, then or ever.

In the new year Edward made another of his periodic visits to London, and was received at Ballincrea House by an Annunciata large with child, clad in a loose cherry-red velvet robe and reclining on a chaise-longue, her newest acquisition, brought over from France at some expense.

'My dear, I didn't know,' he said, taking her hand and leaning down to kiss her. 'When is it due?'

'Next month,' Annunciata said thoughtlessly, and then blushed. 'At least, that is—' Edward smiled wryly, and drew up a stool to sit beside her.

'I understand. And you are a countess now,' he said. 'What did I predict for you, all that time ago, Nance? Was I right?'

'You told me never to let you make love to me,' she said crossly, 'and you were right in that, too.'

Edward's face became bleak. 'I heard about Hugo. I loved him, you know, as much as you did.'

'You had a strange way of shewing it,' Annunciata said.

Edward pressed her hand. 'We both loved him, and we both consented in what we did. It did not affect our love.'

'That's what he said,' she said curiously. 'I didn't really understand. I still don't.'

'You and I, Nance, are a couple of incorrigible rogues. We are thoroughly selfish, and unscrupulous, and that is why people love us. But can we love other people? Perhaps only people like ourselves.'

'Are you trying to tell me that you love me?'

'Do you want me to tell you that? I thought you knew exactly how I feel about you,' Edward smiled, and Annunciata looked at him sharply for a moment.

'No, I don't think I do,' she said, and he did not pursue the matter further.

'But why did you not send a message to me?' he asked.

'About Hugo, or about the baby?'

'Both of course. They are both matters that concern me closely. I would have come at a moment. I could have helped you. You should not have faced it all alone.'

'How else does one ever face things,' she said bleakly, and then shook off the melancholy. 'Besides, the King arranged everything for me, and Birch was very good. It didn't occur to me to send to you.'

'And so you married an earl instead,' Edward said cynically. 'What is he like?'

'He's very kind,' Annunciata said. 'He's in love with me.'

'Poor devil. And will he mind my making love to you? When you are delivered of his child, of course,' he added.

Annunciata rapped his hand with her fan. 'Don't, it doesn't suit you. George lets me alone, that is his greatest virtue. It was a *mariage de convenance*, Edward, as you perfectly well know.' She sighed, and shifted herself uncomfortably on the sofa. Charlemagne pushed the door open with his head and came pattering in, sniffed disdainfully at Edward's stockings, and then jumped up beside his mistress and curled up like a cat.

'Why the sigh, little one? Are you sad?' Edward asked.

'Restless,' Annunciata corrected. 'I thought when I came to London, and then when I married Hugo, that I had found what my life was to be. But even before he died, it had stopped being enough.'

'What do you think you want?' he asked, smiling faintly.

'Love, I suppose. But where will I find it? I don't know where to look next. Perhaps I shall have to take ship for Virginia.'

Edward laughed. 'No need to go to such lengths. Listen, Annunciata, I will tell you something that you will not believe, but it's true all the same. When you finally find love, it will have been there right beside you for a very long time, maybe all your life, only you will not have noticed it. That's where love always is – in your own front parlour, waiting not for you to find it, but for you to recognize it.'

'I don't believe it,' Annunciata said, and they both laughed.

On a wet, cold, bleak January day Ralph laid to rest the second of his sons to die within a year. As he watched

Clem and Arthur seal up the vault he wondered what more fate had in store for him. His body felt leaden, he felt lethargic and useless, and he stood staring at the floor with his shoulders slumped and his hands hanging empty at his sides, he who had always been so cheerful, so energetic, who had always loved life so much. The two men finished their task and walked back towards him, and Clem glanced at his face for a moment and then touched Arthur on the arm and they went past him to leave him tactfully alone.

Ralph looked towards the altar where the candlelight reflected on the heavy gold crucifix and the gold threads in the embroidered white altar-cloth. For the first time in many years the altar bore its furniture with the permission of the law: the Uniformity Act of the previous May had established Anglicanism as the legal religion of the country, and since it was known that the King was sympathetic to Catholics and wished to extend toleration to them if Parliament could be pursuaded, Anglicanism had taken its most Arminian form, and was, in its outward show, indistinguishable from Anglo-Catholicism. The vestments, the candles, the liturgy, the incense, the altar furniture, the Lady-chapel, all had been restored to their former glory, and a new priest, Father St Maur, had taken up residence in the priest's room.

But though Ralph might look at the revived chapel with relief, his heart held back from it. The religious upheavals of his youth, the battle for his conscience between his parents and grandparents, had numbed him. He wished he could turn for comfort to that altar. Sometimes he would walk up to the statue of The Lady and look at Her and wish he could pray to Her with any hope of being heard, but if he began to form phrases, he would find it was Mam of whom he was thinking. Sometimes he prayed to her – Give me your faith, Mam. Let me be able to find comfort as you did. Give me your faith that made you stand up to armed soldiers, so sure of your rightness that death no longer mattered.

But it did not come. The wooden statue remained a wooden statue, its face blurred by time, the slender hands, held forward and down in a gesture of great simplicity, thickened by so many regildings. The Lady was out of his reach, though he did not stint Her, saw to it that She always had fresh flowers or leaves and berries, and Her blue silk robe and Her little crown of gold and seed pearls. 'It is not your fault,' he would say. But he was still lonely, and lost.

A gentle touch on his arm startled him and he turned to find Arabella standing there. Such a *Morland* face she had, he thought. Just looking at her you would have known that the hair under her white cap had been black.

'You should marry again,' she said gently. 'That is the only answer to it, Marry and get more sons.'

'For them to die again?'

'That is God's business,' Arabella said. There it was again, that sureness of Mam's. 'Leave Him to get on with His business – you get on with yours. You are a young man still, and you must marry again.'

There were many things that Ralph could have said, but in the end he just smiled and placed his hand over hers, accepting the intention of comfort rather than the words.

'Perhaps I will, if I find the right person,' he said.

'God will send her to you,' Arabella said. He drew her hand through his arm and walked with her towards the chapel door, and oddly enough, he discovered that he *did* feel comforted. Now how on earth, he wondered, did that happen?

The baby was a boy, and out of courtesy to her husband, Annunciata called him George, and then impelled by a sense of honesty added Edward. The birthing was easy this time, short and uncomplicated, and little Lord Meldon lay in his crib afterwards wide awake and looking, Annunciata said, almost smug. Birch was very impressed with him, and determined that he was going to be even more handsome than little Lord Ballincrea, and the earl hung over the crib gazing at the child with a delight tinged with the faintest wistfulness. Only the twins seemed unimpressed by the new arrival. Brought in to see their mother and their brother they looked down into the cradle without enthusiasm. Then Arabella said, 'I don't like it,' and Hugo said, 'Mama, can we play with Charlemagne?'

George met Annunciata's eyes and she gave a little shrug. He smiled and held out his hands to the twins and said, 'Shall we go and leave your mother to rest? She must be very tired.'

Hugo placed his hand in George's at once, but Arabella, as always when asked to do something, held out for advantage. 'Can we look at your clock? Will you take the case off so we can see it move?'

'Very well,' George said. He came to the bed and kissed Annunciata on the cheek and then led the children away. His clock was his newest acquisition, and the moving parts within fascinated the twins almost as much as their stepfather. Annunciata watched him go with a kind of affectionate pity. She had not allowed him to sleep with her once her pregnancy was established, of course, and she had been wondering how she would make it plain to him that she did not intend to sleep with him again. And then at the door he turned and gave her one last look in which love and sadness seemed equally balanced, and she thought that perhaps he already knew – perhaps he would never ask her.

'It is wonderful how his lordship has taken to the children,' Birch said when the door had closed. 'When you think how some stepfathers are to their wives' children—' She let the rest of the sentence hang in the air, and Annunciata made no comment. She stirred restlessly, and thought, I don't want to be grateful, and I don't want George to make me feel guilty. I didn't ask him to love me – it wasn't part of the contract. Why can't someone love

354

me whom I can love in return? Must it always be so unequal? And she wondered again where she could look next for the man she would love.

Annunciata returned into society at the end of March, just at the time when winter was giving way to warm spring. Born and bred to an outdoor life, she hated long confinement indoors, and was no sooner readmitted to society than she was taking long vigorous walks with the King in the early morning, and riding and hunting with him on Epsom Downs and in Epping Forest. The Court gossip was all about Frances Stuart, a distant cousin of the King's newly come to Court. She was a great beauty, and the King had become very quickly infatuated with her, but La Belle Stuart was virtuous and so far had resisted any attempts on his part to bring her to bed. The two women to whom she refused to become a rival, the Queen and Lady Castlemaine, watched anxiously from a distance as not only the King but his best friends did everything in their power to snare this shy bird – Buckingham and Henry Bennet even set up a Committee For Getting Mistress Stuart for the King. The King told Annunciata about it, and was half amused, half rueful. Annunciata guessed that a considerable part of the lady's attraction was her unnattainability, and that the King was well aware of it.

The Court viewed her return with equanimity. It no longer speculated on her relationship with the King, accepting at last that he had no thoughts of her as a potential bedmate. She had a strong advantage over the other Court women in remaining the King's companion, for she liked hearty exercise, was a brisk and vigorous walker, and had a lively intelligence. While the rest of the fair and the gallant were still abed, or fit for nothing more than a gentle totter to a sheltered seat in the Privy Garden, the King and the Countess of Chelmsford would often be seen walking in St James's Fields. The Countess would be in one of her elegant walking-dresses, the skirt cut to clear the ground and the bodice fitting closely like a man's jacket, her magnificent hair caught with a ribbon and tumbling loose down her back, or pinned up under a feathered hat: a style many of the Court ladies tried to copy but without the same success. Her spaniel Charlemagne would run with the King's pack, and their servants would follow at such a respectful distance that they were as good as alone.

Often that spring they were joined by Prince Rupert, who was also an early riser and liked exercise. The three of them would walk and talk, and then sometimes go on to the tennis court where the King and the Prince would play while Annunciata sat in the spectators' gallery and stopped the dogs from getting in the way. Sometimes they would go back to the Prince's laboratory, for both the King and the Prince were very interested in new scientific experiments, and Annunciata would watch like a round-eyed child as the two men fidgeted with crucibles and flasks. Sometimes the three of them would play pall-mall, with many interruptions from the spaniels, and sometimes they would all three meet on the downs to ride.

One day in May they were strolling in the park when Prince Rupert mentioned the likelihood of war.

'War with whom?' Annunciata asked, and the King laughed at Rupert's shocked expression.

'War with the Dutch, my dear,' he said, drawing her hand through his arm. 'It's no good, Rupert, expecting the Countess to keep up with navy gossip as well as privy-chamber gossip.'

Annunciata was stung. 'I warrant you, Sire, that I have as good a mind as anyone at Court. Why should I not hear navy gossip too? Pray, Your Grace,' she turned to Rupert, 'why should we go to war with the Dutch?'

Rupert looked doubtful, as if not sure she would understand, and then began, 'It is all a matter of trade. Have you heard of the Navigation Acts, and the Staple Act?'

Annunciata nodded. 'The Acts to make sure all goods are shipped in English ships,' she said. Rupert looked agreeably surprised, and she went on, 'My family have been staplers for centuries, and our wealth comes from wool and cloth. Anything that concerns my family concerns me.'

'You must try not to appear so astonished, Rupert,' the King said, still laughing. 'The Countess puts an unusual value on her mind. The Acts also give us a complete monopoly on New World trade,' he went on to Annunciata, 'and that means tobacco, rice, sugar and cotton.'

'And what has that to do with the Dutch?' Annunciata asked.

Rupert said 'Holland, Madame, is a tiny country, and quite unable to grow enough food to sustain its population. It therefore depends for its survival on its power as a trader. It used to have a very important monopoly on the spice trade, but now that we have learned to winter our cattle, spice is not so important. It lost Brazil to the Portuguese during my uncle's reign, and all of the New World it has managed to capture is New Amsterdam. Now with our seizing the shipping trade, it sees its mercantile monopoly in danger. The Dutch have no choice but to challenge us.'

'And that means war,' Charles finished for him.

Annunciata was thoughtful. 'And will we win?'

'Of course,' Charles said cheerfully, but honesty compelled him to add, 'though it may cost us dear.'

'We seem to have so much, that I wonder we need to have more,' Annunciata said.

'We have far more people to feed than the Dutch,' Charles said, 'and more being born all the time. Would you have your three children starve? Of course not. I have five million children, and an empty purse.'

They walked on in silence for a moment, each busy with his own thoughts, and then the King said, 'James is early abroad today. He comes this way – I wonder if it should be

357

me or you, Rupert, that he wants.' They walked on more slowly as the Duke of York came towards them, and then Rupert and Annunciata stopped while the King walked forward to meet his brother, and after a brief consultation the two went on, deep in conversation.

'It seems we are no longer needed,' the Prince said. He smiled down at Annunciata. 'May I have the pleasure of escorting you, my lady?'

'Thank you, Your Grace,' she said, taking his proffered arm.

They stood as they were for a moment, and then the Prince said, 'Where are we going?'

Annunciata began to laugh. 'I don't know. Had you no idea?'

He smiled slowly. 'It seems the King has taken our intentions with him. Perhaps if you have not had enough exercise, you could be persuaded to play a game of pall-mall with me?'

'With the greatest of pleasure,' Annunciata said, and they turned and walked off towards the pitch. The sun was shining strongly now, and the walks were beginning to be peopled by other early strollers. Annunciata felt the strong arm of the tall man under her hand and felt her spine straighten a little with pride, as she thought of the rest of the Court seeing her walking with Prince Rupert. She looked up at him covertly from under her eyebrows. He was a little over forty, perhaps a year or so younger than her husband, but the difference between them could not have been greater. Prince Rupert was tall and broad and vigorous, in the flower of manhood. His hair was dark and curling, his face firm and fine-featured, his great dark eyes giving his handsome face great distinction and power. He was a man any woman could fall in love with. And at that moment he looked down at her, and caught her glance, and they both looked hastily away, she blushing, he thoughtful.

They played their game with vigour, each playing to win

but ready to be courteous to the loser. They were well-matched, and the game went neck-and-neck until the last hoop when Charlemagne, growing bored with watching, darted in and stole the Prince's ball and trotted up to Annunciata to deposit it at her feet. They both burst into laughter, and the dog sat back and grinned at them.

'It seems he has adjudicated, Madame,' Rupert said, bowing. 'May I be permitted to acclaim you the winner.'

'But that isn't fair!' Annunciata cried, her eyes sparkling. 'I was about to win anyway!'

The Prince smiled, his teeth very white in his brown face. 'Then perhaps by way of consolation I might offer you dinner?'

'I should be honoured, but I am engaged to dine with Lord Clarendon,' Annunciata said.

The Prince hesitated, and then looking at her thoughtfully as if gauging how much real regret there was in the polite phrases, he said, 'Then – perhaps supper?'

Annunciata's pulse seemed to move more swiftly, and the blood felt very warm in her cheeks. Supper was so much more intimate an occasion than dinner.

'Thank you,' she said. 'I should like that very much.'

CHAPTER TWENTY

The summer began hot, and Whitehall was soon both intolerable and dangerous, with an outbreak of the pox, and always the danger of plague. The Queen's Household moved early down to Hampton, and Annunciata decided to go with it, though the King's Household would not follow until later, for the move to Windsor. George went to his estate in Essex, and Annunciata took the children, a nucleus of servants, her dog and her horse and left London for the leafy coolness of Hampton with some relief.

In June Edward visited her there on his way to London, and told her the latest news of home: that Cathy's husband had died, and that she and Kit had married and gone back to Stirling, where they would live for most of the time. Annunciata heard the news with a strange pang, and Edward, watching her, was amused.

'Does it hurt, Nance, to lose an admirer?'

Annunciata shook her head and tried to look indignant. 'Of course not! I am not so vain and cruel as that comes to. I am glad that he has found a worthy wife, of course, and that poor Cathy has someone to care for her at last. It is strange, that's all. I never would have thought of Kit wedding her.'

'No one could ever think if Kit wedding anyone but you – that was the whole trouble,' Edward said. 'But though you have lost an old admirer, I am sure you must have got a better to replace him. Have not you?'

Annunciata flicked a glance at him under her lashes, wondering if he had heard of her private supper with the Prince. But he seemed only to be talking idly. Since that meeting she and the Prince had not been alone together, though they had been in company together, and had met again for walks with the King. The Prince was still in London, of course, and would not come down until the King came to Windsor, and Annunciata wondered whether anything would come of his interest in her. Their supper together had been delightful, their friendship warming as they discovered many likenesses between themselves. So far no one seemed to have noticed anything between them; she wondered if Edward would mind if he did know. Probably not, she thought. Edward didn't seem to mind anything very much.

Edward told her the rest of the news from home: that Ralph had found a new chaplain, a middle-aged man of very respectable character who was glad to get away from the agricultural grind of having a living. He not only took care of the spiritual side of life both for Morland Place and Shawes, but he also took much of the burden of doing the accounts off Clem's shoulders, helped Arabella with the household accounts, and had started a weekly class to teach the housemaids to read. Ralph had taken little Ralph away from the school, afraid that he might catch the infection that had killed his brothers, and the chaplain was tutoring the two boys. But Martin still refused to be separated from his little sister, and so Daisy was doing lessons too, and the three children learned their Greek and Hebrew, Latin and Mathematics, Rhetoric and Logic and Philosophy from the chaplain, and learned singing and dancing and music with Elizabeth.

'And Ralph does not think of marrying again?' Annunciata asked idly. Edward shook his head.

'I think he is still much affected by losing Mary. He occupies his days with the estate and the business and his horses, and hunts and shoots and hawks almost every day. He seems cheerful enough, but underneath it all he is melancholy. I feel as if he has lost his way.'

Annunciata tried to imagine a melancholy Ralph and failed.

'But he may have to wed again soon,' Edward went on, 'for Arabella is not at all well, and I think she will not be able to continue with her duties. Unless Ralph seeks to employ a housekeeper, he will have to find one by marriage. He should not have any trouble – there are dozens of good girls of good family who would give their hair for the chance to wed Ralph Morland of Morland Place.' He rolled over – they were lying in bed together – and surveyed Annunciata's thoughtful face. 'And there, my poor little bird,' he said, 'is another of your old suitors lost to you. How shall you do, my hinny, when they are all wed? There will be only me. How dull for you.'

'Tush!' she said crossly, and pulled his hair. 'You are fishing for compliments. Come now, we must get up, before Birch brings the children in.'

'No, no, there is still time,' Edward murmured, kissing her eyelids, and after a brief show of resistence, Annunciata sighed and turned her lips up to meet his.

In July her flux, which was always so regular, did not come, and she guessed with some perturbation that she was pregnant. For some days she was very thoughtful: life, she mused, could become one continuous round of child-bearing, and though she was amused and often touched by the twins, who so much resembled their father, and was fond of little George, she did not want to go on having babies whether by Edward or by George. Besides, she and George had been apart all summer and would not meet again until they went back to Court in the autumn, and everyone would know it could not be his child.

On the third day Birch came into her apartment and found her once again sitting by the window, staring out with a worried frown. The woman considered her for a moment, and then came to stand beside her and murmured, 'There are things that can be done, Madame. I could enquire for you, if you wish. In a village such as this, so close to the Court, there must be a woman—'

Annunciata stared up at her in surprise and with dawning hope, and then, after a brief struggle with her conscience, nodded her head. Two days later Annunciata went, cloaked and masked, to a cottage on the outskirts of Hampton Village, where she met the local midwife. She was a neat, clean, respectable looking woman – Annunciata had expected a weird and muttering witch-like creature – and dealt with the matter very briskly, giving her a noxious dose, and a packet of herbs to take after two weeks if the dose did not work. The first dose gave Annunciata stomach cramps, and made her feel very bad, but it did not have the desired effect. The second dose was even more noxious, and gave rise to very severe pains, a fever, and retching. Birch watched in anxiety, and suggested several times calling in the doctor, but Annunciata shook her head. She felt ashamed of what she had done, and was sure that God was punishing her. But after some hours she began to bleed, and it was evident that the dose had done what was intended. All the same, Annunciata was very ill after it, and had to keep to her bed. She was too ill to move with the Court to Windsor, and when she was able to leave her bed she moved into lodgings in the village and stayed there for the rest of the summer. It was a month before she felt well again physically, and much longer before she stopped feeling depressed and guilty. She vowed that she would never do it again, and privately resolved to change her lifestyle somewhat. The Court habit was to attend chapel on Sundays, but she had been brought up to twice-daily devotions. The King was very tolerant of even Roman Catholicism, and she was sure no trouble would be caused if she added a chaplain to her household and took the Mass daily.

Cheered by her resolve, she spent the rest of the time in Hampton getting to know her children. She rambled in the fields with them, fished with them in the Thames with the aid of a bent pin and a piece of string, taught them to ride on Goldeneye, sang and played to them in the evenings. She discovered the simple joys of feeding the baby, and bathing the twins, and putting them to bed. On hot sunny days, Tom would hire one of the long, flat-bottomed Thames boats, and Birch would pack a hamper with good things, and with Annunciata and the three children and Charlemagne they would pole along the river, drifting under the willows and looking for a suitable place to eat. Charlemagne would stand on the prow, his plumy tail waving, barking defiance at the swans. The twins would hang dangerously over the side shouting with delight when they saw a fish. Annunciata, with the placid baby on her lap, would lie back on the cushions and watch the sky drift peacefully overhead, a string tied round her ankle which led over the side of the boat, on which a bottle of white Rhenish would be suspended in the water to cool. On those days she would abandon the elaborate and elegant clothes she normally wore, and dress in the simple garb of a country-woman, with a big west-country straw hat to keep her skin from browning.

They were idyllic days, and she did not want them to end, and extended her summer stay for as long as the hot summer weather lasted. But finally in October the days began to cool and shorten. One day Annunciata noticed as she was riding that the great triple vein that ran up the back of Goldeneye's ear was no longer visible under his winter coat. That night she shivered in her bed and could not get warm, and the next morning the roofs of the houses were white with frost. It was time to go back. On 5 November they were back at Ballincrea House. George was already there, and shewed her the invitations that had already come in. Amongst them was an invitation for the earl and the countess, if she was back, to attend a private concert at the Palace and sup afterwards in the Queen's private apartments. It was just what Annunciata longed for. Restored and soothed by her long pastoral, she was brimful of energy and longing for some society and conversation.

'Let us go!' she cried. 'Oh, how I long for some music. And a supper in the Queen's rooms – I wonder if the King will be there? And the Stuart – what of her? Oh there will be so much to catch up on! Now what shall I wear? Birch! Birch! What is there that has not been seen yet? Leave the children to Betty and come and help me choose. What would be suitable, I wonder?' And she danced away, gathering up her dog as she did, to go through her closet with her woman, humming a little tune out of sheer happiness. George watched her go, his head a little on one side, like a dog with one ear cocked.

Between them, they chose a gown of pale-gold coloured silk with an overskirt of fine black lace, the sleeves very full, slashed to shew black silk undersleeves, with the lace edging shewing at the elbow. The bodice was drawn together with gold cords, and fastened over pearl buttons, and on it Annunciata wore the cross as a brooch. She had her hair drawn up in a Roman knot, bound with pearls, and the fastening hidden with three yellow rosebuds that clever Birch, by much contrivance, had managed to acquire from one of the gardeners at the Palace. Still she went unpainted, although she was nearly nineteen. In some circles the unpainted look was still known as *peinte à la Vicomtesse*, and she wanted to cling to her fame.

'You look so lovely,' George said wistfully as he handed her into her coach: though it was only a step, it was a very muddy step, and it was unthinkable for an earl and countess to arrive at a royal party on foot. Annunciata felt so elated that she could almost hear her blood singing in her veins. How I have missed it all, she thought to herself, drinking in the sights and sounds around her, leaning forward a little so that the crowds gathered around the entrance to see the coaches arriving could recognize and admire her. They were escorted up the stairs to the little ballroom where the concert would be held, and announced at the door. The room was filled with people, all lavishly, beautifully dressed, all known to her, some friends, some who envied or disliked her, and all looked at her, and she felt their eyes discovering that the Countess was no less beautiful and no less exquisitely dressed than last season.

It was an informal party, but the Queen was seated – she tended to faint if she had to stand for long periods. Annunciata went to her to make her curtsey and kiss her hand, and then the King was there, raising her to her feet, kissing her on both cheeks, exclaiming on how lovely she looked, and how sorry they had all been at her indisposition at Windsor.

'You missed some very good hunting,' he said, and then taking in George with a kind eye, 'and you too, my lord – I believe you had business on your estates? Such a pity you did not see one buck we ran down – I swear to you he was as big as my horse, with horns on him this long—' Talking cheerfully, the King turned George away and drew him towards a group of other gentlemen. Annunciata watched him amusedly, ridding her of her husband, and then the skin on her bare arms and shoulders suddenly goosefleshed. She turned towards the presence which had thus impinged on her. Prince Rupert was standing beside her, looking down at her with glowing eyes.

'I am so glad you came. I hoped you would be back in time.'

Annunciata made her curtsey, her eyes never leaving his face. Her skin seemed to be tingling all over, and she had the maddest desire simply to blurt out 'I have missed you!' but she managed to control herself, though her fingers trembled when he took her hand and placed it on his arm.

'I missed you in Windsor,' he said. 'The company seemed dull without you. May I get you a glass of wine before the music begins? And may I hope that you will sit beside me, and let me read your programme to you?'

Annunciata had no need to answer, and she went with him towards the footmen holding the trays of glasses with her lips parted in such a smile of delight that no one present seeing it could have had any doubts about her feelings at least.

Relations with the Dutch worsened almost daily, and everyone knew that war could not be long postponed. English and Portuguese merchants were complaining of Dutch depredations on the coast of Guinea, and Robert Holmes took a fleet there with orders to try to settle the matter peacefully. But the Dutch burnt his ships, and he seized two Dutch strongholds in retaliation. The Dutch began to draw up a fleet to deal with the matter once and for all. Meanwhile the governor for England on the other side of the Atlantic led a raid and seized New Amsterdam, the only Dutch foothold in the New World. The English people were jubilant, and began to clamour for war to follow up the advantage.

At Court opinions were much divided over the necessity and the wisdom of war. The country was still much unsettled by the events of the past two decades, and needed peace at home more than victory abroad. The King and Clarendon were concerned about the political repercussions, for their policy was amity with France, and France and Holland had signed a defensive alliance; while Rupert was worried about the state of the English fleet, which was not nearly strong enough for all-out war with the Dutch. Yet there was a strong party in favour of the war, led by the Duke of York and the Arlingtons – Henry Bennet, Lord Arlington, had taken over Nicholas's position as Secretary of State, and as well as being ambitious had never been able to tolerate Clarendon – and Albemarle.

Annunciata found herself very much in the centre of debate on the subject, for the King and the Prince were forever discussing it, and she was with them for much of the time. It was equally a never-failing topic with Richard and Lucy whenever they were home, Richard being hotly for war, and Lucy equally hotly against. Annunciata thought that the war ought to be fought, for the sake of the wool and cloth trade, in which she was, by birth as well as nature, interested; but she accepted Rupert's opinion that the fleet was not up to it, and when in company with him and the King, she tended to allow it was a bad idea. When alone with the Prince, however, she argued her case, and it gave them much interesting debate.

They were often alone as winter turned into spring. Annunciata was very much in love: not such a love, this, as she had had for Hugo, a young, foolish love for a lighthearted and careless rake, but a mature love based soundly on respect and admiration. As for the Prince, it was evident that he was completely infatuated with her. The Court had long ceased to wonder about Lady Chelmsford's relationship with the King, but it was delighted to make her the subject of their gossip when it became evident that she and Prince Rupert were in love. They were seen everywhere together, at first only in company with her husband and a large group of other intimates of the King and Queen; but as spring came and the weather grew warm, then hot, they could be seen walking alone together in the gardens and parks; and it became known that she supped alone with him at the Palace, and he with her at Ballincrea House.

They were not yet lovers. Rupert was an old-fashioned courtier, and for him nothing could or should be rushed. He had been brought up in a more formal and leisurely Court, and the preliminaries to love were as important to him, and as enjoyable, as the journey into delight itself. He loved her and made love to her in the old-fashioned way, step by step. He wrote her letters and sent her gifts, and Annunciata delighted in it. For her it was like being young again, as she had been back home in Yorkshire when she had been pursued for her favours, wooed and flattered and petted, made much of in exchange for no more than her smiles and her company. She sat for another portrait, this time a miniature of herself, head and shoulders, by Samuel Cooper; and when it was done she had it set in ivory and gold and gave it to Rupert on 25 March, her birthday. He was delighted with it, and repaid her kindness with a gold locket containing a curl of his hair, presenting it to her at a supper-party in her honour, when it was brought in by a boy bearing it on a velvet cushion and accompanied by six musicians playing a solemn processional.

Annunciata clapped her hands and laughed, and allowed him at once to take off the pearls she was wearing round her neck and replace them with the locket, which she said she would treasure as much as Princess Henrietta's brooch. When Rupert had fastened the clasp, she turned her head quickly and kissed his cheek. For a moment his face was very close to hers, his eye next to hers enormous, and she trembled. It would not be long now, she thought. And all through their long courtship their friendship had been growing. They talked almost all the time, never tiring of each other's conversation. Rupert had travelled so much, fought in so many wars, met so many people, that his experience seemed inexhaustible to Annunciata. But she had a lively and quick intelligence, and he loved to feed her hungry mind. He gave her books to read, and they enjoyed discussing them afterwards. They listened to music together, played and sang together, and tried out some compositions. He introduced her to architecture, and they spent many pleasant hours designing and redesigning buildings and planning towns and cities.

He liked to tell her about his childhood, how he had escaped as an infant in arms from the Hradschin Palace after the Battle of the White Mountain, of his large family of brothers and sisters, and how he had been trained in his early childhood in the martial arts, along with his adored younger brother Maurice, now dead. He told her also about his early soldiering career, and mentioned Hamil Hamilton, Kit Morland's uncle, who had soldiered with him on many a campaign. But he did not like to speak about the war in England, for it had so many sad memories for him; and she never raised the topic, for she felt it emphasized the difference in their ages. He loved her for her youth and vitality, she him for his maturity and wisdom but they did not need to be reminded that he was twenty-five years older than she.

Spring ripened into early summer, and the news from the war front was that the Dutch fleet was to sail under the formidable Admiral de Ruyter to revenge the seizing of the strongholds in Guinea, and it was proposed that Prince Rupert should be given command of the English fleet sent to intercept it. The news reached Annunciata through a delighted Richard, who hoped that the war would thus be hastened. 'It will take time to raise enough money, and to man and ready the ships, of course,' he said.

'How much time?' Annunciata asked, keeping her voice level.

'Oh, a month or so,' Richard said, 'several months. September or October should see the ships ready I hope. Otherwise they will not get out before the gales.'

Annunciata was thoughtful. If he took the fleet to sea, he might be away for a year or more. She had had enough seafarers in her family to know that. She would not see him for a very long time. She went home in a very subdued mood, to discover a letter from him awaiting her, which had been brought by hand from the Old Palace. He asked her pardon for not having been able to wait on her for some days, owing to the urgency of business, and told her about the proposed expedition. He went on to say that he would be prevented by business from calling on her for a few more days, but asked if she would care to join him at Tunbridge for a few days' rest and recuperation, as soon as he had settled immediate business.

Annunciata called for paper and pen and began to compose her reply. Tunbridge was charming at this time of year, and London was growing too hot to be pleasant, and the Prince must need rest after the frantic bustle of the past weeks. It would be delightful to go into the country and taste the cool shade, listen to nothing but birdsong and drink the waters for which the village had become famed. But her hand trembled as she wrote her acceptance. She recognized without a shadow of doubt that, knowing he would soon have to go away for a long time, he had decided not to wait any longer, and that at Tunbridge she would at last become Prince Rupert's mistress.

Edward rode for London as fast as he could get Bayard along, and as he rode his mind turned the problem over and over, trying this way and that of imparting the information without shocking or embarrassing either party more than necessary. Speed was the first consideration, of course. Pray to God he was not too late! His mind went back over the previous day's dinner, which he had been taking at Morland Place with the family. Ruth had been there, one of her rare occasions when she dined with Ralph and Arabella, though she called often enough in an informal way. The conversation had naturally turned to Annunciata, and Ralph, commenting on how well she had done for herself and the family, had asked, jokingly, if she was like to become the King's mistress soon.

'Then she could do a great deal for the family,' he said.

'Not the King's,' Edward said, 'but after all, one of the family. I dare say Prince Rupert has as much influence when all's said and done.'

Ruth had made a small choking noise, and glancing at her he saw that she was staring at him, the blood draining from her face.

Ralph had gone on speaking. 'What's this – our Countess is to be Prince Rupert's mistress, is she?'

Edward, looking sideways at Ruth, had said, 'It runs through the galleries that they are inseparable friends, and that she will be his mistress if she is not so yet.'

A short while later Ruth was taken ill, and with abrupt apologies refused the offer of a bed at Morland Place and insisted on going home.

Edward offered to accompany her, and his offer was accepted. His mind had been working the while, and as they rode away from Morland Place he said, 'Is what I am thinking true?'

'Not now,' Ruth muttered, still looking very shocked and pale. 'Wait until we get home.'

Back at Shawes he had dismissed the servants, brought her to a chair, given her brandy, and begun to ask her questions. A couple of hours later he had been on the road for London, charged in the utmost secrecy with this difficult mission. The weather had been dry and warm recently, which meant at least that the roads were good, and he was able to get along fast, stopping only three nights on the road. When he reached London he had already decided that he could not face Annunciata first; the first interview would have to be with the Prince. His main hope was that he should not find they were together.

But his enquiry discovered the Prince still working at the Navy Office up by the Tower, and Edward sent a messenger on ahead to ask the indulgence of an interview with him on urgent private business. On reaching the Navy Office he was shewn into an ante-room and told that the Prince would be with him in a while. About an hour later the inner door opened and the Prince came out, accompanied by Sir George Cartaret, Treasurer of the Navy, Sir John Minnes, the Comptroller, Sir William Penn, one of the Commissioners, and Secretary Samuel Pepys. The Prince bid them all good night and dismissed them with a nod of the head, and they passed out, glancing curiously at the dishevelled, anxious-looking traveller.

Edward stood up, and the Prince turned to him with the patient look of a very tired man whose attention is being spread too thinly. He looked unwell, Edward thought; yet he greeted him courteously.

'You wanted to see me, Master Morland.'

'Yes, Your Grace. Is there somewhere private that we could go to talk?'

'I am very tired, Master Morland,' the Prince began.

Edward interrupted him. 'I assure Your Grace that I would not trouble you except upon the greatest urgency.'

Rupert did not argue further. He nodded and led the way back into the conference room he had just vacated, and closed the door. 'No one will disturb us here,' he said. 'You may speak freely.'

Edward only wished that he could. 'Your Grace, I have something to say for which I must ask in advance your patience and your pardon. It is a very personal matter – personal to you.' Rupert raised an eyebrow patiently, and Edward plunged in. 'Sir, I must ask you to cast back your mind some years – twenty years, in fact – to the August of 1644.'

If the Prince was surprised, he did not waste any time asking what was the point of this exercise. His eyes, though shadowed with weariness, were alert and intelligent, and he nodded his head and said nothing.

'You were in Yorkshire, Your Grace. You fought a battle on Marston Moor. Your army was overcome and scattered.'

Rupert's face registered even after all these years the grief and pain of that time. His mouth tightened, and he said, 'Go on.'

'You and some other officers sought shelter than night, sir, at a nearby house.' Now he came to the difficult part. He swallowed and licked his lips nervously. 'There was no man of the house – it was owned by a woman. A member of my family. That night you – you – you did not sleep alone.' He avoided the Prince's eye now. 'Sir, a child was born of that liaison. A daughter. She was born on 25 March, 1645.' There was a very long silence, and at length Edward dared to look up. Rupert's face was closed and withdrawn. He looked older, much older, as though some light inside him had been shuttered or doused. He stared sightlessly at nothing for a moment, and then moving slowly, almost painfully, he reached his hand inside his jacket and drew out a gold and ivory-backed miniature.

Slowly he held it out to Edward, and said, 'Is that the child?' His voice was grey.

Edward looked. It was an excellent likeness. He nodded.

The Prince drew back his hand, and looked at the picture for a long moment, before restoring it to his breast. He said, 'I didn't know.' And then, 'Why did she not tell me?' Edward was confused, and the Prince explained, 'The mother, your—'

'Cousin, sir.'

'Your cousin. Why did she not tell me?'

'I don't know. She is a strange woman, sir. She never married. She has lived alone all these years, bringing up the child by herself, with no desire, it seemed, for anyone's help or society.'

'I did not know,' the Prince said again. He looked around him, a restless movement, as of pain. He felt bereft. 'All these years I could have had a daughter. Now I lose her as – does she know? Does the Countess know?' He could not say, my daughter. She was not that to him yet.

. Edward shook his head. 'I have not told her yet. I thought it best to come to you first.'

'I should have guessed – the likeness. Everyone remarked on the likeness. But if you are not looking for it, you do not see it. I saw that she looked like a Stuart, but – so could anyone. Dark hair and eyes – I did not think. How could I have known?'

'There can be no blame attached to you, sir,' Edward said softly. 'There is no harm done – yet.' He said it as a statement, but there was a question in it. Rupert met his eyes and the question wryly.

'We were to have gone away tomorrow. To Tunbridge. She expects me to call for her in the morning.'

Edward said, 'Illness, sir, sudden illness, can sometimes be a useful way to avert danger.'

374

Rupert thought about it. 'But it would be cowardly to avoid the matter. She must be told.'

'Would you think it wise, Your Grace? The shock may perhaps be unpleasant, even dangerous to her. Would not perhaps a gradual withdrawal of your – attentions—' Rupert made again that restless movement of his head. Edward went on quickly. 'Then, at a later date, when she has got over the disappointment, perhaps when her feelings have changed, she might be told – or put in the way of knowing.'

For once in his life Prince Rupert wavered, indecisive, weighing the direct and honourable with the tactful and protective. Edward knew better than to prompt him. He waited in sympathetic silence, and at last the Prince spoke.

'I have been feeling unwell recently. It was partly for that reason that I thought of going away to Tunbridge.'

'Sir, let me take a letter from you, or a message, postponing the expedition.' Rupert hesitated a moment longer, and he added, 'It will seem a postponement only; but you are to go away in any case, I believe, as soon as the fleet is ready. That will give her time to come to terms with it.'

The second part of his task was harder. His decision had been made, as he rode to London, that while both of them, for safety's sake, must know about their relationship, for their feelings' sake it would be better if each thought the other did not know. He arrived unannounced at Ballincrea House to find a ferment of activity in her ladyship's apartments. Dresses lay everywhere in heaps, and two maids were packing the trunks, under the contradictory directions of their mistress and Birch.

'Not that one, my lady,' Birch was saying.

'But I must have a formal dress,' Annunciata objected. 'Suppose we have to receive?'

'Yes, my lady, but if you remember His Highness has

seen that one – at the card party last month at my Lady Arlington's.'

And then Annunciata looked up and saw him. Her face registered first welcome and then indecision, and he smiled inwardly.

'Edward – what do you here? Why did they not announce you?'

'I wanted to creep up on you, unawares, Nance, and here I find you in process of running away. Tell me, has a prince come for you upon a white horse, to take you away to a castle in the clouds?'

Annunciata laughed merrily, her cheeks bright and her eyes alive with the anticipation of love. Edward was sad, seeing that she really did love him, that it was not just vanity and ambition.

'A prince on a white horse – how true that is, Edward. Not just a fairy-tale.'

'All princes are fairy-tales for the likes of us ordinary mortals. And talking of fairy-tales, I have a story to tell you.'

'Oh not now, Edward. I really must finish this packing. I am leaving in the morning.'

'I came here especially to tell you this story,' Edward said firmly. 'Let the admirable Birch go on with the packing, and come you with me into the garden for a breath of air.'

'I can't, I tell you!'

'You can and will,' Edward said firmly. He gave her significant looks, and nodded towards Birch, and then gestured towards the door.

Annunciata sighed with exasperation, but her curiosity was aroused, and she flung down the petticoat she was holding and said, 'Oh very well, I'll come for a moment. Carry on, Birch, as best you can. I will not be more than a moment or two.'

Out in the garden the air was sweet and fresh from the roses that climbed all over the enclosing walls, and somewhere not far away a nightingale sang and paused and sang. Edward led Annunciata to a seat in a bower, and took her hand, and began.

'Now, my dearest, the story I have to tell you. It concerns a woman, not a woman of your rank in society, my little Countess, but a woman of good family all the same. She had, through the death of many of her relations, become mistress of her own fortune early in life; but in consequence of an unlucky love, she had vowed never to marry. Into the life of this woman came a Prince upon a white horse. But he came not in happiness and love, but in the aftermath of a battle, weary, forlorn, deeply grieving the loss of so many of his friends and colleagues.' He paused to assemble the words, and saw that Annunciata had grown very quiet, was listening to him with a strained attention as if she could frame the words he said by the intensity of her desires.

'The woman,' he went on, 'well, she had lost the man she loved in that same battle, and many of her closest relatives. It is not for any of us to judge them. The woman and the Prince lay together that night, and perhaps they comforted each other. The next morning the Prince rode away on his white horse, but he did not take the woman with him, and he never knew that he had left her with child.' He looked at her, and saw the tears shining on her cheeks. 'Do I have to go on?' he asked. She shook her head. In the silence the nightingale sang again, and Annunciata drew breath in a sob. Edward pressed her hand, and held it to his breast, spreading the little fingers in his own. His heart ached for her, but there was nothing he could do to comfort her – not yet. After a long time she spoke, her voice faint and husky with tears.

'What shall I do?' She swallowed and spoke more clearly. 'It is he who is to call for me tomorrow. We were going away together—'

'You cannot go, of course,' he said gently. She looked at him in anguish, but she knew he was right.

377

'What can I say? How can I tell him?'

'Perhaps you should not tell him the truth. Just say you have thought better of it and will not go. He would respect you for your virtue, and forgive you.' Annunciata was still staring at him doubtfully when Birch came into the garden, calling cautiously.

'My lady. My lady.'

'Here,' Annunciata said, with an effort. Birch appeared, holding a folded paper on which the red seal was prominently displayed. The boy Edward had employed had been and gone, as planned.

'A boy has brought this, my lady – a letter from His Highness. I thought I should bring it at once.'

'Thank you,' Annunciata said. She took it automatically, and then stared at it as if it would bite her. It took her a great effort to open it, even after Edward had proffered his dirk to lift the seal. She read it, and he saw her eyes go over the words again, as if not sure she was understanding them. When she looked up, there was no glimmer of relief in the sad dark depths.

'He is ill,' she said. 'He begs my pardon, but he cannot go.' She held out the letter to him with a hand that trembled violently. Edward read it. An old head wound that had long been troubling him – over–work exacerbating the condition – deeply regretted – could not travel in his condition – begged to remain her obedient servant – Edward handed it back to Annunciata, but her nerveless fingers would not grasp it. He saw that she was close to collapse. The tears began to seep from her eyes even as he watched, and he saw she was powerless to prevent them. He looked up at Birch.

'We had better get her to bed. She has had something of a shock.'

Birch's eyes met his, and he read in them her knowledge that there was more to all this than the Prince's illness; but she accepted him as a fellow-conspirator, and together they helped Annunciata into the house and up to her bed chamber. There Edward withdrew while Birch and another maid undressed her and put her to bed, and was readmitted while Birch administered a hot cordial. Annunciata lay back on her pillows, looking bereaved and exhausted, and it occurred then to Edward how like the Prince she looked, not only in her features, but in her expression. His expression had been just such a one of shocked loss: they had loved each other, and the bereavement just then was worse than death. Edward's heart was heavy, for his part in it. He had torn them from each other; one day he must bring them back together, make them both see that they need not lose each other entirely. But not yet, not yet. He kissed Annunciata on the forehead, and left her to her women.

Throughout the summer Edward was there, helping Annunciata learn to live with the knowledge of what had happened and what had almost happened. It was not hard for the Prince to avoid seeing her, and as the shock laid her low for some time it was not without justification that Annunciata pleaded illness as an excuse to avoid gatherings where he might be present. Between them, George and Edward coaxed her back to life, taking her riding and walking, on long boating trips up the Thames, encouraging her to play with her children. Edward would have offered her more physical comfort, but it was evident she did not want it. She leaned on him spiritually, but slept alone.

On 4 October, Prince Rupert finally set off from Greenwich to join the fleet at Portsmouth for the expedition to Guinea, looking ill and old and tired. The news came back from Portsmouth that the fleet was still too badly-provisioned to sail, and then that bad weather was delaying them, and then, alarmingly, that Rupert was too ill to continue his command. The Duke of York sent his own surgeon, Choqueux, to attend his cousin, and the surgeon performed an operation on the old head-wound that had been troubling him. Rupert remained in Portsmouth for some time after the operation, dangerously ill, and then in December came back to London on his way to spend some time at Southampton's house in Tichfield to recuperate.

Edward had kept Annunciata informed all the while of the Prince's progress, and it was he who persuaded her to call on him during his brief stay in London. She was much thinner and had lost a great deal of her sparkle, and it was soberly-dressed and trembling that she went to make the call. The common talk was that he was dying, and she did not know if she could bear to see him thus. But the Prince's man, Will Legge, meeting her at his lodgings, told her not to despair. His Highness, he said, had a strong constitution, and had weathered worse storms, though he would not deny he was in a sorry state. Then he shewed her in, and left them alone.

The Prince was propped up in his bed, a great bandage wound round his head, his face white and drawn with his illness. Annunciata stared in shock and anguish, and felt her legs trembling. I must not faint, I must not, she told herself fiercely through the ringing in her ears. And then the darkness cleared away, and she looked into his eyes for the first time since Edward had told her the story. For a long time dark eyes looked into dark eyes, and they read the knowledge in each other's faces, and the grief of bereavement was suddenly eased, because they did not need to lose each other. Annunciata had no awareness of crossing the room; all she knew was that the next moment she was in his arms, her head against his shoulder, and he was straining her to him, his cheek against hers.

The love was still theirs, as strong, only different. Annunciata was sobbing and laughing all at once, and Rupert closed his eyes, too weak to stop the tears that ran out from under his eyelids, wetting his daughter's dark hair.

CHAPTER TWENTY-ONE

On 14 January 1665 the Dutch declared war, and on 4 March, having received a grant of two and a half million pounds from Parliament, the King followed suit. Prince Rupert was at once given high command in the navy, under the Duke of York. He was back in London, and had been active on committees, though his health was not entirely what it had been, but he was eager for command and was made Admiral of the White, taking the vanguard of the English fleet with thirty-five men o' war. On 22 March he sailed in his flagship, the *Royal James*, to join the fleet at Harwich, and Annunciata was amongst those who saw him off.

Since his return to London, his relationship with Annunciata had returned much to what it was before they had fallen in love. They were constant companions often in the company of the King and other close friends, and the Court supposed that another uninteresting relationship, like the Countess's with the King, had developed. They never talked to each other about their true relationship, though it made a deep and tender bond between them. Each recognized that one day they would talk about it, but not yet. No one else, they determined, would ever know. Birch had perhaps guessed somewhere near the truth, but she was as discreet as an oyster, and apart from Edward, no one else had any idea of the truth.

Annunciata had far more interest in the war, however, than she would otherwise have had, and made friends with all the administration officers in the navy, even the objectionable young man, Samuel Pepys, who had an ungovernable spite against the Prince, for reasons he never disclosed. Through them and through her other Court contacts she heard the news amongst the first: how the fleet had blockaded the Dutch in Texel, hoping to tempt them out to fight, and how Prince Rupert, alone, had predicted that the Dutch would prefer to remain in harbour and force the English ships, through starvation, to abandon the blockade. After a little more than two weeks the Dutch had not ventured forth, and with bad weather and bad provisioning against them, the English had been forced to go back to Harwich to refit, proving the Prince right. Then, while the English fleet was in Harwich, the Dutch fleet slipped out of harbour, captured some English merchantment, and sailed past Harwich and up the east coast. The English fleet pursued them, and at last, on 3 June, engaged them in the great sweep of Sole Bay, near Lowestoft.

It was the hottest June anyone could remember, and the news of the battle came to a sweltering and stifling population in London. The streets were airless and dusty, and cobbles and pavings hot enough to burn even shod feet, and only in the gardens of the city was the heat tolerable. The level of the river was well down, revealing stinking mud that added its own peculiar smell to the miasma of the city, and insects were a pest, congregating in black clouds round the piles of ordure in the streets and settling on the sweating necks of the populace and stinging them to fury. The plague, which came every summer to the city, came early, and from the beginning of June the red crosses were appearing on the doors.

On 5 June Lucy came to visit Annunciata, and found her in the gardens with the children, all of them stripped off, in that privacy, to their petticoats and shirts, and sitting on the grass under the trees. Annunciata called for some cold drink for Lucy, who sat down on a bench and fanned herself vigorously. 'Lord, but I've never known a hotter day,' she said.

Annunciata smiled at her with sympathy. 'It was too hot for me to venture out, though I was wild for news. Even the children won't play – look at them! But tell me, have you heard about the battle?'

'It is won, we have beaten off the Dutch, and they are sailing for home as fast as their crippled hulks will bear them,' Lucy said. 'Eighteen of their ships sunk, burned or taken, and only one of ours – the *Charity* – though two more got separated and it is not known yet where they are. They may be taken. And two admirals killed, Lawson and Sansom, but not many killed besides.'

'And – the Prince?' Annunciata asked quickly.

'Oh, they say he fought famously. The sailors say there is none like him for valour, though it is said he was wounded in the leg—' Annunciata gave a cry, quickly cut off, and Lucy looked at her strangely. 'Bless you, child, it is well enough with him. Not a bad wound. But the King is for calling back the Duke of York, they say, for with the Queen not being yet with child, he is afraid to lose him in battle, and he the only heir to the throne. And with the plague being so bad, he must not take the chance. But I am surprised to see no signs of packing in your house, child. Surely you will be leaving the city? There is nothing to keep you.'

'Oh, it is not so bad,' Annunciata said vaguely. Lucy looked stern. 'I come from Lord Craven's in Drury Lane, and there are three houses there already with crosses on the door. It has never been worse, and most of the big houses are shut up already.'

'Well if it so bad, why don't you go?' Annunciata asked crossly. Lucy shrugged.

'Richard cannot leave yet – he is needed. But why should you stay?'

'I'm not afraid,' Annunciata said. 'It is only the poor people that get the plague. And with the war going on, and news coming in all the time, who could bear to leave? Besides, the King is still here, and one could not leave before the Household.' But really she wanted to hear more about the Prince, though she would not use that excuse in public.

On the fifteenth the Duke of York returned home to London, having left Prince Rupert and Lord Sandwich in joint command, and bringing bad news of the former's health. The wound in his leg had been slight, but his general health had been poor at the beginning of the campaign and the strain of command was aggravating his condition. On the duke's advice, the King called Rupert home too, and Annunciata heard the news with relief tinged with guilt, for she knew that he would not like to relinquish the war at that point. The same evening her husband came home looking very anxious, and bearing the latest mortality-sheet still wet from the press.

'Madame, a hundred and twelve dead in this past week from the plague! Surely you cannot ignore it now,' he said. Annunciata frowned at him.

'You have been speaking to my cousin, my lord, I'll wager. She has persuaded you to try to get me out of London.'

'Well, perhaps she has,' he said, trying to smile. 'But the danger is very great, I assure you. I know that you believe only the poor are vulnerable, but that is not true. Many well-to-do and decent folk have succumbed. The roads are filled with householders leaving the town.'

'You may join them if you wish,' Annunciata said irritably. 'I shall not leave.'

'Why must you be so stubborn?' George said with exasperation. Annunciata looked coldly at him.

'Do not speak to me in such a tone. While the King remains, I shall not leave. You may do as you please.'

George turned away, wiping his brow. 'If you stay, of course I must,' he said quietly, and he went away to order the burning of herbs in all the rooms. Annunciata hated the smell, and spent more and more time in the garden, but did not complain for the sake of peace. She could not leave until she saw that the Prince was not in danger. At the end of the next week the mortality bill told of over seven hundred deaths in the city from the plague. Lucy came once more to beg Annunciata to go, this time bringing Edward with her to add to her pleas. Lucy looked tired and worried.

'It is dreadful to see,' she said. 'I believe there may be more than seven hundred, for some of the poor families are quite wiped out, and who is there to count them? The street next to ours is deserted – I don't think there is anyone left. All are either dead, or fled.'

Annunciata was afraid for the first time. 'But you – you are not in danger? Will not you and Richard leave? Or if you cannot leave, at least come here to me. I am sure it must be safer here.'

'No, I will stay at home. Many of the poor folk look to me for help,' Lucy said.

'But you will go, surely,' Edward said. 'For the sake of the children at least.'

'And my own two sons,' Lucy said. 'I wish they could be got out of the city.' But Annunciata would not go, even for that.

On the 9 July the Court moved from Whitehall, but only as far as Hampton Court, and the King was still in the city most days, travelling by river. Otherwise, Annunciata thought she would have gone mad. A thousand people a day, they said, were dying from the plague. The carts came every night to carry off the corpses and shovel them into open graves on the city's perimeter, and the bells tolled day and night, and in some streets no one survived at all, and grass grew between the cobbles. Those who could leave packed their belongings onto wagons and left, and those who stayed and fell sick mostly died, for the physicians and apothecaries were amongst the first to flee, and there was no help for them. And then in mid-July the Prince finally came back to London. He came almost at once to see Annunciata, astonished that she should still be there.

'I thought you must have gone, or I would have called before,' he said. Annunciata brushed that aside, eager to know how he was, and though he tried to speak cheerfully, he looked far from well. Only his tremendous physique and vitality had kept him alive through so much strain. He was exhausted now, and desperately needed long rest. 'The Court is moving to Salisbury tomorrow, I go with them,' he said. 'You will come, of course? It is madness to stay here any longer.'

Annunciata looked at him unhappily. 'It is too late,' she said. 'I cannot go now. My cousins Richard and Lucy are sick and there is no one but me to care for them.'

'But – they live in the city, do they not? You cannot go there, into the worst area.'

'Their house is there, but when they fell sick, I had them brought here,' she said. 'They are upstairs now, and my cousin Edward. I cannot leave them. I cannot go with you.'

The Prince bit his lip. 'God forbid that I should persuade you against your will,' he said at last. 'I shall pray for your preservation. But will you let me at least take the children?'

'Oh, please, please do. I should be so glad if you would. And Richard and Lucy's sons, who are with the King's chapel choir – you will look to them as well?'

'Of course. I had better go, then. Will you send the children to me tonight? Very well. I shall care for them until you come. God bless you, Madame. God keep you.'

'God keep Your Grace.'

The next day the Court moved on, taking Annunciata's children with them, but she parted with them in relief rather than regret. That night her husband felt queasy after his supper, and later vomited, and tried to convince himself that he had eaten a bad piece of meat. But the next morning his body was burning with fever, and he stared at her with terrified eyes when she insisted that he should not get up.

'I'll send your man to you,' Annunciata said quietly. The earl shook his head.

'No, it can't be, it can't be,' he whispered. 'Dear God, not that, not the plague.' He stared at his hands, terrified of what he thought he might see, and then suddenly he screamed at Annunciata, a thin high scream of delirious fear. 'It is your fault. If we had gone before, I should not be sick now. But you would stay. It is your fault. It should be you who is sick, not me.' Annunciata turned away, sickened and horrified, while the terrified babbling went on. Perhaps it *was* her fault, she thought. Perhaps her stubbornness and selfishness had led to other people's suffering. But she would surely suffer herself. Her wrongs were always punished. Perhaps she would die. She didn't think she cared very much.

She went downstairs, sending the earl's manservant to him, and walked out into the garden for a breath of air. It was stifling hot, even outside, and the grass was turning brown already, and the roses hung limply, their scent sickly sweet in the still air. And then a group of sparrows flew down into the tree nearest her and began quarrelling fiercely, one of them hanging upside down and beating its wings furiously at the other two. A tired smile touched her lips. 'Dear little birds,' she said aloud. They lived, and while they lived, they fought. She thought of her mother, of her family in Yorkshire, her children, the Prince, and the King, her friend. So much to be thankful for. Yes, she cared. She straightened her back and turned towards the house. The sick ones there needed her now. She would fight for their lives with all the strength she had.

At the end of September the Household of the Countess of Chelmsford was on the road north. She travelled fast, on horseback, for she was in a ferment to be home, taking with her three maids and three men, her own three children and the two young sons of Richard and Lucy, leaving the rest of the household to follow behind in its cumbersome train of coaches and wagons. She rode as if in flight from memory, or death, or guilt – perhaps all three.

Lucy and Richard had died. She had almost expected it, for they had been working and living amongst the poor sick, and they were already tired, and their strength impaired from travel in foreign countries. When she had moved them, at night and by closed coach to her own home, she had known more or less that it would not save them. She had had to tell her servants what she was doing and ask them if they wanted to leave, for she could not impose such a risk on anyone else. Their reaction had touched and impressed her. With no more than one or two exceptions they had all offered to stay with her and nurse the sick; she had chosen a nucleus household and sent the rest to join the Court and the children.

Edward had caught the sickness, she supposed, because he had been living with Richard and Lucy. He had not found it in himself to leave them and flee for safety, for they had been good to him when he first came to London, and through them his advancement had come. Annunciata had nursed him, and for a long time had thought she might bring him through, for his symptoms were not like Richard's; but that was one of the deceptive faces of the disease. He died quietly one evening, holding her hand. When the servants came to lay him out, they found that his other hand was clasped round a miniature of Annunciata, a copy of the one she had had done for the Prince. Edward must have got Cooper to make it for him without telling her; she told the servants to put it under his hands, and it was buried with him.

George seemed only to have the sickness lightly. His fever soon broke, though it left him very weak. As soon as he was well enough to travel she had taken him and the remaining servants out of town, up the river as far as Hampton and there had taken her old lodgings, with their memories of a happier time. They were all relieved to be away from the city of death, where the passing bells and funeral processions were a constant reminder, and even George, though still weak, had grown more cheerful. Then one morning a servant had come running to fetch her from her bed: he had found his master dead when he went that morning to wake him. George seemed to have died quite peacefully, in his sleep, and Annunciata thought his heart must have been weakened by the fever and failed.

So there had seemed nothing to do but go on to join the Court at Salisbury. It was good to be reunited with her children, and to see that the Prince was growing gradually stronger. She thanked him for caring for the little ones, and he smiled and said he had enjoyed it; though neither of them said it, the awareness was in their faces as they looked at each other that these were his grandchildren, after all. Annunciata had had no thoughts for the future when she rejoined the Court, but after two weeks she sought interview with the King and asked permission to withdraw herself and go home.

'To Yorkshire?' he said. 'Well, yes, of course you may go. We shall not be a true and complete Court again until we go back to London, and the Lord knows when that will be. We shall winter in Oxford, and I dare say the more people I can persuade to go home, the happier Oxford will be. But are you well, my lady? You are looking drawn and fagged.'

His genuine concern brought tears to her eyes. She cried easily these days, at the merest suggestion of sympathy.

'I am well in my body, Your Majesty, but sick in my heart and soul,' she said. 'My cousins – my husband – I feel almost as if I brought their deaths on them. All I can think of is to go home. I want to see my mother again . . .'

The King pressed her hand. 'Go then, but come back if you can. I should miss you very much if you were not to come back. And so would Rupert.' Some message was in the depths of his dark eyes – dark Stuart eyes, like Rupert's, like her own – and she wondered if Rupert had told him, or if he had finally guessed. Saying goodbye to the Prince was harder – she could not think of him by the word father, having once been his lover – and she saw that it was hard for him, too. They both made the parting brief.

He took both her hands, and kissed her on both cheeks, and said, 'Go safely. I must see you again soon. I have lost you twice in my life already, and I cannot bear to lose you a third time.'

He pressed her briefly to him, and they parted. 'I will come back,' she said, and she meant it.

She reached home after sunset, and rode up to Shawes as darkness was beginning to draw all shape and colour from the world. The squat grey house looked just the same in the blue dusk; she had been away for five years, and there was a tightness in her throat as she rode in through the gate. *Home*, she thought, and then, *Mother*. Wherever she went and whatever she did, those things were constants in her life, and would always have the power to call her back. They were not expected – no messenger could have travelled faster than she, so she had sent none – and the yard was empty. The servants and children drew rein and waited apathetically for her to command them. They were all tired: the babies were asleep in the arms of the footmen, Clovis and Edward drooped wearily in the saddle, though Clovis still had enough energy to look around with surprise and interest at his surroundings.

And then the door to the house opened, and Parry and Ellen came hobbling out, closely followed by two footmen, and then at last, Ruth.

'It's the little mistress come home! Holy sweet mother be blessed! Our little lady come home!' Ellen cried. Parry, whose gout had got much worse since she left, Annunciata noted, could only gaze in inarticulate pleasure, but he directed one of the footmen to help her down, and in a moment she was on the ground. Her feet were numb, and it took her a moment to get her balance, but as soon as she did, she restrained herself no more and ran to her mother.

Ruth was standing on the step of the door, and looked immeasurably tall and straight. To Annunciata she was unchanged – if there was more grey in her hair and more lines in her face, Annunciata was not in a state to notice just then – but as she put her arms around her and buried her face for a moment in her mother's bosom, Annunciata felt the unyieldingness, and she stepped back, hurt and rebuffed.

'Mother, what is it? Aren't you pleased to see me?' Annunciata cried, and then saw that her mother was dressed all in black – so many people were in mourning in London that one hardly noticed it any more – and that she seemed dazed, as if not really understanding that her daughter had come home. I should have sent a message, Annunciata reproached herself. I forget that she is old. 'You are wearing mourning,' she said gently. 'Who is it?'

'Ralph,' Ruth said woodenly. 'The funeral is tonight.' Annunciata felt her heart turn a sickening somersault.

'Ralph?' she said through dry lips. He couldn't be dead, he couldn't be, not Ralph. Ralph was Morland Place to her, he was home; she realized then that it was as much to him she had been returning as to Shawes and her mother. Ralph, the keeper of her childhood, her champion, protector, admirer, friend, who alone had understood her, who had shielded her from the frowns of her elders, to whom her faults had been part of her perfection. 'Ralph, dead?'

'Little Ralph,' her mother corrected, without seeming to notice the shock she had caused. Her eyes wandered vaguely over Annunciata's black mourning garb. 'You had better come with me. It has all had to be arranged very quickly, because of the heat.' She was beginning to take in what she saw; Annunciata saw her eyes going over the assembled company with more of their usual alertness. She looked at her daughter again, searchingly. 'These are your household? You are well? We have heard terrible things from London.'

'Yes, I am well. We do not bring the sickness. My three children, and Richard and Lucy's two boys. They are all tired and hungry, Mother. It has been a long journey.'

'Of course, let them come in. You must tell me all your story, but it must be another time. My dear, I am glad to see you – I am sorry I did not welcome you as I should. But we are all so shocked – I cannot think of anything else yet. William, tell Ann and Betty to take the children up to the nursery and care for them, and then take these servants and make them comfortable. Parry, the horses. Annunciata, will you come with me?'

'Of course, Mother,' Annunciata said. She was bone-weary, and had had a surfeit of death, but duty to the family could not be denied. It was lucky, she thought wryly, that I am correctly dressed. She turned back to Goldeneye, whom the second footman was holding, and with a grimace took the reins and placed her foot in his hand to be thrown to the saddle. Every bone ached in protest as she settled herself, and poor Goldeneye sighed and shook her head.

'Never mind, old lady,' she said, leaning forward to stroke her neck. 'It won't be a long journey this time.' Her mother's horse was brought out, and she mounted, and with the two servants behind they set out for Morland Place.

The chapel was crowded with flowers and candles, and the mixed scents of beeswax and flowers were powerfully evocative. One of Annunciata's earliest memories was of the funeral of Mary Esther Morland. She had been taken into the chapel to pay her last respects, and had been lifted up to look into the open coffin, at the white wax doll dressed in a white gown and wearing the fabulous black pearls. Today the coffin was closed, and the wax doll would be wearing a likeness to little Ralph's face.

All the family and servants were gathered, the men sober-faced and red-eyed, the women weeping, many of them passing the long-forbidden beads through their fingers as they prayed for the soul of the dead one. Ruth and Annunciata made their way to the front where the immediate family were seated, and Annunciata was glad that no one gave her more than a cursory glance as she passed; but when they reached the front row, Ralph turned to look at them. His face was marked with great distress and he looked much older than she remembered, but when he saw her, after staring for a moment in astonished disbelief, his face softened with pleasure and gratitude. He took and pressed her hand, and drew her into the place beside him as the chaplain came out from the vestry to begin the service. The thurifers came forward swinging their long chains, and the sweet, heartbreaking smell of incense mingled with the scent of the flowers; and as the boys began to sing in their pure trebles, Annunciata wept too, for the dead child, for all the dead ones, for all the sadness of life.

Ruth had told her, briefly as they rode, the sad story. When Ralph's oldest son died, he had given his horse, Torchlight, to Edmund. When Edmund died, little Ralph had expected to be given Torchlight in his turn. But Ralph, in an unconscious desire to break the pattern, had refused him. Little Ralph had brooded on the refusal. He felt that it was up to him to take his brothers' place, to be the oldest son in everything, the heir, the *young master*, and he began to feel his father did not think him up to it. He longed to prove himself, and to shew he was capable of riding any horse, however fine, he had stolen the stallion Kingcup out of the stable, saddled and bridled him, led him to a paddock, and tried to ride him.

The stallion had been hand-reared by Ralph, and was gentle enough to handle if one was firm and strong and calm; but like all stallions he was highly-strung, and had never been ridden. Ralph's nervousness upset the horse. The boy mounted, and after a short struggle the stallion had succeeded in bucking him off; but little Ralph's foot had caught in a stirrup, and he had been unable to free himself. The stallion was terrified by the inert thing trailing behind him, and being equally unable to free himself, had been maddened by fear. Before anyone had been sufficiently alerted to help the boy, the stallion had dragged him into a corner of the paddock and trampled him to death.

After the funeral Mass came the funeral feast. This was the other aspect of death – the glory and triumph. The pain of loss was with those left behind, but the soul that had left the earth was winging its way to the Father's Court to live in everlasting joy. The company passed from the chapel into the great hall. The whole house was lit with candles and decorated with flowers and evergreens, wreaths of laurels and sprays of ivy; the yard outside was as bright as day with dozens of flaring smoky torches, and at the gates the poor from ten miles around had gathered for the dole, of farthings, biscuits and burnt ale. Later, of course, anything left over from the feast would be distributed at the gates, as after any feast, and many would stay for that, and had brought baskets with them to take away the broken meats.

Within, family and friends ate and drank and spoke the praise of the departed child. Because of the terrible heat and the fear of pestilence it had not been possible to delay the funeral, and this meant that the family far away had not been able to get here. It also meant that Ralph and the other close family were still dazed with the shock of the terrible accident. Ralph did his best to do what was expected of him, but Arabella simply sat with her hands in her lap, looking shrunken and old. Annunciata remembered what Edward had said about her – that she would not live long – and saw the truth of it. Elizabeth greeted her with a warm clasp of the hand and swimming eyes. She could not take Arabella's place as hostess, for she could not stop crying, and stayed in the background holding tightly to the hands of the remaining two children as if she thought death might snatch them away if she let go. So it fell to Ruth to direct the servants, and Annunciata, with her well-developed social instinct, moved amongst the guests as, in easier circumstances, the mistress of Morland Place would have done.

From time to time Ralph came to stand beside her, not saying much, but seeming to draw comfort from being near her, as a dog draws warmth from a fire.

'It is so kind of you to come,' he said. 'Will you be able to stay long?'

'I have come home for a rest,' she answered. 'I shall stay all winter, at least. After that – I don't know what I shall do. My husband is dead, of the plague, and there is nothing to take me back to London. Perhaps I shall stay here.'

Ralph's eyes warmed a little at that. 'I wish you would,' he said. 'There seem to be so few of us left. Sometimes I feel as if God has a spite against my family.'

Annunciata nodded. 'I have felt that too, that He has a spite against me. But it cannot be, of course. God is good, and all that He does is good.'

Ralph looked haunted. 'Three of my sons,' he said. Annunciata knew what he meant, and it was a thing she might have said herself in the same circumstances. But hearing it from someone else, she heard the falseness of the ring.

'Death is sad for us,' she said, 'but our grief is for our own bereavement. For them, it is release, and glory.' A wraith of a smile touched Ralph's mouth, and she shook her head. 'I see that you have spent too long with dissenters, cos. They lead such sad lives, their faith giving them no comfort.'

Ralph thought of Mam, and all those he had seen face death unafraid, with the knowledge of the faith strong in them. He thought of the calm, sweet face of the Holy Virgin, and he looked at the beautiful strong face of the woman before him. If he could believe his children gone to the circle of loving arms, he could free himself of the burden of his guilt.

'You must teach me, Countess,' he said. 'You must help me find my faith again.'

She nodded gravely, but the touch of her hand was warm before she moved away again to see to his guests.

Spring came early, and by Lady Day the weather was warm enough for picnicking. Ralph organized one for Annunciata's birthday. They did not go very far, because of the children and Arabella's infirmity, just to the beautiful water-meadows across the river from Clifton, which had once been Morland lands, belonging to the Watermill estate. Some of the servants went ahead to prepare things, and when the riders finally arrived a silken awning had been put up to shelter those who did not care for too much sun, and the cloth had been spread, and the delightful delicacies laid out upon it. The little group of musicians had set themselves up nearby to provide the proper music for a birthday feast.

Annunciata was delighted with everything. 'It was so kind of you to go to so much trouble,' she said to Ralph.

'It was no trouble at all to me,' Ralph smiled, and Birch, as she shewd Annunciata to the place of honour, on Ralph's instructions, gave her a significant look. Birch had got very thick with Ralph through this winter, Annunciata thought. It might be coming time to remind her whose servant she was.

Everyone ate and drank and the company was very merry, and the children danced for them, and then ran about happily in the spring sunshine, enjoying their release from the tyranny of lessons. Eight-year-old Martin, now the heir to Morland Place, was quieter even than usual, seeing that he had rivals for his adored sister Daisy's attention. She had abandoned his side to play with the twins, now four and a half, and even now that their novelty had worn off, she often seemed to prefer their company to his. Daisy petted Arabella like a life-sized doll, brushing down her dress and straightening her curls and attempting to carry her about – though both the twins were well-grown for their age and Arabella was far too heavy for six-year-old Daisy to lift. With little Lord Ballincrea her relationship was very different. He ordered her and bullied her and demanded homage from her in a way her own brothers never had, and it intrigued her enough to allow it – though Annunciata privately thought that Hugo would one day soon find a small but determined fist planted in his eye. Hugo was growing extremely bumptious, and though it was partly because he was very clever for his age and therefore easily bored, Annunciata thought she must do something about it soon. The one sure way to quieten him was for Birch to remind him, coldly, that though he may be a viscount, his younger brother was an earl, and should always take precedence over him. Birch was rapidly becoming a younger and more intelligent version of old Ellen, ruling her adored charges with a rod of iron. She would have beaten them far more often than Father St Maur ever did; but Annunciata could see that, though Hugo bullied where he could, he was more sensitive underneath than perhaps Birch realized, and the knowledge that little George would always come before him really hurt him. She made a mental note to speak to Birch about it. Hugo needed to feel that he was loved for himself, not for his rank.

Martin sat quietly with Lucy's boys, fourteen-year-old Clovis, and twelve-year-old Edward. Clovis was restless, and eager to go back to London to further his career. The King had returned there in February, and though Clovis's voice had broken, he could still be a Gentleman of the Chapel, which would lead to other things in time. The King would never ignore a word from Annunciata, and it was in her power to help the boys greatly.

'What are you thinking about so deeply?' Ralph asked, breaking in on her reverie.

'Oh – that it was time Clovis went back to Court. Edward too, really – it is a pity to waste his voice while he has it, and he may not have it long.'

'Oh,' Ralph said, and his voice sounded dejected. After a moment he said, 'Will you go back too?'

'I don't know,' she said. 'I can do more good to the family there.' She beckoned to Birch, and as she came over said, 'Birch, Daisy seems determined to drag Arabella along by the arms. Can you stop her?'

'Yes, my lady. Shall I bring Arabella to you?'

'No, just keep an eye on her. Daisy doesn't seem to realize she's alive, and Arabella is too patient.'

Birch went away, and Ralph laughed softly. Annunciata looked at him, and he said, 'I just cannot quite get used to you. Little Annunciata, always in trouble for torn dresses and unladylike behaviour, and look at you now – mother of three children, and a Countess.'

Annunciata smiled. 'I am just the same underneath. I still long to ride cross-saddle and paddle barefoot in streams and do the things boys always managed to do without being punished. I dread to think how many more punishments I would have had if you hadn't covered up for me so often. Do you remember, Ralph, how it was always you who sorted out the troubles I got myself into.'

'I remember,' he said quickly. 'I didn't know if you did.' She met his eyes for a moment, and felt her face grow warm. Suddenly he stood up. 'Let's just this once do something unconventional. Can her ladyship abandon her dignity far enough to ride with me up the river a little way – alone?'

Annunciata glanced about her, and then grinned up at

him. 'Why not? If being a Countess doesn't mean I can do what I please, then what is it for?' He took her hand and pulled her to her feet, and they ran towards the horses. Tom was sitting near them, talking to the maid Pal, and he started to his feet as they approached.

'It's all right, Tom, we are just going off for a short ride,' Annunciata said. 'We shall be back very soon. Tell anyone who asks.'

Tom nodded and unhitched Goldeneye. Ralph threw her into the saddle, and a moment later they were cantering off along the riverbank, laughing with the excitement of freedom. Ralph pressed Fox into a gallop, and soon they were racing each other, the horses pulling in excitement, and they did not pull up until they had rounded the bend of the river and the willows hid them from view.

Ralph hitched the panting Red Fox to a tree and came back to Annunciata. 'Come, then, jump down,' he said. 'I want to walk and talk with you.'

He put up his arms, and she yielded into them, and he lifted her down and for a moment did not let her go. She was very close to him, could smell the distinctive sweet scent of his skin, see his grey-gold eyes looking into hers from very close, and her body trembled with anticipation. Suddenly he released her and led Goldeneye away to tether her, and then came back and took her hand through his arm in a very friendly way and began to saunter with her along the bank. Annunciata looked sideways at him. He looked strangely pleased with himself, and there was a little secret smile on his lips, and he hummed quietly as he walked. He looked happier, she thought, than she would have imagined possible last September, and after a moment, to open conversation, she said so.

'Do I?' he said. 'I feel very differently, it's true. After Mary died, and then I lost the boys, I felt as if winter had come, and there would never be any more spring. I was in darkness, and I couldn't see any hope. Now I feel as if life has begun again. It is all ahead of me, Annunciata. Do you know why?'

'No, why?' she asked.

He seemed to forget he had asked a question, and after a pause he went on, 'What do you see as your future? Do you plan to go back to Court, or will you stay at Shawes and take your mother's place?'

'I haven't decided,' she said. 'I can't imagine *never* going back to Court—' Never to see Rupert again? No, that was unthinkable. '—but on the other hand, I should not like to live there permanently. Perhaps it would be pleasant to spend some months there each winter, and the rest of the time here. But then, I can't imagine taking my mother's place, either. No, while she lives, she will be mistress of Shawes.'

Ralph stopped and turned to her quite abruptly, as though he had suddenly made up his mind about something.

'Do you know, I think I have been in love with you all my life, without really noticing it. I think we all were when you were a child – Kit and Edward and me – but you were always meant for Kit. And you, were you in love with all of us? No, I think perhaps you too were in love with yourself.' He did not say it unkindly, as a criticism, but as if it were natural. 'Many people have been in love with you, do you know that? Edward told us about Hugo, and about the earl. He told us quite a lot, one way or another.' He looked at her smiling eyes. 'Some of it I think he did not mean to tell, but I was very close to Edward, and I knew what he was thinking. He loved you, as he never loved anyone else. And little George – he is growing to look strangely like Edward, don't you think?'

Annunciata frowned a little, and as if he read her thoughts, Ralph said, 'No, I don't say these things to hurt you. How could I ever hurt you, or want to? Only to shew you that I understand you. I know everything about you, Annunciata, and I always have, because I've always loved you. When you came back last September, I thought it was simply because you are so beautiful and intelligent and alive. But it's more than that. I don't want you to go away from me ever again. You are the sun to me.'

Annunciata's eyes were filled with tears, and she saw that Ralph's were too, and she understood with her heart as well as with her mind. She could not have spoken then, for she had no words for what she felt, the sense of being at home in him, of coming back to where she belonged.

Ralph spoke again. 'You cannot be mistress of Shawes, you say, while your mother lives. Would you consent, then, to be mistress of Morland Place?'

'Yes,' Annunciata said, the only word required or possible. He took her into his arms, and laid his cheek on her hair, and she put her arms round him. She felt so safe, as if there was an inevitability about being here, as if it had always been her fate, and she could never have escaped it.

The legal settlements were immensely complicated, and so it was not until August that the marriage documents could be drawn up; and finally, on 3 September 1666, the dowager Countess of Chelmsford married Ralph Morland in the chapel at Morland Place. She was dressed all in cloth-of-gold covered with silver lace, and looked magnificent, and around her throat she wore the priceless heirloom, the mark of the Mistress of Morland Place, the black pearls.

It was a beautiful hot and sunny day, another in a succession of golden days that had made that summer remarkable, and after a sumptuous feast in the great hall the company moved out of doors to dance on the carefully-tended grass of the Long Walk, to the music of twenty-five of the best musicians that could be found; while children and young couples sought the maze-like hedged walks of the Italian Garden, to play hide-and-seek or other games;

and older folk sat wherever there was shade and discussed the wonderful good fortune of the Master and the Countess, predicting a golden future for them, and many children.

As dusk came on, torches were lit. It was still so warm that the servants were directed to bring the supper out of doors, and the guests ate and drank in the warm twilight along the banks of the moat, while the swans came gliding silently out from the place where they had hid from the heat of the day and eyed the guests regally, as if indifferent to pie-crust and bread.

'Are you happy, my lady?' Ralph asked Annunciata as they strolled from group to group. Her hand was through his arm and she leaned lightly on him as she walked.

'Very happy,' she said, smiling. Then there was a disturbance around the front of the house, out of sight of the Long Walk. Annunciata and Ralph glanced at each other, and then began, slowly so as not to alarm the guests, to stroll that way. As they came round the side of the house they saw a travel-stained man on a panting horse leaning down to talk to a group of servants, who were talking amongst themselves in consternation and asking the traveller anxious and eager questions. One of the servants detached himself from the group and came running towards them, his mouth moving even before he was within earshot. It was Tom.

'My lady! Oh sir – it's from London, terrible news from London.' Annunciata felt her heart leap painfully. The plague again? The Dutch? The King dead? 'A fire, my lady, there was a fire in a cookshop near Cheapside, and they couldn't put it out. It spread to the warehouses – tar and pitch and tallow and cordage, my lady – and then there was no holding it, and what with strong winds as well, and everything being dry as tinder after this summer—' He swallowed and licked his lips, staring at them but seeing something else in his mind's eye. 'The whole city's going up, my lady, and no one can stop it. London's burning!'

DYNASTY 1: THE FOUNDING

Cynthia Harrod-Eagles

Power and prestige are the burning ambitions of
domineering, dour Edward Morland, rich sheep farmer
and landowner.

He arranges a marriage, the first giant step in the
founding of the Morland Dynasty.

Robert, his son, more poet than soldier, idolises his proud
young bride, Eleanor, ward of the powerful Beaufort
family. But she is outraged. Eleanor's consuming secret
passion is for Richard, Duke of York, but duty is held
supreme and she must obey.

Against the turbulent years of the Wars of the Roses, the
epic unfolds, a passionate saga of hatred, war and
fierce desires.

978-0-7515-0382-1

DYNASTY 2:
THE DARK ROSE

Cynthia Harrod-Eagles

The marriage of Eleanor Courtenay and Robert Morland
heralded the founding of the great Morland Dynasty.
Now Paul, their great grandson, is caught up in the
conflict of Kings and sees, within his family, a bitter
struggle bearing seeds of death and destruction.

And Nanette, his beloved niece, maid-in-waiting to the
tragic Anne Boleyn, is swept into the flamboyant intrigues
of life at court until, leaving heartbreak behind, she is
claimed by a passionate love.

A magnificent saga of revenge, glory and intrigue in the
turbulent years of the early Tudors as the Morlands crest
the waves of power.

978-0-7515-0383-8

The complete Dynasty Series by Cynthia Harrod-Eagles